The LifeLine Signal

Cover art by Laya Rose.
Interior design by Key of Heart Designs.
Interior graphics by Kristina Kuznetsova, Sham Canggih and Pavel Konovalov.

The LifeLine Signal

Chameleon Moon Book 2

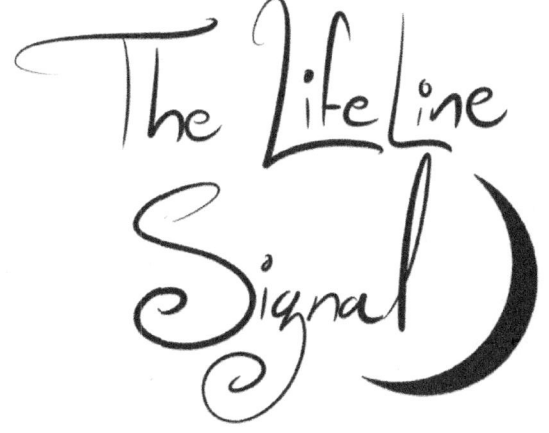

ROANNA SYLVER

To Moo and Kevie

I love you forever.
I'll like you for always.
As long as I'm living, your Bunny I'll be.

♡

PROLOGUE

Letting Go

PEOPLE DIDN'T USUALLY SHARE DREAMS. BUT CITIES DIDN'T USUALLY BURN FOR YEARS AT A TIME either. The odds of anything surviving those flames were fantastic, unbelievable—but most things that happened in Parole were. And people did stay alive.

The only thing rarer than a city that burned for years and survived was three dreamers sharing the same dream, like sitting around a radio for a favorite song. Tonight, when they tuned into their shared frequency, they listened like it was the only song that mattered in the world.

They sat in a tree on what felt like a mild summer night. Darkness surrounded them like a gentle curtain and soft lights shone through the

branches, so close they seemed like fireflies or flowers instead of stars. The trunk stretched up into darkness and down into the same, so thick around it felt like leaning against a wall.

"Can you hear the sirens?" one asked suddenly. She sat up straight on her branch, holding perfectly still. The starlight above them died and a new light ignited down from below and grew brighter. They looked at each other, fearful eyes lit up in a harsh orange like the glow from a Jack-o'-lantern.

The trunk was burning and the fire was rising.

"I know what this is!" The tree swayed as wild winds began to rise around them, rushing on all sides as if they were caught in the center of a cyclone. As she spoke, there came the sound of running feet beating in time with a pounding heart. Like the roar of the fire and howl of the winds, the sound came from all around and she shouted above the noise. "I've been waiting for it my whole life, I'd know it even in a dream. Parole is collapsing!"

"No way." The second dreamer's voice was incredulous, a snorted laugh over the sound of shuffling cards. A coin flipped into the air and fell, shining in the firelight—heads or tails, heads or tails? "Not real and not funny. Just knock it off, whoever's doin—"

Another sudden light from overhead cut him off, entirely unlike the soft light that belonged there. The branches were blazing as brightly as the roots, every one wreathed in flames. As above, so below. Sparks and burning twigs fell, shaken loose by impacts like blows from heavy axes.

The dreamers reached for one another, but they were too far. The tree shuddered under one last, terrible impact—and fell. For a few endless seconds gravity disappeared. There was nothing but empty space, reaching hands, and the fire below.

Then everything stopped with a jerk. The fire still raged, but the terrible shaking stilled as the figure of a boy appeared. He was suspended in the air before them, upside-down... and then he slowly turned, righting himself.

"Gabriel?" The first dreamer squinted through the heat, shielding her eyes from stray sparks. Her voice was accompanied by the far-off sound of a revving motorcycle's engine.

"Yes!" The boy shouted above the roar of the inferno. He still had the round, soft face of a twelve-year-old. Now he always would. His thick black curls caught the sparks falling from the blaze above but they didn't burn. His large, dark eyes shone bright in the void and they did not reflect the flames. But unlike the three in the tree, his image was partially translucent as if he were only half-solid, half-there. "I'm still here a little longer!"

"Thank God." She slumped against the tree trunk, weak with relief. "Thought we lost you again."

"Ten years was long enough." The second shook his head, still laughing, nervous, not looking down even as the flames climbed higher below them. "Now seriously, whoever's shaking up the tree, cut it out. We're finally back together, nothing's gonna—"

"What did you mean 'a little longer?'" the third dreamer asked with a flare of nervous realization. An overpowering surge of crackling energy flowed around everyone in the tree. Electrical currents raced white like lightning through a curling cloud of dark hair and shone from behind dark mirrored glasses. "Is Parole really collapsing?"

"It's falling." Gabriel nodded, young face serious. Behind and through it, they could see rising flames. "And I don't have much time. You have to wake up. *Icarus!*"

"What did you say?" the first dreamer asked in a whisper. Her eyes went wide with shock as sirens and alarm klaxons bled through the wailing wind. "I know that word. What does it mean?"

"You have to let go." He stared directly into her eyes. "The barrier is down. Sixty seconds. Run."

"Wait! Will I ever see this place again?" she cried, seizing her branch with a renewed strength and pointing to the other two. "Will I ever see them again? Or you?"

"Once you wake up, find each other. Then find me!" Gabriel shouted over the wind. "But you have to let go. There's nothing left for you in Parole!"

"I can't." Tears streamed down her face but they would never be enough to put out the fire. "Parole is my home! The people I love are here!"

"If you want to save them, you have to let go!"

"Where are you?" She looked around desperately. "How do I find you?"

The one whose energy sparked like a live wire shouted above the roar of the flames. "I'm in the lighthouse! Find me in the lighthouse!"

"Wake up." Gabriel reached out and gently touched her forehead with one small finger. She froze, staring at him—then silently slipped off her branch and fell out of sight.

"No!" the second dreamer screamed, finally shaken out of his anxious, smiling denial. Below his cry came the fluttering of wings, like dozens of panicked birds flapping to escape a hunter's gun. "Fuck you, Gabriel! Bring her back! Just—just stop! We're happy here! We're finally back together, don't take that—"

"You have to wake up too." Gabriel's young face was set, determined. He bit his lip and reached out, even as the terrified dreamer flinched away.

"The lighthouse!" the third yelled again. The words sounded like wrong notes on a piano, discordant, desperate. "We'll keep the light on for you! Find me!" Before the words were out, the second dreamer fell too.

Gabriel slowly turned to look up at the third dreamer, the last one left in the tree. "I'm sorry. This isn't how I wanted it. It took me so long to wake up and find you again, and now I have to split us up..."

"Why? Parole's collapsing, but this is a dream! Even if everything burns, nothing can hurt us here, right?"

"There's still so much to do," Gabriel said, sounding more tired than anyone in a dream should. The last dreamer's mirrored sunglasses reflected his tear-filled eyes. They looked many years too old and less solid every second. "And we can't do it here. I'd love to stay here with you, but..."

"What's happening to you? You're fading away, where are you going?"

"You were my best friends in the world. I know I'm just a ghost now, but I wish we could..."

"We're still your friends." A cool breeze rushed past them, soothing against the searing heat of the fire. The last dreamer reached out for his hand. "We never forgot you. We never stopped looking. You were never a ghost."

"Let go," Gabriel said softly, watching as the branch shook in the dreamer's tight grip. He did not take the offered hand, averting his gaze as if it hurt to even look. "Wake up. So we can start."

"I'm scared." Clinging to the tree might be futile, but the choice between that and falling into the darkness was simple. There was no choice.

"Trust me. Trust you. Let go."

"I'll fall," said the dreamer. Some fears never went away even in dreams.

"Yes. But sometimes falling isn't the last thing that happens to you.

Sometimes it's the first thing."

"How do you know?"

"I don't know a lot of things," Gabriel said, voice somehow sounding as faded as the outlines of his face. "But I know you'll be okay."

"But what about you?"

He didn't answer. They sat in the tree together for another moment. Then Gabriel watched the last dreamer slip away—falling into the dark, but not into the fire.

"Find them, Shiloh." Gabriel was alone in the darkness, watching the tree burn. As he spoke, the sound of static distorted his voice, as if he were speaking on a radio channel with another signal bleeding through. There was a girl's voice below, just barely audible. *Celeste, where are you? We have to go...* "Find them, and I'll find you."

CHAPTER 1

Lightning in a Bottle

THREE THOUSAND MILES FROM THE FIRES OF PAROLE, A DREAMER SAT IN THE WARM MIDDAY SUN, leaned against a cool concrete wall, and drew the dream.

Shiloh Cole's hand moved quickly, recreating the visual details before they faded. A trunk stretching up into darkness and down into flames. A city with fire underneath. A ship that sailed on the land. Memories of that tree and the people in it were clear and strong, much stronger than any memories of a childhood in Parole, ten years removed from this quiet moment.

But there was still a barrier overhead. Like the one over Parole, it blurred the sky and made everything look wavy, like ripples on water or thick glass. Staring at it was a recipe for a headache—but that could be said for a lot of

things. The barrier did nothing to block out the sun, there wasn't enough shade in the world to deal with that monster. Not even with an oversized hat and dark, mirrored sunglasses that always stayed on, even inside and at night. For someone who lived in a lighthouse, Shiloh put a lot of time and energy into trying to avoid the glare. Avoiding pain, drawing, remembering...and now, waiting. Shiloh hated waiting, even more than the sun.

At least the waiting wouldn't last too much longer. Today the air seemed charged, filled with palpable electricity. Like the air before a storm. Shiloh couldn't sit still and it wasn't because of the usual cabin fever or coffee jitters. Something was about to happen. Soon. Today.

In a sea of strangers, familiar faces were about to appear. Everything would change; Shiloh could feel it. Two of them. Any minute now.

"Shiloh!" A tanned, white girl with strawberry blonde hair and a dusting of freckles strode closer, walking with purpose in her step and smile. Brianna. She wasn't one of the people Shiloh was waiting for but it was never a bad thing to see her coming either.

"Hey, Bri," Shiloh said. "Catch anything?"

"About to head out now." She waved with one bare hand. A pair of thick gloves were tucked into the strap of a bag slung over her shoulder, along with a metal canister for collecting toxic samples. "Just couldn't leave without seeing the sketch of the day."

"Sure. Pull up a wall." Shiloh smiled at her approach and the one Brianna gave in return was reflected in upside-down miniature in Shiloh's sunglasses. The eyes behind the mirrors were bright and sharp and there wasn't much that escaped their notice. Shiloh's sense of humor could cut too—but the hard edges ended there. The rest was soft. Round cheeks that curved and dimpled with easy smiles, a soft body that felt at home in gentle colors, warm brown skin, and loose-falling natural curls.

"Good people-watching today?"

"It's not creepy if I'm an artist." The half-joking answer was only partially true. Shiloh had been waiting by Meridian's entrance for the past hour. The large gate in the surrounding high walls was open, the barrier arcing overhead. Traffic was picking up today, a couple of men in white uniforms stood inside the cubicle at the gate, waving people and vehicles through. A boxy delivery truck. A small group of relief doctors on foot. But no one Shiloh especially wanted to capture on paper. Today's people-watching wasn't for art inspiration.

"You're still feeling like a princess locked up in a tower, aren't you?" Brianna asked, looking up at the barrier above and the walls below. The barrier was a dome, not a sphere, and only extended down to the top of the wall that encircled Meridian, but that wall was high, thick concrete, and just as impassable. When Shiloh didn't answer she looked over. "Sorry. Is there a better word? A more nonbinary word?"

"It comes closer than prince," Shiloh said with a shrug. Neither word quite fit. Nothing like them did; even the pronouns 'he' or 'she' didn't work. 'They' came closer, but it was still worse than the sun on a hot day. "But the rest sounds about right. I'd rather face a dragon than one more day of nothing."

"Well, between you and me," she grinned, "if it ever came down to you versus a dragon, I'd bet on you every time."

"Keep it under your hat." Shiloh smiled back, pulling the floppy brim down, immediately feeling better when shaded from the harsh sun. There were a lot of words that didn't work and searching for one that fit had taken a long time. Finally finding one was worth it, because it felt something like this—but a thousand times better. Some words could be worn like healing armor. Some brought the cool relief of putting on sunglasses at high noon. Out of several prescription pairs, Shiloh's favorites were round and mirrored.

When xie looked into them, xie saw xirself, and smiled.

Brianna was quiet for a moment, then asked something a little more serious. "How's Arnold?"

"Not being an asshole for once." Shiloh went back to xir drawing. It took painstaking attention to accurately recall each detail—emphasis on pain. That focus came with a price, and if the hand cramp wasn't steep enough, the headache was. "Pretty good day so far."

Arnold wasn't a person, but he was a major pain in Shiloh's ass. Or more accurately, xir head. Arnold-Chiari Malformation was a condition—technically a genetic mutation—that involved the skull putting pressure on the brain where it shouldn't, with problem areas in the spinal cord, cerebellum and occipitals. Scientific words to say there were a lot of ways for Arnold to ruin Shiloh's day. On a bad day, the pain in the back of xir head and neck could be piercing, blinding, nauseating. Sneezing hurt. Even laughing hurt. Vertigo. Blackouts. Dizziness. Disorientation. Dissociation; the lightheaded feeling that nothing was real—but Shiloh was starting to feel that one even without Arnold.

"I like those two," Brianna commented on the open sketchbook page and drawing-in-progress; two people and a less-practiced attempt at a ship with sails. Shiloh held very still, heart pounding, watching her reaction. These images had been stuck in Shiloh's mind like a catchy song and right now it was like that song was playing in surround-sound. "Punk rock Asian girl? And this guy... sorry, his eyes. Dreamy."

"Punk rock Vietnamese girl. American." Shiloh started busily drawing again and didn't look up, focusing on looking intense and artistic instead of anxious. "And dreamy Indian American guy. Like the country India, not Native like my mom and me."

"Love her jacket," Brianna said, resting her chin in her hand. "It's like 80's vintage punk—I hear that's totally coming back now. What's she wearing, armor?"

"Uh, metal braces," Shiloh said. "But they work as armor too."

"Awesome. Oh, I like dreamy guy's scarf too. Little hipster for me, but it goes nice with his skinny jeans. It'd look better on you."

"Ha, thanks," Shiloh said with a head-shake, but not an annoyed one. Long as she didn't start asking questions Shiloh didn't know how to answer, Brianna's happy chatter made it easier to relax. "She has this huge, cool motorcycle but I can't draw vehicles to save my life—see?" Xie pointed at the ship in the upper right corner. "The sails aren't right. People are easier, though. This guy can do all kinds of magic tricks, like cards and flocks of doves and... always staying one step ahead of... um, together, they fight crime?"

"You gave them a whole little story? Do they have names?" Shiloh didn't answer right away, but Brianna didn't seem to notice. "You're right, you are good at people. They almost look real."

"I've been practicing. A lot." Xir smile faded and xie closed the sketchbook. "Not much else to do. I'm done with the semester already. That's how bored I am, homework sounds fun."

"At least they're online courses?" Brianna suggested. "I would've done that if my dad actually let me make a decision."

"Yeah, they're okay," Shiloh mumbled.

"Well, maybe next semester, you can take some in-person classes, get out of

Meridian for a while."

"Maybe. But my mom needs help with her research and that's gotta be more exciting." Now Shiloh looked up at her. "What else is there? Drawing, that's still fun. My rogue-mage is almost to level thirty-seven."

"Really? I must have missed—Oh." Brianna's own serious expression was reflected back in Shiloh's dark lenses. The mirrors made anyone talking to xir look themselves in the eye as they spoke. That was about as close as most people looked. "I'm sorry. I know I haven't been around with all the field work. We'll make time, okay?"

"No worries." Shiloh tried to smile. "It's cool you're doing more with Radiance, I'm just trying to keep busy too. Only so many *Star Trek* episodes I can re-watch alone without losing it a little."

"There are five whole series and tons of movies, that's like a million hours," she teased. "Sure you can't do without me?"

Shiloh gave a world-weary sigh. "TNG takes four seasons to grow the beard, Enterprise I'm still not sure about, and you know how I feel about Chakotay."

"You've told me a couple times, yeah." Brianna smiled. "I'm free this weekend, you can tell me again."

"Thanks, Bri," Shiloh said, but there wasn't much hope for change behind it. The days here stretched on like lines on a highway toward a far horizon. Days spent with walls on every side and barrier up above. Shiloh felt trapped underwater. Cut off. Half-real. Half-alive. Life on pause. Frustrated, isolated, bored to tears, ready to scream, paralyzed, over-caffeinated—the list went on. Shiloh made a lot of lists. It felt productive. It wasn't really, but somehow it helped. "So, how is the field work anyway?"

"*Awesome!*" Brianna gushed. "I get to crawl around in the dirt, make sure no nasty Tartarus contamination spreads too far, watch for ghosts. It's almost fun. And so is assisting the foremost genius in the field, while I do my field work...in an actual field. Ha! Come on, that was great, why are you looking at me like that?"

"Because you keep saying stuff like 'foremost genius' around my mom," Shiloh groaned. "And I have to live with her. She already thinks her tech's gonna save the world and—okay fine, it probably is. But it really goes to her head."

"Sorry." Brianna held up her hands but she was grinning. "Guess I still can't believe she's letting me help with her projects at all. I mean, she's a—she's *Maureen Cole,*" she corrected. "And all her designs are way over my head. But they're gonna help in a big way, so I wanna help in a small one."

Unsure what to say to that, Shiloh re-opened xir sketchpad and tried to regain xir focus on the details of the two familiar faces. Inventing practical uses for advanced technology was xir mom's expertise. Drawing was one of Shiloh's. Maybe not as practical, but just as important. When both your parents were geniuses or revolutionary leaders, basically superheroes, it was kind of nice to have some things of your own. Even if most of them were problems.

"Your dad still mad you joined Radiance instead of his...people?" Shiloh finally asked.

"His little secret private army, you mean." Brianna leaned her head back against the wall and stared straight up at the barrier.

"There, you said it so I didn't have to," Shiloh said with a smile xie didn't really feel. "And it doesn't really look that little. Or secret."

She hesitated, slowly lowering her head to look Shiloh in the eye or at least in the glasses. "You ever wish you weren't good at something you were good at?"

Shiloh opened xir mouth but no sound came out. Xie made a conscious effort to hold still while an electric current surged inside. The pencil tip tapped against the sketchpad in an echo of fast heartbeats, fluttering wings, and running footsteps.

"He's not giving up on me being a sniper," Brianna continued. "Keeps talking about me joining his corps, now more than ever. I don't wanna join anything that makes me carry a gun, even if it didn't have the creepiest name in the universe." She gave a little shudder. "Eye in the Sky. No thank you."

"Creepy's definitely one word for it," Shiloh said, thinking of several stronger words and resisting saying any of them. "What do you think they're watching?"

"You think the Major tells me anything?" Brianna laughed; it wasn't a happy sound. "You gotta tell me what it's like to have a dad who actually communicates sometime. Any new music?"

"Oh," Shiloh hesitated while xie tried to figure out exactly what she meant, then formulate a believable response. "Nah, it's been a couple weeks. But I told him how much you liked his and Evelyn's last concert."

"Awesome." She gave a wistful sigh. "London must be amazing. Think they'll ever come do a tour here? I'd love to see a show live. And meet your dad! Can't believe I've never met him."

"He's... pretty busy. You know. London." There was a reason Brianna had never met Shiloh's father, Garrett, but this relatively mundane one wasn't it. Sometimes truth really was infinitely stranger, stronger, and more powerful than fiction. "Your–I mean, the Major really doesn't tell you what Eye in the Sky actually wants or does?"

"I don't even know what he'd have me do if I joined." Brianna shook her head. "Be a sniper, okay, but where, why, shooting what? I know he wants to ship me out somewhere deep into Tartarus but not where. Just that I wouldn't be able to help your mom with her work anymore."

"I kind of thought you'd jump at the chance."

"At what?"

"Getting out of this bubble." Shiloh glanced up at the wall, the barrier. "It's just about the only thing I've *ever* wanted."

"Don't wanna get out if it means I have to shoot a gun," she shrugged, looking the wrong way to catch the relief on Shiloh's face. "Besides, I go outside every day now. Tracking ghost movement. Search and rescue for survivors when Tartarus decides to lash out a hundred miles in a random direction and eat up some poor unsuspecting town. Picnics. You can come any time you want, you know."

"That's not what I mean," Shiloh said. Xie had the feeling Brianna knew exactly what xie meant and was evading the real question. "We've been living in a snow globe for ten years. Doesn't this place feel like a cage?"

"No. It's a shield," she said as she scooted sideways into a small bit of shade. It sounded like she had the phrase memorized, automatic. "And almost everywhere has barriers now."

"That doesn't make them good." Shiloh didn't have much hope of changing her, or anybody's, mind but xie still watched her reaction carefully.

"Out there be monsters," Brianna said easily, not sounding very troubled about it. "Like, real, actual monsters. I'm fine right here, figuring out how to keep people safe."

"Without a sniper rifle?"

"Yep. Don't need one, not with your mom's special projects and Radiance Technologies," Brianna affirmed. "I like their motto, 'be the light in the darkness.'"

"Light hurts my eyes," Shiloh said, only half joking as xie gestured to xir dark glasses and kept scanning the people coming and going. No familiar faces yet. No world-change.

"You okay?" Brianna gave xir a hard look. "You seem distracted or something."

"What? Oh! Sorry." Xie came back to the present. "Guess the ratio was a little off this morning."

"Ratio between what?"

"Coffee and my bloodstream." Shiloh grimaced. "Might just try injecting it next time."

Brianna gave xir a sympathetic look. "Can't sleep?"

"I've been having some...weird dreams," Shiloh said in what might be the greatest understatement ever to escape xir lips. "I thought sleeping pills might make them stop but it didn't really work."

Impressively, that lie managed to be the exact opposite of the truth in more than one way. The pills had been an attempt to make the disjointed dream imagery clearer. They'd worked a little too well, just not in the right way. The intensity had been off the charts. But the imagery was surreal and jumbled, nothing xie could easily make sense of. The tree was clear, but not the city. Falling. Upside-down, backwards, static, garbled sound effects, it was like watching an ancient videotape with dust and scratches. Shiloh suspected the distortion was Arnold acting up again—it almost felt like the vertigo before a blackout and the pain the back of xir head started to flare when xie tried too hard to remember.

The only things really clear about those dreams were the faces and names in them.

"Trade you weird dreams for insomnia." Brianna shook her head. "I can't turn my brain off at night at all."

"Running numbers?" Shiloh guessed.

"Nah, that'd actually be productive. I'm just worrying. What I said about Tartarus eating up towns, growing in random directions—if that sounded specific, it was." She curled her knees up to her chest and bounced her fists against them, as if unable to keep still and think about this concept at the same time. Shiloh knew the feeling. "Happened again last week. This thing's getting meaner every day. What if its runoff reaches epidemic levels? Can't have another Parole on our hands."

Shiloh kept silent for a few seconds. Everyone at least knew the word Parole, but not in xir vibrant, urgent present tense. Parole *had* been a great city. People's relatives *had* lived in Parole. Parole was the past tense. The present was something else entirely. "You really don't think there's anything out there?" xie asked at last.

"How could there be?" Brianna gave xir a confused look. "Parole was the first place Tartarus wrecked."

"It's a thousand miles from the center."

"Yeah, and we've seen Tartarus branch out farther than that," Brianna maintained. "That's what it does, it grows out, wrecks everything, and then scoots back. Just because someplace is safe now doesn't mean it always was. Or will be tomorrow."

"It's not like Parole was blown up or anything, though," Shiloh pointed out.

"It's gotta still be standing."

"Sure, standing and infected by a deadly, toxic wasteland."

"SkEye must think something's still going on there or else they wouldn't be keeping everyone away from it."

"Or maybe they're keeping everyone away from the poison storms and dangerous monsters? So they don't get wiped out just like Parole?" She dropped the sarcastic tone and shook her head. "It's gone. Nobody could survive that."

"That's what SkEye says, sure," Shiloh countered. "But what if the answer is *in* Parole? And we're all too busy dealing with this new terrible stuff to pay attention?"

"We have to make sure the present is safe before we think about the past, or the future," Brianna said, again sounding as if she were reciting memorized rules. "Remember, but don't carry ghosts around with you. Don't treat ghosts like they're still alive. Let them go."

"I've never been very good at that," Shiloh returned. "Especially when things won't let me go."

"Parole's gone. We have actual ghosts to worry about now and people in the Tartarus Zone need help." Brianna jammed her hands in her pockets. "Sick and displaced because their whole cities got destroyed by monsters that shouldn't be real, but are. *Those* people are the ones I'm worried about. Ones we can help, the ones who are still alive. Not Parole. Forget—"

"But what if people are still alive there and they need help?"

"No one is alive in there!" Brianna snapped, voice rising for the first time. She was panting as if she'd just been sprinting, staring not at Shiloh but something only she could see. Shiloh waited, recognizing the signs of hitting a nerve, setting off a flashback and knowing waiting was all there was to do. Xie'd felt that way often enough.

"It's been ten years," Brianna said after several seconds. "But I still wake up thinking I smell smoke. Or hear fire. I remember how it roared. Or rushed, like a river. Sirens, screams, people trying to get away..." Brianna paused. Leaned in closer to whisper, "you know how people say it's still there, just burning?"

"Yes!" Shiloh whispered back, feeling hopeful in the strangest way. "That's one of the biggest theories out there. I didn't know you listened to that stuff, Bri."

"I don't," she said quickly. "But sometimes I just—hear things. I mean, it's probably nothing, just because it's on the internet doesn't make it true, people say the same conspiracy-nut stuff about Atlantis, or Area 51, but..."

"But you can't get it out of your head," Shiloh supplied. "Me neither. Not for a minute."

"I can't forget about Parole just because I'm supposed to," Brianna whispered, as if telling the most dangerous secret she knew. "It's where we used to live."

"I can't forget it either," Shiloh said carefully, like a sudden movement might startle her out of the fragile memory. "But it's hard to remember sometimes."

"I remember..." She didn't complete the thought, eyes drifting out of focus again.

"I've, uh, heard a bunch of theories too," Shiloh said with deliberate casualness. "Like, about two years into the quarantine, everything caught fire."

"Uh-huh," Brianna said noncommittally.

One of the nice things about wearing dark shades around ninety percent of the time is that people could never tell where you were looking. When xie spoke again, the words came out light and casual. "Do you remember a kid named Gabriel?"

She shook her head, still tugging at her sleeve. "Doesn't ring a bell."

"Are you sure?" Despite the bright sun and pain that came with it, Shiloh pulled xir glasses off to look directly into her eyes. Or at least make it more obvious. "Think back to when there weren't walls everywhere, or the big bubbles. Or Tartarus."

"It hurts to think about," she said and Shiloh could feel the distance between them growing.

"I know." Shiloh let the memories go and focused on the present. They were very much linked, anyway. Sometimes they were even one and the same. "Listen, Bri, I didn't come down here to people-watch, not today." On the next street, the sound of a motorcycle engine rose and fell. "I'm waiting for some... friends."

"I thought I knew all your friends," she said, sounding a little disappointed in spite of the tension rising between them.

"I'm leaving." Shiloh couldn't take it anymore, xie just blurted the words out. "And I want you to come with me."

"Come where?" In the time it took for Shiloh to hesitate, it seemed like Brianna had already made up her mind. She stood up and took a step away. "I'm staying here. Looking for answers."

"You really think you're going to find them here, stuck in a bubble?" Shiloh got up too and replaced xir sunglasses. "The answers aren't here, Bri, they're out there, I know it."

"Please, stop. I never want to think about that place ever again." She took another step back, and Shiloh felt their connection slipping out of xir fingers like loose sand. "It's too dangerous."

"To even think about?"

"Yes!" She whirled around to face Shiloh. "I know you think I'm just being stubborn or a coward or something, but you don't know what he's like!"

"Your dad?" Shiloh asked, already knowing the answer. "I mean, the Major?"

"I didn't say that." Brianna stared at her pale, curving reflection in Shiloh's sunglasses. "Just like I didn't say—"

Tap. Tap. Tap.

The unexpected sound, like knocking on a windowpane, came from an equally strange direction: directly above their heads. Shiloh and Brianna both looked up—and immediately gasped.

The barrier curved above them like the wall of a fishbowl. And sitting on the outside, crouched like a hungry cat, staring directly at them, was a dragon.

"What in the..." Brianna started, looking transfixed.

Shiloh couldn't reply, only stare at the creature overhead. Its long, curving neck, four limbs that ended in huge taloned feet, its folded wings—and most of all, its matte-black eyes, fixed on the two small humans below. To say it didn't look like an 'ordinary dragon' would have been ridiculous, xie thought, overwhelmed with surreal wonder. But it was true. Shiloh wasn't sure what xie expected of a dragon, but it wasn't this. Instead of looking anything like a living thing, this one was...wrong. It had no color in its scales or eyes, from the tips of its pointed horns to the end of its serpentine tail. It almost looked like a computer glitch, entirely rendered in greyscale, shadows an absolute black and highlights a harsh white. Its movements were jerky, unnatural. Most of it held completely still, as if it were a freeze-frame image—except for one 'hand.'

Tap. Tap. Tap.

Very slowly, very deliberately, the ghostly dragon—*ghost*, Shiloh's brain latched onto the word, *ghost was right, important, that meant something*—was poking at the barrier's iridescent surface with one long black claw. As it moved, it left behind trails of smoke; black vapor so thick and solid that it moved like ink in water. Then, as they watched, paralyzed, it slowly began tracing a circle. The energetic barrier fizzled and disappeared where it touched. It peered through the impossible hole it had made in the barrier, staring at Shiloh and Brianna unceasingly, its dark eyes like bottomless holes. As it slipped through, Shiloh heard a voice. It was familiar.

(It's finally happened, babies. Parole is burning.)

Shiloh started to shake, and Brianna let out a small frightened noise. They didn't hear the voice with their ears. Instead it rattled inside their skulls like a ball bearing in a can.

(They say we started out in a blaze of glory and now we're all going down in flames.)

The sound was like whispers in a crowded theatre before the rise of a curtain, a hundred people hiding just out of sight, giggling at something nobody could quite see. And it wasn't just the two of them who'd heard it—a clamor of screams and honking horns started to rise up from the people and cars on their way through the gate.

(But it's going to be okay. I promise...)

Shiloh and Brianna stared in horror as the dragon wormed its way inside the barrier and hung above them, upside-down, as if rooted to the barrier's inside surface by magnetic force. Then, slowly, it spread its black wings and kept spreading them. They were so huge Shiloh thought they might block out the sun itself. Which, for once, wouldn't be a good thing.

"Bri," Shiloh whispered, shaking her arm. "Bri, it's—it's—"

"HEY! HELP!" Brianna yelled, voice cracking. She looked around but the street was emptying fast. Two gate attendants ducked inside their booth and disappeared, possibly out the other side. "There's a thing! There's a ghost, it's inside—"

The dragon launched itself from the wall and dropped to the ground. Strangely, it made no noise when it landed. But the air around the ghost wasn't silent. It started to thrum with a strange whirring like the sound of a swarm of locusts, combined with a low, rumbling droning and rapid clicking. Shiloh realized with a chill that the sound didn't just come from the dragon, but, like the voice, from inside xir mind. Some people, those who'd never seen the Tartarus Zone and its creatures in person, said waste ghosts like this one were just urban legends. Ghosts being telepathic met with even more skepticism. But Shiloh felt the hums and scratching sounds inside xir brain more than heard them with xir ears, and they were starting to almost sound like whispers too.

(*Whatever you do, sweeties, stay out of the light.*) The dragon moved closer, stepping delicately and slowly like a stalking cat. People ran, the crowd quickly scattering, though some lingered to record the scene with their phones. But the eerie dragon wasn't looking at them at all. It wasn't looking at anyone but Shiloh. Thick smoke swirled around its head and neck but, oddly, it didn't seem to permeate the rest of the air, staying close to the dragon's head almost as if it were an extension of its body. *(Just try not to fall into the fire, okay?)*

"This is Meridian Research and Resupply Beacon requesting immediate support! A ghost has breached the barrier!" a voice cut into Shiloh's reverie. Brianna had run up to the now-vacant gate post and grabbed a dangling walkie-talkie. "This is a Radiance research and resupply facility, I repeat, there's a ghost here, and—"

(If you ever thought the law was on your side, let this open your eyes.)

"*Anyone* in range, this is Meridian!" Brianna shouted. "We need immediate aid!"

The dragon paid no attention to Brianna's pleas. Its eyes were fixed on Shiloh as if xie were the only person in the world. But Brianna's cries shook Shiloh out of xir mesmerized haze and xie ran over to her and started trying to pull her away from the gate.

"No! You run!" Brianna yelled, shaking Shiloh's arm off, not putting the walkie down or moving.

"Not without you!" Shiloh was starting to panic, knew it, but xie couldn't help it. Not with those eyes still fixed directly on xir. The dragon's unblinking gaze paralyzed Shiloh mid-step as xie and Brianna struggled to run, move, or do anything but stand there helplessly. Neither of them could breathe as it moved closer. That thick smoke started to rise from its nostrils. Slowly, never taking its eyes off the shaking teenagers, it opened its mouth.

Something whizzed by Shiloh's shoulder, smacking the ground near the dragon's talon—and its oblong head whipped down to look at the stone that had almost hit it. At the same time, Shiloh and Brianna whirled around to see where the thrown rock had come from.

A young man shakily stood his ground, dark eyes wide and russet-brown skin washed out with fear, holding a handful of rocks. Shiloh gasped, immediately forgetting everything behind xir. No dragon, no terrified crowd, no gate, no barrier, no Parole. Nothing mattered except the young man getting ready to throw another rock.

He might as well be lit up in a spotlight. Not because xie wanted to draw him but because xie already had—and like Brianna said, he rocked the cerulean scarf and skinny jeans. Shiloh's head and heart buzzed with the electric feeling of Déjà vu. Of importance. *Pay attention,* everything in the world seemed to whisper. Don't miss this chance. *Chance,* the word—the name—reverberated in Shiloh's head like an echo.

As he—Chance, yes, Shiloh had never been more sure of anything—tossed one of the rocks up in the air in preparation for another throw, Shiloh had the wild thought that it really should have been a coin. But just before he let the rock fly the young man seemed to lose his nerve. He stood frozen for a moment. Then he dropped the rest of his stones and sprinted away.

"*Theres-a-freaking-dragon-why-aren't-you-running?!*" he shouted at them as he flew past, nape-length black hair flying behind him. That shook Shiloh and Brianna out of their paralysis and they turned to follow the only person showing any sense. The rock hadn't even hit the dragon but it at least distracted it for a few microseconds—and that was all they needed to get a head start.

Somewhere behind them a motorcycle roared to life.

They ran chaotically, in a clump of three, sticking close together out of instinct with no direction except *away*. Behind them came a rushing sound like rising wind and Shiloh knew if xie looked back it would be into a pair of black, shineless eyes. Everyone kept running, rounding the next corner—

And almost tripping over one another as they scrambled to a stop.

The dragon stood directly in front of them in the middle of the street, huge wings almost stretching from sidewalk to sidewalk.

"No," Shiloh said, lightheaded with fear and shock. This had to be a dream. A bad one. "How did it..."

(Icarus,) said the dragon-ghost, staring impassively down. *(The word.)*

"What?" The words cut through Shiloh's fear and xie was able to grasp them enough to be confused. The voice was different; it didn't sound like the girl from the radio anymore.

(Icarus. Exchange.) Definitely not the same voice as before. Or the same words.

"What does that mean?" Shiloh called, taking a tiny step forward, hands coming up.

"What are you doing?" Chance said in a loud whisper. "You can't talk to these things!"

"We can't run from it either," Shiloh said slowly. "And this one's talking." Xie couldn't decide which voice was stranger, the dragon's new one, or Chance's voice, which xie knew, despite hearing it for the first time in—

"It's just repeating!" he protested. "This is from the radio! It must have heard it too, that's all it's—hey! Where are you going?"

Shiloh stepped forward, hands raised not in a surrender, but extended in front, palms facing out. Slowly, xie moved past Chance, past Brianna, toward the dragon.

Chance was right. Ghosts didn't actually talk, everybody knew that. They made all kinds of eerie, click-whisper noises that weren't really sounds; you heard them in your head, not your ears. But this one was using words. And it didn't seem about to stop trying to get its point across, whatever that was. Shiloh kept eye contact as xie came to a stop right in front of it. The day's electric charge seemed to sweep across xir skin and Shiloh didn't blink or move an inch. "What did you just say?"

The dragon held perfectly still. So did Shiloh. Xie'd started the day feeling like a princess in a tower. Maybe the first step toward freedom was facing a dragon.

(*I know it's scary, but I'll be right here with you, just listen to my voice,*) it said, tilting its head in what almost looked like confusion. (*I'm your Radio Angel, and–*)

"Don't just repeat old words," Shiloh interrupted, probably surprising xirself more than the dragon. "Talk to me. I know you can."

(*Icarus,*) the dragon-ghost said, in the voice from before, the one that sounded nothing like the one it had been using.

"You said that before. What does that mean?" Shiloh's hands almost dropped, but from surprise more than fatigue. That word was familiar too. But it wasn't from a girl on the radio. Shiloh had heard it from a boy in a tree.

(*The word?*) Now it sounded almost uncertain. It tilted its head the other way, seeming expectant and waiting, like Shiloh was supposed to know what came next. The fact that xie had no idea what it wanted or what response wouldn't get them all eaten was almost as terrifying as the dragon itself. (*The word you need?*)

"I don't know what that means," Shiloh said, not sure if admitting this was the right thing to do at all. "What does 'Icarus–'"

The thundering roar of a motorcycle filled the air, startling Shiloh into silence. Gravel flew as a pair of huge wheels came to a skidding halt beside the small group and a booted foot slammed down against the pavement. The girl before them rode the biggest motorcycle any of them had ever seen, wore a black helmet with a dark visor, and bounced her leg impatiently on the ground. She quickly swept a hand over the glass in front of her face and the lens went transparent, revealing the upper half of her face.

Like the dragon, her intense eyes were fixed directly on Shiloh. But unlike the dragon, xie recognized her at once, feeling a surge of excitement instead of terror.

Anh Minh Le. Annie. Like 'Chance,' Shiloh knew her name as surely as xir own. But even more absolutely, xie knew her face. Over and over xie'd drawn the seeking expression in her eyes, their unwavering focus. The angle of her sharp jaw. But this was not paper, *she was finally here.*

"Didn't you hear me?" She asked—again, apparently, since Shiloh hadn't heard her the first time—glancing at the dragon-ghost which still waited passively in the street, then back to Shiloh. There was something new about her, xie realized, something xie hadn't drawn. She wore a large, sharp-pointed shark's tooth on a chain around her neck. "What did it say?"

"The dragon?"

"Yes, the dragon!" She turned back to face it. There was something on the back of her leather jacket in metal studs xie couldn't read, but her urgency was much clearer.

"It said 'Icarus,'" Shiloh said, scrambling to get over xir shock at her sudden appearance, and the fact that the dragon was still staring at them.

(Icarus,) the ghost repeated. *(The word you need.)*

"What do you mean by that?" Annie demanded before Shiloh could, staring straight at the ghost without hesitation. "How do you know that word?"

"Hold it right there."

It wasn't the dragon's voice. Shiloh and the rest of the small terrified group turned to see two men standing in the middle of the street.

"Oh no," Brianna whispered, as if realizing her call for help had been answered in the worst possible way. "I didn't... I didn't mean..."

The Eye in the Sky enforcers carried long-barreled assault rifles, footsteps heavy from steel-toed combat boots weighed down with black body armor. They wore helmets that obscured their entire faces, black visors, and gas mask breathing apparatuses shaped vaguely like skulls. They scared Shiloh more than dragons, ghosts, or Tartarus itself. "Don't move."

That wouldn't be hard. Shiloh was frozen to the spot. The men in the black masks had never been here to help before. But this time they weren't looking at Shiloh or any of the other young people huddled near one another. Their guns were pointed at the dragon.

"Take it alive if we can," one said, voice muffled by the helmet but audible. "The Major will want–" he cut off, holding perfectly still, paralyzed by the cold, alien eyes.

There was a moment of complete silence–then gunfire erupted in the street as the first soldier opened fire. Terrified, Shiloh clapped xir hands over xir ears and stumbled backwards, running into someone else as they all scrambled to get away. The only one that didn't move an inch was the dragon. Every single bullet sailed directly through its ghostly body and kept going, as if it were made of light and shadow instead of flesh and bone.

But people weren't made of light and shadow. Some had remained at the edges of the street to stare at the dragon but most of them scattered, running at the first gunshot. Not all of them made it. Bullets were faster, and now they passed through the ghost's insubstantial form and into the terrified and much-more-solid human beings around and behind it.

When the clamor of gunfire and the metallic jangling of shells against sidewalk quieted, the street was almost empty. But the dragon was still there. It stood exactly where it had before, staring at its assailants. Slowly it opened its jaws.

"Shit," one soldier whispered, before he was hit with the first blast.

Out of the dragon's maw, frighteningly fast, poured a torrent of–*something*, that looked like smoke but much more solid, almost a liquid, and it caught the men full in the chest. They flew backwards, slamming into the concrete wall and crumpling to the ground. Over the next few seconds, their armor and the bodies within withered like burned paper, dissolving into moist ash, thick smoke curling into the air.

The dragon's head whipped around to face the four frightened teenagers who'd taken refuge behind Annie's motorcycle, which was barely scratched despite deflecting several bullets. Now its teeth were bared and dark plumes of smoke poured from gaps between its fangs in irregular bursts as if it were panting from exhaustion or panic.

"It's okay," Shiloh said, climbing shakily to xir feet from behind the familiar vehicle and wracking xir brain for the right words. Out of the corner of xir eye, xie saw still forms lying in the street. The soldiers? It had to be them, Shiloh's brain refused any alternative. "They're gone now. We're not gonna–"

The dragon's head plunged forward like a striking snake's, almost faster than xie could register. But not faster than defensive instinct. Shiloh's hands shot up; hands that now pulsed with a brilliant amber light.

Something surged inside, like a gust of warm air or sunlight, starting from xir solar plexus and radiating out, shining from xir eyes behind dark glasses. Shiloh couldn't see, couldn't hear anything except for the sudden pounding of blood in xir ears, couldn't feel anything except intense, scorching heat and power. Xie was blinded by blue-violet afterimages. The light was disorienting, but not harmful to xir sensitive eyes. It didn't hurt. When the light faded, the ghost was gone. All that remained was scorch marks on the pavement, as if it had been burned in white-hot flame.

Shiloh stared. Brianna and Chance stared from where they still crouched behind the motorcycle. Everything was still, except the thick smoke rising from Shiloh's hands.

"Get on already!" Annie yelled, jumping back onto her bike and, waving one arm. She wore a metal brace on it, shining and strong as armor.

She didn't have to tell Chance twice; he scrambled up to sit behind her immediately. "It's about time!" he yelled, grinning.

When Shiloh and Brianna didn't move, Annie revved her throttle and the engine roared. "*Come on!* We have to go!"

"That's right." Brianna said quietly, still staring at the scorch marks where the dragon had once been. But when she turned, her eyes were clear. "You know those two, don't you? They're the friends you were gonna meet?"

"Yeah," Shiloh said at last. The only words that existed would never do reality justice. How did you cram a lifetime's worth of memories and loss and heartache and yearning into words they were quickly running out of time to speak? Force them to make any kind of sense? Tell any kind of truth? "They're pretty important."

"Your friends are from Parole, aren't they?" Brianna looked past Shiloh to where Annie and Chance waited on the huge motorcycle. Her eyes were glassy, and Shiloh couldn't tell if she was going to cry, or just in shock. "Is that where you're going?"

Silence stretched between them like the sky beyond the barrier. Somewhere out there was a city that never stopped burning. Toxic storms screamed across a wasteland stretching thousands of miles across the American Midwest. Radios answered when Shiloh asked questions, even if their signals were never meant to leave Parole. The smell of smoke never faded away. Somewhere, flames were buried in dreams, and shut behind walls. Barriers, with monsters inside and out. Beams of light that could burn—or protect. Slay dragons. Light up the night with crackling energy that sung in xir veins.

"Yes." Shiloh heard the whispered answer, only then realizing it came from xirself. "Listen...I know that thing just kind of ruined the words—but everything's gonna be okay."

"No. It's not," Brianna said, and the certainty in her voice was jarring. "But maybe it still can be. Go, more soldiers will be here soon, and someone needs to head them off. I'll catch up to you when I can. Go!"

Shiloh stumbled away from her and toward the motorcycle, climbing up to sit behind Chance. The thing was big enough that three people could comfortably fit even without using the sidecars, and the dashboard was so covered in buttons and displays it looked like it belonged in the cockpit of a spaceship.

"Ready?" Annie asked, voice tight with what might have been excitement, fear, or the mix Shiloh felt. In her voice, xie heard the sound of running feet, a pounding heart, and the crackling of flames.

"Feels good to wake up," Chance said, smiling in a way that was loose and shaky and brave all at once. Somewhere in Shiloh's memory a coin arced through the air. When the wind swept through his hair, it sounded like rustling of leaves in high branches and shuffling cards. "Doesn't it?"

Annie twisted the throttle in reply. "Hang on."

Meridian had the right name, Shiloh thought as the engine roared and the bike shot forward, tearing through the streets. The edge of one place and the next. Three dreamers started out in a tree, and now they were all standing together on a high precipice, knowing they were about to fly, not fall. Shiloh didn't look back as the motorcycle peeled away, and didn't even think about being afraid. Now, xie was finally close enough to read the back of Annie's jacket.

HERE WE GO AGAIN.

CHAPTER 2

Turn On The Lights

THE LIGHTHOUSE WAS THE TALLEST BUILDING IN TOWN. IT WAS ALSO THE STRANGEST. THERE WERE no dangerous seas to illuminate or ships to guide into a waiting berth. But even without a sea, after today, Shiloh definitely felt like a ship tossed about by a hurricane.

"We almost died," Shiloh panted as the bike came to a stop around back, hidden from the main street. It wouldn't do much about anyone who really wanted to find them but at least they were out of plain view. Xir head spun from excitement and terror and was starting to ache, but that was background noise.

"I know!" Chance laughed, free and easy. "But it was fun!"

Shiloh nodded and climbed off the motorcycle onto unsteady feet. "Coming about an inch away from death is fun?"

"Forget that! Remember that the first thing we did together is *slay a dragon!"* Chance jumped off too, taking a few excited, almost dancing steps, like the adrenaline just wouldn't let him sit still. He moved with ease and smiled with a brightly beaming charisma that instantly caught attention and held it. "Wow. This is it, isn't it? The lighthouse."

"You mean the beacon." Annie slung her helmet under her arm and stood with her feet planted far apart, as she always did due to her ankle braces. When she stepped closer and unabashedly stared, Shiloh met her gaze easily. Her eyes were intense but not intimidating and their searching focus felt nothing like a stranger's. She held very still except for one short finger, which twirled around a thick, tightly coiled strand of hair that hung down past her jaw, the nervous motion continuous. "That *is* what it actually is, right?"

"That's right. The Meridian Beacon." Shiloh nodded, raising xir arm in a little presenting gesture. The tower's concrete exterior was smooth and looked like the newest thing in Meridian. Nothing decorated the plain walls except for a heavy steel door and a numeric keypad beside it. "This was the first one my mom ever built. The ten big ones around Tartarus are based on it. Not much, but it's home."

"Well, I'd call it much," Chance said, craning his neck to look straight up. "Kinda obvious, don't you think? Doesn't seem great for hiding. While we're at it, that big-ass motorcycle's probably gonna catch some eyes if we just park it here."

Annie glanced at her motorcycle, then back up at him. "We won't have a problem," she said, as if this explained everything.

"I'm just saying, that was kind of... conspicuous," Chance said with a raise of his eyebrows. "We were supposed to meet up quietly, like normal people. Instead we blow up a dragon."

"We're not normal people," she said, not meeting his eyes. Annie tended to look longer and harder than people expected or considered polite—or not look at all. "And I didn't want it blown up either but it didn't leave us much choice."

"Oh, I'm not complaining." Chance smiled and brushed his smooth hair out of his face. Instead of seeming at all troubled by the strange circumstances, or the fact that they'd just narrowly escaped death, his smile was relaxed, as if he found the world endlessly entertaining. Shiloh recognized the way his eyes crinkled at the edges when he smiled. "Shiloh kept us all alive and put on a good show at the same time."

"I never told you my name," Shiloh said, but instead of feeling disturbed, xie felt a rush of joy, confirmation.

"I know, but it's right here in my head." He shrugged, smiling in a way that was awkward and apologetic and relieved all at once. "Do you know mine?"

Shiloh thought for a few seconds. "Chance? That's all I'm getting." Xie rubbed xir temples, then the back of xir head and occipitals where the Chiari pain still rested as a dull ache. "Is that really your name? It seems more like—I don't know. I think your dreams might have made more sense than mine."

"Chance is good." He nodded, looking satisfied and maybe a little relieved. "Call me that, that's fine."

"That's what I heard in the dreams too," Annie said, frowning.

He shot her a nervous look. "Is there a problem with that?"

"Not really. Where I come from, a lot of people don't use their given names."

"But you don't seem convinced."

"You seemed different in the tree."

"Lemme guess, you thought I'd be taller?" He gave her a flashing grin, but this one seemed pained if anything. "We're all a little different when we're awake. You wear a lot more spikes, for one thing. And seem a lot more on edge. Which I understand, being awake is terrible. And Shiloh's not as... sparky? Electric? Xie's human, not made of energy. So really..." he turned to see Shiloh staring at him, a grin spreading across xir face for the first time. "Hi there."

"What did you just say?" Shiloh stared at him, heart leaping; suddenly xie remembered cool shade on a hot day, dark lenses that cut a harsh glare.

"I just said a lot of things. I like to talk." He shrugged—then realized. "Oh! You mean..."

"You said 'xie.'" The feeling of confirmation was back, a thousand times stronger. Joy, relief and *absolute certainty* surged through xir chest in a warm rush.

"Was it right?" Chance asked, turning fully to face Shiloh.

Xie hesitated, trying to find the words. They failed but xie just nodded, smiling so hard xir cheeks hurt.

"Okay," Chance said, more quietly than his usual charismatic tone, and the smile that spread across his face was less brilliant and gentler than before. "So that should tell us we're not making this dream thing up. He's really talking to us. Gabriel."

"Yeah." Annie frowned, deep in thought; she didn't seem nearly as convinced.

"Isn't this a good thing?" Chance asked. When she didn't answer, he pressed on. "I thought Gabriel died in Parole. I never thought I'd see you two again either—but here we are. How often do you get a second...chance?"

Annie didn't smile, or answer. Her hand went to the shark tooth on the chain around her neck and she rubbed its smooth surface with her thumb, looking lost in not-quite-pleasant thoughts. Then she busied herself with something Shiloh couldn't see on the dashboard and the air around the motorcycle somehow went dark, as if a very solid cloud were passing over it like a curtain—and then it was gone.

"Are you going to explain that?" Chance asked as she walked past them toward the beacon entrance, wide-eyed.

She shrugged, looking almost bored. "Custom model."

Shiloh considered pressing further, but didn't think xie'd have any more luck. Xie didn't want to linger outside anymore, either. So xie entered a code in the keypad beside the solid steel door, which slid smoothly open. They stepped into one long curving room that looked more like a spaceship corridor than the interior of a building. The walls seemed made of humming machinery, dials, and consoles, every conduit and bit of wiring alive with electricity. A tight, spiraling staircase led up to the next level and more complex machinery that only got more intricate until it reached the huge light on top.

"Wow." Chance turned in a complete circle to look around. "You live in here? Like, all the time? Sleeping and everything?"

"Yeah. It's not as weird as you'd think, just kinda bright and loud." Xie wiggled xir dark glasses, which xie didn't remove inside. "And it's not all like this, we have normal rooms too..." A fast, rhythmic clanking came from overhead and Shiloh turned to look at the spiral stairs. "Mom?"

"The damn thing's got an attitude," a woman's voice called down, echoes bouncing off the metal walls. When she appeared, they could all see that the clanking came from her steel-toed boots as she quickly descended the metal steps. "But I reminded it who's boss. It should cooperate now."

Maureen Cole stood as tall and solid as the tower that was both her home and biggest ongoing project. Like her child, the Tsalagi Native American woman had a quick, perceptive stare that took in small details and an urgency about her, an electric impulse to move. With her long black hair tied back in a thick ponytail and old work shirt that smelled like a combination of coffee and motor oil, Shiloh didn't have to guess at what she'd been doing just now. She only got quite this messy—or this sweaty and keyed-up—from digging in the beacon's guts itself.

"I saw the flashes from all the way up here. They probably saw it all the way across Tartarus." As she spoke, she turned to check a screen on a nearby console. It must have confirmed something, because she gave a quick nod before turning her full attention to Shiloh. "Something exciting happened down there, didn't it?"

"A ghost. Down at the barrier. Tore a hole in it like it was wet kleenex."

"Crap. Is it still there?" she asked as she wiped her hands on her jeans in two fast, efficient swipes. Her movements were a combination of confident physicality and intense, precise focus. Her hard muscles came from running up and down stairs and more heavy lifting than anyone would believe engineering involved. The lines on her face spoke of hours spent squinting at equations and blueprints, swearing at delicate equipment until it got its act together.

Shiloh hesitated. "Uh, no. It's definitely not."

Maureen's eyes narrowed. "What exactly happened? Are you okay?"

"I'm fine," Shiloh said after hesitating just long enough to be suspicious.

"Mmm, no, definitely not fine. I think you'd better start at—who are they?" Maureen's eyes landed on Chance and Annie, immediately narrowing as if she'd seen them for the first time, and wasn't sure she liked what she saw.

"Uh, that's Annie, and this is Chance," Shiloh said quickly, glad to be out of the spotlight.

"New friends?"

"...Sort of."

"Okay, great, nice to meet you." Her words were short but not terse, expression softening as soon as Shiloh confirmed they were friends. Then she turned right back to Shiloh, concentration unbroken. "Tell me about the ghost."

"I...it was..." Shiloh bit xir lip. "Bri and I were down at the gate. Suddenly it was just *there*, on the outside of the barrier. It looked like... a dragon. Then it cut a hole in it, with its hand, or claw, then it was inside, then Eye in the Sky showed up and it panicked and SkEye shot—"

"They shot at who?" Her eyes flashed. "At you? Are you—"

"I'm fine, really! I don't even think they saw us, they were shooting at the dragon."

"SkEye shot first and asked questions never?"

"Pretty much."

"Look at my surprised face. I am so surprised." Maureen gave a disgusted snort. "How'd that work out for them?"

"I don't think it did anything. It just kind of stood there, then it breathed back at them."

"Breathed what, fire? Points for commitment, I guess."

"No, just Tartarus poison," Shiloh made a face as xie tried to explain the awful almost-liquid toxic air. "Or something."

"That does make more sense. Then what?"

"Then it turned to look at me, and I could tell it was gonna breathe again, so I just—zap." Shiloh held up xir hands again.

"Zap?" Maureen's eyes narrowed again. "Right down there in broad daylight?"

"I didn't have a choice!" Shiloh protested. "And I don't think anyone saw. They were kind of, either not there, or, probably, not... alive."

"Not alive?" She stopped, breaking off her and Shiloh's rapid-fire back-and-forth. "Are you telling me the ghost fried actual people?"

"Just the soldiers." Shiloh shook xir head, suddenly feeling a wave of... xie wasn't even sure. Once xie remembered the sight of the bodies in the street, nothing else existed. "SkEye did the rest."

Maureen stared, intensity slowly fading from her eyes, replaced by devastated horror. "Bastards."

"Yeah," Shiloh murmured. Xie knew what xie was feeling now. Faint, numb, and more than vaguely sick. "So then—"

Xie was interrupted by a very fast, firm hug. Maureen's arms wrapped tight around Shiloh and pulled xir in close. Xie let out a deep, exhausted sigh and rested xir face against xir mother's shoulder. "You saw this? This happened while—you were right there?"

Shiloh couldn't answer, but xie nodded, and Maureen's embrace tightened in reply. After several seconds of very tight hug, xie thought xie could open xir mouth and say words instead of crying, so xie tried again. "SkEye shot people. Then the ghost blasted them. Then I blasted it."

"Sounds like Eye in the Sky got what they deserved for once." Maureen released Shiloh and held xir at arms' length, taking another close, careful look. "And you did the right thing."

"You forgot something," Annie cut in, not seeming to think twice about interrupting.

"Yeah you did," Chance nodded, looking rattled. "That thing opened a hole right in the barrier. What happens if more attack?"

"The barrier isn't the only defense, we've got the beacon here." Maureen nodded up, indicating a higher floor. "Not as big as the ones around Tartarus, but just as powerful. Don't worry about the ghosts, even if this one sounds a little bigger than most."

"No," Annie said more firmly. "I mean you forgot the most important part. The dragon was talking."

"Talking?" Maureen turned her head to quickly zero in on Annie's face. "Saying what?"

"It said, 'Icarus.. The word you need,'" Annie answered slowly. "I know I've heard that word before somewhere. It has to be important."

"Icarus..." Maureen said, then mouthed the word again. "Well, I know it too. Couldn't tell you where from, though." She shook her head, seeming to dismiss one enigma in favor of another. "Did the ghost seem alive? Intelligent? More like a projection? A program?"

Annie hesitated, looking overwhelmed. "It said more. 'It's happened, Parole is burning.' In... her voice. From the radio."

"I've heard ghosts make a lot of noises," Maureen said, stepping toward Annie with the same kind of searching look xie'd given Shiloh a moment ago. "And when they're not just parroting, a lot of those noises sound like some kind of language. But I've never heard one say anything new, like 'Icarus.' And I've never heard one repeat anything from... that radio station. Because no one is supposed to hear it."

"I heard it," Annie said, still looking anxious. "But not from a dragon. I heard it when it first played."

Maureen stared at her with what looked like equal parts suspicion and curiosity. "Who are you?"

"Anh Minh Le." She was suddenly so tentative, with none of her usual confidence. "Or Annie. It's an honor to finally meet you, Dr. Cole."

"You're the messengers from Parole," Maureen realized, eyes going wide.

"I am," Annie said, then turned to face Chance. "He's not."

"No, I lived in Parole ten years ago," he explained. "But I guess it's not the kind of place you walk away from. I tried, but I just ended up in a tree."

"In a tree?" Maureen looked up at him, as if seeing him individually for the first time. "You're Shiloh's brain friends."

"Brain...? Sure, I guess." He shrugged, looking untroubled by the fantastic idea. "Not sure what else to call recurring dreams about a tree and a few old friends."

"Gabriel said we had to find each other," Annie filled in. "And him. He warned me about the collapse so I could make it out of Parole in time, so I knew it wasn't just dreams. They needed someone to get to you and your project, Dr. Cole, so I volunteered. I thought it was my only chance to find out what was going on."

"Well, looks like you were right. When were you going to tell me this?" Maureen turned to Shiloh. "These aren't just random kids, they're the ones from the dreams you've been telling me about all this time?"

"Sorry," Shiloh said, embarrassed. "I kind of forgot ... there's been a lot going on." Second major understatement of the day.

"I'll give you that much," Maureen said, then turned back to Annie. "We lost contact with Parole weeks ago, total radio silence, it's been a nightmare. Then we get through for two seconds and they tell us they've got people coming out to meet us. Is that you?"

"Not people," Annie said quietly, eyes flicking away. "Just me."

"You got my message." It wasn't a question.

"That your project plans are complete, yes ma'am. So I drove here."

Maureen's eyebrows knit together in concern. "You can't be more than what, seventeen?"

"Eighteen." She gave Shiloh a sidelong glance that almost looked like plea for help.

"Radio Angel said someone else was coming. Ash Price. Is he meeting us later?"

"I..." Annie stuck her hands in her pockets and looked down at the floor between her shoes. She opened her mouth to say something, then shut it again.

"You escaped from Parole?" Maureen questioned further. "And traveled three-thousand miles to pick up my project? Alone?"

"I wasn't alone. It's a long story." The color was draining from Annie's face. Her hands, still in her pockets, curled into fists. When she spoke, her voice was higher than usual, fainter. "Some of us got out in time, though. Not all of us. We..." She paused, licked lips that were suddenly dry, and she blinked several times. She trailed off, staring—but not at Maureen. Past her. As if she'd forgotten any of them were there.

"Ash isn't coming, is he?" Maureen asked quietly.

"No. He's not." She squeezed her eyes shut and shook her head. "They didn't send me alone, they wouldn't do that. Ash said you'd help us and if we could just get to Meridian we'd be safe, then we could go home. But..."

"When?" Maureen asked quietly.

"Yester–yesterday. My shields burnt out. Eye in the Sky. Snipers." Annie swallowed. She took one hand out of her pocket and reached up to hold the shark tooth hanging around her neck. It seemed to help calm her down a little. "But I'm here now. I made it."

"Yes, you did." Maureen took in a breath and let it out, looking shaken and awed. "We knew the Parole collapse was coming. This is exactly what we planned for. You did the right thing coming to me."

"Thanks," Annie answered, sounding faraway and still not looking at any of them. She hadn't let go of the shark tooth either.

Maureen was quiet for a moment, then shook her head, eyes wide. "Can I maybe get you kids something to drink?"

"I'm good," Chance shook his head, staring at Annie with something between admiration and pain. She continued to stare vacantly into space, then suddenly looked up at Maureen.

"Ice cream," she said. "Uh, please. If you have it. If that's okay."

"You bet," Maureen nodded and a faint smile spread across her face for the first time since they'd arrived. "What's your favorite kind?"

"Favorite..." Annie mouthed, then shrugged, shaking her head. "Anything. Whatever's cold. We don't have much cold stuff back in–I haven't had it in a long time."

Maureen just looked at her for a few seconds, then headed off to the kitchen. "Cold it is."

A few minutes later, it seemed like Annie might actually eat all the ice cream in the whole house. She tore into the cookies and cream almost before there was a spoon in her hand and only stopped to press the heels of her hands against her eyes. Shiloh thought she was crying, until she mumbled the words 'brain freeze.'

"Better?" Chance asked when she finally slowed down, looking equal parts fascinated and impressed.

"Mm-hmm," she mumbled, tossing down the spoon and leaning back against the couch cushions. "I like cold things. Sweet things. Don't get much of any of that in Parole."

"That's—that sucks." He started to smile, but it faded.

"It's fine. I'm out now." Annie shrugged. Then she looked up at Maureen and Shiloh, as if realizing something for the first time. "You used to live there too. You escaped."

"Ten years ago," Maureen said with a slightly rueful smile. "If you call...yeah, I guess we did escape. Out of the fire, but back into the frying pan."

"You can escape Parole," Shiloh said. "But you never really escape *from* Parole."

"No. We're three-thousand miles away from Turret's mess and he's still making our lives harder." Maureen's voice turned bitter. "We kept our mouths shut. I made the beacon prototypes to keep away the ghosts. I made the barriers that protected every big city in the U.S. from the worst of Tartarus—and places nobody else gave a crap about, small towns, poor towns, reservations, they weren't his priority—well, they're priorities to me! And all the while Tartarus keeps spreading and Parole keeps burning. Was it enough?"

"Mom," Shiloh said quietly when she stopped to take a breath. "You did good."

"I know—I know, just... I guess I'm not that good at sitting still in a bubble while I know the world's going to hell outside."

"So, what are we bringing home?" Annie asked, right back to business.

"Got it right here." Slowly, Maureen reached into the pocket of her jeans and drew out a small object. It looked like a floppy disk, a worthless relic of office supplies and old movies, nothing anyone would use anymore. But Maureen held the plastic square delicately in the palm of her hand, gazing at it like it was worth a fortune or maybe a lost masterpiece. "I haven't put this baby down for a second since I finished. Don't you let it out of your sight either, not for anything."

"Good." Annie gave a resolute nod, usual determined energy returning. The ice cream seemed to have done wonders. As did getting back to the goal. "That's all I need. I'm ready to go right now, how about you?"

"I've been ready for years."

"Wait—what is that?" Chance asked, looking at the unassuming square.

"Hope on a floppy disk." Maureen smiled. "Actually, it just looks like one. This thing holds about a thousand times more data than anything you can get right now. But it's what's on the disk that's important."

"Hope for Parole?"

"It starts there, but it doesn't end there," she said slowly, suddenly seeming reluctant to let the disk go. "An old friend of mine in Parole will know what to do with these schematics."

"Danae?" Annie asked quietly, as if the name were a secret code word.

Maureen gave a short laugh. "We're gonna have fun."

"So what is the plan?"

"The plan *was*..." Maureen answered Annie's question but looked at Shiloh as she spoke. "That we'd take the data, find your dad, and then make tracks for Parole together." She looked at the other two, and the disk. "But we just added a ton of variables I'm not sure what to do with yet. And this disk needs to get there fast."

"I drive fast," Annie said with a nod. "But I'm not going all the way back to Parole. I'm meeting some friends halfway."

"What friends?"

"The crew of the FireRunner," she said with a hint of pride. "They got me out. And they got me halfway here. They're making a circuit of Tartarus' main beacon ring now, then they'll pick me up and take the data the rest of the way to—"

"The FireRunner? *Jay's ship!*" Maureen and Shiloh looked at each other. "Oh, this just got a whole lot easier. There are three people in the world I'd trust with this data—one of them is Jay. And the FireRunner's gotta be safer than Parole, especially now."

"Jay, like..." Chance frowned, looking like he was trying to remember something important, but not having much success. "That name rings a bell. Are you saying a name or a letter?"

"Both," Maureen said, but didn't elaborate, or seem to intend to.

"He's my uncle!" Shiloh smiled, the kind that went with an inside joke or juicy secret. "Everything amazing my mom does with inventions and machines, he does with computers."

"He wishes," Maureen snorted. "There's no comparing. But he'll be able to unlock my encryption, eventually. Might need some help from a friend, though." She smirked, clearly not about to say more. "He'll know who. Gonna drive him nuts."

"So I'll get this to him." Annie's pokerface was back, but the determination was clear in her voice. "The FireRunner should be about halfway around the Tartarus Zone. I can make it in four days, tops. From there, it's about three to Parole."

"Good. And when you do reach Parole, find Evelyn. If anybody knows what's happening, it'll be her." Maureen shot Shiloh a somewhat conspiratorial glance. "Your dad's probably been in contact with her too."

"We have to find Gabriel too," Annie said quietly but insistently. "He warned me about the collapse. I would have died if he hadn't woken me up."

"Yeah we do," Shiloh readily agreed. "None of this would have happened if he hadn't linked us up, however he did it. I still can't really believe it, but it's important."

Annie still looked pensive. "If I wasn't living it, I'd say this was bull. And I'd walk away."

"Even coming from a city full of superheroes?" Chance shot her a grin. "Thought this kind of thing was normal in Parole."

"None of this is normal. Nothing has been normal for a long time. And maybe I should be scared, but I'm not. I've been in your head and there's nothing to be scared of."

"It's an awful place, isn't it?" Chance's smile became a grimace. "Sorry about that. But I know what you mean. That tree is pretty much the one good thing in my life that stayed, while everything else changed."

"Or collapsed."

Shiloh gave a nervous laugh in the silence that followed. "Listen, I've been waiting for something to happen for so long, so we could get back to Parole and start living. Now that you guys are here, maybe I can get rid of the sleeping pills and coffee."

"And we *will* find your dad." The second Maureen said those words, nothing seemed nearly as frightening. Reality came into focus, like so many threads forming one coherent picture. Somewhere out there, the city still burned. Everything was lining up, falling into place, and starting to happen very fast.

"Not to be a killjoy," Chance said, sounding a bit apprehensive. "But once we get to Parole, how do we get in there? It's still locked up under a barrier."

"Don't worry about that." Maureen reached into another pocket and pulled out a small device, a black cylinder with a red button on top, like a remote-control detonator from an action movie to go with the floppy disk. "I designed that barrier, I can get us past it just as easily."

Suddenly, the metal doors slid open behind them and they all turned to look. Chance stumbled a few steps backwards and Annie raised her fists and lowered her head—but instead of the monster they'd anticipated, Brianna rushed through the door, disheveled and panting.

"Bri!" Shiloh ran to hug her, so weak with relief it almost felt like the precursor to a blackout. "Are you okay?"

"Am *I* okay?" She pushed Shiloh back enough so xie could see the incredulity on her face. "I'm not the one who shot a laser out of my hands!"

"Yeah, about that," Shiloh grimaced. "Did anybody see—?"

"You know, until now I never really believed in miracles." She shook her head. "But I don't think anyone actually saw where you went. Oh, they saw the energy beam, but not where you went."

"Mm-hmm." Annie smiled and nodded, as if confirming something to herself.

"But listen, the hole in the barrier's still open, it's not closing up like it should," Brianna said, worry clear in her eyes. "Somebody has to give it some extra juice from here. I still can't believe that thing actually tore a hole in it, like it was nothing!"

"I know," Maureen replied grimly. "I've been working on that problem for a while. But Meridian's still got its beacon."

"Good," Brianna said, though she didn't look very comforted "Because there's a lot more on the way."

"What?" Maureen's eyes widened.

"Yeah! Like, a whole swarm. I've never seen so many at once!"

"More firsts. Never heard of anything like this." Maureen frowned, voice sharp with alarm. "They must have been attracted by the discharge. Or maybe the hole in the barrier. Or maybe they were following..." She continued indistinctly as she began manipulating the controls on a nearby console.

"This day just keeps getting weirder. I'm about ready to send it back and ask for a new one..." Brianna said, then stopped, taking in everyone gathered around in the corridor. "Are you guys going somewhere?"

"Can't stay here," Shiloh said, looking back at Maureen and xir two new-old friends. "Not after today."

"You don't mean..." Brianna's eyes widened and her pale, sweat-damp face lost even more color. "Not Parole. You can't be serious."

"I've been serious about this for a long time."

She stared at Shiloh and tried to speak. No words came out the first couple tries, though the noises sounded like protests. At last, she just shook her head. "You really think you're going to find the truth out there?"

"Won't find it here," Shiloh answered. Somehow xie felt more serene than xie'd felt in a long time.

"And there's nothing I can say to make you stay?"

"Bri," Shiloh said gently. "We've lived here for ten years. We've been preparing to leave this bubble for about nine."

"Go find your answers, then." Brianna nodded, blinking hard. "Don't look back. But—call me? Somehow? Just let me know you're okay."

"When I get there, I'm gonna be more okay than I've ever been in my life." Shiloh pulled her close. Her arms went immediately around xir as well and they held each other tight. When they broke apart, Shiloh was still smiling. "And I'll call you. Somehow."

"There," Maureen said, striding up to the pair and giving Brianna an appraising look. "The hole's started closing, but it'll still need some babysitting. You'll be okay here on your own?

"Yes, Ma'am." Brianna straightened up, hands behind her back. The only thing missing was a salute. "I had an excellent teacher."

"Just keep it from falling down," Maureen shook her head, almost laughing. "And watch out for any new tears. Then we're good."

"I can do that."

"Good." Maureen grinned and took a deep breath, like it was the first fresh breath she'd had in a long time. "I've got a lot of unfinished business in Parole. Been waiting a long time to get back to it. Did you drive here?"

Annie looked up at that last question directed at her, and nodded, heading toward the door. Shiloh cast a last, half-sad, half-excited look back at Brianna as everyone else hurried outside; she followed them to the doorway and watched with wide eyes as Annie located her invisible motorcycle and did something that made it reappear from thin air.

"Now come here," Maureen said, holding up the black cylinder with the red button. "Everybody get in close like it's a group selfie." Everybody squeezed in tight, and Maureen pushed the button.

In a heartbeat, they were somewhere else.

☆

Brianna worked feverishly, guiding Meridian's barrier-and-beacon system through the regeneration process. Closing the hole took more energy than she'd thought, and it stayed stubbornly open until she re-directed power from the backup generators. Slowly, the wound in the energy dome healed. As soon as it was safe to let her mind wander, she started running over the next few minutes to come. Rehearsing the conversation. Deep, calming breaths. Eyes steady, no blinks.

After not nearly long enough, an insistent buzz from the intercom warned her that someone wanted to come inside. Brianna savored one last second of blissful silence and an empty room to herself. Then she flipped a lever and the airlock decompressed with a hiss. "Come in!"

Major David Turret's pale face was weathered and his close-cropped hair was silver-white. He was not a tall man, or a broad one, or heavily muscled. He was not physically imposing, and he did not raise his voice often. He didn't have to. He'd made a long career out of getting results long before that became necessary.

"Major. Sir." Brianna stood straight and tall, making herself look unwaveringly back when he fixed his cobalt-hard, pale blue eyes on her. Not many people in the world could hold their own under the intensity of his stare, not even her. Today, several lives might depend on the steadiness of her eyes. On one blink. "What can I do for you?"

He took his time, movements unhurried and purposeful as he studied the conspicuously empty room containing the beacon's primary control. It and the curving corridor outside were silent except for softly humming machinery. He seemed entirely unsurprised by the apparent vacancy and sounded like he knew the answer to his next question before he asked it. "Where is Dr. Cole?"

"I don't know, Sir." Brianna pushed all the confidence she had into her technically honest answer. She kept her voice and gaze steady and prayed for no uncomfortable follow-up questions. "I just saw there was a hole in the barrier and I came here to repair it. Maybe she's doing some field work."

If he suspected this was anything but the truth, he didn't pursue it or alter his surprisingly soft, measured voice that anyone not intimately familiar with it might have called calm. "I received a disturbing report today of an incident that resulted in the deaths of several civilians. Shiloh Cole was involved, as well as two other unidentified youths. I'm told you were an eyewitness. Can you verify any of this?"

"There was a disturbance," she said carefully, not liking the direction this was headed. "But it was because a ghost—"

"Thank you," he interrupted in the same level tone. With that, he turned to leave.

"Dad, no," Brianna said quietly and her tentative objection was enough to make him stop in his tracks but not turn around. "That's not what I said, Shiloh didn't kill those—"

"*Major.*" A sharp edge emerged for the first time.

"Major. Sir." She corrected herself, standing up straighter until her back began to ache. "I said Shiloh didn't kill anyone, the ghost did. Shiloh dissipated the *ghost*."

"With an electric discharge," Turret continued, his tone once more carefully controlled. Slowly, he turned to fix her with an unblinking gaze, but there was no trace of the annoyance that had flared in his voice. "It charred the bodies of two Radiance volunteers beyond recognition."

"No, it didn't," she said firmly. "That was the ghost's venom. And it killed armed Eye in the Sky officers—not unarmed volunteers." She took a breath, then spoke very quickly. "Your report is wrong. Whoever gave you that information is wrong or lying."

"My source is reliable," he said just above a thoughtful murmur but, as he spoke, he watched her very carefully. She wondered if she'd ever worn that pensive expression while assisting on one of Dr. Cole's many projects. Evaluating a new and untested resource, one whose fate remained undecided. Maybe limitless potential, maybe a pile of scrap.

"But like you said, I was an eyewitness. If you actually look at the bodies, you'll see the cause of death is much closer to being doused in acid than struck by lightning."

Turret said nothing. Nor did he move, blink, or seem to breathe. He waited, and Brianna started to sweat.

"And before that...it spoke."

Again, nothing, just a continued, unbroken stare. Face reddening and heart beginning to pound, Brianna scrambled to say the right words, give him what he wanted, say anything to make what suddenly felt like an interrogation come to an end.

"The ghost–the dragon. It said...words, it sounded like some kind of radio broadcast. Staticky, hard to understand."

"What words?" His voice dropped to just above a whisper. Brianna began to shake.

"'It's going to be okay.' That's what it said. It almost sounded...nice."

"Is that all?"

Brianna forced herself to straighten her back, suck in a breath and look her father in the eye, transform every bit of her being into the soldier he wanted. It was never more important than when she was about to lie to his face. "Yes, sir."

Without another word, he turned to stride out the door again.

"Where are you going?" The question was out of her mouth before she knew it. She just couldn't let him disappear again, taking all the answers to this bizarre day with him.

"Parole."

The answer was plain, abrupt, and the last one Brianna expected. Her mouth hung open. Then she shut it, and forced her spinning brain back into enough operation to form words. "I was under the impression that Parole was–lost. Sir."

"It was. But not in the way you've been told."

"Then the conspiracy theories are correct–Sir?" She barely remembered to tack the last word on, or to mask her surprised reaction. "I never believed them. Or I would have mentioned–"

Turret stopped and she fell immediately silent. When he turned, it wasn't all the way. But when he looked at her, it was with his undivided attention. Once again he carefully studied the way all the color drained from Brianna's face, her wide eyes, her clenched jaw that couldn't hide her shivers. "Parole wasn't destroyed in the Tartarus Blast. Parole caused it."

"What? I... I thought—"

"You were supposed to. You focused on the immediate problem, Tartarus. There was nothing anyone could do for Parole, or needed to. The problem was designed to correct itself. You didn't need to know." The words almost sounded comforting.

"Sir?" Behind her back, her palms began to sweat. She balled them into fists. "Are you saying that—that *there are still people in Parole?* Could Mom and Liam still be alive? And Aunt Cass—"

"No." His low voice cut her off as easily as if he'd shouted. "I'm not saying that at all. There are no people left in Parole."

Brianna couldn't answer but she nodded, eyes stinging and teeth and lips pressed tight together. Her fingernails dug into her palms and fists shook behind her back.

"The priority remains the same," he continued, never deviating from his calm but unwavering tone or course. "Contain Tartarus. Neutralize it. By going back to the source and ensuring Parole does no more damage."

This time, when he turned to leave, Brianna was ready.

"Wait! I want to go with you."

"Why?" he asked immediately, as if he'd been waiting as well.

"To stop Tartarus from spreading, like always," she said, throat and lips suddenly very dry. "But if Parole's really there, and it's making things worse... if it'll hurt anyone, I just—even if they think it's—I just don't want anyone to get hurt. Please."

He considered her for a few seconds, a sensible evaluation period, but the wait felt interminable on her end. At last, he gave a slow, deliberate nod. When he left, she followed.

CHAPTER 3

Radio Silence

THE FOUR OF THEM REMATERIALIZED A FEW FEET OFF THE GROUND AND DROPPED. MAUREEN landed smoothly on her feet, Shiloh clung to her to keep from falling, Annie dropped into a half-crouch, and Chance face-planted directly into the dry grass.

"What was that? What the *hell* was that?" Chance sputtered, spitting out dead leaves.

"Portable transport device," Maureen said much more calmly. "One of my handier little toys."

They stood a few yards away from where Meridian's barrier arced into the sky. Barriers like it protected major cities and isolated outposts, insulating them from most of the Tartarus Blast's effects. Unlike Parole's, these weren't meant

to imprison everyone inside. Instead, they kept toxic storms and ghostly pests out.

Parole was a world unto itself. But while everyone inside hoped and dreamed for escape, the world outside was changed for good. And not necessarily for the better.

The ground was hard and powdery from long weeks of drought, and the air was unseasonably warm and dry for November in Maryland, where humidity usually lingered long into the fall.. It was the day after Halloween and it felt like summer. Clouds hung low like heavy smog. There was no wind, no cars or people left on the visible stretch of highway leading back into Meridian. The stillness was unnatural, as if everyone had vanished or run away in a hurry. Seeing a dragon (or SkEye police) would do that.

Annie eyed the transport device as she grabbed onto the handlebar of her huge motorcycle, which had reappeared beside them. "Sure could have used one of those in Parole."

"Parole's got a few, they're just in SkEye's hands. That'll change," Maureen resolved. "I've been out of the game a long time, but I haven't given everything up yet."

"What's that?" Chance looked down at a black backpack on the ground near Shiloh's feet. Like the motorcycle, and all of them, it hadn't been there a moment ago.

"Bug-out bag." Shiloh said as xie unzipped and started to dig through it. It was packed for what appeared to be a long road trip—spare sunglasses, several changes of clothes, toothbrush. Some canned food, can opener. Maybe most importantly, a spare sketchpad and the medication that would lessen xir head pain and the likeliness of blackouts. "Good, looks like everything made it. We are good to go."

"Finally," Maureen whispered. Shiloh looked up to see an intense expression xie rarely saw on xir mother's face. "Been waiting for this moment for ten years. Can't believe it's finally here."

"I know the feeling." Shiloh smiled up at her. "But it was just a matter of time. I knew we'd bust out of here someday, get out from under Turret's thumb, and go home. We were always going to end up heading back to Parole."

"Yeah we were," Maureen sighed, but she didn't look disapproving or even sad. The look on her face was pensive, but oddly hopeful.

"Great!" Chance clapped his hands; he sounded genuinely excited instead of sarcastic. "Always wanted to go on a breakneck motorcycle road trip across an apocalyptic wasteland."

Annie blinked, giving him a confused look. "I don't think I've ever met anyone who actually wanted to go to Parole before."

He shot her a winning smile. "Well...hey."

"You know, you never did tell us exactly why."

"Same reason as you," Chance shrugged. "Just because I haven't lived in Parole for a while doesn't mean the love is gone. And it must be a pretty great place if so many people are ready to give everything to save it. I just gotta see for myself."

"Yeah... people really did give a lot," Annie said slowly, turning to look up at Maureen. She suddenly seemed very young, and obviously scared. "I know you can't tell me what's on that disk. But just tell me, will it be worth it?"

Maureen took in the mingled hope and pain in her face, the question that was more like a plea. "A lot of people died to give Parole a fighting chance. We don't know all their names. We know one of them, though. Ash Price."

Annie couldn't answer but she nodded. Her hand went to the chain she wore around her neck; the shark tooth was under her shirt but she held onto it anyway.

"It was worth it," Maureen said without a trace of doubt. "Even if all he died for was to get you here safe and get us out of Meridian, it was worth it. But it doesn't end there at all."

"This will really help Parole?" Annie asked, voice more tentative than ever before since she'd rode into Shiloh's life.

"I'd say this would help bring Parole back to life, but it's already alive and well." There was a passion in Maureen's eyes now that usually lay just beneath the surface, like fire raging under a city's streets. "It's surviving, even after the collapse, even..." She stopped, closing her mouth before her voice broke. Took a breath. "I've done my best to make everything worth it too. Now it's up to you."

"Wait," Shiloh's stomach dropped as something behind her words clicked, and xir stomach dropped. "Kind of making it sound like you're not coming with us."

Maureen bit her lip. She said the next words quickly, like ripping off a band-aid. "I'll catch up with you as soon as I can. But you just have to keep moving no matter what. Get to Jay's ship, that's the safest place in the world right now."

"But why can't you come with us?" A note of desperation entered Shiloh's voice.

"I have to find your dad," she said quietly. "There is so much he and I have to do. And Garrett and Parole aren't quite in the same direction."

"You know where he is," xie realized, eyes widening. "He told you where he's hiding. Why didn't you tell me?"

"Sometimes the less you know, the safer you are."

"I won't tell anyone," xir voice dropped. "Please."

"Garrett?" Annie said, sounding baffled but alarmed. "Your father is Garrett Cole?"

Shiloh hesitated, shooting a questioning glance up to xir mom. When she nodded, xie turned back to Annie with a smile. "That's right."

"But he's dead!" Annie blurted. "Everyone knows he's dead!"

Instead of looking stricken or any kind of upset at all, Maureen let out a snort of laughter. "Do they? Does everyone really know he's dead?"

"Not everyone. Brianna thinks he's a music producer in London," Shiloh supplied, not laughing but not at all troubled either.

"Oh good! He likes that one."

"My dad's fine, he escaped from Parole," Shiloh explained before Annie got any more confused or frantic. "About a week before the collapse. We only just lost contact with him a couple days ago."

"That's not a good sign," Maureen said a bit more seriously. "But it's not a horribly bad one either. He's gone dark before and always come back all right. Still, it's about time we caught up with him. About ten years past time."

Annie stared at them. "Garrett Cole's not dead?"

"Nope," Shiloh said; xie couldn't stop smiling. "Faking his own death is kind of one of his favorite moves. It's worked really well before."

"He escaped from Parole," Annie murmured, as if the words would somehow make more sense if she said them. "How?"

"Sorry," Maureen shrugged. "Even I'm not sure. Like I said, sometimes the less you know, the safer you are."

"But he's not dead." Annie couldn't seem to get past that point. But now, her own eyes were lighting up with slow-building excitement. "That means nobody killed him. That means R—" she cut herself off and shut her lips tight but her eyes stayed wide and awed.

"It means he's out there somewhere," Maureen said when Annie didn't continue. "And he's got a plan. Those are the only two things I know for sure."

"And he's waiting for us to come find him!" Shiloh's excited smile faded as xie looked up at Maureen. "Or... you. I guess he's waiting for you."

Maureen hesitated as if she didn't want to say the next words, trying to make the moment last. "Do you remember what I told you, if you ever had to find me?"

"Keep watching the stars," Shiloh said in a soft voice.

"Right." She put both her hands on xir shoulders and gave them a squeeze. "They're still up there. Right where they've always been. That hasn't changed, I promise."

"So," Shiloh said, voice thick. "Just look for the lifeline?"

"Yes." She nodded firmly. "Find it and you'll find the answers. Or we'll find you. Whichever comes first. But you just worry about getting that disk to Jay first. That's the next step. Everything else will fall into place."

"Okay," Shiloh whispered. "I'm scared."

"I know, baby. But you are never alone." Maureen pulled Shiloh close and held xir very tightly. When they parted, xir mother pressed a kiss against xir forehead and didn't pull away for several long seconds.

"Okay. I can do this," Shiloh whispered, though tears finally spilled out of xir eyes. Xie didn't know who xie was trying to reassure, Maureen or xirself. "This is what we've been waiting for. Blowing out of Meridian, no walls, no barriers, nothing holding us back. We find Dad, we get to Parole, we find the truth. We live." Shiloh looked down at xir hands, which were not glowing, but so easily could be.

"You're going to shine so bright." Maureen shook her head, smiling. "We'll be able to see it no matter where we are." Blinking rapidly, Maureen stepped backwards, holding up the small cylinder with the button on the end. "Shiloh! Remember what I told you!"

"I will! I'll find you!" Shiloh didn't know how it could be true. But like the truth about burning cities on the horizon, some things you just had to take on faith.

"Not if we find you first, kiddo. Now I better get out of here fast," Maureen half-laughed, half-cried. "Before I change my mind." She pressed the button as Shiloh forced xir stinging eyes to stay open and on her until the last second. When she was gone, xie squeezed them tightly shut.

☆

The motion and bumps in the road made Shiloh's head hurt. But then, almost everything did. Except, oddly, for the helmet. It was light and comfortable and fit perfectly, almost like it was molded to Shiloh's tender head. They blocked out all but the loudest outside sound and they were linked by a radio channel, speakers sensitive enough that everyone could hear each other whisper. The visor diffused harsh sunlight into soft, purplish twilight; it was the kind of subtle but advanced technology Maureen would have given her left arm to study for five minutes. Annie rarely took hers off even when they stopped and Shiloh wondered if she liked the way she felt behind the darkened lens. Maybe it insulated her from a too-bright, too-loud world like xir sunglasses.

The motorcycle itself was far from uncomfortable. It was *huge.* With two sidecars and wide rows of trunks and storage compartments between them, Chance and Shiloh each had their own seat and space and could spread out as they wanted.

Even empty, the sky was one of the most beautiful sights xie'd ever seen. Xie couldn't remember the last time xie'd seen the open sky at all, much less a lovely fuscia sunset fading to indigo-blue as pale, small stars appeared all around.

When they stopped for the night in a sparse clearing surrounded by bare, unhealthy-looking trees, Annie jumped off and started unpacking without a word, instantly launching into what looked like an automatic routine by now. Shiloh moved to help, but quickly stopped dead as she pulled something out of her motorcycle's trunk.

She held a large, sealed jar filled with transparent greenish fluid, with an indistinct, soft shape floating inside. As Shiloh stepped closer, xie could see that it held some kind of organ. Large enough to be human. Carefully, Annie turned the jar around in her hands, studying it from all angles like she was inspecting it for damage.

"Annie," Shiloh called at last, after exchanging a worried glance with Chance. Suddenly xie had the strange impression they were interrupting a private moment between her and the anatomical object. "What's—"

"Right," she said abruptly with a slight jump, as if she'd forgotten the other two were there, where she was, or that anything else even existed. "Time to set up camp."

"Are you going to explain *any* of that?" Chance asked, echoing his previous question about the disappearing motorcycle.

"No," she said, not looking up as she carefully replaced the jar.

"Well, I'd kinda like to know why you're smuggling body parts before we go much further."

Annie tipped her head back and sighed, as if the whole thing was too annoying for words. That, or she was having trouble finding them. "I'm just... holding it for a friend."

Chance stared. "That's a spleen or something—"

"Pancreas," she corrected automatically.

"That's a pancreas. And you're holding it for a friend? Are we on our way to or away from them? Because that makes a difference."

Annie let out an aggravated groan, almost a growl. "I didn't hurt anyone and I didn't steal it. Sharpe stole it from *us.* It belongs to—somebody I care about and Sharpe could have really hurt them with it, so Ash and I went..." She stopped, holding very still. She had the same thousand-yard stare from back in Meridian, when she'd told them about Parole, Ash, and what came after. Then she seemed to snap out of it, shaking her head and moving on. "We got it back safe, that's all. Setting up camp now."

Shiloh looked over at Chance, who nodded at Annie, eyes still wide and obviously concerned. Shiloh shrugged and shook xir head. She hadn't given nearly enough of an answer, or explained just who Sharpe was, but it didn't seem like pushing more would yield any results. Xie moved to help her unpack and, after a moment of incredulous hesitation, Chance did the same.

Annie didn't seem to need much help. She was clearly a more experienced and efficient camper than both of them put together. If Shiloh couldn't remember the night sky, xie definitely couldn't remember ever spending time outside like this. Annie had a substantial cache of preserved food and bottled water, along with tents, flares, emergency medical equipment, and several large sleeping bags, more than one person would use on a trip like this, even with backups. A sad reminder that even though Annie had run into them on her own, she hadn't started out that way.

"Preparing for a zombie apocalypse?" Chance raised his eyebrows. "Guess it makes sense, considering the creepy..." He paused, smiling nervously when she gave him a warning glare. "The, uh, item. That you have. For a good reason, I'm sure."

Annie didn't smile back. "Might be the apocalypse. Get prepared or get dead. Sometimes you still get dead. If Ash..." She shook her head as if to dismiss the thought. "Four people would be a squeeze on one bike anyway. And I'm already running low on food. Here, put one of these on the ground every few feet around the perimeter," she said, handing him several small objects, shiny and round like quarters, but thicker. "In a big circle. Try not to leave any gaps."

"You got it," Chance said, holding one of the discs up and starting to deftly flip it end over end across his knuckles. "What are they?"

"Proximity alarms," Annie answered, glaring at his hand until he stopped playing with it. "They'll make a big noise if somebody tries to sneak up on us. Be careful if you go to take a leak in the middle of the night."

"I'll keep that in mind," Chance said with a slightly awed shake of his head. "So, uh, you want a campfire or something? Looks pretty wildernessy, probably nobody around to see it. I'm actually pretty good at making—"

"No fires," Annie said flatly. "Really don't like them."

"Oh—that's right, I'm sorry," he stammered, seeming to realize what he'd just suggested, and to whom. "Um, never mind. I'll just—can't believe I said that. Like you're gonna want to roast S'mores, what am I thinking..."

But Annie didn't seem to be listening. She stood up and headed back to the bike, opening its trunk and taking out an object about the size of her head. But it wasn't her helmet; it was the jar again. "Won't get far without a shield," she murmured, staring into it as if it were a crystal ball that might solve her dilemma. "Hope she won't mind me dropping in."

"Who?" Chance asked, seeming eager to make up for his mistake. "Are we seeing a friend of yours?"

"I have a contact at Radiance headquarters in Chicago," Annie replied, but didn't look up from her jar, seeming to find the bizarre object comforting. "When SkEye cuts off Parole's water shipments, or food, supplies, anything, Lakshanya Chandrasekhar's always been the one to get them through. I've never actually talked to her, Kari or Ash handle—handled—that, but she should still listen to me."

"Uh—Radiance HQ? We're stopping there?" Now Chance looked up sharply from placing the perimeter alarms, voice a good half-octave higher than normal. Shiloh glanced up at the interruption and paused briefly, but soon went back to xir project, turning the dial with steady determination.

"Yes," Annie said slowly, turning to face him just as deliberately. This gave him and Shiloh a very clear view of the jar she hugged to her chest. Shiloh looked long enough to confirm that yes, it really was a disembodied pancreas and then looked anywhere else. "Is that a problem?"

"Well, no, but aren't they—I mean, we should really just be getting right to Parole, huh? Why take a detour? We should just—"

"Chance." Annie shot him a look. "Why are you acting so weird right now?"

"I'm not acting weird!" he folded his arms. "Anyway, how would you know? We just met, this could be how I always act when everything's trying to kill me."

"Our bodies just met, but our brains didn't. But I don't even have to know you to know you're *really bad* at lying." Annie replaced the jar and opened another compartment, revealing a large radio with headphones connected. "And you're acting weird."

"Am not," Chance insisted. "I'm just saying, we are on a mission, to get an important thing somewhere, and this is not—important!"

"A shield that protects us from deadly toxins and keeps us alive isn't important?" She picked up the headphones and held one to her ear as she switched the radio on.

"But aren't your friends coming to meet us halfway? I dunno, I say we keep going, right for Parole."

Annie put down the headphones and stared at him. "We need shields if we want to survive. I don't have one. Radiance HQ has one. How aren't you getting this? Am I saying it wrong?"

"No," Chance looked slightly confused. "I don't think so. I just think it's a bad idea."

"It's not," Annie said, turning back to the radio as if that settled everything.

"Then maybe I'm the one hearing it wrong!"

Shiloh suppressed a sigh and wondered exactly what xie was in for. It was only the first night, and already the potential for misunderstandings and bickering seemed high. "We all seemed to get each other pretty well in the dreams. After that, basically being able to hear each other's thoughts, no wonder talking's hard."

"So, what then, we go back to sleep and talk it out in the tree?" Chance gave a skeptical shake of his head but Shiloh just shrugged in reply.

"Couldn't hurt. Understanding everything seems easier there."

"I hear that," Annie muttered. She was turning the radio's tuning dial now, slowly cycling through the frequencies. But from what Shiloh could hear from the headphones, each one was nothing but static. "I hate words sometimes. And they hate me."

"Yeah, but we're still connected," Shiloh gestured to all of their heads. "You guys already understand me better than just about anyone else."

"Why do you say that?" Chance looked caught between vague suspicion and intrigued curiosity. Curiosity won out, and he seemed to lose some of the defensiveness he'd acquired over the last exchange.

"*Xie,*" Shiloh said at last, simply. "I knew your faces the minute I saw you. But when you said *that,* when you called me 'xie' without being told—that's when I knew it was real. It wasn't a dream, I wasn't making it up. This was really happening. And it was a good thing."

"Wow," Chance said quietly, eyes widening. Annie stopped tuning and looked up as well. "It's that important, huh?"

"Yeah. More than anything in the world."

"Even superpowers?"

"A lot more." Shiloh smiled. "So thanks for getting it. And you didn't even make me explain anything. I think that's the best part."

"Yeah, sure, uh. No problem." He shook his head, looking a little downcast instead of awed now. "People suck. In lots of ways. I'm glad we didn't."

"I knew you wouldn't," Shiloh shrugged. "I told you about it in the tree, so I knew you got it. I could feel you get it. If you hadn't, I wouldn't be here now.

But then, I'm lucky. If someone has a problem, I can shoot lasers from my hands."

"Always a good thing," Annie nodded. She'd put the headphones down and stepped away from the radio. Nothing in range, Shiloh guessed. "Someone doesn't like it, blast 'em."

"Yeah." Xir heart was pounding again, but not in a frightening way. "I know it's easier when we just know things in the dreams—but some words are still really important."

"Shiloh," Chance reached out to touch xir shoulder, brought xir gaze down—to xir hands. "Look."

Xie didn't even have to look to know they were shining. The warmth came with every warm, galvanized, brave, *alive* feeling, and being called by the right words, being heard and seen, made xir feel very alive. A soft glow suffused every finger, shining through the skin, brighter at the tips. Shiloh drew in a slow breath, holding up xir hands and turning them, staring at the golden glow. The veins in xir wrists lit up the brightest, branching strings of light under xir skin.

"How does it feel?" Annie asked quietly. She didn't look shocked. Instead, on her face was something like confirmation, something like hope.

Shiloh's answer came in a faint whisper. "I think I leveled up."

Then, a strange noise broke the spell. Nearby, the radio hummed faintly, lights flickering as if it were trying to turn itself on. Static issued from the headphones again, but the signal remained faint and sputtering, lights flashing like Christmas tree bulbs that weren't screwed in all the way.

"The heck—are you doing that?" Chance stared at it, then back at Shiloh.

"You said you couldn't get a signal to Parole?" xie said to Annie at almost the same time.

"No, not for weeks." She shook her head as she unplugged the headphones so the audio would play through the speakers. "It's never done this before, though. If I find the channel I need, can you boost it stronger?"

"Worth a shot," Shiloh nodded, then put one hand on the radio. The volume increased sharply and the display needles on the front jumped at the contact, but still no coherent sound above the static. Annie went back to her slow frequency-search, while Shiloh frowned at the radio, certain xie was forgetting something. After a few seconds xie almost laughed, then held xir free arm up straight in the air. "There, now we got an antenna."

The static ceased immediately, and at first Shiloh thought xie'd done something wrong. A broken radio was the last thing they needed. But then xie realized the radio wasn't silent at all. Instead of the static, they could now hear a human voice, very faint, but clear. And familiar.

"*Hi, babies...dio Angel...*" it said, sounding like it came from farther away than any broadcast in the world, maybe from another planet. "*Don't kn...if you...me at all...*"

"Holy crap." Chance stared. "How are you doing that? What are you even doing?"

"Signal boosting." Shiloh grinned, excitement flowing like the humming, crackling energy. "Did this all the time in my mom's lab. A lot more practical than laser beams."

"*But I'm gonna keep talking anyway,*" said the voice as Shiloh concentrated, turning dials with xir mind's eye instead of xir fingers and tapping into stronger signal. "*Just in case. It's what I'm here for. Oh, Celeste, I miss...*"

"Kari?" Annie called, crouching down in front of the radio as if to speak to it on its own level. "Hello? I'm here! Can you hear me?" A burst of static crackled through the air, and Annie gave her head a frustrated shake. "We're losing her!"

"Let me give it some more juice." Shiloh shut xir eyes and focused harder, tried to reach into the static and pluck the voice out like a shiny pebble in thick mud.

"...Only took out the rider."

It was not Radio Angel's voice. It wasn't clear who was speaking; the signal was so distorted and static-filled the words were barely intelligible. It sounded like a man, but anything beyond that was impossible to say.

"Moving target's a hard one. Messy job, no clean wrap-up. Loose ends. But that's a temporary problem."

All three of them looked up at each other with surprise. Shiloh started to ask what they were hearing but held very still and stayed quiet after xie saw the look on Annie's face. It wasn't surprised anymore; instead her expression was one of absolute horror.

"Mission still accomplished. Ten years' worth of headaches, gone in one shot. Would've liked to get an interrogation in first, but we can still salvage something useful. Dead men tell no tales, but their bones might."

Annie mouthed something but no sound came out.

"The other one got away. Almost pursued–but no target's a higher priority than Price. Besides, there were extenuating–"

"Turn it off!" Annie got the words out at last, voice higher and more urgent-sounding than ever before. "Just–just make it–"

Shiloh pulled xir hand away from the radio like it was a hot stove. Immediately the static stopped and the lights went out, but all three of them kept staring at the dormant radio as if it were still going, unable to look away.

"That was him," Annie whispered, breaking the shocked silence. She repeated the words a few times, more mouthing than speaking them, then started to pace around the edge of the campsite, just inside the perimeter lights. "Sharpe, that was him, he was talking about me, me and Ash, that's what—bones? Their bones, what does—"

Annie's sudden panic was almost as alarming as the frightening voice and its chilling words. Shiloh's dumbfounded brain searched words that would help, but xie still couldn't speak at all, much less offer any coherent comfort.

"And nobody knows," she continued, finger twisting rapidly at her hair. "Nobody knows but me, everybody thinks we're coming back and he's not coming back, nobody knows we were both supposed to die but I didn't, or what he—the only ones who know are SkEye, they shouldn't know, not when even—not when we—"

"Maybe they do," Shiloh thought xie grasped her trauma-jumbled meaning and knew that words had little chance of helping. But xie had to say something. "Your friends might have heard somehow—"

"That's worse!" she snapped. "They hear about it from Sharpe? No! No, they should hear it from me, but they can't. And now that bastard is talking about it—bragging—"

"Annie, it's not your—"

"Maybe there's nobody left to tell anyway, maybe Parole's burned up completely or collapsed into the ground," Annie shot back as if she hadn't heard, pacing faster and kicking at pieces of gravel. "Maybe everyone I love is gone and I'll hear about them on the radio next. Maybe this is a dream and I'll wake up and I'll be falling too!"

"You're not gonna fall," Chance spoke up for the first time, though he didn't sound convinced; as her nervous energy increased, he sounded more desperate too, like he could see this was headed somewhere bad, but didn't know how to help. "And I'm sure everyone in Parole is fine, they can take care of themselves, right? We just have to get there and then everything will be fine."

Annie said nothing. Instead she held perfectly still, staring at him. Then, with a sudden explosion of movement, she turned and ran a few steps in the other direction. She stopped a small distance away and kept her back toward them, then threw her head back, letting out a half-strangled scream. "God! It's not fair!"

Stricken, Chance turned to look at Shiloh, whose only answer was a firm shake of xir head. They both remained silent and still.

"We were supposed to be safe out here!" Annie screamed at the vast night sky. Mercifully, it stayed silent. No horrors emerged, no searchlights or flames or monsters. Instead, her voice was swallowed up in an infinite darkness. "The night Gabriel found me, the ground crumbled! People were dying—we're still trapped inside! And then the wall came down, and I finally escape and—I'm free, I can go as fast as I want! But there's monsters out here too!" She kicked at a rock on the ground, missed, stumbled, almost fell. "Ash is dead and I left him behind just like I left everybody behind in Parole and—I'm still trapped! And we're still! Falling! Into! The fire!"

Slowly, Shiloh took a tentative step forward. "We just need to get some help—"

"I had help! An actual adult, who knew what he was doing—Ash had this all figured out, he was supposed to protect me—but he died!" She turned around, and her face was the palest xie'd ever seen, standing out blood-drained and stark like a ghost in the inky dark. "He died, okay? I wasn't supposed to be the leader here, I don't shoot guns, I don't have superpowers, all I do is drive—I drive a bike, okay? I get us places, and I drive the bike while..." She caught her breath, shoulders dropped. "I wasn't fast enough to save him either."

"Annie, it'll be—"

"Don't tell me it'll be okay! It's not!" Annie's voice cracked. She went to kick at another rock in a frustrated jerk but overstepped; her foot shot out from under her and she fell, landing hard in a heap on the pavement. "It's gone! Everything's gone, it burned up and sank into the ground, and everybody's waiting for me, and I have to tell them—that I'm sorry—about Ash—*aggh!*" She slammed her fist on the ground, letting out a shout that was more of a sob. "THIS. IS. WHY. WE. NEED. A. SHIELD!"

"Hey, Annie, I'm..." Chance started to say, uncharacteristically quietly. He moved closer to her, reaching out.

"No! Don't touch me!" she gasped, flinging out one arm to stop him, turning away from him and choking back tears. It sounded like she was having a hard time getting a breath. Shiloh and Chance exchanged an apprehensive glance as she scrambled the short distance to where her helmet lay on the ground and jammed it back onto her head, swiping the visor to black it out. Then she seemed to cave in on herself, curling her knees up to her chest, sucking in deep, fast breaths, forcing oxygen into her lungs.

Holding up his hands, Chance took a few steps backwards to where Shiloh stood. Xie hadn't moved from beside the bike or shut the still-open trunk, figuring movement or sudden noise might startle Annie and make everything worse.

"She'll be okay," Shiloh said, hoping it was true. The two of them waited, trying not to intrude, while Annie sat curled around herself on the ground, one hand clutching the shark tooth around her neck, other arm pressed against her helmeted head like she was trying to shut out the light.

After the second minute, Shiloh glanced down into the open compartment, hoping to see some water or maybe a blanket in easy reach, anything that might help. Xie didn't find either, but there was something helpful inside.

Gingerly, and trying not to look too closely, Shiloh picked up the pancreas jar. It was heavier than it looked, the glass probably protectively reinforced. Still, the thought of it breaking and Annie being crushed beyond recovery made Shiloh treat it with extra care as xie took the first step toward her. Its importance was still a mystery, but its clear significance to Annie wasn't.

She looked up sharply at the quiet sound of Shiloh placing the jar on the ground beside her. She didn't move away, or say a word, or seem to notice Shiloh quietly backing away. She held perfectly still, staring at the jar and disembodied organ—until all at once, she grabbed it up, wrapping both arms around it like it was a treasured childhood stuffed animal. Now she did start to audibly sob, but at least she wasn't shaking so violently anymore.

Slowly, Annie relaxed by degrees, muscles gradually unclenching. After several more minutes, her rocking and sobs finally stopped. At last, she got up and walked back to her friends, still cradling the jar close to her chest.

"I'm good now," she said, placing it back in the trunk and shutting it. She passed a hand over her visor and it lightened just enough so they could see her eyes. "Thanks. I needed that."

"Listen, um..." Chance said haltingly. "Just forget what I said. About Radiance, and the shield. It's fine, we can—"

"Okay. Great." Annie swept her hand back over her visor, darkening it again.

"It wasn't your fault," Shiloh attempted as she turned away again. "What happened to Ash. They're not—"

"You weren't there."

"Didn't have to be," xie called as she disappeared into the treeline, head hanging low.

She didn't come back until some time later that night, but she did come back.

☆

The next day was a long one and the air grew hotter and drier with every mile. Annie put the pedal to the metal and kept the bike screaming down the empty highway and, slowly, the world around them began to change.

Trees thinned out. Abandoned cars dotted the sides of the road, rusted and sun-scorched frames stripped of paint and lying bare like metal dinosaur bones. They crossed a bridge and the sluggish stream below was black. The ground hardened and slowly bleached a pale white. Shadows from the rare, bare and leafless trees stood out like charcoal drawings, reminding Shiloh of radioactive landscapes after a nuclear blast, how shadows got etched in permanently.

They stopped for water under the shade of an eerily silent highway overpass, a tiny island of relief from the beating sun. Annie often kept her helmet on, even when she wasn't driving, and this time she put it back on immediately after she was done with her drink.

"From here on in, we should keep these on as much as possible," she said, urgency sharpening the edge of her voice. "And make sure your filters are on."

"Didn't think we were close enough for bad air yet," Chance mumbled, one of the first complete sentences he'd said all morning. Something last night had shaken him out of his groove and he hadn't quite regained his animated energy. "You know something we don't?"

"Tartarus' edges shift all the time. And we don't have a shield. Until we do, we just shouldn't take any chances... Chance."

"Very funny. You're hilarious," he groused, and jammed his helmet back on his head as if tired of looking at both of them. Shiloh felt a mild tinge of worry as xie and Annie exchanged a glance and it wasn't for the first time. This didn't seem normal even in their waking reality. In dreams, Chance's energy was kinetic, playful, quick and infectious as his smile.

"We have to make some serious miles if we wanna beat the sun." Annie shook it off and took a few steps away, shielding her eyes as she cast another glance at the sky. "Once I get the shield installed, we'll leave the highway, be able to go at least twice as fast—and *then* we'll hope it's enough to keep out some vapors and ghosts." She let her hand drop and turned away. "A good one will even keep out bullets."

"So what's the plan with Radiance?" Shiloh asked, not at all sure about the next step. "Your friend will really just give us a shield?"

"I don't know," she said slowly. "I've never met her in person—it's really Kari who took care of all this stuff. Kari and Ash, or Celeste."

"Celeste?" Shiloh repeated; that was a new name from Annie, but xie had heard it before. "Kari said that name on the radio last night."

"Right," Annie grimaced, as if she'd just remembered something discouraging. "Celeste was—I guess you'd call her like an intelligence expert? And negotiator, kind of? She used to handle stuff like this, whenever we needed to know something or get something, she'd just... make it happen. She disappeared in the collapse, along with half of Parole. Now that she's gone, we're all picking up the slack."

"Think we can still make this happen?" Shiloh was already trying to think of alternatives, any kind of backup if this one fell through. Unfortunately, xie was in so far over xir head xie didn't even know how deep the water was anymore. Xie had nothing.

"Radiance has helped us enough in the past. They should still help."

"And if they don't?"

"Then I'll figure out another option," Annie said in the grim kind of tone that said she'd allow no arguments, because she had no other options after this one.

"Listen, Annie..." Chance sighed and his shoulders dropped. Both she and Shiloh turned to look as he took his helmet back off to look her in the eye. This was one of the first times he'd spoken today. "Lakshanya will help us."

Annie slowly turned to fully face him. "You sound pretty sure about that."

"I am." He pinched the bridge of his nose, then shut his eyes and pressed down on them too. Shiloh had done that often enough when xir head threatened to split in two. But the next words made it clear that this pain wasn't physical. "She'll help her brother."

"*Indra?*" Instead of narrowing in anything like accusation, Annie's eyes went very wide. "All this time?"

"Yeah." He gave a listless little wave. "Hi there."

"It's been a year since he—you disappeared!"

"You heard about that?" He sounded a little surprised, but still didn't look at her. "Parole doesn't know who's president, but you heard about me running away?"

"Yeah, it was kind of a big deal! Everyone thought you died! You ran away?" She waited. When he said nothing, she kept pulling teeth. "And you've been here all along?"

"Well, not here. A lot of different places. Trying to find Parole. Didn't have a whole lot of luck until the dreams started."

"Indra Chandrasekhar..." Shiloh said under xir breath, trying the name out as xie worked to place it. Xie couldn't remember it from waking life, or any recent time. But it pulled at the back of xir brain, not just into a dream, but ten years. "How did you keep this from us?"

He didn't look up. "Sorry. Didn't mean to keep you in the dark. At first, I mean. Just couldn't think of a way to bring it up. Then it just kind of happened."

"No, I'm not mad. I'm almost impressed. It couldn't have been easy. It almost took all of my energy just to get anything to make sense. To keep back that big a secret..."

"Didn't really mean to, actually." He shrugged, looking away. "I push painful shit into the back of my mind when I'm awake. Guess being asleep's no different. I kinda liked the name 'Chance' anyway. It was fun."

"Why didn't you want to tell us? Everyone in Parole knows your—"

"*There.* That. That's exactly why, right there!" His head whipped up and now his eyes were open and filled with an intensity neither of the other two had ever seen in them before. "Everyone knows my family, and everyone knows my... brother's name," he looked away again. "Not my name."

"This would be why you didn't want to stop by Radiance?" Annie asked, a much calmer counterpoint to Indra's sudden flare.

"It would be. Kind of hard to keep that particular secret with my sister standing right there, yeah."

"Feel like telling us anything else?"

A beat of silence. "No."

Annie sighed. "You still want us to call you Chance, or...?"

"No. Indra is fine." He closed his eyes and folded his arms. Shiloh thought his shoulders were shaking. "If you're still with me when we get there, that's all you'll hear anyway."

"If we're still...?" Annie shook her head firmly. "You have a lot of explaining to do, yeah, but I'm not about to just cut you loose."

He was quiet for a few seconds, nodding slowly while still looking at the ground. "Okay. So. Let's just go. We won't have any trouble getting in, but I should probably call ahead first. I haven't been home for a while."

When Shiloh got back on the bike, Chance—Indra Chandrasekhar—wrapped his arms around xir waist and buried his face in xir back. He stayed that way for a long time.

CHAPTER 4

Welcome Home

CHICAGO'S BARRIER BUBBLE WAS A MARVEL. THEY ALL WERE, MAGNIFICENT SHIELDS THAT ARCED over major cities and protected them from airborne Tartarus vapors while the main beacon ring, and smaller city beacons, repelled rogue ghost activity. Maureen Cole had mixed feelings about their construction for years, the lives they saved by design, the thousands in Parole trapped by their misuse. The way the gleaming bubbles had become iconic, visible even from miles away. So even as Annie brought the motorcycle to a stop in front of their destination, Shiloh caught a glimpse of the barrier overhead, and froze. Xie couldn't help remembering Maureen's clashing pride and shame, wondering if she could see one like it from wherever she was right now.

When xie finally took a step, xie almost ran right into Annie. She was staring too, but not at the barrier. Her eyes were fixed on the bright glass towers of this upscale corporate district like they were the strangest things she'd ever seen, in a world full of strange things.

"You okay?" xie asked gently, trying to get her attention without startling her.

"Yeah," she nodded after the moment it took for the words to get through to her. "Everything's just really... clean." As they moved, she kept turning her head to stare at things like the smooth, well-maintained sidewalks, undamaged cars, and people walking by like they'd never once felt the ground crumbling beneath them or felt the touch of flames. Then they stopped at the brightly lit, large sign outside one of the tall, modern buildings. "Radiance Relief Coordination Center" gleamed in polished brass.

A few hours earlier, Indra had stared at his emergency cell phone and made himself dial a number, doing his best to keep his hands from shaking. The wait for an answer was interminable, every ring making it harder not to just hang up and call the whole thing off. He was about a half-second away from doing so when someone picked up on the other line. The conversation that followed was whispered, awkward, and very short. But afterwards, they had a plan.

Now Indra led the way up the marble stairs leading to the large glass building in front of them, hands in his pockets and head hanging low. He hadn't said a word except to direct Annie to the Radiance HQ building and now headed directly for the entrance again without speaking, steps quick but mechanical as if he were forcing himself to get this over with as soon as possible.

The sliding glass doors reflected the glare of the setting sun, obscuring what lay inside. So, when they slid open, it was Indra's turn to come to a hasty halt, step aside, and mumble an apology as someone emerged.

The man who strode from the Radiance lobby didn't change course or break his stride as the three teenagers hurried to get out of his way. His steps were slow but their unerring rhythm suggested he would have happily bowled them all over and just kept walking. He kept his hands hidden in his pockets, elbows sticking out at angles that made them all give him a wide berth or risk collison. He wore a grey-camo SkEye uniform and short-cropped brown hair, just like any other of the dozens, maybe hundreds of Eye in the Sky paramilitary officers and volunteers. There were only two reasons this average-height, average-build, white, uniformed man stood out to them at all.

First, it was rare to see these uniforms inside a city bubble. SkEye operations visible to civilians were small, and usually took place outside, guarding against ghostly advances. Nobody witnessed their major operations—but nobody saw Parole itself either.

The second reason they noticed this man was that he clearly noticed them.

Even at his leisurely pace, it didn't even take a full second for him to pass by. But that was all the time his sharp, bright blue eyes needed. As the man's eyes flicked from Annie's helmet over to xir face, Shiloh had the strangest feeling that they were all being evaluated and felt a sudden surge of panic. Being under his penetrating gaze felt like being studied under a microscope, or caught in a hunter's crosshairs. The urge to escape was almost overpowering, and now it was a struggle to stand xir ground instead of run.

But the man didn't say a word or stop moving. His only reaction was a small, tight-lipped smile Shiloh couldn't even be sure xie'd seen, the same way xie couldn't be sure if it was xir imagination the man had eyed Indra for just a fraction longer. It was too fast, too subtle to know for sure before he turned his head and continued on his way.

Still, xir heart was pounding as the man reached the sidewalk and turned a corner, disappearing as suddenly as he'd appeared. That was xir first close encounter with an Eye in the Sky officer since Major Turret's occasional, unexpected visits and they barely counted. They'd been cold, always with a threatening undercurrent, but civil.

This man's gaze almost felt predatory. When he'd fixed his eyes on them, what had he seen?

But he was gone now, and they'd come here for a reason. Shaking off the unnerving encounter, the small group continued into a spacious foyer with marble floors and bright, gleaming surfaces that almost seemed like a luxurious hotel rather than an office building's lobby. Not for the first time, Shiloh was glad for xir sunglasses.

Suddenly Indra stopped dead again, not moving when the other two came up level and moved past him, looking back to see him frozen. This time, he didn't even seem aware of their presence, like someone had hit 'pause' on the playback of his life, while the rest of the world continued around him. Annie and Shiloh turned to see what had captured every bit of his attention.

A young woman stood with her back to them, straight and tall in the center of the wide open floor, giving directions to two assistants with clipboards in clear, measured tones; something about restorative functioning, beyond expectations. The two others hurried away, leaving her alone—she watched them go, but didn't move or turn, waiting. From behind it looked like she wore a fancy ballroom gown or something with about as many ruffles, strange for an office setting, but Shiloh's attention was more caught by Indra's powerful reaction. His eyes were wide and his mouth hung open slightly. Silently he sucked in a breath.

"Shanni?" When he spoke it was in a whisper.

His voice was soft, but the echo from the excellent acoustics was enough to catch the young woman's attention. She turned around and looked up, eyes going wide. This had to be Lakshanya Chandrasekhar, but Shiloh had always envisioned somebody older whenever someone had talked about the head of Radiance relief operations. She wore heavy eyeliner and dark makeup, her short black hair swept at an asymmetrical angle. But despite the superficial differences, her features were strikingly familiar. If she'd been smiling—or, at the moment, wearing an expression of unabashed awe—she'd have looked a lot like Indra.

He raised his hands as if expecting to pluck the right words out of the air, then turned them toward her as if presenting her to a captive audience of one. Now a smile did spread across his face, tentative and crooked, but genuine. "You cut your hair."

There was a moment of stunned silence, broken by the girl giving a soft gasp, and then she rushed forward to meet them; arms flying around Indra's neck and pulling him close.

"*Indra!*" she breathed; hand on the back of his head and fingers running through his hair. She held him so tightly the air rushed from his lungs and it was a moment before he recovered enough to hug her back. "Is that all you're going to say to me?"

"I'm so sorry, Shanni." His voice was muffled as he buried his face in her shoulder, so it was difficult to tell if it broke or not. "I'm sorry, I—"

"Hush," she said firmly. After a moment, she held him at arm's length so she could look into his face. His eyes were much redder than they had been a moment ago and his breath caught in his throat. He looked like he'd just been awoken from a bad dream to find himself safe in his room, but still disoriented, half-caught under a nightmare's spell. "You're here now, that's all that matters."

Her hand came up to cup his cheek and smooth away hair from a face that looked, in profile, almost identical to hers. They were mirror images of one another, almost certainly twins. But there were differences as well as similarities, and not just because of the clothes or makeup. Maybe it was the heeled boots and corset she was probably wearing, but she stood straighter than Indra's easy slouch. Her expressions were clearer, eye contact more direct than his often tuned-out or flippant glances. If he was a feather on the breeze, she was a knife cutting through the nonsense, right to the chase.

"I—we really didn't have to meet here," he said, glancing around the glass foyer, the clean corporate facades and smooth glass surfaces. He shifted uncomfortably, as if afraid his shoes would stain the gleaming floor. "We don't wanna just barge in on your—"

"Nonsense." She shook her head, fixing him with a firm gaze. "You called me asking for help. Said it was an emergency. What did you expect me to do, make us meet under some bridge in a thunderstorm at midnight?"

"Well, I dunno, an anonymous place might be safer." He shrugged, bouncing on the balls of his feet. "Less chance of getting ambushed, or spotted, or traced some other way. Actually, the bridge thing might be better."

The young woman rolled her eyes, but her smile didn't fade. "Be more dramatic, Indra."

"You're the one who looks like Lydia from Beetlejuice." He smirked now, taking in her deep violet eyeshadow and lipstick, the tiered velvet skirt and petticoat, the shining black lace-up boots. This was why she looked out of place for a corporate work setting; instead of a day job, she looked like she might have just stepped out of a sumptuous oil portrait that would hang in the parlor of a haunted manor. Or from the neon purple accents, maybe a rave. "What is...going on here?"

"Classic high Victorian gothic," she chided, shaking her head in mock disappointment. "I thought you of all people would appreciate a good aesthetic."

"I do! I mean, it's just kind of different." He tilted his head, taking in the meticulously arranged layers of lace at one sleeve. "Last time I saw you, you were rocking the cyberpunk look. Didn't expect you to roll back the clock five hundred years. Not that it's a bad thing! I like it, I do. It's very...dark."

She studied him for a moment, as if trying to decide if he was making fun of her or not—then seemed to decide she didn't care. "Thank you. I felt it was time for a change, so I made one. Enough's certainly happened *to* us; I thought it was about time I was actually in control of something."

He smiled like he was about to make some other joke, but changed his mind halfway through. "It looks nice. Sad, but nice. Good look on you."

"Thank you, Indra," she said without further question. Her dark eyebrows came together. "Or are you still going by—"

"Chance? No, don't worry about it," he mumbled. "Miss me?"

"Yes. So much." She was smiling now, wide and warm. Even her voice was a contrast to her brother's. Where his was fast, expressive and with a natural Western-neutral American, she spoke in a calm, measured cadence and a slight but decidedly present Tamil accent. When her dark eyes were on her brother they were warm and wide, taking him all in as if trying to memorize his features, afraid he would disappear again. But after a few seconds of giving him her undivided attention, she made herself look up at the other two.

"And you've brought some very important friends with you, I see." She cleared her throat and stepped away then, clasping her lace-gloved hands in front of her, using the motion to recover her composure. Her eyes were as bright and animated as her twin's in their own way—or were—until she seemed to make a concerted effort to control her expressions. Her joy at Indra's sudden appearance had interrupted her poker-face, but it came back easily enough. "Anh Minh, I presume?"

"That's right. Annie's fine," she said with an incline of her head. She still wore her helmet, but now that they were inside and away from the noise and crowd of the street, she seemed more comfortable. There was an intensity in her voice that came through loud and clear, a rare eagerness that caught Shiloh's attention as much as anything else in a new city. "Our mutual acquaintance, Kari, said if I ran into trouble, you're the one to call."

"Yes—and I do hope she's doing all right," Lakshanya said, a note of concern entering her voice. "I know everyone's a bit... short-staffed, as of late. And you're another mutual acquaintance?" She turned to Shiloh with a significant look and raised eyebrows.

"Shiloh. Nice to meet you." Shiloh gave her a sincere smile in contrast to Annie's guardedness. Xie meant it as well; there was just something wonderful about Indra having a twin sister who clearly loved him. Xie weighed the possibility of using Maureen's name and Radiance connection for about a second before dismissing the thought. That information was too sensitive and important in several ways to go waving around. At least until xie knew a lot more about what *she* knew.

"Great, so we know who everybody is," Indra stammered, still looking around as if expecting to be burst in on and attacked any moment. He shot Shiloh a glance that was probably supposed to be subtle. "But no last names. Because they don't...have them."

"That's reasonable." His twin was a great deal more calm and unruffled. "Most of my contacts don't. Much safer that way. In any case, thank you for taking care of Indra. I must say, I'm quite curious to know how my brother got mixed up in your... exciting business."

"Some days, so am I," Indra muttered.

"I'm sure you've got some stories."

"You could say that." Annie nodded. She swallowed as if her throat was suddenly dry, but didn't break her focus. "But probably not very fun ones."

"If there's anything I can do to help, say the word." Lakshanya met her eyes with a sharp, yet sincere look. "I can't tell you how much I regret hearing about... your difficulties this trip."

"Just the shield," Annie said in a flat voice, gaze dropping to the floor. "We really need to keep moving."

"Then please, step into my office."

"You have an office now?" Indra gasped in mock surprise. "Moving up in the world."

"Yes, quite literally," she said, throwing him a deadpan glance. "It's upstairs. I have a small *presentation* planned in a few minutes, which you're welcome to join." She cast Indra a pointed glance and raised her carefully shaded eyebrows.

He clearly didn't get whatever she was trying to communicate, because he just raised his eyebrows in return, as well as his shoulders in a shrug. She rolled her eyes, and just started walking.

"Are you sure?" Shiloh frowned slightly. "We don't want to interrupt anything. We can wait; let you have some catching up time."

Lakshanya hesitated; she looked like she wanted very much to say something, but couldn't find the words. Finally, she smiled again. "Please. Today is an important one–it should be shared."

☆

Lakshanya led them through the high-ceilinged glass foyer. Every wall seemed to be made of glass, transparent or frosted, with high, bright lights reflected and magnified by planes of glass and white and amber accents, gold and brass, warm yellows and red woods. Even the staircase they ascended was made of glass. The building inside radiated daylight, sunshine, warmth. Shiloh wished for darker shades.

Indra and Lakshanya kept their eyes on each other as they walked, seeming to hold a silent conversation. Or at least trying. By the time they reached the top of the stairs, Indra looked confused, as if she'd 'said' something strange. Shaking her head, Lakshanya pushed open a door, and led the small group into her private office. Now she dimmed the lights, heavy curtains already drawn over the window. Instead of the modern, high-gloss metal-and-glass theme of the outside building, Lakshanya's office seemed to match her classic Victorian Gothic style.

"Here," she said, unlocking and opening a lower desk drawer and pulling out what looked like a tiny CD. Shiloh had to smile; xir mother's nostalgic aesthetic was immediate recognizable. "One state-of-the-art portable shield generator, guaranteed to hold up against all but the most deadly airborne poisons."

"How about bullets?" Annie asked, tone as grim as the subject.

"It's new and improved, yes," Lakshanya nodded, clearly proud of the little device. "Should deflect just about anything, even at point-blank range."

"I'm not worried about point-blank range."

"Long-range is even easier. Shock gets absorbed and redistributed and the integrated force actually gives the shield strength a temporary boost. Saves lives by design."

"Thank you." Annie took the round disc, giving a slow nod. "We'll put it to good use."

"One more thing." Lakshanya took another small object out of her desk drawer: a small, ordinary flash drive. "Please make sure this gets to the FireRunner safely. It contains a message of great importance."

"Who's this message from?" Annie stared at the offered drive with mixed curiosity and slight unease.

"A confidential informant," Lakshanya said readily. "I can't say anything more. Just that its contents should prove quite interesting to whoever properly decrypts it."

Annie stuck the shield generator into a pocket where it was hidden completely, then handed the flash drive to Shiloh. "Here. No sense in keeping all the important things together. Thanks," she said with a nod to Lakshanya.

"You're quite welcome," Lakshanya said, turning back to Indra. "Now, our parents should be here in a few—"

"Our *what?*" Indra yelped.

"Shut your mouth." She gave him an exasperated look. "You knew I was planning this. I told you I had a special project I was working on and that I was going to reveal it today."

"Well, yeah, but how was I supposed to know—"

"Because you were invited, along with *our parents.*" Now she looked disappointed. "I thought you'd come back specifically today, just to see it! And them! And you brought friends!"

"Shanni, please," Indra said, a note of desperation creeping into his voice. "Does that sound like something I'd do? On purpose? Ever?"

She opened her mouth and shut it again. Then she threw up her hands. "They're already on their way. It's not my fault you just happen to drop back in on the very day of—"

"All right! All right, fine!" Indra held up his own hands. Suddenly the twins were exasperated mirror images of each other.

"Are you sure you want us here for—?" Shiloh started, having no desire to intrude on a family moment and an increasing desire to leave before anything got awkward.

"Nope! Nobody move." Indra spun around to point at xir, then Annie.

"Are you and your parents...not doing great?" Annie asked slowly.

"It's not that," Indra sighed. "They're good people. I just...really wasn't expecting this. I need a while to prepare. Emotionally."

"You have about four minutes." Lakshanya nodded at a small, ornate clock on her desk.

"Oh. Great." Indra looked at it too, then turned his attention to a candy-filled bowl beside it. He took one plastic-wrapped piece, then an entire handful. "I'll just be preparing over here."

"Is there anything we should *know* before they get here?" Annie prodded, eyes flicking from Indra to Lakshanya and back again.

"Don't talk about Parole," Indra advised around a mouthful of candy. "Just don't."

"Of course not." Anxiety tainted Lakshanya's little laugh, like a performer's before the curtain rose above the stage. "My project is a great deal bigger than one city."

"What exactly is your project?" Annie looked back at her quickly, instantly on alert.

"Nothing less than–"

"Shanni! Hello, darling!" A knock accompanied the woman's voice, both from right outside the door.

"Hello! It's open!" Lakshanya called, shooting Indra a nervous grin. "There's someone here I think you'll want to see!"

Indra dropped the remainder of the candy back into the bowl and wiped his mouth, swallowing fast and coughing as the office door swung open.

It was easy to see where Indra had gotten his smile. The tall, long-limbed Indian woman who strode through the door wore one very much like his, but instead of flashing bright and quick before melting into a smirk, hers stayed where it was. She wore a deep magenta, modern salwar kameez suit with a lovely, long scarf around her shoulders woven through with intricate patterns of gold. Her black hair shone in a thick, ornate braid that hung down her back. She stood studiedly tall and composed, every motion projecting poise and strength. She radiated confidence, and in her large, dark eyes that resembled Lakshanya's, a swift, perceptive intelligence. And something about her was familiar to Shiloh besides the family resemblance. Like the feeling of Déjà vu when xie'd first met Indra and Annie, xie was certain xie'd seen her before–but not in a dream.

The man beside her had a salt and pepper beard and seemed content to let her command the spotlight. Once he may have been handsome and robust, but long years of fatigue and clear sorrow had worn deep lines into his face. His hair was slightly untamed, his shoulders rounded in a slouch as he stood somewhat caved into himself.

Both of them automatically looked to Lakshanya's desk when they entered, as if accustomed to finding her sitting there, but they soon saw she was not the only one in the room.

"Indra!" they exclaimed together, faces shifting into matching expressions of shock—and then joy. The woman immediately rushed forward, arms flying open, and Indra stepped forward, falling into the hug with a grateful sigh. "How did—where have you—are you all right?"

Indra shut his eyes and wrapped his arms around her in return, shoulders dropping slowly. His every movement was slower now, in a stark contrast to his brittle tension from before. For the first time, he seemed fully relaxed instead of studiedly cool. Relaxed, relieved, and exhausted. "Better now."

His mother held him at arm's length, looking him over with palpable relief and brushing the hair from his face. "You look...good."

"So do you," Indra said after a moment, seeming to notice her outfit's vibrant colors for the first time with slight surprise. "Like seriously."

"A special occasion is an invitation to indulge." She shrugged, still smiling and staring at him as if he were a dream that may disappear at any moment. Now Shiloh realized where xie'd seen her before: on television public safety announcements, assurances that Tartarus was being carefully monitored; reminders to be vigilant and report new sightings to local volunteers. "And now even more so."

"Son." Her husband had come up behind them and placed a hand on Indra's shoulder, pulling him into a much slower embrace. He moved like someone laboring under bone-deep fatigue, or pain, and Indra returned the hug gently. "You are safe. I can breathe again."

"Yeah," Indra sighed, dropping his head to rest his chin on his father's shoulder. "Hope you weren't holding it. Dad, I'm not here to stay, I just—"

"Not now. You are here safe and sound. Forget everything else for a little while." The older man's kind eyes flicked to Shiloh and Annie. "And you brought friends."

"Ah! The more the merrier. Splendid." Now that Indra's mother was over her initial shock at seeing him, her energy changed again. Now her bright smile held the same magnetic charm that Indra had in so many spades. Maybe it was a family gift, or a shared skill, but Indra had it and so did she. And now that she was composed again, it was back, turning the room's energy into one of excitement and engaging electricity. And something else—an air of authority. This might have been Lakshanya's office, but Radiance was hers.

She crossed the room with long strides and immediately shook Annie and Shiloh's hands in both of hers. "Welcome to Radiance. I am Rishika Chandrasekhar, and this is my husband Bhanu, and daughter Lakshanya, whom it appears you've met. I must thank you, so very much for bringing our Indra back to us safely. I can't say how worried we've been."

Annie said nothing. She simply stared at both of them, face entirely blank.

"Shiloh," xie said just before the silence would have become awkward. "And you're welcome. For bringing Indra home, glad to do it. Not that we want to get rid of him," Shiloh amended, feeling painfully awkward and out of place in the expensive building with the beautiful family. "He's been awesome. We just met not that long ago, but he's—just really great. Seriously, amazing. Uh, the first time we met, we were attacked by one of those—those things that come out of the Tartarus Zone?"

"A ghost?" Rishika's eyebrows shot up as a look of concern flashed onto her face.

"Yeah—we're fine! Because Indra distracted it, he threw a rock at it!" Shiloh laughed, nervous. Why had xie said this? Why couldn't xie stop talking? "He gave us time to get away—anyway it was the bravest thing I've ever seen, he probably saved our lives. That's all."

"Thanks, Shiloh," Indra mumbled, looking at the floor but smiling, a slight red tinge in his cheeks. But it wasn't his ordinary flashy grin, or even the softer, genuine one Shiloh had caught a glimpse of and liked. It looked like it hurt. All of his body language screamed pain, ever since they'd walked in the door.

"That's wonderful," Bhanu said quietly. He had a soft voice and a face that looked like it would have been much more at home smiling. But all his gentleness was accompanied by a heavy sadness, the kind acquired over many painful years. "Bravery clearly runs in the family. I'm proud of you. And so glad to see you home."

"Thanks," Indra whispered. Oddly, he looked like he was about to cry, and not from happiness from his father's praise. "I'm—yeah."

"We...weren't expecting anyone but the family when Shanni called us here tonight," Bhanu continued, eyes lifting to take in the unexpected guests. "But you are most welcome. Perhaps it will make a good change."

"Yes, always." Rishika exchanged the same kind of glance with her husband that Indra had shared with Lakshanya—instant conversations to which no one else was invited. "We've certainly had enough staff and reporters to last us a lifetime. Surely we can open our doors to our son and his two young friends. If we're about to see what I suspect..."

"I'm actually glad they're here," Lakshanya said. She smiled and took a deep breath as if to center herself as she crossed the room to the table with the white cloth. "They can spread the good news, give people some comfort and hope. And I must say, I do love an audience."

"Who doesn't?" Indra grinned, seeming somewhat recovered and actually curious.

"Distinguished guests," Lakshanya picked up one corner and looked up at everyone with an almost mischievous smile as they gathered to watch the show. She cleared her throat, and spoke the next words with deliberation and drama. "I give you..."

She snapped her wrist and pulled back the white cloth in a grand gesture, revealing her secret with a whoosh, and took a small bow. When she straightened up, she was still smiling, looking nervous and proud and pleading all at once.

"Is this what I think it is?" Bhanu's gentle brown eyes lit up when he saw what was beneath the sheet, and the terrible heaviness from long years of sadness seemed to lift.

"We finalized the plans last week," Lakshanya said, as if she could barely believe it herself. "The model might be a bit premature, but you know me...I like to get a jump on things."

It was a model of the Tartarus Zone, showing the toxic area with its bleached-white land giving way to a 3D holographic projection of the poison storms swirling in the center. In a ring surrounding the worst of the contagion and its constant storms stood the ten major beacons—enlarged far beyond scale, for demonstration. White lights on the tops of the lighthouse-like towers gave off a soft glow.

"For the past years, this has served us passably well," Lakshanya began, gesturing to the familiar arrangement. "Thanks to Maureen Cole's brilliance and our dedicated Radiance staff, we've kept Tartarus fallout from spreading any further than its concentration in Nebraska and outer edges expanding in its..." she paused, considering. "Approximate circular expanse from mid-South Dakota to Utah, to northern Texas, to Illinois."

"That's a pretty big 'approximate,'" Annie observed. "You really don't have any more specifics on this thing's actual borders?"

"The only predictable thing about Tartarus is unpredictability," Rishika said without looking up, her probing gaze locked on the model. "The contagion flares at random. Completely unaffected areas reach epidemic levels of toxicity overnight. Then the contaminated land recedes just as quickly. Absolutely no rhyme or reason."

"No, but if anyone can find one, it's my mother and Maureen Cole," Lakshanya said with a nod. "Their work has allowed us to slow the spread and develop some protective measures. Otherwise it would have eaten up the entire country—maybe the entire continent—like a hungry wildfire. But is this really good enough?"

"Certainly not," Rishika replied, studying the arrangement with a scrutinizing gaze very reminiscent of her daughter's. "Nothing will be good enough until Tartarus is neutralized and no longer a danger."

"And it's only getting worse," Lakshanya responded, with certainty but not despair. "Ghosts are getting bolder. We don't know if the beacons are deteriorating or if Tartarus' effect is intensifying. The sad fact is, the contagion is spreading, and we've been unable to decisively stop it."

"I am, as always, open to suggestions. I'm sure you have them."

"Of course. We've been unable to stop it...until now." Lakshanya smiled. "Watch."

She pressed a button on the side of the display counter, and every beacon light went out, like candles snuffed by a sudden wind. Shiloh felt a sudden pang of alarm and xir stomach dropped. After growing up with the constant illumination of beacons and barriers, there was something viscerally terrifying about sudden darkness.

But soon it became clear that the light wasn't entirely gone, because xie could just barely see Lakshanya's face, illuminated from below in an eerie purple. She held up one finger, then pointed back down at the display to reveal the change.

The beacon lights had changed from plain white to neon violet. And now instead of general light, they projected thick, arcing purple beams that connected each of the towers. Not just in a ring around the Tartarus Zone, but crisscrossing it, each tower reaching to each of the others, and curving up in a dome until it formed a net over it, containing the storms within.

"Is this..." Rishika took a step closer, eyes lit up by the beams and what might be hope.

"Yes." Lakshanya's smile grew. "We've been using plain light based on halogen gas so far. But my modifications will alter it to a specific wavelength on the visual spectrum, proven to be hundreds of times more effective. The web itself will be invisible."

"Ultraviolet. Of course." Her tone was hushed, admiring, and a little self-amused, as if she couldn't believe she hadn't thought of it herself.

"Not exactly, but close enough," Lakshanya amended. "Actual UV rays at the required strength would be deadly to human life—most forms of life, actually. I'd rather not have us all develop cancerous lesions. This was our primary concern and biggest puzzle, but I'm proud to say we're at full power and no risk for that. I've also assigned one of our most dedicated and reliable crews," she added, voice casual as if it were an afterthought, but she looked up from her model to watch her mother's face.

"Which one is that?" Rishika asked, but still seemed absorbed in the demonstration.

"The FireRunner," Lakshanya said just as casually, and now her eyes flicked over to Annie, Indra, and Shiloh. Annie turned toward her, eyes widening, but said nothing, soon looking away again to hide her reaction. Shiloh was once again glad for xir dark glasses that hid xir own surprise. "I figured the project could use their experience and expertise. They should be around halfway done right now."

"A good choice," Rishika said, not looking up but sounding thoughtful instead of simply impressed. "I know the captain well. They'll get the job done."

"Quickly and safely," Lakshanya agreed. "This barrier will stop the spread of Tartarus contagions and the ghosts inside with no damage to the surrounding environment."

As they watched, the ever-present central storm gradually dissipated, until there was nothing left inside the ring of beacons but calm air. The bleached land slowly regained its natural color.

"This is a time-lapse demonstration, of course. The real process will take years, even decades. But I'm confident that with consistent monitoring and care…recovery is possible."

"Oh, my darling…" Rishika's eyes grew wider, bright with excitement.

"This is what you've been working on this whole time?" Indra asked a little breathlessly. "This is amazing!"

Lakshanya nodded. "It's been a long time coming. You might call this my star project."

"Our girl is a wonder," Bhanu said proudly, obviously tearing up. "He'd be so proud. I'm so proud. We've suffered so much pain—I believe now we'll turn a corner."

"That's the plan," Lakshanya smiled, her own eyes shining. "One of many. I simply can't wait to put them into motion—not just for the Tartarus Zone, but for our family as well! Things are going to get better, I can feel it, and if we all work together we can start to heal our lives, and the world. I believe this with all my heart."

"Listen to you, talking about healing the world! After all that's happened. If it were anyone else, Lakshanya, I'd call them raving mad!" Bhanu laughed, the first spark of pure joy returning to his tired eyes. All the while, he couldn't help glancing back at Indra and a smile kept creeping across his worn face, lighting it up anew whenever he looked at his son. "But seeing this? And now Indra back with us? I think I can start to believe you."

"Thank you," Lakshanya whispered, and now she blinked hard, her eyes shining for a different reason. "Thank you for believing in me. I know we can make a difference in—"

"So what's the plan for Parole?" Annie spoke up. Silently, every head in the room turned to look at her.

"What?" The smile faded from Lakshanya's hopeful face. For the first time, she looked distinctly nervous. “The Tartarus Zone has been my primary focus. It will help everybody affected by these terrible disasters.”

“What about Parole?” Annie pressed. “What are you doing about the collapse? The barrier’s still up, thousands of people are still trapped in there, and they need help!”

“The ‘collapse?’” Rishika asked, taking her first long, undivided look at the strange girl who knew too much.

Annie shrugged in what looked like an attempt to look casual, but the motion was jerky and stiff. Her eyes were narrowed and the corners of her mouth turned down, hands slowly curling into fists. “I just want someone to actually help.”

“We will, of course.” Rishika spread her hands. “Radiance’s primary aim is to ascertain the exact nature of the poison ravaging the Midwest and provide relief to its victims.”

“So what about the Parole quarantine?” Annie pressed, sticking her hands in her pockets as they began to shake “And the soldiers there, killing people?”

“You seem to know a great deal about the situation.” Rishika observed. Nobody was even pretending not to listen or stare anymore. “Perhaps even more than me. I wasn’t aware of soldiers killing anyone.”

“Well, they are.”

“Um, hey,” Indra spoke up, voice unnaturally high-pitched. “Maybe we shouldn’t, uh—can we not—”

“No, let your friend speak.” Rishika shook her head. “Although I hope she listens as well. Radiance Technologies is responsible for saving more lives than any other independent group in the history of the United States. Our current project is Tartarus, unraveling its mystery and healing its catastrophic damage.”

"By ignoring Parole and letting everyone there die?"

"Annie, no!" Indra hissed through clenched teeth.

"Let her speak," his mother said again, slowly. "I'm listening."

"The relief you're talking about?" Annie said in a low, rasping voice that didn't sound like her own. "It's not getting there. Not enough, anyway. Water, medicine, food—you're sending it, but we're not getting nearly enough." She looked up, directly into Rishika's eyes, then Bhanu's, then Lakshanya's, then back up at Rishika. "And people are dying."

"How did you come to know all this?" Rishika asked, studying her very carefully. "And what did you say your name was?"

"Anh Minh is an independent contractor," Lakshanya said hurriedly. "One of several I work with directly while overseeing relief efforts to Parole's survivors. If there's a problem with our system, I want to hear it."

"You do?" Annie wasn't looking at her, but her mother.

"Absolutely, I do," Lakshanya said nonetheless, gesturing for her to follow as she stepped toward the door. Please, Anh Minh, come with—"

"No," Rishika shook her head. "I'd like to hear this as well."

"I just told you." Now it was Annie's turn to stare at Rishika in confusion and disbelief. "Parole's still quarantined, everything fell into the fire a whole month ago, people are still trapped inside, and *help. Isn't. Getting. Through.* You're supposed to be in charge here, how could you not know any of this?"

"I will admit that Parole has been..." Rishika trailed off. Did not finish the sentence. Her eyes drifted out of focus. Like her son, she had moments where vulnerability shone through, raw and real, and her composure faded, leaving only sadness and fatigue. But soon, she made her eyes re-focus and looked directly into Annie's. "You must understand; the problem is so much bigger and more deadly than just one city. Tartarus has absorbed my attention for good reason. This monstrous contamination threatens us all. Parole may simply be casualty in a greater war. It's tragic, but sometimes we must mourn and move on."

"We can't move on," Annie said flatly. "Not while we're still trapped and burning."

A shadow crossed Rishika's face—another momentary crack in her armor. But then it passed, and she was looking at Annie with a new resolution, as if she'd made the decision to reveal one more layer. "You're right about one thing. This 'collapse,' as you call it, may be dangerous beyond measure. If the barrier were damaged, and anyone escapes into the general population, if it spreads...we have to be prepared for the worst possible outcome."

"What outcome?" Annie asked quietly.

"Overwhelming loss of life, of course," Rishika replied calmly. Her voice never rose above soft conversational tones that still carried through the entire large room. "A disaster far worse than Tartarus and its plagues. You have no idea of what Parole's citizens are capable."

Shiloh held very still and said nothing. Xie was afraid even to breathe.

Annie clearly had no such fears. "Parole isn't dangerous. It's full of good people, and they don't deserve to be hurt or killed or forgotten or ignored—and they definitely don't deserve Major Turret, or Lieutenant Sharpe, or anything else!"

"Guys," Indra cut before anyone could respond, sounding increasingly desperate. "Fighting about all of this, when we should be..." he gestured helplessly. "Is this what Mihir would want?"

Shiloh didn't recognize the name, but it was impossible to miss the instant effect it had on everyone in the room. Rishika and Bhanu looked as if they were in physical pain at the sound of it. While Annie kept her mouth shut, her eyes did go wide, as if she'd suddenly remembered something terrible. And Indra just stared at the floor.

"We don't know what Mihir would want," Bhanu said quietly and every head except Indra's turned toward him. He'd been so still and quiet during the heated exchange they'd almost forgotten he was there. "Did you forget why we cannot ask him?"

"No, I..." Indra didn't look up. "You don't have to remind me."

"When I saw you tonight, I had some hope." Bhanu stared at his son, voice barely above a dry whisper. His eyes were wide, whites around their irises stark. "I thought surely you'd come back because this nightmare was over. And that after this we would go home and remember him. And begin to heal."

"Dad," Indra whispered, slowly shaking his head. "Dad, I'm sorry, I–"

"It's all right, Indra," Rishika said, and when she looked at him her eyes were warm, along with her voice. "We're very glad you're safe. Please don't let grief and pain make you forget that. Make *any of us* forget that." She glanced at her husband. Then, folding her hands, Rishika turned back to her guests. "I am...truly sorry you are seeing us like this. We have something of a personal interest in Parole, as well as a professional one. Our eldest son was one of the first lost there." She spoke with dignity as if she'd rehearsed these words countless times.

In the silence that followed, Bhanu drew in a long, shaking breath. "Parole is a monster that eats the good people that try to help it. It took his life and all of us along with him. It didn't deserve Mihir and it doesn't deserve you."

"We should go," Shiloh said quietly. "We are so, so sorry. Indra, we'll be out—"

"No," he said quickly, shaking his head, eyes wide. "Don't move. I knew this would happen the second we stepped in here. Just stay with me, please."

"It still stands, they still live, and he is gone," Bhanu whispered. "My son is gone, and they still—"

"It's what he wanted," Indra said slowly. "He said he had to—"

"Indra, please!" Bhanu shook his head, slowly at first, then faster. "If Mihir had listened, if he had stayed safe at home, if he'd never heard of it, Parole or that—that Syndicate—he would still be alive!"

"Dad," Indra said, voice shaking. "I'm—"

"They've already taken one son from us!" Bhanu cried. "As he was trying to save them! My beautiful, kind, brilliant son, dead—for being too generous! He is gone and for what? For scorched earth, fire, and poison! His murderers still living and that place, that city, still standing above it all!"

Rishika moved then, closing the distance between her husband and herself, arms wrapping around him. She said something into his ear that none of them could hear, eyes flicking to Indra. He buried his head in her shoulder and sobbed, holding her very tightly.

Shiloh stared at them without seeing them. Xir brain had ground to a halt several seconds back, and xie hadn't heard anything that came after. After that single, innocuous word from Indra's father, nothing else existed. By the time xie rejoined the present and prepared to ask, someone had beaten xir to it.

"Syndicate?" Annie whispered. When Shiloh slowly turned to look at her, she was very pale and looked as disoriented as xie felt.

"Dad—I'm sorry!" Indra hadn't heard her, or noticed Shiloh's reaction. His pleading eyes were fixed on his father and suddenly he looked very young. "I'm sorry I left. But I had to. I just had to see—"

"See what, Indra?" Bhanu slowly shook his head. "Why this fascination with that damned place? All it does is take, and take—it steals the best people we have, the best of our lives."

"No it doesn't!" Annie shook off her shocked paralysis and nearly shouted the words. "Turret does! He's got his own private army and the whole city just collapsed into a lake of fire like we *knew* it would for years and nobody is listening—"

"Major Turret has been nothing but an ally, to Parole and Radiance both," Rishika said firmly, mouth a straight line. "If there was a danger, I would have been informed."

"How can you trust him?" Annie stared at her, uncomprehending.

"Because he knows what that place does." Bhanu's voice was much softer, but still cut through the increasingly heated exchange. "He lost a son there as well. And a wife, a whole family gone. Nobody has more reason to care."

"He didn't lose his whole family!" Annie retorted and proceeded to say what Shiloh was thinking but would never say out loud under the circumstances. "His daughter's alive, we saw her just a couple days ago."

"Brianna? Yes, she's a Radiance volunteer, I believe," Rishika said with increasing incredulity and disbelief. "She alone survived because of her father's bravery and he is very proud of her—and grateful." She cast a bittersweet glance toward her own children. "We all are."

"Well, you shouldn't be." Annie pulled her hands out of her pockets just to fold them across her chest. "He's lying. He didn't lose his son. Liam Turret is alive and well—actually he's not that great, he's arrogant, and annoying, and nosy, and nobody really likes or trusts him or his dad. But he's fine."

"What did you say?" Rishika stared at her, eyes widening.

"I'm telling you the truth." Annie stared right back, unblinking. "If Turret told you his son was dead, he lied to you. And I bet he's done it a lot more times."

"David Turret told us the truth when no one else would." Rishika's eyes narrowed and her skepticism hardened into a steely defense. "He gave us a name. The CyborJ Syndicate."

Shiloh felt as if xie'd been punched in the chest. Xie couldn't say a word, or for a moment, breathe.

"Then he took the burden of Parole from my shoulders," Rishika continued in the same calm, cold tone. "And allowed me to leave it behind. He swore to bring the Syndicate to justice. And to protect, monitor, and resolve Parole: a volatile and deadly place where his own family lost their lives, so that mine could withdraw, and perhaps someday heal."

"And that is the place you want to go," Bhanu said, looking at Indra with more despair than Shiloh had ever seen on a person's face. "A doomed city, ruled by murderers and burning to the ground. As well it should. But it need not take you with it!"

"I have to know what he was thinking. I have to see what he saw!" Indra clenched his teeth but a sob choked out anyway. Shiloh's heart was pounding; no matter what Indra said, this was something xie should not witness—*none of them* should be seeing this—but xie was paralyzed into awful silence.

"Is that why you left?" Bhanu sounded bowled over. Then he almost laughed. "You will never see what he saw, because if there was anything good in that place, it died the moment he did. None of us can know his mind. Because he is not here to ask. But you are! You're finally home—"

"And I'm starting to remember why I couldn't stay here another minute!" Indra nearly yelled. "Everywhere I looked I saw Mihir. You and Mom and Shanni fighting all the time about who did it or if we should even think about Parole anymore. Everybody keeps saying we have to move on, but nobody moves on! Ever! I definitely can't, not like this! How am I supposed to just forget everything?"

"That wasn't what I meant." Rishika shook her head. "I would never ask you to forget your brother. None of us would. We only wanted—"

"I had to go," Indra said vehemently. He sighed, shook his head. "And I couldn't stop wondering why he did it, it's all I thought about. I just had to see Parole for myself."

"And did you?" Bhanu sounded caught between grim laughter at an impossible notion, and fear that it might not be impossible after all.

"No," Indra said, suddenly calm. "I tried, the entire time I was gone, I was trying. Might have made it if there weren't SkEye barricades and armed soldiers keeping anyone from getting within fifty miles! And everyone who *isn't* SkEye, or us, thinks it's just a toxic ruin thanks to Tartarus. Real convenient excuse. Not a whole lot of planes, trains, or anything else heading that way."

"Because regardless of its condition, Parole is dangerous," Rishika said without a trace of doubt. "The area itself was grievously effected by the Tartarus blast; it wouldn't matter whether it's standing or not—"

"It's standing," Annie said with the same immediate confidence. "And it hasn't been poisoned at all. People are alive in there, you know they are, or else why would you send relief?"

"Nobody here is denying Parole is alive," Rishika said, remaining calm with what had to be a great deal of effort. "But that situation is stable, and we must focus our attention on a greater concern, the Tartarus—"

"It's not a greater concern!" Annie snapped, anger finally flaring without restraint. "It's a distraction! A lie! Turret lied to you, now you're lying to everybody else, and while all that's going on, we're all dying! And we deserve better! Parole is full of good people and we work to keep each other alive every day—but we *will* die unless you listen!"

"There, that." Indra's eyes slipped over to her, then back to his mother. "That's what made me keep trying. Hearing how people talk about it, how they're trying to make it safe, make it a home? I've never really...wanted to *go* anywhere before, just away. But I think I want to go there."

"That place killed your brother," Bhanu whispered. "The CyborJ Syndicate thought he posed some sort of threat and they killed him for it. He should never have been there."

"He was there because he wanted to be," Indra said back, voice almost as quiet. "He *saw something* in it. Something that made him want to give everything so it could live. I couldn't come home."

"You can *always* come home," Bhanu insisted.

"I couldn't! Not until I knew for sure!" Indra's voice broke again. "Not until I knew what really happened—why he did what he did. And if it was really worth it. Because if it wasn't..." Indra trailed off. Shook his head, slowly at first, then faster, until his hair flew. Then he half-ran across the room, wrenched the door open and slammed it behind him. Shiloh felt the wall-shaking force in xir chest along with xir sinking heart.

With rapidly clicking heels and without a backward glance, Lakshanya followed.

"Indra!" Bhanu choked out, reaching for the closed door, blinded by tears. "Wait! Come back!"

Annie grabbed Shiloh's arm and bolted for the door as well. Maybe to follow Indra, maybe just to escape from the increasingly claustrophobic room and its raw, excruciating grief upon which they were unwelcome intruders.

"I'm so sorry," Shiloh managed to get out before xie followed Annie. "This wasn't how—I'm sorry!" The words didn't even begin to be good enough. Nothing could. But there was nothing they could do here, not about the family's pain or the disturbing implications surrounding Turret and The CyborJ 'Syndicate.' Like Indra, the only possible good they could do was outside. They left Rishika and Bhanu alone to hold one another together.

☆

Outside it was quiet, except for the soft humming of night crickets and Indra's furious stomps down the sidewalk.

Indra said a four-letter word. Then he said it louder. Finally, frustration and pain boiling over, he pulled his foot back and let it fly. It hit the large Radiance Technologies sign and bounced off, accomplishing nothing except a stabbing pain in his toe. He clenched his teeth over more angry words and salty tears. His fists clenched so tight his fingernails dug into his palms and he almost didn't hear the footsteps until there were arms around him.

"You have nothing to prove to us," Lakshanya said quietly, pulling him close as he turned and wrapped his arms around her neck, burying his wet face in her shoulder. "Nobody expects you to—"

"I can't stop," Indra said, voice muffled. "And I can't help it. Mihir wouldn't be fucking up left and right and backwards and forwards, he wouldn't be running away and leaving you alone, leaving this family a mess, Mom running herself ragged and Dad's just as much a mess as I am, I know he is—"

"Stop!" She took a step back, gripping his shoulders and holding him at arm's length. "Mihir *isn't* here. He's gone, but you are still alive, you're still with me, and all we can do is try to keep going." She took a deep breath. "Keep picking up the pieces. Keep studying the Tartarus Zone and rebuilding Parole, making sure what went wrong there never happens again. Somehow try to hold this family together... and myself." She swallowed hard. "I haven't been having the best time of it either, you know."

Indra stopped. For a moment he held very still and just breathed, staring into his twin's eyes. They were wet, red and puffy under their black liner and heavy purple shadow, and just as exhausted as his. "I'm sorry. I didn't think—"

"No, you rarely do," Lakshanya sighed, shoulders sagging. She gave a long sniff and blinked several times. Raised a hand to wipe her eyes, then immediately realized what she was doing and lowered it. "This is so impractical. Didn't wear the waterproof, didn't plan ahead. How unlike me."

"Hey. We've all had a rough couple years." This time Indra pulled her into his arms. "Feel like taking a long road trip?" he said thickly, smiling through his tears. "Room for one more on the bike."

"I've thought about it." She sighed and disentangled one of her star earrings from his hair, but didn't pull back. "Just leaving everything behind and starting fresh. Quite a bit. But there's so much for me to do here. More than you'll ever know. That's not a barb, just a fact."

"Don't care if it was." Indra shook his head, then changed tactics. "So Mom really didn't know how bad it was in Parole?"

"No, but I did." Her eyes narrowed, but it didn't seem to be in response to anything he'd said. "I didn't see a need for her to step in or even know. Or you. You were both grieving, and knowing would only bring more pain—so I handled it myself. Maybe not being more open about the reality was a mistake. And now an entire city's paid for it."

Indra thought about Annie's white knuckles, her shaking fist clenched tight around the shark tooth as they listened to the strange and frightening voice over the radio. "Well, I know now."

"I believe she does too." Lakshanya said, glancing back up at the bright windows. "At the very least, you've got her attention."

"Should have gotten it sooner. Mom never would have let any of this happen in the first place."

"No." Lakshanya's black-lined eyes hardened, but again the glare wasn't aimed at him. "That she would not. What is it they say, evil triumphs when good men do nothing? Change that to good women, I suppose. Grieving women. Women who are quite understandably distracted when their lives are nearly destroyed." She smiled, eyes staying hard. "Women who will *not* let this imbalance continue."

"And Turret is the evil that's...triumphing."

"I said inside that he approved of my plan to raise a new-frequency barrier over Tartarus, yes? Well, that was a bit of an understatement. He couldn't be happier. He's been more than generous with his support, he's given me resources, staff, donated private funding. We're more than capable of getting the job done but he wants it done yesterday." She paused. "And that alone is suspect."

"I thought this was your plan." Indra shook his head, head spinning from too many details and not enough answers. "You don't trust your plan anymore?"

"I don't trust Turret. If he supports it this readily, maybe it's time to reconsider. His hands are so bloodstained they leave red fingerprints on everything he touches. So I've had to take matters into my own."

"Shanni…what are you plotting?" When she didn't answer right away, his heart sank. Not because she hesitated, but because he recognized the return of her poker face. Indra felt like he'd been punched in the gut. That was their look to share, to use on others and laugh about later. She was never supposed to use it on him.

"I've had my eye on Major David Turret for a while. He's gained far too much power, far too quickly. Our mother is an excellent judge of character and she didn't make her choice lightly. He may have been a deserving man once but, like many denizens of Parole, that man is dead now." She looked at him steadily. "I'll be watching him very closely."

"I believe you."

"You'd better. If something goes wrong, you'll hear from me."

"So…you're letting me go?" Indra raised an eyebrow.

"Are you still going to Parole? After everything that's happened? After everything our parents have been through? And *we've* been through?"

"What if I am?" he countered. "Are Mom and Dad gonna send anyone after me?"

"You're an adult, Indra, they respect your decisions. Even when they don't understand them." She shook her head. "As for me, that depends," Lakshanya spoke just as carefully. "What exactly are you and your friends trying to do?"

"Just get to Parole and see if Annie's family is okay. She wants to find them.

Shiloh has missing people too." Indra didn't dare mention the data from Maureen they carried, or Shiloh's powers. Or his remaining personal agenda: Gabriel. Not even to Shanni. Was this the first lie he had ever told his twin sister? He wasn't even lying, just omitting some truths. Was omitting some truths still a lie? It sure made his stomach twist. "And I—"

"You want to see what Mihir believed in so strongly that it made him give up his life."

"I have to," he said, looking steadily into her eyes. "I have to see if it's worth it."

"Did you ever think that perhaps there's nothing special about Parole? That it's just a place, no different from anywhere else? And our brother was a just good person who believed thousands of people, no matter who they were, didn't deserve to die?"

"I've thought of everything," Indra said quietly. "I still have to stand where he stood."

"Then yes," Lakshanya said simply and without hesitation. "I'm letting you go."

Indra smiled through his tears, leaned forward and kissed her on the cheek. "Best sister I've ever had."

"Best twin, period."

"Fine, you can have that one."

"One more thing," she said, growing serious in an instant. "The girl on the radio. I heard her again, just a little. Just for a few seconds."

"Yeah, I know," Indra smiled, even though he had no idea where this was leading. "I've been listening too."

"If you find her..." She hesitated again, and again Indra had the impression that she was holding back far more than she was saying. Deciding how much to reveal, how much to trust him with. Out of all the disturbing, frightening things he'd seen on this strange journey, this was the most disconcerting. "Just find her."

"Okay." They only stood a few feet apart, but Indra felt the distance in miles. Like they were staring at each other from across a great divide, wide as the Grand Canyon. Or maybe like they were on different planets. He'd lost another sibling. In a different way; he could still see her and reach out and touch her but the connection they'd had their entire lives now seemed far from reach. The realization slapped him in the face, and it stung. "I'll tell her you said...hi?"

"No. Give her this." She pulled something out of her purse—a small, sealed envelope, with no writing on either side. "She'll know what it's for. Do *not* open it yourself." She glared directly into his eyes. "Do you hear me, Indra? Do *not*—"

"Don't open the thing, got it." Indra nodded a couple times, giving her an incredulous look. "Be more dramatic, okay?"

"I'm serious. Get it to her." She looked directly into his eyes, unwavering. "And yes, I know very well, the moment I tell you not to do something, you'll do it—but this one time, I ask you to resist. More is at stake than you know."

"I mean, I'd probably wait until we got back on the road, but—"

"Indra." Her hard, low voice cut him off mid-word. "I've never believed it was vengeance you were after. But if you want Mihir's death...vindicated? If you want to help me prove he was right and Parole was *worth* saving? Give that envelope to the girl on the radio."

Indra stared, mouth hanging open. Moments of silence stretched. "Who *are* you?"

Lakshanya bit her lip, eyes wide. Words in her mouth fought to come out, while she was fighting just as hard to keep them in. "The best sister you've ever had—remember?" She held him close one more time.

"You're the best twin. Period."

"I hope you find what you're looking for."

He held on very tightly, suddenly terrified of letting her go. "I'll—I'll see you—"

"Just go!" She released him, barely stopping herself from rubbing at her own eyes before she smudged her eyeliner further. "It's not goodbye. It's *not*."

"Yeah. Okay, Shanni."

"Take care of your friends—and let them take care of you. And remember what I said about the radio girl."

"Got it. And tell Mom and Dad I'm sorry. They won't believe me, but I am. I'm sorry about so *much*."

"I know. Now go."

☆

When Indra walked shakily back out into the dark sidewalk, he passed right by Annie and Shiloh, who waited outside. He sighed, beckoning for them to follow with a loose, tired wave of his hand. "How much did you guys hear?" he asked in a resigned sigh.

"Just now?" Annie shook her head. "Nothing. Wasn't gonna eavesdrop on you and your sister."

He shot her a glance as if that hadn't been the answer he expected, but didn't stop walking or trying to excuse the disaster they'd just left behind. "Listen, about inside—"

"It's fine. You don't have to talk about it. It's your business."

"My mom really doesn't—"

"We'll talk later. For now we keep moving. Find someplace safe for the night. I don't think this place is safe for you."

Indra stopped walking. Eyes wet, he looked back up toward the towering building, the lights within. Silhouettes of people moving around inside high windows. "I'm sorry," he whispered, lips barely moving. Now his shoulders shook. Now the tears fell.

"I'm sorry too," Annie said quietly.

"I should have told you. You didn't know." Indra's words came through clenched teeth, little more than exhaled air with faint consonants attached. It sounded like speaking hurt. Like everything hurt. "God, I just wish...I wish..."

Shiloh hadn't said a word since they'd all come outside. Now xie stepped forward and wrapped xir arms around Indra. He let out a soft, broken noise—a sob that wracked his entire body as if he'd been struck a staggering blow—and collapsed into Shiloh's embrace. His knees shook and buckled; he would have fallen if xie hadn't been there. Annie too, he dimly recognized, she was holding him up on his other side like a wounded soldier; together they guided him back to the bike.

Indra let himself be led. He put his trust in their arms and they put him on the bike, held safely between them this time. He didn't ask where they were going. He didn't say anything at all. Dim streetlights swept past, then disappeared as they left the city lights and barrier behind. Soon, darkness stretched out before them, so infinite and complete that he could pretend they were the only ones left on the planet. Indra rested his helmeted head on Annie's back and felt Shiloh's warm hand rubbing circles on his while he shook. White lines on the pavement blurred in his tears as they sped off into the night.

CHAPTER 5

See You In My Dreams

INDRA DIDN'T SAY A WORD AS THEY SET UP CAMP WHEN THEY STOPPED FOR THE NIGHT. WHEN HE did, he kept his eyes on the ground instead of either of his friends. "Sorry about back there. I didn't mean for you guys to see that."

"It's fine." Annie shrugged, sounding truly unfazed by the dramatic, somewhat traumatic evening. "You've seen enough of my meltdowns."

"Those are different," he said, shaking his head but still not meeting her eyes. "Or they seem different. I don't know, none of my business. Still didn't mean to drag you guys into my crap."

"You didn't drag us into anything," Shiloh said firmly. "We wanted to be there."

"Yeah, well?" He ran both hands through his hair and kept his eyes fixed on his shoes. "I don't know what I expected, being in the same room as my family again, but I have to think it could have gone a little better. I don't know why it matters, you've been in my head, you've probably already felt the bad stuff in the dreams, but I just..." He trailed off, as if too exhausted to even complete the sentence.

"You deal with it however you can." Annie picked up where he left off. "Everybody's got stuff. You figure out your stuff, whatever makes it easier to survive. Forget what anyone else thinks. If you mess up sometimes, forget that too. You didn't mess up tonight, though. Sometimes everything else messes up for you. Sometimes it's your own brain."

Slowly, he looked up at her, expression tentatively quizzical. "You really do get this, don't you? Being numb, your own brain making everything harder?"

"Sometimes everything's too much, too loud and bright," she said, nodding at her helmet that sat on her bike nearby. "So there's that. Doesn't matter if people stare at me then, I don't have to look at them. Or I remember some stuff that happened and it's..." She stopped, unwilling to go back there. "Words are hard sometimes. Can't always say what I want, can't make people understand. Even if the feeling's there in my head, sometimes I can't get it out in words. So my jacket does it for me." She waved at her back where the studs had somehow rearranged themselves into a single word that definitely hadn't been there before: BRAINWEIRD.

"Nice." Indra nodded, and now he was looking less ashamed, less shut-down, more open. "I wouldn't mind one of those."

"Make friends with someone who can basically make magic clothes and robots." Annie half-smiled.

"So you didn't make that?"

"*Pff*, I don't have superpowers."

"Or eyebrows." He paused in the middle of smiling, then hurried to correct. "Not that that's a bad thing. On you it works."

"Thanks." She said it as seriously as ever, sincere where someone else might have joked. "I get scared, stressed, whatever. Start pulling out my hair. Head hair, eyebrows, whatever. Shaved the sides of my head so you couldn't tell, then just shaved my eyebrows clean off, no more mess. Done." She sniffed, finger going to the long, loose coil of hair hanging down past her jaw. "Except this piece. I fiddle with this, it calms me down."

"You've really thought all this out," he said, taking in her appearance with a new appreciation. "I thought you were just making like, a punk-rock fashion statement or something, but it's all designed to help you deal, isn't it?"

"Pretty much. Forget superpowers, you try growing up autistic, or with wobbly joints, or anything else—*in Parole* of all places. And that's just my stuff, lots of people have it way worse. So we learn how to survive hardcore."

"All alone?" Indra's eyes slid away. He seemed to drop back into himself, lost in some distant memory he'd rather not revisit, but did nonetheless.

"No." She said it so definitively it brought his focus right back. "We stick together. Parole freaks... and the rest of us who are just supposed to curl up and die. Anyone 'normal' or 'important,' like the mayor, or doctors, anyone with useful skills or whatever—or just a lot of money, power, whatever—they didn't get trapped in there with us. They got set free first thing."

"Basically, people the world likes."

She nodded. "We're on our own. We're not supposed to exist. So we take care of each other. Protect each other. Remind each other we do exist." She said all of this completely matter-of-factly. "The world is a nightmare. If I wanna survive, gotta get creative."

"So what about the armor?" He was smiling now, actually seeming excited. "That's gotta be something. Besides just armor, I mean."

"Yeah, 'cause they're braces." She wrapped her knuckles on one of the metallic plates covering her shoulder. They were molded into shapes like large scales, somehow between modern and medieval. "They keep my crappy joints from dislocating out of nowhere. Shoulders and knees especially. They pop out if the wind blows on 'em wrong. Which sucks because–"

"Because you need to run to feel normal," Shiloh said automatically. Xie'd been quiet most of this exchange, lying on xir back and looking up at the stars, glasses off and hair wrapped in a soft scarf. Again, xie had the odd-but-not-unpleasant feeling that xie knew everything Annie was going to say before she said it. It was more like being reminded than hearing anything for the first time. Or remembering a dream.

Annie slowly looked down into xir face, making and holding steady eye contact. It was odd to think this was one of the first times she'd seen Shiloh's eyes. Awake, anyway. "Yeah."

"Whenever you'd talk in my dreams, I'd hear running. Does being out of Parole help?"

She hesitated, then nodded. "It's nice not having walls around. I can move. I can breathe."

"I know the feeling." Xie smiled.

"You've felt trapped?"

"Kind of." Shiloh searched for the words. "Not behind an actual barrier. Or in a city on fire. But like...I know what you mean, when you say you have things that make you feel normal, or let you breathe."

"What things?"

"The shades, for one." Shiloh picked them up from where they rested near xir head and put them back on. Even at night, xie felt better wearing them. "Not just because light literally hurts. It's sort of like something you said about your helmet—it doesn't matter if people stare, because you don't have to look at them. Wearing these makes me feel safer, a little removed. Free, I guess?"

She didn't speak, but she nodded. All her words seemed used up.

"Sort of like when you called me 'xie,'" Shiloh said, looking over at Indra with a smile and a realization that made xir heart beat a little faster. "Sometimes it's words that help the most. You have to go with whatever gives you that feeling."

"I still wish you hadn't seen what happened back there," he said quietly, but didn't sound as flattened as he had a few minutes ago. "But thanks. I'm dealing with everything the best I can. Don't know how good that is, but..."

"But you keep going." Annie sounded sure. She usually did. "It gets easier or it doesn't. If it doesn't, we'll handle it when it comes."

"Thanks," Indra almost laughed. "You know, that really doesn't sound like something that should help. It gets better or it doesn't? But it did help, thanks."

"Probably because I'm not bullshitting you about it."

"Yeah, that's probably it. Or just you guys listening at all. Thanks."

They fell asleep under the stars.

☆

"This isn't the tree," Shiloh murmured, head swimming in a warm, dizzy way xie would never quite get used to but recognized immediately. "Definitely a dream, though."

"I know," Indra answered. "Is it yours?"

"No, I've never been here before." Shiloh turned around slowly, trying to get xir bearings. "But I think I've heard about it. Annie?"

"Yeah." She nodded slowly, looking at the room around them like it was the most beautiful place she'd ever seen. "We're home."

The club was small and windowless but comforting without feeling claustrophobic. The curtain at the back of the stage was thick burgundy velvet and the lights were low, atmosphere intimate. Dark shapes shifted as people moved around, indistinct shadows against the colorful lights. But there was no crowd chatter, no music, no ambient noise, or any sound at all. It was like they'd entered their own soundproof room where they could watch the world going by.

Even silent, the stage was lit up. A gorgeous woman with a curling cloud of gravity-defying violet hair stood in the spotlight. The sequins on her shimmering magenta dress cast thousands of tiny points of light on the walls and ceiling and the intense joy on her face lit up the room almost as brightly. But just like everybody else here, when her lips moved, no sound came out.

Two girls danced in one corner of the stage. The one in the floating chair was short and curvy with bubblegum-pink, fluffy hair, a smile on her round, pretty face. The other was tall and thin, more like a black silhouette than anything. As her long limbs moved through the air, something trailed behind them and Shiloh instantly thought of ghosts—but instead of thick smoke, the trails she left were glowing, bright green binary code. Ones and zeroes floated in the air as the two girls spun together. When the tall girl turned, the three dreamers saw that she wore a harlequin-like mask, and her eyes seemed made of stars. They twinkled as the two continued their surreal, but happy, dance.

"It's the Emerald Bar," Annie whispered, sounding reverent as if they'd stepped into a sacred space. "I never thought I'd see it again. Or them."

"I know Evelyn," Shiloh said, following her gaze to the the singer in the spotlight and the slow-dancing girls. "But who are–"

"Evelyn! Kari!" Annie was already running flat-out toward the stage, pushing past the shadowy shapes of other people. The crowd didn't seem to have faces but all that seemed to matter were the three she knew. She reached the stage and stopped just short of climbing up onto it, looking up at the still-silent figures. None of them reacted to her shout or presence; the show went on uninterrupted. "Hey! Can you hear me?" She paused for breath and slowly the excitement faded from her face. "They can't hear me."

"Maybe it's because we can't hear them?" Shiloh suggested, taking a closer look at the nearest shadowy audience member. Again, xie thought of ghosts, but these forms were even less substantial. No music, no chatter, no laughter. The silence was almost peaceful but the oblivious performers and ghostly audience made it far too eerie to be relaxing. "I'm not sure how real all this is. Maybe it really is just a dream."

"No," Annie insisted, sounding breathless from desperation. "No, this is real, I know it. We're here and they're here, they just can't see or hear us. I don't know why, but–this is the Emerald Bar, I can feel it!"

"It's not very emerald in here." Indra seemed a lot more laid-back, or maybe resigned, as he looked around at the primarily burgundy and deep purple decor. "You'd really think there'd be more green."

"There's some," Shiloh said, nodding at the audience, front row, center. Someone was there xie hadn't noticed before, almost as if he'd appeared from nowhere. He must have, since nobody could have possibly missed his entrance.

The small, wiry man's skin was covered in what looked like scales and it was green. His large, pointed ears stuck slightly out from his head and his eyes were yellow-gold with a vertical black pupil in the center. Like a cat's eyes, or maybe snake's, since the rest of him looked undeniably reptilian. His appearance was almost frightening. But instead of looking menacing or predatory, the lizard-like man seemed more sad and tired than anything; he was curled up in his seat, chin resting on his sharp-looking knees and arms wrapped tight around himself. He held very still, wistful snake-eyes fixed on Evelyn as she silently sang in the bright pool of light.

"Regan!" Annie cried, shoving shadow-figures aside as she made her way toward him, every bit as urgently as her rush to the stage.

"Annie?" He looked up immediately at the sound of her voice, startlingly quickly. Shiloh hadn't quite expected him to hear, or move, much less that fast. He uncurled and stood up, but much more slowly, hesitantly, as if unsure his senses were telling the truth.

The second she reached him, she jumped into his arms, wrapping her own around his neck and its frilled flap of loose-hanging skin. He wasn't a tall man or very strong-looking, but when he hugged her back, he picked her right up off the ground. Now he smiled. They both did and laughed, or maybe cried as he gave her a little spin and she pressed her face against his shoulder and frill. When he set her down and she picked up her head, she left his scales wet with tears. The ones on his face were damp as well.

"You can hear me!" They said it together, then definitely laughed, drying their faces. In what seemed like an automatic reflex, the man gently wiped away one of Annie's tears she'd missed the first time.

"Yes, I can hear you!" The man Annie had called Regan was looking at her like he hadn't seen her in months, or longer. "And see you! I can't believe it, I thought I'd n—Annie, I'm just so glad you're here."

"Where have you been?" she asked eagerly, still hanging onto his hands as if afraid he might disappear if she let go. "Everybody's been looking for you, they're so worried—so am I! I mean, I was! But..." She paused then, glancing around and seeming to realize where she was. "Wait. This is a dream."

"That's right," he said, smile fading as if he'd forgotten too and didn't like remembering. He coughed a little, then cleared his throat. His voice was a little raspy, as if he hadn't used it in a long time. "It's still good to see you."

"You too. Where have you been?" Annie asked again, letting go of his hands and taking a small step back to take a better look, starting from the tips of the crest running down the center of his head and back of his neck. "We didn't know what happened, we thought—well, first we thought you were dead," she said, looking upset at the very thought. "Or that he—that Sharpe had you again."

"No," Regan said quickly and visible relief washed over her face. "Nothing like that. He's never getting near me ever again."

"Okay. Good." Annie still looked troubled and kept looking at him hard, like she was trying to memorize every scale on his face. "That scared the hell out of us."

"I know. I'm sorry for scaring you. I wanted to tell you everything, but..." He paused, seeming to struggle to find the right words, or maybe try to figure out exactly how much to reveal. "I thought some things were better off...

forgotten."

"It's not your fault, he's the one who kidnapped you for two days—then you disappeared again!" She didn't seem upset at him, but his eyes still dropped to the floor. "I mean, we found out you were alive eventually, but you were already gone, you escaped in the collapse—that's what Jay said anyway. What happened? Why didn't you come back? Are you okay?"

"I'm fine, I'm with friends," he said, then frowned a little, tongue flicking in what might be annoyance. "Hans shows up sometimes too."

"Who?" Annie blinked, looking confused.

"Never mind," he said. His eyes flicked over to Shiloh and Indra as they came over to join him and Annie, then widened, as if he were noticing them for the first time. Annie turned around and gave a slightly embarrassed laugh; maybe she'd forgotten they were there too.

"Uh, yeah," she said in a more composed voice than her excited squeal from a few seconds ago. "Guys, this is Regan. He's... family."

"Hi, Regan. I'm Shiloh," xie said with a little wave. It might have startled Regan, because he gave a little jump, eyes widening. It almost seemed like he recognized xir, but Shiloh was sure xie'd never seen him before. Regan would be pretty hard to forget.

"Jay's Shiloh's uncle," Annie said before anyone could speak. "If Shiloh looks familiar, that's why."

"You know him?" Shiloh asked when Regan's eyes widened; he looked as surprised as Shiloh felt. But then, maybe xie shouldn't be. Jay lived in Parole and people like Regan—and Shiloh, though xie was usually less obvious—were supposed to be normal there.

"Yeah," Regan said with another little cough and throat-clear. "I—I've known him for a long time. He's one of—he's a good guy."

It didn't seem like Regan was going to say much else, so Shiloh shot Indra a glance, waiting to hear how he introduced himself.

"Indra," he said after just a split-second's hesitation and Shiloh made a mental note. He'd been serious about dropping 'Chance,' evidently, even to strangers. He gave Regan an odd look then, prompting Shiloh to turn around and look. "Everything okay?"

Regan was staring at them as if he'd seen a ghost and not the kind that lived in Tartarus. His round eyes flicked from Indra to Shiloh and back again, vertical pupils shrinking until they were nothing but thin black slits. For a second it seemed like his eyes were going in different directions, one on each. But no matter who he looked at, his expression of total shock remained. Finally, he shook his head as if to clear it. "Yeah, everything's fine. I just haven't seen, uh. Much of anyone lately."

"We've never seen anyone else in one of our dreams either," Indra said, taking in Regan's dully shining scales and brightly gleaming eyes, his delicate-looking frill and slightly clawed hands. "Especially someone... Annie knows," he finished, shutting his mouth and briefly sucking in his lips. Shiloh was sure that wasn't what he'd been about to say and from the way Indra was looking at him, xie had a pretty good idea of what he actually meant.

"Our dreams...?" Regan didn't seem to notice Indra's last minute switch, looking curiously from Annie to Shiloh, to Indra and back again.

"Oh." Annie's eyes widened, as if she'd never realized it wasn't common knowledge. "I forgot, I never got the chance to tell you before—uh, we're all kind of... we've been calling it brain-linked," she said, looking back at her friends as if for confirmation.

"It's not like, actual telepathy or anything," Indra said with a shrug and a bright, disarming smile, like he was trying to downplay any strangeness. "I don't think. We just show up in each others' dreams!"

"Usually we meet up in a tree," Shiloh explained, a lot more calmly. Xie did understand Indra's point, however—one of them, anyway. It was impossible to explain in a way that didn't sound ridiculous. "We've never been here before."

"It's Gabriel, isn't it?" Regan asked, unexpectedly casually. It seemed like he already knew the answer. "He brought me here for the first time too."

"How do you know about him?" Annie stared, as if that were the most surprising thing about this dream so far. "I definitely never told you about him. I was going to, but..."

"But I was gone," Regan said simply, without excuse. "And it's a long story. The short version is, he's been hanging out with me while I take care of some things. He said he was going to find some friends of his, and I guess that's you."

"Yeah, us and Gabriel go way back—and I guess you do too!" Indra gave a nervous laugh, and only then did Annie look over as if to ask what the hell was wrong with him. But the second she saw his face, she shut her mouth and turned back to Regan with a slight shake of her head.

"So if he's in your head too," Shiloh said. "Did he ever show you anything like a giant tree?"

"No," Regan said, looking out at the Emerald Bar and its shadowy patrons. "When we talk in dreams, we're usually here. Or in the library, back in Parole. I hope that means they're both still standing."

"When you talk in dreams," Shiloh repeated thoughtfully. "Does that mean you see him when you're not dreaming?"

"Not see exactly, but I usually know he's there. He kind of goes to sleep during the day, but he's pretty good company."

"Well, he linked up our dreams, so we could all find each other again," Annie said, sounding like she wanted to keep the conversation moving. "Then he told us to find him."

"That would be... difficult now," Regan said; his bemused expression made Shiloh suspect this was the biggest understatement xie'd heard in some time. But it wasn't the first time someone had downplayed a fantastic and/or bizarre reality. In fact, it seemed to happen more and more the closer they got to Parole.

"Why difficult?" Annie asked. "If he's in your dreams too, don't you know where he is?"

"Only in...spirit," Regan said, looking increasingly anxious. "By that I mean, he projects himself, I guess, like a ghost but not. He doesn't use his own body anymore."

"Then how are we supposed to find him? In real life, I mean?"

"I'm not sure you can," Regan said slowly. "He's not dead—but when Parole collapsed, his body went with it. He survived because I let him project into my brain and stay there, or something—we're not really sure."

"Well, he definitely told us to find him," Annie said, sounding certain of this at least. "And now you're here. Maybe this is what he meant."

"That's probably why you're here. I dream about this place a lot," Regan said softly. He seemed fond, looking at the burgundy velvet curtains, the stage, even the shadow-figure audience. "Gabriel probably knows it's one of my favorites. He might have even made it quiet, because it's usually too loud and bright in real life."

"Quiet is right." Indra gave the silent stage an incredulous look. "Has anyone here ever said a word?"

"No," Regan sighed, shoulders sagging. "I've tried talking to them every time. Nobody ever talks back. No one's ever heard me until you. Probably because we're all connected through Gabriel."

"That has to be it." Annie nodded, seeming convinced at once. "He wanted us to find you in a dream and then for us to all find each other in the real world. That's how it worked with us, now we can do it with you!"

"I've been… looking for some important answers," Regan said, obviously evading. "But it's not safe for me to come home yet or contact anyone directly. Gabriel's got a lot more freedom than I do right now. I asked him, if he ever found someone I knew, who I could trust, to let me know." He smiled at Annie. "I guess this is him letting me know."

"I'm just so glad you're okay." She smiled back, blinking fast; no tears this time, but it looked close. "And I can't wait to tell everyone I saw you! It'll be a couple days, because I'm not on the FireRunner and not everyone's even on it, but they'll still be so happy!"

"You're not on…" Regan looked unsettled. "Why aren't you on the ship? You're not still in Parole, are you?"

"No!" Annie shook her head vehemently. "We got a message from Meridian, Dr. Cole—I know you've heard of her," she said, shooting Shiloh a glance. "She had some important data, or a project or something—but it'll save Parole!"

"Hopefully." Shiloh nodded. "She's my mom, but she didn't even tell me exactly what it is. I hope it helps."

"It will," Annie declared. "It has to. It's what—" she broke off, as if struck by a sudden, awful thought.

When she didn't continue, Regan turned to face her, face serious but voice gentle. "Annie, who besides you made it out of Parole?"

"Aliyah and Stefanos," she said in a small voice. Shiloh didn't know those names, or many of the next, but Regan clearly did. He relaxed a little with every one. "Jay. Kari. Rowan. Uh, Ash."

"Good. Okay," Regan whispered, nodding slowly; he'd closed his eyes and seemed almost weak with relief. But he must have realized something troubling; when he opened his eyes they were concerned and his neck frill started to twitch the slightest bit. "What about Rose?"

"Haven't seen her since leaving Parole. Actually not for a while before that." A look of surprise came over her face. "Wait, I didn't know you knew Rose."

"We met recently," Regan said, not meeting her eyes. "If—when you see her, can you... tell her I'm sorry?"

"Yeah, sure." Annie looked confused by the question and slightly apprehensive to hear anything more. But she asked anyway. "Sorry for what?"

"She'll know." Regan's gaze had dropped to the floor, but now he looked back up at them. Mostly at Annie. "She's alive, I know that much. And if she's alive, it shouldn't be too hard to find her in Parole."

"I'll tell her," Annie reassured him and he seemed to relax a little. "Whatever it is, I'm sure she won't be mad."

"Thanks." He seemed to be making an effort to smile but it didn't quite reach his eyes. "There's a lot of people I need to say that to, but she should come first. Evelyn and Danae too." He shut his eyes again briefly. "And Zilch. They're not...?"

"Back in Parole," she said and Regan's faint look of hope faded. "But we know they're okay. Rowan saved their organ jars. Almost all of them."

"Almost?"

"I have their pancreas," she said, looking nervous. "It's safe and so is Zilch, because it looks fine." She paused, then blurted the rest. "We couldn't find their heart, I'm sorry."

"Don't be." Regan didn't sound surprised or even upset. "Just tell them I'm sorry too, if you see the rest of them. Tell everyone I'm sorry."

"Why don't you come home and tell them yourself?" Annie asked, sounding actually hopeful. "They'd be so relieved!"

"I'm sorry," Regan said, with a small, real smile. "There, that's one of you down."

"It's fine! You're here now, you're alive, and everyone wants you back so bad. Especially Rowan. And—and Jay," she stammered a little on that last one. "They've been... worried."

The smile dropped off Regan's face and he began to slowly shake his head. "Still have too much to do out here." It sounded like he was recommitting, convincing himself he was doing the right thing. "At the very least, I have to help Gabriel first."

"How?" Annie looked impatient but Shiloh knew her well enough to recognize fear in her eyes behind the frustration. This was a dream, xie thought. They had to wake up sometime and then Regan would be gone.

"I'm trying to give him another shot at life." Again, Regan's answer was evasive. He seemed unlikely to explain specifics. "All that time stuck underground, burning, soaking up everybody's fear and despair? He deserves better."

"You deserve better than to stay out here all alone—almost alone!" Annie was getting more worked up by the word. "Far away from Parole... and I know that's probably a good thing right now, but you can at least be around people who love you, or let them know you're okay!"

"You can tell them," Regan said, quietly but firmly. "I'd love it if you did. But I can't go with you."

"You don't have to stay away, nobody wants that!"

"It's not about what I want." His self-convincing tone was back, but his voice didn't waver. "It's about what's safe for everyone. And I am home, in a way." He looked up at the stage, the lights above, the thick curtain. "It's nice to have good dreams for a change."

"But where are you when you wake up?" Annie asked immediately. "In the real world?"

He seemed about to laugh, a fond smile replacing his heavy fatigue and lonely determination. "You haven't changed at all. Good. Hang onto that."

"Yeah, I'm stubborn," she said, folding her arms and looking up at him, but not glaring. "Almost as much as you. Just tell us where you are and what you're doing, then we'll stop worrying so much!"

"I'm..." Regan hesitated, tongue flicking in and out. He seemed to consider his next words very carefully. "I'm not in Parole."

"We know." She let her arms drop but stayed just as focused on his face. "Jay saw you leave, he said there's a recording of it."

"It worked?" Oddly, Regan seemed happy to hear this. "That's good, that means he saw..." He stopped, thoughtful and vaguely worried look coming back. "Never mind."

"If you're not in Parole," Shiloh started. Xie'd been quiet until now, letting Annie and Regan focus on each other. It meant xie could watch and listen for as much information as possible. "Does that mean you're in Tartarus?"

"You're not, right?" Annie jumped in before Regan could answer the first question. "We didn't know how bad it was until we got out here,"

"I'm not in Tartarus," he said, again in his measured tone; his voice caught for a second and he cleared his throat, frill rippling. "I'm with a friend. I'll have to go there for a little before I come home—but don't worry. I know what I'm doing, and I'll be fine."

"What are you looking for, exactly?" Shiloh asked as Annie opened her mouth, clearly ready to contest Regan's definition of 'fine.' "Maybe we can help."

"You can't," he said, only sounding a little disappointed. "But Celeste might. Talk to her. When you wake up, I mean."

Shiloh turned back to the stage in time to catch the mysterious girl come to a slowly rotating stop with her dance partner. "Celeste? The missing hacker?"

"Not missing." Regan didn't seem worried about the possibility and, not for the first time, Shiloh had to wonder exactly how much more he knew than they did. Oddly, Annie didn't seem that surprised to hear this either, but Shiloh didn't pursue it. She knew the situation better than Shiloh, xie reasoned. Instead she was focusing on the girl on the stage, so Shiloh did the same. "Just doing her own thing behind the scenes, like always."

"Who is she?" Stars twinkled in the eyes of the mystery girl's mask as she smiled down at the pink-haired girl. They rested their foreheads together even though they'd long since stopped any pretense of a dance. "If we can't see her face, how do we find her?"

"You don't. Not if she doesn't want you to."

"What if she doesn't want to give us anything?" Annie asked now.

"Then she doesn't." Regan shrugged. "And she has to have a good reason for staying under the radar. Celeste always does."

"But you know who she is," Shiloh countered. Some of Annie's frustration had to be rubbing off on xir. If Regan had told them a single concrete thing, Shiloh didn't know what. "And *where* she is. You know everything!"

Regan looked at the ground. "No. I really, really don't."

"You know more than any of us," xie countered. Maybe it was a risk, but xir chance for actual answers beyond glowing lights in the sky could end any minute. If Shiloh never heard one more vague, nebulous hint ever again, it would be too soon.

"Believe me, I don't like keeping you in the dark." Regan sounded more insistent, and his frill gave a bigger twitch. He cleared his throat again; it took several deep coughs before he could continue. "I've had enough of that to last a lifetime."

"Regan?" Annie sounded genuinely worried for the first time. "Are you okay?"

"I'm fine," he said quickly, voice still raw.

"You don't sound fine." For the first time, Shiloh noticed the chain and shark tooth around her neck when her hand closed over it. Maybe it hadn't been there before.

He shook his head like shaking off a question he couldn't answer. "Listen. There's nothing I want to do more than tell you everything and—and come home. But I can't, not yet."

"Why not? Regan, we need you back!" She was definitely close to tears now. "You don't know what it's—"

"I'm so sorry," he said, reaching out to put both hands on her shoulders. "I'm not doing this because I want to. Tell everyone. Tell them I didn't mean to hurt them. And I never quit thinking about them or wanting them back. Jay...Rowan..." His shoulders shook, with either a stifled cough or a sob. "Tell them I still—God, I love them so much!"

"Okay." Annie let go of the shark tooth and reached up to hold his hands. "I promise I'll tell them. Pretty sure they already know, but—what?" Her weak attempt at a smile faded as she saw Regan's eyes open wide, filled with what could only be fear. But he wasn't looking at her. His eyes were fixed on the shark tooth she'd just released.

"Annie," Regan whispered. "Why do you have Ash's necklace?"

She didn't answer. Maybe she couldn't. She seemed paralyzed, sick.

Very gently, Regan reached out to pick up the huge tooth between his pointed finger and thumb. He stared at it, unblinking; his facial scales started to look grayish, where someone else might have gone pale. Slowly, horror dawned in his eyes and the hand that held the tooth began to shake.

Regan seemed about to say something, but never got the chance.

CHAPTER 6

Don't Go Out at Night

(PAROLE...BURNING...)

Shiloh's eyes snapped open and xie shot upright, completely disoriented. Regan was gone. So was the bar. The night was still and calm, and Annie and Indra were asleep on either side, though Annie's sleep looked fitful. But Shiloh had definitely heard something, a voice. Neither of theirs, not Regan's. But xie did know it and recognition sent a cold shock through xir heart. Xie held absolutely still, hands clutching the sleeping bag, ears straining to hear past xir own breathing and pounding heart. For several long seconds there was nothing. Then—

(Blaze of...flames...)

Xie struggled out of the sleeping bag, half-awake. Xir head hurt, as it often did on just waking up, especially if xie'd slept in the wrong position. It was even harder to find a pain-free one sleeping on the ground. But Shiloh hadn't woken up from pain. It was the voice. Familiar. So were the words.

(*Okay...promise.*)

But it wasn't just one familiar voice; now it sounded like many were all speaking at once. Different pitches, modulating, changing, hundreds of whispers from all different directions. It sounded like whoever was speaking was circling the camp, voices becoming a surround-sound whirlwind.

(*Stay out of the light. Open your eyes.*)

A chill ran down Shiloh's spine despite the warm night as a familiar shape emerged from the darkness. Xir heart skipped a beat, then another, as the serpentine figure drew nearer, an inky blot against the stars. The dragon's black, tunnel-like eyes were just as alien as xie remembered.

"Annie, wake up!" Shiloh said as loudly as xie dared and slowly crouched down, trying not to make any sudden movements. "Don't move fast, but wake up. Right now, please."

"What?" Indra mumbled, sitting up behind them. "Where's the lizard guy?"

"Don't freak out," Shiloh whispered as the dragon undulated closer, huge claws moving silently across the ground. "Turn around very slowly. There's—"

(*Listen to my voice.*)

"Rega-Ash!" Annie gave a huge jerk awake, seeming to yell out two things at once. But she wasn't stunned for long. Wriggling out of her sleeping bag with a flashlight she must have slept with, Annie jumped to her feet. As she stomped on the ground, the night lit up. Small, piercing columns shot upward from the proximity ring—the ghost was already inside. In a flash she pulled another object from her sleeping bag neither of them had seen; Shiloh half-expected a gun but the familiar silhouette and her new stance showed it was a baseball bat. "Indra, get down! Shiloh!"

They stumbled backwards in a terrified clump, but the dragon followed. As it moved, it began to change. Its outlines blurred and its shape elongated in some places and shrunk in others, twisting and transforming until it resolved itself into an entirely different shape. Almost as impossible as a dragon—but much more familiar. Annie let out a gasp, said something in a shocked voice but Shiloh couldn't grasp the words. The world could have ended and xie wouldn't have noticed, because now nothing else existed but the man standing before them. He often had that effect.

"Dad?" Shiloh whispered, trying not to let xir voice shake, but unable to care when it did.

"Icarus." Garrett Cole's voice made cities rise and fall. It was full of presence and persuasion, it could move mountains. But all of that was secondary to it simply being his. Shiloh felt like xie could wrap xirself in the warmth of xir father's voice like a blanket, swim in the reassurance and safety. If he said everything would be all right, Shiloh would believe it. *"Turn out the lights."*

The only things more powerful than Garrett Cole's voice were his elaborate, meticulously layered plans. Parole's master-strategist hero knew that the real work was done behind the curtain and, if he did his job right, nobody would ever see his hands pulling the strings. They were supposed to be watching the show. So he dressed for the part: master of misdirection and ceremonies. The ghost had recreated his top hat and glittering tuxedo down to the last sequin. But it gleamed in a monochrome, shine dulled like an image captured on film centuries ago. He stood too still, too silent. His smile appeared frozen. This was not Garrett Cole. No ghostly facsimile could hope to compare with the original.

Still, the details it got right were perfect. Looking at the thing Shiloh *knew* was not xir father, memories surfaced before xie could think. A complex series of notes floated through Shiloh's spinning head but xie couldn't even tell if it was Rhapsody in Blue or Bohemian. The important part was standing on tiptoe to watch xir father's hands—thick fingers, deceptively nimble, nobody expected them to have so much skill the way nobody expected such a voice to come from such an unassuming-looking man—fly across piano keys. Now xie stared at those same hands rendered in greyscale. Shiloh knew every line, every crinkle in the corner of his eyes when he smiled.

But these eyes were not his. Instead of the bright, quick, and warm expressiveness Shiloh remembered so well, xie stared into flat, starless voids.

The wave of nausea brought Shiloh slamming back down to Earth. Reality hurt.

"You're not really here," xie whispered. Shiloh's eyes were filled with tears; xir chest felt like it was caving in. Xir heart wasn't skipping beats anymore but it might be breaking. "You're not really him. You're not my dad."

The face that looked like Garrett's mimicked confusion. His eyebrows knit together in deep thought and again Shiloh felt the impact of memory like a physical blow, mingled with a nauseated chill. Xie knew that expression, but it only belonged on Garrett's face. Not this one, not with these eyes.

"No." Shiloh shook xir head. "You're not. You look like him and you sound like him but you're not. Why are you doing this?"

"*Exchange.*" The voice had Garrett's rich, melodious timbre but the words came very slowly, as if each one was a tremendous effort. "*Showing you…the way.*"

"The way to what?" Shiloh's voice shook but xie didn't let it break. "Parole?"

The ghost did not respond. Not a word, not a nod, not a shake of the head. The look of confusion bordering on frustration remained etched into Garrett's features.

"The FireRunner? We know the way there," Annie said, with a similar look of confusion but with an underlying wariness instead of frustration. "What are you trying to show us?"

The ghost with Garrett's face hesitated, seeming to wrestle with an insurmountable dilemma. Finally, it raised its recreated hands, gesturing to Garrett Cole's face, then spread its arms. If all the world was a stage, he'd just stepped into the spotlight.

"Him," Shiloh said in an awed whisper. "Where he's hiding. Where my mom went to find him. You're going to show us how to find my parents."

A pause. Then a slow incline of Garrett's head. His fingers went to the brim of his hat. Then one hand slowly came up again, reaching, not toward any of them, but the sky. Shiloh turned to look, eyes following the outstretched finger.

"Oh..." Xie took in a breath, slow and shaking.

Something came into view above their heads, like the fullest, brightest moon possible emerging from behind a curtain of heavy clouds. But it wasn't the moon, or the stars. Even at night, it seemed to shine almost as bright as the sun. A silver-violet stream curled in a shimmering path like a comet's tail. It ran parallel to the highway, a glittering aurora borealis, curling in sibilant whirls and curves arcing toward the horizon. Shapes and swirls, like someone took a paintbrush and started making an iridescent watercolor across the sky.

"What is that?" Annie's eyes narrowed and she took a step back. But she was the only one suspicious. The other two were staring, motionless at the lights in the sky.

"You asked what I was looking for when I looked up at the stars. Well, there it is." Shiloh's voice was hushed. Xie adjusted xir sunglasses, smiling, and the other two didn't need to see xir eyes to tell they were wet behind them.

"What is it?" Annie stared up at the metallic swirls. The light started faintly at first and then grew, thicker and wider, until it looked solid enough that they could have walked on it. Tiny glittering particles danced in its spread, sparkle snow cascading gently like dust in a sunbeam. The motion almost made it look alive.

"My mom's lights!" Shiloh laughed, but swiped at xir eyes. "Remember back when we split up, we kept talking about stuff like, 'you know what to look for,' and 'what we planned?' This was it!"

"Pretty," Indra said appreciatively, then saw the look Shiloh was giving him. "What?"

"You can see it?" Shiloh looked at him, then Annie, then up at the sky. "You can see that, is that what's going on?"

"What are you talking about?" Annie turned to stare at her friends now, as if they were just as strange a sight. "Of course I see it. Am I not supposed to?"

"Not without these," Shiloh said, tapping xir mirrored glasses. "All my life, there have been two kinds of light that didn't hurt to look at. The kind that I make...and the kind my mom uses to write in invisible ink. Invisible unless you're wearing something that lets you see it."

"Then why can we see it?"

"I don't know." Shiloh shook xir head in wonderment. Xie experimentally removed xir glasses; as expected, the lights faded.

"What—where'd they go?" Indra said in a startled voice, then turned to look at Shiloh. "Did you—"

Shiloh put xir glasses back on and the lights seemed to re-appear, bright and shining as before. Apparently, not just to xir eyes, because Indra and Annie looked back up at the sky immediately.

"This is weird," Annie muttered. "Really weird."

"It's gotta be the brain-link stuff." Indra shrugged. "Nothing else makes sense."

"None of it makes sense at all," Annie said.

"Yes it does!" He sounded like he was trying to convince himself, and shot a suspicious glance at the Garrett ghost. "Shiloh can only see the lights with those glasses, so, same for us."

"This is so weird," Annie repeated under her breath.

But Shiloh was only half-listening. "Don't you guys know what this means?"

"Weird."

"It means my mom's okay!" Shiloh laughed with sheer relief. "She's writing in the sky, she's pointing the way to my dad, she might have even found him by now—and she was right about them!" Shiloh turned to look back at the Garrett ghost, who was also gazing serenely up at the starry night sky and glittering lights. "They communicate, she must have found a way to talk to them and—she was *right*, I knew it!"

"That's a lot to take on faith," Annie said warily, looking not up at the sky but at Shiloh's face, lit up from the inside with relief. "But I'll agree with one thing. That light is pointing us directly toward the rendezvous. Your family and mine must be going the same direction."

"You think they're all together?" Shiloh asked in a small voice. "You think when we get to the FireRunner, my parents will be there?"

"I don't know," she said, turning away from the hope in Shiloh's eyes to look back up at the stream of light flowing toward the horizon. "But it's in line with our next step."

"*Move along,*" boomed Garret's voice, and Shiloh turned around with a slight jump. Somehow xie'd almost forgotten the ghost was there.

"Thank you," xie whispered, blinking back tears. For some reason xie was sure the ghost could hear even the softest whisper.

"Um, am I the only one having a hard time with this?" Indra eyed the glittering lights, then peered around Annie at the ghost wearing Garrett's face. "Like, where did that light come from? How did that even happen? Was it always there, and the ghosts were like, hiding it until now? Do the ghosts have your dad? Is he a prisoner, or are they working together? And if your mom made the lights—is she with them too? Is that good or bad? Is *any* of this good or bad?"

"And those are all good questions." Annie leveled a hard stare at the Garrett ghost again. "Garrett Cole is very important to us. So is Dr. Maureen Cole. Are you friends with them?" She waited for an answer. When the ghost didn't give one, she tried again. "You haven't attacked us. You keep trying to talk to us instead. Why?"

"Icarus." The word rang low and settled warmly in the deepest part of Shiloh's chest. Maybe the questions were sensible. They might even be right. But xie couldn't stop looking up at Maureen's encrypted invisible ink pointing the way, or stop listening to Garrett's voice and just hearing confirmation that everything would be okay. Just for a minute, Shiloh wanted to see, hear, and believe. *"Exchange."*

"And then there's that," Indra said quickly, sounding less and less reassured by the word. "That 'Icarus' thing again—and 'exchange,' what the hell does it mean by that?"

"*Exchange,*" Garrett's hands gleamed silver-bright in the light of the proximity ward circle; strange shadows danced across his face as he stepped closer, lit from below as if he stood inside a ring of tiny stage floodlights. "*Turn out the lights.*"

"What?" Every bit of the warm glow Shiloh had felt the moment xie'd looked up into the sky was gone, as if xie'd been plunged into cold water. Something about the enigmatic words in xir father's voice sent a shiver down xir spine. Was it a mere request? Or a threat? "My mom's lights? No, we can't turn those out, we need those, they're important—"

"*Exchange. Icarus. Turn out the lights.*"

"Exchange for what?" Annie cut in as Shiloh opened xir mouth to protest again. "Just tell us what you want."

Before the ghost could answer, a long, high-pitched howl split the quiet night air, so strange and sudden everyone fell silent and very still.

"Was that a freaking wolf?" Indra inched closer to Annie and Shiloh. "There are wolves out here too?"

"There shouldn't be," Annie said, though she sounded just as unnerved and raised the baseball bat she still held. "I don't remember ever seeing an actual animal around here. Only—"

(*Enemy.*) It wasn't Garrett's voice anymore and it wasn't even the dragon's. The sound like a ghostly choir rose up from every direction again, many voices all together raising the hair on the back of Shiloh's neck.

"What?" Xie looked up, shaken alert by the cold surge of panic. Above the eerie voices, a new, strange sound rose up through the cover of darkness. Something was running toward them. It sounded like a horse's gallop, without the sharpness of hooves.

("*If you ever thought the law was on your side...*") The voice shifted again, back to a single girl's that everybody knew. Everyone here had heard these words before, when an Angel on the radio talked a frightened city through a disastrous collapse. The ghost shook its head, borrowed face twisting into a furious scowl. Again, its outline began to twist and shift. *(Think again.)*

"Wait!" Shiloh cried, suddenly overwhelmed with panic at the thought of Garrett disappearing again. Even an imitation, even a ghost. He'd still be gone.

But nothing could stop the change and Garret's features began to morph into something else. His features disappeared into the dragon's sharp, snakelike face and, soon, any trace of humanity was gone. The only things that stayed the same was the pair of tunnel-like eyes.

A terrible metallic screech erupted as something slammed into the dragon at high speed. The suffocating pressure vanished and the lights flickered back on. In an instant, the whispers were gone and all that remained was a struggle between two very solid creatures: a huge canine shape wrestling with the dragon on the ground.

A surreal battle unfolded before them. A giant metal wolf rolled across the desert floor, fighting the dragon tooth and nail. The bear-sized animal had paws the size of garbage can lids and glowing blue eyes, which gave off sparks and metallic glints when it moved. It didn't look entirely robotic—it moved with the fluid grace of a real wolf—but had enough metal and synthetic parts to suggest a blend. And all of it was focused on slaying the dragon.

"Annie, suggestion, maybe we should get back on the bike." Indra pulled at her arm, trying to edge all of them toward the motorcycle and hopefully the open road. "They look busy, we can probably get away while—"

"No, we're fine!" Annie wasn't going anywhere. She was actually grinning, relief shining through the fear on her sweat-drenched face. "It's Dandy!"

"Are you kidding?" Indra stared at her as if she'd grown another head. "Fine and dandy? Fine and—"

"No!" Annie pointed directly at the robotic wolf. "He's here to help us! Good boy, Dandy!"

The cybernetic wolf shot Annie a glance as if he'd been called by name. Then he lunged toward the dragon's head, but that wasn't the only weapon at the dragon's disposal. Its tail cracked like a whip through the air, then slammed into its opponent's skull, slipping away while its opponent was off-balance.

"Wait... what?" Annie whispered, joy at seeing the wolf dissipating fast, replaced by horror. "No, they're not supposed to be solid. They're not supposed to be real!"

The ghost almost seemed to hear her. It turned with frightening speed, and dove away from the wolf—and directly toward Shiloh.

Xie stumbled backward and tripped, over a rock or maybe just xir own feet. Xir back hit the ground and the wind rushed from xir lungs before Shiloh could react or even process what was happening. The dragon was there in an instant, looming over Shiloh and staring straight down. In shock, Shiloh stared back, immobilized under its terrifying, empty eyes.

(*Turn out the light.*)

"No!" A flower of light, defiantly blazing, bloomed from Shiloh's hands. Unlike the flashlight or the harsh halogen lamps, it didn't hurt xir eyes. It grew into a sphere, brilliant and prismatic, filled with the full color spectrum instead of the sterile white of the lights on the ground—which exploded in rapid pops and showers of sparks. It enveloped the dragon, then Annie and Indra and the entire camp and beyond it, below them and above them, the entire world—

It was almost impossible to see through the flare but Shiloh could just make out a long, curving silhouette. The dragon reared back, head and neck poised like a cobra about to strike. Curls of smoke so thick it seemed almost solid poured from its nostrils and between its teeth, cascading to the ground. Shiloh squeezed xir eyes shut and waited for the blast of killing smoke, but it didn't come. After a few terrifying seconds, Shiloh opened xir eyes—and gasped in horror.

Indra stood between the dragon and Shiloh, one arm raised in a defensive block as swirls of the dragon's oily-smoky breath curled around it. It must have burned where it touched his skin, because his mouth was open in a silent scream of agony. Still, he didn't make a sound or move an inch—until he slowly fell to his knees, eyes wide in horror.

"Indra!" Shiloh gasped, scrambling to where he lay in a heap, curled around his right arm, shoulders shaking.

"Stay down!" Annie shouted, swinging her bat wildly at the dragon's head, gasping as it connected. Shock waves shot up her arm, nearly jarring the bat from her hands. Slowly the dragon turned to stare at Annie and, in a horrifying flash, Shiloh remembered the soldiers in Meridian, the torrent of poison, the way they'd burned—

Shiloh's brilliant light sputtered and went out. Snarls and screeches filled the air but Shiloh couldn't move, paralyzed with terror. Xie hunched down over Indra, who reached out in the dark to catch hold of xir hands and held on. Every instinct screamed to run but the fight sounds seemed to come from everywhere, one wrong move would take them right back into swiping claws and razor teeth. After a terrifying, disorienting moment, xie felt a hand on xir elbow—Annie. Behind her something sputtered and struggled to stay lit: the last remaining perimeter light, pointing the way. Together, she and Shiloh half-dragged Indra toward it and out of danger.

The fight wasn't going nearly as well for the ghost anymore. Needle-sharp metal fangs tore at its impossibly solid flesh, unaffected by its toxins. Curved razor claws raked, huge, heavy paws crushing its skeletal frame, blue gem-bright eyes staring down at it. It didn't fight back or even move, instead just slumping to the ground with what looked like a tired sigh.

Then, after one last swipe of the wolf's steel talons, the dragon was gone. It dissipated into the dark as quickly as it had come, leaving behind nothing but a thin trail of curling smoke and a puddle of viscous black liquid on the ground. Toto-Dandy turned with a satisfied flick of his tail, to look at the trio of exhausted, and in one case wounded, young humans.

Indra curled protectively around his arm, breathing in harsh, painful hisses. He didn't look up or seem aware that the fight was over, or even that Shiloh or Annie were there.

"Let me see," Annie reached out to gently take his arm for a better look. Indra didn't flinch, but he did turn away and shut his eyes.

"Indra, are you..." Shiloh stopped. The question didn't deserve to be asked.

Of course he wasn't okay. He hadn't been okay since they'd arrived at Radiance Headquarters and maybe not for a long time before that, certainly not now. "Say something."

"Like what?" He gritted his teeth against the pain. The skin of his injured arm was beginning to crack and peel, as if it had been touched by an open flame. It didn't look melted or as destroyed as the SkEye soldiers had been, but the damage was still clearly severe.

"I need to clean this, at least get the surface poison off," Annie said in a low voice, shaking her head to keep from sinking into a painful reverie. "Shiloh, there's a first aid kit in the left front compartment. Grab it. And a water bottle. And a jacket or blanket or something." She looked up as xie hesitated, still staring at Indra's arm in horror. "Now!"

"Okay!" Xie snapped out of it, scrambled hurriedly off, and Annie looked up at Toto-Dandy.

"You—I don't know how you found us, but good boy. Good." The synthetic wolf did not loll out his tongue or prance around like another animal might have. Instead he met her eyes and dropped his head in a strangely human response, almost a nod of agreement. Praise acknowledged and accepted. "Now... make sure none of those things come back." He trotted a small distance away and sat down at the edge of the faint light of the halogen lamps. Dandy looked alert and on guard, but the night air was still. No sign of ghosts or anything else.

"Here we go," Shiloh reappeared at her elbow, kneeling down with xir arms full of the items she'd listed and clearly still running high on adrenaline. "What can I do to help?"

"You can take some deep breaths." Annie opened the white and red crossed box and started digging around. "Then help Indra do the same thing. This might sting."

"Okay." Shiloh cradled Indra's head, smoothing his hair back and trying to get xir own panicked breathing under control. "Hey, Indra, look at me. You're gonna be okay. We're both right here with you, we got you. We're not gonna let anything bad happen to—"

"Aaaghh!" Indra cried as Annie poured water over the burn-like wound, then followed it up with antibiotic ointment and an ace bandage.

"That's all we have?" Shiloh cast her a worried look.

"I lost a lot of supplies on the trip," she answered shortly. "I have bandages and I can keep it clean, that's about it. But it really wouldn't matter anyway. Not much anyone can do for Tartarus infections." The burnt texture continued to spread across Indra's skin, as if it were still slowly burning with an invisible fire. "We just need to reach the FireRunner. They have treatments, prototype antitoxins Radiance hasn't even made public yet. They can help."

"Sorry, Indra," Shiloh murmured, remembering the dragon-ghost's head looming high above xir. "We'll get you some real help as soon as we can. How are you feeling?"

"Fuzzy...hot...I don't feel good," Indra sniffed, suddenly looking about five years old. Then his eyes slipped shut.

"Hey, you awake? Don't go to sleep." Shiloh reached forward to touch his uninjured shoulder, but Annie stopped xir with a shake of her head.

"Don't worry, sleeping it off is pretty normal actually," she sighed, rubbing her forehead and shaved-smooth brow, as if she wanted to pick at hairs that weren't there. "He'll wake up in around fourteen hours, probably. Won't be very symptomatic until after that."

She fell silent then and held perfectly still, staring at Indra's unconscious form. Her face might have appeared blank, but it was the kind of deceptive neutrality that simply hid too big of a tangle of emotion, too intense, too overwhelming to express. Shiloh had seen this look on her face before and it wasn't a good one. Xie remembered boosting a weak signal and tapping into Radio Angel's broadcast. Then the strange, frightening voice that interrupted. When xie looked down at Annie's hand, xie wasn't surprised to see it holding onto the shark tooth around her neck in a white-knuckled grip and shaking.

"I know you're not okay, so I won't ask," Shiloh said quietly, not sure how much she was aware of xir presence anymore or wanting to startle her. "But I'm here."

Annie did not look up. But she did tuck the shark tooth into her shirt, hiding it from view. "Early symptoms are a lot like the flu," she said, getting to her feet and starting to put the first aid kit back in order. "Fever, vomiting, diarrhea, fatigue, shakiness...delirium, hallucinations."

"Yeah, I know," Shiloh resisted the unhelpful sarcastic note that wanted to creep into xir voice. "My mom and I have studied this a little bit, but not firsthand or actually treating anyone infected. Think someone could help back at Radiance HQ?"

Annie shot Indra an appraising glance. Like people so often did when they slept, he looked peaceful, younger, free of worries or the effort of showtime deflection maybe for the first time since they'd met him in the flesh. "Pretty sure he spent a long time trying to avoid going back there."

"I know!" Shiloh said again. Xie let out a frustrated noise, hating the feeling of helplessness and indecision almost as much as the outright fear. "But if it'll save his life, I think it's worth the risk."

"I say we keep heading for the FireRunner." Annie folded her arms tight around her upper body, as if trying to hold herself together. "We're almost there and if there's anyone who can help Indra, they're on that ship. We get Indra there, everything will be fine," she said like a declaration of an immutable fact.

Shiloh nodded and tried not to let xirself shake. "Sounds like a plan."

"Just gotta hold it together, for a couple more days." She sucked in a deep breath through her teeth. "If we can just—not break down. For a little more."

"Just let me know how I can help," Shiloh said quietly. "We're alone here and we shouldn't be. But we will get to a safe place, with actual adults, who know what they're doing. I want us to make it. I want you to see your family again." Xir voice nearly broke, because in speaking those words xie realized exactly how alike their desires were. Shiloh had never missed xir parents more than when Garrett had seemed to stand before xir just a few minutes ago, and the pain still settled deep in xir chest. Did Annie feel like this every day too?

"Thanks," she whispered. "I just want to go home. Right now that's all I can think about. I want to stay alive and get to where things make sense. I'm so tired."

"You got this. You're so much stronger than I ever—"

"Stop it. I don't want to be strong," Annie said suddenly. "I'm strong because I don't have a choice. None of us do."

"I know," xie said, swallowing hard. "But you're not alone. We're not going anywhere. And soon you'll be home."

She didn't speak but she breathed a little easier. "We gotta keep moving."

Shiloh cast a concerned glance at Indra. "We're not waiting until morning?"

"Does spending another minute out here really sound like a good idea to you? No. Every mile we go is another mile we don't spend out here." She glanced at the giant wolf that waited patiently by her bike. "You did good, boy, you protected us. Who knows what would've happened if you hadn't shown up."

"Well, the ghost might have told us what 'exchange' meant. Or 'Icarus.'" Shiloh eyed Toto-Dandy's huge paws with their curved, wicked-looking claws, protruding teeth and gleaming blue eyes. "He's definitely friendly?"

"What? Yeah!" Annie looked up, face still pale and shiny with cold sweat, but smiling. Still, her joy had a desperate, almost manic edge that threatened to overtake her as easily as fear. "Since I was a little kid. From Parole. Danae made him—she makes amazing machines. Like your mom, except Danae's are alive. Kind of, they're kind of alive. He's alive."

"It's okay, Annie," Shiloh cut in, recognizing how close she was to being overwhelmed on either side, good or bad, terror or relief. If they were going to keep moving tonight, she had to stay in the middle of the road and they both knew it. "Breathe."

She tried, keeping her hand on the wolf's thick neck and thicker fur. It seemed to help, and when she looked up again she seemed more grounded and focused.

"The FireRunner crew must have sent Dandy after us when we didn't come back right away," she said, speaking at a slower, regular pace. "They must really be worried."

"Okay. Then let's...move along."

When they did, Annie put the pedal to the metal even more than usual, gripping the handlebars so hard her knuckles turned white. Anxiety growled in the back of Shiloh's brain like an angry dog snapping at xir heels. Xie was sure xie could feel Indra's fever burning through xir jacket, hear his shallow, labored breathing in xir helmet even with the radio turned off. They passed the dark hours in silence.

Shiloh did not try to remember xir father's voice or mother's eyes. The ones xie'd seen tonight weren't real. Instead, xie focused on the strings of light above and the fact that real love, real warmth, and real, true safety and rest lay at the end.

CHAPTER 7

Move Along Home

BY THE TIME THE SUN CAME UP, THE INFECTION IN INDRA'S ARM HAD SPREAD OUT FROM UNDER its bandage, up to his elbow and down to his wrist. His veins stood out, stark black under his skin's dry, burnt-paper texture.

"Sorry," Shiloh said and quickly looked away, realizing xie'd been staring again. It was so hard not to look once xie caught a glimpse and felt the cold, tight squeeze of fear. Nothing compared to what Indra had to be feeling. "I'm—sorry."

"No, please, look, feel free." Indra held his arm up and wiggled it, then winced and lowered it, instantly looking like he regretted the motion.

"It's just...any other circumstances? This would be really interesting, because

I've never seen—no!" Shiloh grimaced, shaking xir head. "God, I can't turn it off. This is what you get, growing up with a...foremost genius mom. Observe variables, take notes..."

"I mean, it's for a good cause," Indra mumbled. "Make sure this doesn't happen to anyone else. I guess. So go ahead. Observe all you want."

"You won't have to," Annie cut in from in front of them. "There'll be nothing to see in a little bit. We'll get you help, I promise."

"Thanks," Indra murmured, still staring at his arm and sounding not at all comforted. "Reassuring."

As the trio rode—at a breakneck, desperate pace down the empty highway—he leaned heavily back against Shiloh, who wrapped xir arms tight around Indra's waist as if trying to keep him from disappearing. Annie drove in silence while she opened up the throttle all the way, clearly pushing herself and her bike to their limits. The giant robotic wolf loped effortlessly alongside at sixty miles per hour, long metallic legs eating up yards of highway with every stride.

They kept the glowing stream in clear view overhead as they drove. A shape slowly appeared over the horizon, and soon they recognized it—an energetic barrier dome encasing buildings. Annie pulled off the main highway about a mile away from the city, veering away from the iridescent light pathway above their heads. Traffic now lined up in a long queue to get in through turnstiles and security checkpoints—mostly semi-trucks and military jeeps.

"We're right on the edge now," she said, sounding distracted as she stared out at the buildings in the distance and the scorched expanse beyond. "But Tartarus has never gotten this far out before. Transports resupply here, refill the water tanks that go out to whatever cities actually still exist in there. Pretty important to hold onto and keep safe from the ghosts and storms and...

whatever else."

"How are we going to get in there?" Shiloh asked as they came up on the outpost bubble. "There's no way they'll just let us through. And even if they do, they'll recognize us in two seconds and Turret will be on us so fast..."

"Meridian's barrier wasn't airtight, was it?" Annie didn't sound worried.

"No, sections would burn out sometimes." Shiloh frowned, trying to see where she was going with this. "But my mom would patch them ASAP. Kind of a long shot that would happen here, isn't it?"

"Not what I mean. There's always a way in." She brought them in close to the energy barrier—and luckily found a gap in the concrete wall to let a side street through. There was a gap in the shield, the kind everyone in Parole would kill or die for, but rarely went noticed unless the town it protected was right on Tartarus' ephemeral edge. They (and the quietly trailing Toto-Dandy) slipped in through the side street unnoticed.

"How the heck'd you know that would be there?" Shiloh couldn't help but ask. "Did you scope this place out on your way?"

"I've never seen anywhere besides Parole that's totally locked down," Annie said with a shrug. "I dunno why, it's not very smart. But every place we passed had at least one way in or out besides the main gate."

"People like to pretend everything's normal," Indra supplied, sounding like he was trying to keep in a groan. "Even when it's not. Especially when it's not."

"To the point of leaving doors wide open?" Shiloh couldn't quite believe that. People had to know better. After the past ten years, xie couldn't imagine not looking over xir shoulder just in case. "That's... really not safe at all."

Annie didn't seem to share xir confusion or even interest. "Whatever gets us in."

The streets didn't stay vacant for long. As they pulled out into the main drag, full of semi-trucks and other transport vehicles, the most noticeable thing was the sheer number of people on the sidewalks. Not driving, but walking or standing. In clumps and lines leading up to buildings and tents with Radiance's insignia on them, in dirty, ragged clothes, with duffel bags and backpacks and small children and tired eyes.

Medical staff handed out small disposable gas masks and eye flushing kits. Information sheets and diagrams on what to do if someone inhaled a lung full of toxic air hung outside—nothing to do really except get them back here for detox.

"These are Shanni's people, aren't they?" Indra seemed to realize all at once, as if his feverish fog had cleared a bit. "This is what she was talking about, the Radiance relief teams, medical response."

"We saw a bunch of them on the way to Meridian," Annie said, not sounding quite as impressed. "Nothing like that back home."

"Looks like my friends are doing good work out here." Indra sounded determined to hold onto this small bit of hope. "We might actually have a chance against Tartarus."

"Yeah. Someone should really tell them Parole exists."

In the slightly awkward silence that followed, Annie steered them into a relatively empty side street, a temporary refuge from the crowd.

"See anything familiar?" Shiloh asked when she brought the bike to a halt and hopped off. Toto-Dandy continued ahead and rounded a corner a short distance away but Annie didn't seem to notice or care.

"I just needed a break," she said, leaning against the nearest brick wall without removing her helmet. "Crowds. Never liked 'em back home, then I got used to wide open space outside. Those are weird, but better."

"When you're done, maybe we should ask around or something, try to find the the ship itself," Shiloh suggested. There was no water here, or anywhere around, so xie wasn't sure where to start looking, but surely someone would. "That's gotta be hard to miss."

"Well, they're pretty hard to miss too. I mean, Rowan has actual..." She broke off, sucking in a loud gasp as Dandy reappeared from around the corner. The usually-calm, metallic wolf was dog-smiling and frolicking like an enormous puppy—and he wasn't alone. Two people were following close behind: a towering man with long, thick black hair and a just-as-thick beard, and a much shorter, slight woman with very dark skin in a white hijab and what looked like a loose-flowing poncho. Both wore large, dark sunglasses and Shiloh thought of red-carpet movie stars. But Annie clearly recognized them from somewhere else.

"Aliyah! Stef!" She pulled her helmet off, face lit up with more excitement and joy than Shiloh and Indra had ever seen from her. She started to actually bounce in place, as if unable to contain the happiness. Then she sprinted forward, arms outstretched. The woman was slightly ahead of the man and she threw her arms open wide, catching Annie as she leaped into them. Dandy sat down beside them, without a trace of predatory tension or sharp teeth, all wagging tail and lolling tongue.

"I'm so glad to see you!" Annie squealed, a young-sounding, joyful noise neither Shiloh nor Indra ever expected to hear from her. "I missed you so much!"

"And we you, darling!" The woman she'd called Aliyah squeezed her tight, planting a kiss on the top of her head. Aliyah spoke with an accent Shiloh had never heard before; xir inexperienced ear landed on some kind of English but wasn't sure which, or even if that was right at all. Her words definitely came out faster than most xie'd heard, clipped but expressive and airy. "We've been counting the days."

"I got here as soon as I could," Annie said, sounding like she was caught between laughing and crying. "I—I'm sorry if I made everyone fall behind schedule, I didn't—"

"Oh, no, don't worry about a thing!" Aliyah was definitely laughing as she held Annie at arms' length, taking a good, hard look as if expecting her to have visibly grown up in their time apart. The ends of her sentences tended to rise, making everything she said sound free and lively. "I meant that quite literally, had you pegged to meet us in six days since you left and, look, you're right on time!"

"Heard it was quite the trip," the man said in a rich, gravelly voice, mock-stern but clearly covering laughter. He spoke much more slowly than Aliyah, in deep, earthy-sounding tones that fit the rest of him: a bear of a man with deep bronze skin, worn leathery from years in the sun and wind. His face was etched with deep lines from countless smiles and deeper laughs and a thick mane of black hair fell in waves from his head and beard. Whenever he looked at Annie he smiled, full and broad; everything about him was wide and expansive as the sea or open horizon. "The kind of road that's good to put behind you."

"Hi, Stefanos." Annie blinked hard as she looked up at the giant, meeting his gaze with a shaky smile of her own, seeming overwhelmed with more emotion than she knew what to do with. "Yeah, it was... We ran into a few bumps in..." She couldn't make herself finish.

"We heard. Bad bumps," he said, and his voice was full of sympathy instead of reproach. It also had undertones of a soft, metallic whirring or some kind of tone adjustment, making it sound as if he were talking through some sort of speaker.

"But you made it through," Aliyah said, her voice natural and a good deal more energetic. "Just like we knew you would."

Annie opened her mouth, but no sound came out.

"You got there and back again, didn't you? You recovered the data?" Aliyah asked, tone softening. It sounded as if she already knew the answer, not at all surprised when Annie nodded. "That's right. You did all of that. And I never doubted for a second, I mean it."

"Well, I did," Annie said thickly, hands beginning to shake. "I doubted for a lot of seconds."

"You've never let us down before." The man removed his sunglasses to reveal golden eyes that shone like a pirate's doubloons. They were made of metal, intricately crafted with multiple layers of delicate moving parts. They looked like the lights that burned in Dandy's mechanical, intelligent wolf eyes, and moved with the same gyroscopic rotation. "And you're not starting now."

"Yes I am," she whispered, eyes filling with tears. Her hand went to the chain around her neck, the shark tooth. "I let him down. He was... I just..."

Annie ran out of words. Instead, head hanging low, she took a step toward him, and Stefanos bent forward, huge hands going under her arms to pull her right off her feet into a bear hug. Shiloh caught a metallic flash, and realized one of his hands looked artificial, made of intricate metal parts. Annie's arms went around his neck and she buried her face in the thick mane of his hair. When he set her down, she swiped her forearm across her face.

Annie turned, eyes widening as she saw Shiloh and Indra, like she'd forgotten they were there. "Oh. Sorry. She's Aliyah, and he's Stefanos.

They're..." she shrugged, words not seeming to come easily. "They're family."

"I'm Stefanos Argyrus," the big man said, golden eyes traveling over both of them. "And if you're friends of hers, you're already friends of mine."

"Yes, indeed." Aliyah turned away from Annie for the first time to face the pair of them. She paused almost imperceptibly, and Shiloh had the feeling she was sizing them up very quickly behind her dark glasses. She must have liked what she saw, because her smile came back quickly. "Aliyah el-Khalil. Very pleased to meet you both. If Anh Minh's carted you thousands of miles, she must think you're quite nice indeed."

"We think she's pretty cool too," Indra said. He seemed to be feeling slightly better, because he gave her a winning smile back. "Call me Chan...Indra. I'm Indra."

Aliyah didn't answer right away. Instead she removed her sunglasses and both Indra and Shiloh tried not to jump, stare, or otherwise be rude as hell. Aliyah's eyes were entirely black, no white sclera, even around the edges. "Are you really?"

"I think so," Indra said a little faintly. Both as in volume and because he looked like he might faint. "Is that...good?"

"It's very good," Aliyah answered, explaining nothing but seeming satisfied just the same. "And you must be Shiloh."

"Yeah, that would be me," xie said, watching both of their faces for another reaction. Aliyah and Stefanos looked at each other, sharing a grin at the name, and then back. "How'd you know? Are my parents here?"

"No, I'm sorry." Aliyah truly sounded like it as she watched Shiloh's face fall. "Fortunately, your uncle tells us we're headed in the same direction. We're bound to meet up with them sometime."

"My uncle Jay?" xie asked, feeling another small flutter of hope.

"Indeed. Says we're right on track following your mother's guideline. Most of us can't see the thing, but he tells us it's bright and shiny right overhead. Sounds quite pretty."

"It's leading around the beacons?" Shiloh asked. Xie wasn't sure why xie was surprised. Maybe just because xie expected it to be harder.

"Seems to be," Aliyah nodded. "Or at least pointing to the next one."

"You're halfway done, right?" Annie asked.

"That's right. Five beacons down, five to go." Aliyah gave a slightly annoyed click of her tongue. "Should've gotten more, but we ran into a truly, *exceptionally* nasty storm, nearly all died, ran into some Eyes up in the Sky, nearly all died again, shield generator bit the dust at last, and now we're running naked. Quite nippy even in this heat." She said all this so casually it was as if she were commenting on some mildly inconvenient weather. "So we've been stuck here a bit until we can dig up a new shield. Besides, seemed like we could all use a couple days' shore leave after that. And real showers."

"Your shields broke down too?" Annie looked troubled by the very concept.

"Indeed they have. Wait, what do you mean 'too?'"

"Ours got—ours was damaged so badly we had to stop at Radiance HQ to pick up a new one. Lakshanya gave us a better replacement, but we were 'running naked' too for a while."

"Well, now I'm even more grateful you made it back in one piece," Aliyah said as Stefanos headed a short distance away, hand to his ear as if he were making a call on a cell phone. Xie couldn't catch much of what he was saying, but it sounded like 'Tell Rowan it's Annie. No, he's...'

"Yeah," Annie said, but she didn't meet Aliyah's eyes. "So how long are we staying here?"

"No word yet, I'm afraid. Ship-sized shield generators are apparently a hot-ticket item, because we haven't seen a single one. We'll try for a couple more days but after that we may have to brave the storms without shielding."

Annie didn't answer or seem to notice Aliyah had stopped talking. She was hanging onto the shark tooth necklace again and biting her lower lip. She seemed to struggle to find the right words even more than usual and Aliyah waited patiently until she did. "I...did Kari tell you about... where's Rowan?"

"Back at the ship," Stefanos said, coming back to stand beside Aliyah. His voice was lower than it had been, softer, and straight to Annie as if it were meant for her ears only and everyone else was just listening in. "They'd be here, but we thought it was better if somebody met you and called ahead."

"They'll be so happy you're all right," Aliyah said as Annie's eyes went back to the ground. Shiloh didn't know what painful ground they'd stumbled onto and xie wasn't about to ask. "We all are. Turning that corner to find you standing there? That was one of the sweetest things I've ever seen. Wasn't sure I'd ever see it again."

"Yeah, me..." Annie stopped, looking puzzled. "Wait. You knew I was coming back with the data, though. You had to. How else did you know to wait for me?"

Aliyah hesitated, then seemed to recommit to whatever she planned to say and just powered through. "We knew one of you was coming back. But not which one."

"Oh." Annie stared at her, eyes wide. Shiloh recognized the look on her face; whatever she was seeing, it wasn't any of them. "How did... how'd that happen?"

"Kari picked up a weak signal," Aliyah said, glancing quickly at Stefanos. At least it looked like she did; her eyes made it a bit hard to tell. "A SkEye frequency. Someone reporting in, saying they'd sighted a motorcycle outside Meridian. And shot one of the two riders."

Annie didn't reply. She had the now-familiar expression of looking but not seeing and it took her a second to come back. "Is Jay around?" she asked at last, as if the last exchange hadn't happened. "I know he'll want to meet Shiloh first thing."

"Also back at the ship," Stefanos said, after just a moment of hesitation. "He's with Rowan."

Again, Annie didn't answer. Instead, her eyes slipped back out of focus, as she slipped back into her reverie.

"So you guys keep talking about a ship," Shiloh had to ask, despite the heavy mood, or maybe because of it. "Are you the captain?" Stefanos reminded xir of a storybook pirate, like he would have been right at home striding across a pitching deck in ocean spray.

"Me?" Stefanos looked down at Shiloh with a slightly surprised smile. "No, and it's a good thing." His golden eyes went down to Aliyah, smile turning warm and fond. "The FireRunner's in much better hands than mine."

"That's right, captain-ing would be my job," Aliyah said with a proud nod. "And I love it. The job, though, *not* the title, please don't call me 'Captain', just Aliyah would be lovely." She glanced up at Stefanos. "People always think you're the captain for some reason, don't they?"

"I wish they didn't," he returned. "I wouldn't last a minute doing your job."

She seemed to like that answer, but her smile faded into something more serious as she focused on Indra and Shiloh. "Now, unless there's anything else, why don't we walk and talk? We've hung around here too long already—and there are several people on the ship who'll want to see you ASAP."

"The ship's right here?" Shiloh asked, realization and confusion dawning for the first time. "I didn't think there was even a lake around here. Everything dried up in the Tartarus Blast."

Captain Aliyah grinned, white teeth and black eyes flashing. "Won't keep me from sailing."

☆

"Some ships sail upon the ocean. Some go blazing off through space," Captain Aliyah explained, hands clasped behind her back and leaving them all hurrying to keep up, even the towering Stefanos. Annie walked her bike alongside the small group as they followed. "And some are made to cross this new toxic nonsense splattered across the country, delivering basic medical supplies and clean water to places that don't exist anymore. Technically."

"Technically?" Shiloh panted, taking three steps for each one of the captain's long strides. "You mean Parole, right?"

"Of course." Aliyah shot a grin back at Annie. "Wouldn't be much point in bringing water to a smoking crater in the ground. Our operations are dangerous, but strictly anchored in the realm of sense and practicality."

"Sense. Yeah, that's the word I'd use to describe us." Stefanos shook his big head of black hair, golden eyes glinting with what might have been a smile. It was hard to tell sometimes under all the hair.

"Well, I can think of several more, yes," Aliyah conceded. "But why not let our guests decide for themselves?" She raised one long hand as they rounded a corner. The tents and prefab buildings gave way to the 'docks', loading bays jutting out not into the ocean but the desert. And just beyond them, standing tall and impressive even on dry land, was the ship. "Say hello to Water Transport Carrier 359. We call her the FireRunner. Or just 'Home.'"

The FireRunner gleamed a dull bronze in the setting sun and was nowhere near as elegant as its name might suggest. Once, the enormous craft might have been something out of a storybook. Its four masts had sails tightly furled around them and must look majestic fully opened. The rest of it told a different story. One of being torn apart and rebuilt many times over many years. It was a jigsaw puzzle of replacement parts salvaged from other vehicles and entire sections that looked like small houses. Its metal hull was pockmarked and scarred from slashing winds, rough sand, and what looked like huge, deep claw gashes. It was a patchwork quilt of a ship and had clearly been through its share of storms, but it was still floating. Even with no water within a hundred miles. The FireRunner and all its scars silently hovered about ten feet in the air.

"Technically, the FireRunner is an official Radiance ship," Aliyah said, looking at the vessel, mismatched and repaired and gleaming in the sun, as if it were the only thing that mattered in the world. "Tasked with relief efforts organized through Lakshanya Chandrasekhar."

Shiloh only half-heard. Suddenly xie felt lightheaded from a now-familiar sense of impossible recognition. Xie had seen this ship before. Drawn it–xie'd carried its image all this way in xir sketchpad. Xie had been inside it, walked around in it. In a dream.

"Yeah, she said she assigned you guys when we were at Radiance HQ," Indra said, looking as awed by the ship as Shiloh felt. "Guess she's really serious about helping Parole."

"You might call us independent contractors." Aliyah grinned. "But yes. She's been instrumental in its survival. Thanks to her, Parole *isn't* a smoking crater where a city used to be. Well, less of one. The situation is—complex. We'll speak more later."

"Come on," Stefanos gently prompted them. An electronic whirring gave his voice a metallic quality. "All aboard."

They climbed a long metal staircase that looked like it might have once been a building's fire escape and stepped onto the lower deck. Up close, the FireRunner's improvised construction was much less obvious. It might have been largely or even mostly salvaged but whoever had actually done the repairs had fit everything together well; actually standing on board, nothing felt out of place or ominous. Rather, Shiloh couldn't say why, but felt somehow reassured the moment xie stepped on board. Even the harsh sun overhead seemed less painful.

"The hovering deal? That's Radiance tech right there, even I know that," Indra remarked excitedly, looking around with an eager gleam in his eye. Although, judging by the sheen of sweat on his forehead, his eyes might have been glassy from fever, Shiloh realized with some concern. "My mom's people developed that a while ago. Or, uh, maybe that was your mom, Shiloh."

"The engine design was Rishika's," Aliyah supplied when Shiloh hesitated. "The shielding was Maureen's—as it was meant to be used, to withstand toxic atmospheres and ballistic assaults, not to box thousands of people in over an inferno. The FireRunner itself is all mine." She grinned. "The world's been through a change or two, but I'm still captain of this ship, this is my world, my home, and that means..." Aliyah let out a huge sigh of relief, stretching her arms to the sky as if it were the first time she'd been allowed in a week. Then, something else stretched out behind her that made Shiloh gasp out loud. Sprouting from her upper back was an enormous pair of golden wings. She'd been hiding them under her loose poncho-like top layer and must have been keeping them folded very tightly across her back, because now they exploded out with a sound like a huge umbrella opening. They were the biggest wings Shiloh had ever seen and actually looked large enough to lift a human being, certainly the small Aliyah, off the ground.

"Please don't say the 'A' word." she grinned at the looks on their faces as she folded up the poncho and adjusted her hijab—which stayed exactly where it was. "Unless it's my name. Or Kari's alias. I'll never understand the idea of people with halos sitting on clouds playing harps all day. I've got much more important things to do, anyway."

"Speaking of 'A' words," Stefanos cut in, looking Indra over carefully. "Antitoxin. The infirmary should be your first stop. I'm surprised you've been on your feet this long."

"Aw, I feel fine!" Indra protested, earning him several skeptical looks. "We just got here! I want to see more, just a little!"

"You're not going to see much more if you pass out or have another attack." Aliyah's firm voice allowed no argument. "You feel fine now, but in a minute? Heaving your guts out over the side and that's if it goes easy on you. Now, you only got a breath and we're catching it early, you're lucky. Don't waste that luck. A lot of people haven't got it."

"Okay, I hear you." Indra's smile faded, and once it was gone they could all much more easily see the way his eyes slipped a bit out of focus, how he wavered slightly on his feet. "Um, yeah. Maybe that's not a bad, um... idea."

"Of course." The captain shot Stefanos a glance and a nod toward Shiloh, then stuck out a wing to guide Indra along as they kept moving. "Sickbay's a bit of a hike, walk and talk."

Shiloh watched them go with rising concern. Indra had so much performer's charm and charisma, xie'd almost forgotten he was sick—then it all came back in a rush and Shiloh immediately felt terrible. The truth was obvious the moment Indra stopped making what had to be a monumental effort to simply appear normal, fine, functional. Something Shiloh deeply understood, or at least thought xie did. If he felt half as bad as he looked...

"He'll be fine," said a rumbling voice and xie turned to see Stefanos smiling down at xir and Annie. "Tartarus tries to pick us off. But we've got it beat."

"You can treat the infection, right?" Shiloh asked, grasping for a glimmer of hope that had been rattling in the back of xir brain for some time. "Annie said you had a prototype antitoxin."

"Have it? Who do you think developed it?" Stefanos let out a deep chuckle. "Half of Radiance's best tech and medicine comes right out of Parole. Don't worry about Tartarus on this ship—or the sun." He held up his metallic hand, and it should have flashed in the sun, but the reflection wasn't blinding. Actually, the entire ship wasn't unbearably hot like one might expect from all the reflected heat from metal surfaces. "The blast ten years ago punched a new giant hole in the ozone layer. That much raw UV light is deadly, so we've had to improvise." They looked up to see that it was suddenly twilight. Or that's how it appeared.

"Dampening fields," Stefanos said almost lazily, as shade fell around him like a translucent curtain. It reminded Shiloh of the Aurora Borealis, but instead of being iridescent light, it was soothing darkness. When his golden eyes glittered, they looked a bit like stars. "Which help cut out the worst of the sun. Nobody dies of heatstroke on this ship."

"Always a good thing." Shiloh adjusted xir glasses, trying to smile and shake off some of the nauseating worry from a few moments ago. "Me and bright light aren't friends."

"Remember how I hid my bike along the way?" Annie said with an excited smile. "Same deal, bending the light. Good for hiding things. Not really invisible, but hidden unless you're standing right next to it."

"Yep," Stefanos's voice resonated with pride. "They can't hide something as big as the FireRunner if you look out a window, but they can mask it from radar and most other sensors. And keep us all from frying like eggs out here. Jay did good work."

"Hope he can open my mom's disk too," Shiloh said quietly.

"If he can't, not sure who can. CyborJ's got a bag of tricks that's saved Parole more times than any of us can count over the years, including him, probably."

"I can't wait to talk to him." Shiloh's heart was pounding but this time it wasn't from fear; xir cheeks ached from smiling. "In person, I mean."

"You will. And he'll talk to you. A lot. And you'll probably only understand about a third of what he says—part of it's techno-babble, part of it's just Jay being Jay—but the important part is he's glad to... see...damn it!" Stefanos grimaced in sudden pain as his mechanical hand began to jerk and twitch as if it were having some kind of spasm. He glared at it in frustration. "Not again. This is fine, just a little Tartarus corrosion."

"Oh no," Annie said quietly, blood draining from her face. She looked about to continue, but suddenly a nearby metal door burst open.

"All right, nobody panic, I'm here!" A lanky man strode out, his gait reminding Shiloh of xir mom's clanking steps descending the stairs, except that he wore black sneakers instead of steel-toed boots. He made a direct beeline for Stefanos, single-minded focus entirely on him and his malfunctioning hand, as if he didn't quite notice anyone else was on deck.

"Nobody's panicking." Stefanos sighed at the dramatic entrance. He always did know how to make one. "This is just a little corrosive buildup."

"Good, keep not doing that." A thick pair of goggles with purple lenses covered the top half of his face, but his visible skin had the same coppery tone as Maureen's and he wore his long black hair the same way: tied back in a ponytail, keeping it out of his face and quick movements. He glanced up at the sky—to where the shining trail was still visible—and Shiloh realized the visor must allow him to see ultraviolet light. Then he flicked the side and the lens opacity lowered until they were mostly clear, giving him a better look at Stefanos's seizing synthetic hand.

"Mm-hmm." Stefanos' broad shoulders slowly lowered as he relaxed, but he said nothing more. The new man in the torn jeans, wrinkled black T-shirt, and fingerless gloves, by contrast, never stopped talking.

"Of course, even if it was basically the end of the world as we know it, there'd still be no need to panic, because I'd still be here." He flashed a grin and climbed up to sit on the metal railing for a better angle; his bare knees poked out of his jeans where they were nearly ripped to shreds.

"Right, Jay. Then everything would be fine." Stefanos glanced over at Annie and Shiloh, as if asking if they were hearing this, but held still and let Jay examine his hand.

"What, you think the only superheroes are the ones who can fly and punch things really hard?" he snorted, pulling something out of a belt holster that resembled a small flashlight. He tapped it against one fist as he studied the damage and the object made a clinking noise against a metal stud in the knuckle of his gloves. "This looks like about a week's buildup right here. Why didn't you tell me? Even I can't work miracles if I don't know there's a problem, hard as that is to believe."

Stefanos looked down at the much smaller man with something between exasperation and fondness. "Maybe because it comes with so much running commentary and self-congratulation."

"I congratulate myself when I do good work." Jay stretched out his wiry arms, flexing his long fingers to release an obscenely loud series of cracks. Then he gave the cylinder he held a flick, and the end ignited into small violet flame. It was apparently a custom, handheld blowtorch. "And I always do good work."

"Did this happen a lot while I was gone?" Annie frowned, worry clouding her face as she watched Jay hold the flame to Stefanos's metal hand. The big man kept his flesh and blood hand on Jay's shoulder so he didn't fall backwards and overboard, serenely looking into the sky toward the glowing trail. Shiloh was about to ask, but caught a flash of Stefanos' golden eyes glinting, and realized they must do more than just see the standard naked-eye spectrum.

"Depends on what you mean by 'this.'" Stefanos smiled, voice steady, but Annie didn't seem any more at ease. A tiny shower of sparks fell onto the deck, but she didn't move. It looked like that was the last thing she wanted to do right now. "Corrosive air and mechanized parts don't mix, we know this—but that doesn't give me nearly as much trouble as *Jay being a mother hen.* I can take it from here." Stefanos shook his head, but he was hiding a smile in his thick beard.

"Fine, you go rest," Jay said, shutting off the flame power. "That means sit down on something and don't move, I don't know if you're familiar with that concept. Actually, I know you're not, so you can start de-gunking your gears." He pushed the goggles up onto his forehead, and Shiloh was again struck by the resemblance to xir mom. And the differences. They had similar long features, square chin, angular jaw. Their eyes moved in the same quick way; they both gestured and spoke with their hands. The biggest difference was that where Maureen tended to fix anyone she talked to with a piercing gaze that made them immediately shut up and listen, her younger brother looked like he was trying not to laugh. Jay had the same intense eyes and sharp focus, but always looked like he knew a secret. And it was a good one. He handed over the dormant blowtorch with a little flipping toss and flourish. "I'll check on you in a little bit."

"When we find Danae, I'll see if she can add a blowtorch extension to my next upgrade." Stefanos flexed his synthetic fingers and the movements were smooth. "Along with the can opener."

"Good. Then maybe you can stop 'forgetting' to give mine back. Annie," Jay hopped down off the railing and spread his arms wide, not missing a beat. "Get into my arms, now."

"Welcome home." Stefanos gave Annie a smile as she complied. "You're going to miss the quiet."

"No, I'm not," she said in a soft voice, chin on Jay's shoulder as he held her close. As Jay moved, Shiloh caught a glance at the back of his black T-shirt; it read BAD REPUTATION in white block letters in a way that looked very reminiscent of Annie's jacket. Shiloh stole a glance to see if the text on hers had changed, and smiled when xie saw what it read. LOVE IS ALL AROUND. "Never stop talking to me, okay? Or them. I want to show Indra and Shiloh everything, and nobody's gonna do it better."

"*Shiloh?*" Jay looked up after he and Annie parted. His eyes were wide and face slack, as if he'd truly been so hyperfocused on Stefanos's hand, then Annie's presence, that this was the first time he'd realized anyone else was here. Now that focus shifted onto xir. "I—I'm..." for the first time, Jay hesitated. For a few seconds all he could do was stare into Shiloh's face, the mirrored lenses. But then, an open and honest smile spread across his face. "Really glad you're here."

Shiloh figured that was an understatement, one that did nothing to encompass the complex and overwhelming wave of bittersweet emotion, loss, joy, relief, awkwardness, and feelings too big and important for too-small words. Shiloh studied his face right back, trying to match the living person to the still images at home and the faint childhood memories. It wasn't hard, and Shiloh was oddly relieved. All this time, xie'd been worried xir uncle would be a stranger, but Jay's animated face and bright eyes had so much of Maureen in them and so much kinetic energy, it was easy to forget any lingering anxiety. It was harder to form the right words. "It's good to see you again too."

"I got so much to tell you, I don't know where to start," Jay said, sounding overwhelmed and excited and maybe a little scared all at once. Shiloh could empathize.

"Jay—you know about Ash, right?" Annie cut in awkwardly. She stared at the deck instead of him.

Shiloh froze, happiness dissolving so fast xie almost felt dizzy. Jay turned to fully face her. For the first time, his smile vanished and his shoulders fell under the heavy weight of fatigue and grief. “Later. You gotta take five minutes to land and breathe. And don’t push Rowan, okay? They’re dealing with it in their own way. Everybody is.”

“Mm-hmm.” She nodded, neutral-blank expression not changing a bit.

“Anh Minh. Don’t beat yourself up. Nobody blames you.”

“They’re taking it hard?” Annie whispered. She kept her eyes trained on Jay’s face as he forced the pain from it.

“It’s not on you,” he said more firmly. “It’s just...I don’t think there’s an easy way to lose a brother.”

“Annie, why don’t we go check on your friend?” Stefanos said in a low voice, resting his large, warm flesh and blood hand on her shoulder. “I’m sure the captain’s dropped him in the infirmary by now.”

“Huh? Oh!” She still jumped a little despite his gentle tone. Once shaken out of her reverie, her eyes flicked down to his other hand and its corroded joints, then quickly away again. “Yeah. That’d be...okay.”

“Don’t worry about this, it’s all under control, see?” Stefanos nimbly flexed his newly repaired hand in Annie’s direction. “Maybe then we can go tell Kari you’re here. She doesn’t come up for air much anymore but I know she’ll be happy you’re home.”

“Yeah. I know I am.” Annie managed a smile as they headed to a door leading further into the depths of the ship. “Uh, I just got one thing to pick up from my bike first...”

“Will he really be okay?” As xie followed Jay inside, Shiloh cast a concerned glance back toward the deck where Stefanos had disappeared with Annie.

“Oh, yeah. We’re used to that,” Jay answered with an easy shrug and nod. With every new turn past doorways and hallways that appeared identical,

Shiloh counted new ways to get lost. But Jay seemed to know exactly where he was going, because he moved with confidence, until he stopped, turning to face Shiloh. "I'll have to go help in a minute, but right now, let me look at you."

"I've got so much to ask you," he said, voice softening a little as he took in everything about Shiloh he could see, starting with the usual hat and mirrored glasses. Probably wondering about the face and eyes behind them, like everybody did, even if he knew them better than most. "Damn. Sorry, almost forgot you came here for a reason. We'll catch up later—you have it?"

Shiloh hesitated, then nodded. Dug in xir pocket and pulled out the drive, rubbing the familiar shape between xir fingers. Xie'd done this so many times over the long journey it had become something like a worry stone, squeezing it like a stress ball and remembering that it wouldn't be a good thing to accidentally break. Xie knew every molded corner and smooth plastic expanse and metal ridge, so much that xie was strangely sad to let it go. Still, it was one huge thing they'd come all this way for and it would help a lot more people in Jay's hands than anyone else's. Xie handed it over with a silent goodbye and mental thanks to xir mother for getting them this far. "Yeah. Mom said it's for your eyes only."

"Mine are probably the only ones that could understand it." In an instant the disk disappeared as fast as a card in one of Indra's tricks in their dreams. Maybe it had actually gone up Jay's sleeve. "That it?"

"Oh!" Shiloh reached into xir opposite pocket and held up the thumb drive with Radiance's logo on its side. "This is from Lakshanya Chandrasekhar. She wanted me to give this to you, it's supposed to have a really important message from a contact on it."

"Huh," Jay took it much less eagerly than he had the disk, holding it up and squinting at it as if it were either very valuable or potentially explosive. He reached up and slipped his thick goggles on, sliding a dial on one side and continuing to examine the thumb drive with an intent focus. Shiloh remembered looking for the hidden light-trail with xir own glasses, and the fact that Jay could see it too with the purple-lensed goggles. Xie wondered what else they let Jay see. "She…say… who's it from?"

"I don't know. Just a contact." Shiloh took a closer look at it too now, wondering if there was something unusual or important about it xie'd missed despite having it in xir pocket for the last thousand miles. "Is it okay?"

"Huh?" Jay looked up quickly, as if surprised to see Shiloh, or anyone at all, with him in the corridor. "Oh, yeah, it's fine! This is great, good, very good, uh, information." He slid his goggles off again, and like the disc, the thumb drive disappeared along with his intense focus. "I gotta say, I'll feel better once we're moving again," he said, easy smile and use of full sentences returning. "Our shields have been giving us hell. We've been cooling our heels here for a week waiting for a new one, and nobody likes being cut off from Parole."

"Cut off—so it's not just us who couldn't talk to you, you can't talk to Parole either?

"Kari's working on it. And so am I. Together we got radio and internet covered and if we can't do it, no one can."

"But no word yet."

"Right. So I guess that means no one can." He shrugged, giving an almost-successful smile. "Relax. I'm sure they're working hard on their end too. Nobody's gonna leave us out here in the dark. In the meantime, I'll get working on this. Maureen probably wrapped it up in a million layers of paranoid encryption. I sure would." He was still grinning when he looked up from studying the device. "But there's never been an encryption, firewall, or certain-doom scenario CyborJ couldn't beat."

"Really, certain doom?" Shiloh couldn't help the teasing note. Xie'd talked with xir uncle enough through encrypted messages and very rare video calls to get a sense for his talent of exaggeration. It was harder to tell when he was joking or not. Maureen liked to say that even Jay didn't know for sure, but right now, he looked pretty serious to Shiloh.

"Hey, Parole tried it a million times, then it tried one more time, just with murder, betrayal, and everything on fire—you know, that wasn't already on fire—and look, here I still am, still kicking. You'd think they'd learn."

Shiloh stared at him for a few seconds, eyebrows raised and a slow smile spreading across xir face. "Sounds like you got some stories I haven't heard."

"Yeah." He nodded, smile fading into a grimace, as if he regretted that last round of bombastic confidence. "Please don't ask me to tell them."

"Okay, no new stories," Shiloh conceded, though it almost hurt to let that intriguing hint drop.

"Probably for the best." The smile Jay flashed wasn't nearly enough to cover his exhaustion and Shiloh quickly realized xie'd made the right decision not to push the subject, no matter how xir curiosity burned. Xie had a feeling Jay had seen things xie couldn't even guess at and wasn't sure xie wanted to know. Probably enough actual burning to last a lifetime. "Got a bunch of oldies-but-goodies if you want those."

"Sounds great. And I still want to catch up for real when you get the chance. Oh, and I know Indra will want to meet you when he feels better. I think he said he'd heard of you before." Shiloh had to smile at the memory, even as xie felt a pang of worry, thinking of Indra in an infirmary somewhere in this huge ship and the burn-like wound on his arm. "He might even know some of your cooler stories already."

"Oh—yeah. Great." Oddly, Jay looked startled by the suggestion, as if he'd never even considered it and, when he did, he didn't find the idea altogether pleasant. When his smile came back it seemed strained. "Well, listen. You're probably about to drop right there, huh? Well, one good thing about the ship being basically empty right now, tons of rooms to choose from." He turned and headed down the corridor, motioning with his head for Shiloh to follow. "I'll show you where to crash—on a bed, a lot better than the floor! Then I better get to work on these. Hey, how long do you think it'll take me? A minute? Less?"

Shaking off xir confusion, Shiloh hurried to catch up. Xie couldn't help but wonder what had prompted the sudden change or even if xie had said something wrong already. But it was probably just the fatigue of the long day and longer trip and, by the time Shiloh caught up to xir uncle and his apparently happy monologuing, xir worries were forgotten.

CHAPTER 8

Recovery

THE MOMENT INDRA SAW THE INFIRMARY DOORWAY, HE POINTED HIMSELF DIRECTLY TOWARD THE first bed he saw and fell right down, unable to take another step. He'd never been happier to see a bed, but after that he didn't see much else. He'd been following the captain, or maybe she'd been steering him along, and he thought he heard her say something and hurry out but his feverish brain couldn't understand the words. Then she must have come back in, because he heard rapid footsteps. But he also must have been sicker than he thought; they sounded like hooves against the metal floor.

"...on. Have you feeling better soon." It wasn't the captain speaking. Or Annie, or Shiloh. A new voice. Hard to latch onto with all the rushing in his

ears. He didn't recognize the voice but held onto it like a lifeline while his head spun like leaves caught in a whirlpool. "Seen this before, you hold out for a while and then collapse all at once. Indra, can you hear me?"

"I hear lots of things." Even his own voice sounded like it was underwater or a million miles away. He almost laughed; the hoof noises were back. How could a horse be inside?

"It'll pass. Just keep breathing, in and out, nice and slow."

"'Kay." He let out a giggle at the clip-clops that accompanied the voice. Where was the horse? Maybe he could find it if he opened his eyes. He did and immediately regretted it. The room was spinning even worse than his head. Indra groaned and shut his eyes again.

"These things come and go in waves. You'll make it through this. Just keep breathing."

Waves. More like a tsunami. He had to be underwater because it was getting hard to breathe. He reached out, fumbling, until he touched something, a hand steadying him as he careened through a black void. It felt like the hand was pulling him up from the depths of the ocean. He sucked in a breath and held on.

Slowly, the roiling chaos in his head ebbed. He let go of the hand, only now realizing how tight he'd been clinging. He breathed deep, relieved to find that he could. It felt wonderful. So good he felt safe opening his eyes. He blinked up at the unfamiliar ceiling—metal, slightly curved, with recessed lights. It looked almost like the inside of a spaceship. Maybe he'd been abducted by aliens.

"Feeling a little better now?" The voice was still here. Was the horse? Indra couldn't see who was speaking laying down like this, so he raised his head a bit off the pillow.

He immediately started to scream.

"Are you all right? Where does it hurt?" The voice was still gentle despite sounding a good bit more alarmed. Indra was alarmed too, to say the least. Because now he could see where it was coming from.

There was no horse. But there were hooves. They were the kind Indra couldn't remember the name of, split into two parts, and bigger than he'd ever seen. They went up to a pair of furry reddish-gold legs that looked like they bent back the wrong way—then the person looked like a person, he thought wildly, except for the horns on the top of their head. Huge, spiraling things a good foot high and wide and, below them, ears that looked soft but not human. Their eyes didn't look human either, they were completely black, like—no, not like the ghost eyes, those had been dull, matte, more like holes, these were shiny, just black all—

He stopped screaming to take a breath.

"I'm so sorry," the more-than-slightly-demonic-looking person said quickly. "I promise, I'm not going to hurt you."

Indra stared, but silently. Partly because screaming made him feel even more lightheaded and partly because their voice that didn't match his expectations at all. No hellish growling, didn't sound like an old record being played backwards. It didn't even sound like a forward-played death metal song, though the horns, hooves, and dark eyes would have made an amazing Satanic band mascot.

He didn't say any of this. He could hardly think of any words that fit. Except for one. "Centaur."

"No," they said in the same nice, non-evil-sounding voice.

"Dreaming?"

"You're not dreaming. But you probably have a very high fever."

"Oh." It was only when Indra sank back down that he realized he'd been halfway to his feet, apparently ready to run. "Weird."

"Yes, this has to be a shock," the strange, not-centaur person said, holding up their hands as if to show him they were empty and unarmed. And human. "Ordinarily we'd meet after you were more used to—us, but it looks like we had to get you in here right away."

"It's—yeah okay, but," Indra stammered, still trying to catch his breath. "Who are you?"

"My name's Rowan," the strange person said, sounding more calm and level than Indra felt or could imagine ever feeling again. "You're on a ship called the FireRunner, and you're safe."

"You're really not a centaur?"

"No." They didn't seem to find the question strange. Maybe for them, it wasn't. "But I am a doctor."

"Cool." Indra still felt like he was trapped in the weirdest dream he'd ever had but, if he was dreaming, he might as well go along with it. "You can fix..." He gestured to his arm, then all of himself.

"Yes. I'm here to help you."

"Good. Also, hi. My name's Indra, and *I'm* here to..." He didn't know, so he stopped talking and went back to staring.

"You're here to get better," Rowan said as they moved—clip-clopped—over to a nearby cabinet, but Indra only half-heard. He couldn't take his eyes off their horns, ears and—

"Eyes? What are—what's going on there?" He gasped. "The captain lady had those too!"

Rowan lowered their eyelids, hiding their all-black eyes and looked quickly away. It seemed like a reflex, automatic once they remembered. "Yes, a few of us do. It's not contagious or painful, but sometimes we do forget they look a little...different. Again, I apologize."

"But she had them too," Indra insisted; about half of that had gone over his dizzy head. "Will that happen to me?"

"Not unless you've been consistently exposed to Tartarus' atmosphere, for years." They shut the cabinet again. "When did this happen?"

"Uh, yesterday, I think. Yesterday-ish." His panic subsided a bit as he tried to remember the sequence of events.

"Good, then you have nothing to worry about." They came back and only now Indra noticed they had something in their hand that looked like an asthma inhaler. When did they—the cabinet, he realized, feeling very proud of himself for having solved that mystery. "What kind of exposure was it? It looks like very close-range."

"It breathed on me," Indra said, nodding his head a few times—a mistake, because it made the room start spinning again. He shut his eyes until it stopped a couple seconds later. "A dragon. Ghost dragon. Dragon ghost?" Indra laughed, just a little hysterically.

"Indra?" Rowan interrupted his latest round of half-panicked giggles, not unkindly. Despite their somewhat disturbing appearance, their face and voice were mellow and soft.

"Yeah?"

"It's going to be okay." They smiled and, for the first time, Indra realized the small tuft of hair on their chin was...a *goatee*. Indra groaned softly. He couldn't even appreciate a good visual pun feeling like this.

"What are you going to do?" He made himself breathe deep and slow as Rowan gently lifted and examined his infected arm and peeling skin.

"First, I'm seeing how severe the infection is and how far it's spread. That'll tell me how much antitoxin to give you." They held up the inhaler. "Then you breathe this in."

"Okay. And that'll fix this?" He tried to wiggle his arm, but the sharp pain made him stop. "Please fix this."

"The inhaler works from the inside," Rowan explained. "It'll help your entire system from the lungs out. But for skin damage like this, you need something more direct." They held up their other hand and showed him another small object. It looked like an ordinary squirt bottle and Indra hadn't known it existed until now. He must be worse off than he thought.

"You're gonna spray me?"

Rowan nodded with a slight smile. "Just a small amount covering the damaged surface area. I know it seems odd, but topical works much faster than systemic treatments sometimes. We're working on an even stronger form, an injection, but it hasn't been tested—I don't think you're quite to that point yet, anyway. The inhaler and spray should work just fine."

"Lemme guess, won't hurt a bit, right?" Indra made a weak attempt to smile back.

"It can burn depending on how bad the infection is," Rowan said. "But I've seen an incredible range of contagion intensity. Yours doesn't look severe, so the pain shouldn't be either."

Indra started to shiver. He didn't know if it was from the infection, or because he was getting nervous, or both. "Hey, thanks for just telling me the truth."

"It's your body. You go into this with your eyes open or not at all."

"How much do I do?" Indra eyed the inhaler nervously. Somehow, inhaling a strange substance seemed riskier than spraying it on his skin.

"Just one puff, at least for now." Rowan studied his arm again. "And two sprays should do it. I know it looks bad and must feel worse, but this is really one of the less severe cases I've seen."

"I'd hate to see the bad ones." Indra gingerly took the inhaler with his undamaged left hand, wishing for the first time that he was born a leftie, or... another word he couldn't remember, when both hands worked just as well. "Shake it, right? That's what people do on TV."

"It's the same in real life." Rowan nodded. "Give it a good shake, hold it in your mouth, then push the top down and take a deep breath. Try to keep your mouth shut and hold your breath for the count of ten."

The puff of vaporized antitoxin tasted vaguely of citrus and made the inside of his mouth tingle. Not in a bad way; it felt like he'd just used some very minty mouthwash, cool and refreshing. The feeling traveled down his throat and into his lungs; it felt like he'd taken a deep breath of icy winter air. When he let it out in a rush, the feeling didn't fade completely.

"Not bad," he said appreciatively, as if he'd just tried a new food and was now considering seconds. He held up his arm with an only slightly loopy smile. "Spray it on me, doc."

The medicine came out in a fine, amber-colored mist and had the same kind of cool, clean tingling where it landed on his burned-looking skin. This time it was more intense, the feeling intensifying until it stung a bit.

"Ow, yeah, that's happening!" Indra grimaced, but he was still glad to feel anything aside from the constant burning from that arm. He'd been afraid his skin was so damaged it might never feel anything else again. He was about to say as much to Rowan, when he noticed something that made his eyes widen in wonder. “And so is that...”

The infection was healing before his eyes. Like a time-lapse video, the burnt top layer of his skin started to flake off in papery pieces and fall away. Underneath it was raw but healthy-looking skin. The edge was receding as well; just a few seconds ago, the infection had come all the way up to the inside of his elbow, but now barely reached halfway down his forearm.

He stared at the seemingly magical transformation, then looked up at Rowan, face lit up in an excited grin. “You’re seeing this, right?”

“I certainly am.” They nodded, seeming unable to keep from smiling as well after seeing his joyful reaction. It was a nice smile, Indra thought. Not demonic at all. “It’s looking very good. How are you feeling otherwise?”

“Better,” Indra realized with some surprise. “Not as dizzy, or out of it. No more room spinning—wow, I can actually think.”

“I’m so glad,” Rowan said, setting the inhaler and aerosol bottle aside. Although their tone and face stayed around the same level of calm and it was a little hard to read their all-black eyes, Indra did get the feeling that they meant it. “You might get very sleepy in a minute and that’s fine, also normal. You’ll sleep like the dead for about a day and wake up feeling more alive than ever.”

“Okay.” Indra was still staring at his now almost-completely-healed arm. Then he remembered something else, not nearly as good, but just as strange. “Uh, I’m sorry for yelling when I first saw you.”

“Think nothing of it.” Rowan shook their head—slowly, he noticed, because of the big, heavy-looking horns. Instead of being angry, they seemed almost about to laugh. “You’re far from the first and probably won’t be the last.”

"Yeah, I blame the fever," he said, giving his fingers an experimental wiggle. They were still a little sore but no lances of pain shot up his arm, which was now smooth, if raw and tender. But no hint of the burnt-paper texture and no black veins underneath. Even his fingernails were their right color again. It was bliss.

"Exactly. But even without it, I wouldn't blame you. I still scare myself in mirrors sometimes. It's the horns mostly."

"I probably would too," Indra said, taking a better look at Rowan's face for the first time, instead of any of the strange animal-ish additions around it. They had curly hair the same reddish-gold color as their fur. Or maybe it was wool. But aside from this, and the sound of hooves instead of footsteps when they walked, Rowan appeared entirely human. Pale skin with a few freckles, pinkish on their cheeks and nose—sunburn, maybe, from the harsh Tartarus sun. "But you seem pretty chill about—oh."

"Does it still hurt?" Rowan asked in response to Indra's wince and soft groan.

"No," he said in a small voice, feeling, appropriately, sheepish. "Uh, I'm sorry about the centaur thing too."

"That's also fine," Rowan said and their small, almost-smile came back. But for the first time, Indra noticed the dark circles under their darker eyes. "You're not the first there either."

"Satyr," Indra said suddenly, something else clicking in his increasingly clear brain. "That's what I was trying to say. Centaurs have horse legs. Four of them. And... aren't real. Probably." He was starting to wonder.

"I've never seen one, but you never know in Parole. Satyr or faun comes close for me, though. Goat hooves, ram horns. Not much horse." They paused for a moment, then amended, "'Rowan' is also good."

"That's right." His fever was fading, but he still felt a little warmth in his cheeks. "You said that before, didn't you? Sorry."

"It's fine," they said with another faint smile. "Thank you for remembering, actually. Most people don't remember a thing when they're that feverish."

"You're wel–wait, no, I should be thanking you!" At least he thought he should. The worst might be over, but he was still exhausted and foggy.

"It's what I'm here for," they said easily, taking the inhaler and aerosol bottle back to the cabinet across the room.

"Wait, are you leaving?" Indra's voice shook, and he felt a small surge of panic for the first time since his arm healing. "Can you stay for a little? At least until I sleep, right? Like I'm supposed to?"

"Yes, of course," they said, coming back to stand beside his bed. "I'm right here. And so are you."

"I'm really gonna be okay?" He was already fighting to keep his eyes open. The wave of exhaustion seemed to come out of nowhere, as if all his fatigue had been saving up to hit at once.

"We were very lucky, and caught it early," Rowan assured him. Like everything else they'd said, he believed it. "When you wake up, you'll feel much better. And if you don't, we'll do it again."

"Good..." Indra murmured, eyes closing. "Yeah, I feel the sleepy."

"That's normal. You've been through a lot, but you're safe now. It's all right to sleep."

"Be here when I wake up?"

"Either here, or very close by," they said. Again, Indra somehow felt better hearing the truth instead of a comforting absolute. "I'll certainly be here as much as I can. If I'm not, just call, out loud, and I'll be back in just a minute."

"Shiloh...Annie?" he managed to say, eyes opening just a crack.

"They're safe too." Indra was awake enough to notice the slight hesitation, but not awake enough to know what it meant. "I'll let them know where you are and they'll come by later."

Indra didn't answer. His eyes were closed again and his chest gently rose and fell. Pulse normal. Color starting to return to his face. Instead of lying unconscious, he rested in a peaceful, restorative sleep. Stable.

With Indra asleep and out of danger, Rowan stepped away from his bed and stood by themself for a moment in the now-silent room. Once they were alone, a change seemed to come over them. Their shoulders and head sagged, as if their horns were too heavy to hold up anymore. Once poised and attentive, now their entire being seemed weighed down with deep-seated exhaustion and sadness. They turned, quietly left the infirmary and closed the door behind them—then stopped dead.

Annie stood in the middle of the corridor outside, as if she'd been waiting. She said nothing, and held just as still as Rowan. She also held the large, fluid-filled jar and pancreas she'd been carefully guarding for thousands of miles.

They stared at one another—Annie wide-eyed, tangibly nervous and more-than-vaguely sick, and Rowan just looking shocked. Awed. At her, at the jar, at seeing both of them here in the hall. Neither of them could move, but finally she was the one to find her voice first.

"Here," she said, holding up the jar with shaking hands, voice shaking as well. "Here, it's—"

The rest of her sentence was drowned out in a flurry of hoofbeats as Rowan ran the short distance between them and threw their arms around her, pausing only to ensure they didn't send the jar flying.

The moment she realized what was happening, Annie let out a soft cry, eyes squeezed shut. "I brought their–it's Zilch's–"

"Pancreas, I know," Rowan whispered, stroking her hair. "Shh. You made it. You're safe now, everything's all right."

"No it's not, I'm so sorry," she sobbed. "He's–I'm so–"

"I know," Rowan's voice broke. "I know, I know..."

"Outside Meridian," Annie gasped, still trying to force the words out. She wrestled one arm free, digging at her shirt collar, pulling out the chain she wore under it. The shark tooth. "This. This, here, take it–"

"No." Rowan pushed her hand–and the tooth–back and away but didn't let it go, their own hand curling around hers, holding it tight. They spoke through clenched teeth. "Just... *who?*"

Wordlessly, again, she held up the chain and the large tooth held tight in both of their hands.

Rowan couldn't speak. Neither could she. The tooth and chain fell from her shaking hand, clinking softly against the jar.

Annie buried her face against Rowan's chest, curling her fingers into fists around the soft, clean fabric of their shirt. Her mouth hung open in a silent wail as Rowan pulled her closer, the precious jar held tight between them. Together they half-stumbled down the corridor toward a room away from the infirmary and sleeping patient, where their grief didn't have to stay silent.

☆

As soon as Indra was physically able to get out of bed, he did. This ship begged to be explored. There were things to see and people to meet and he couldn't wait for another single second. Annie had been waiting just as eagerly, only too glad to introduce her new friends to her old ones.

Shiloh thought the tour would have started on the upper decks and gone top to bottom. But Annie surprised them by leading the way down several decks, into the deepest parts of the ship, through twists and turns and squeezing through tight tunnels. It had the feeling of burrowing deep into some industrial rabbit's warren or wending through forest paths, finding secret passageways and discovering something precious few knew about. The constant hum of the ship's engine made the metal floor vibrate and xie quickly lost track of every tight turn. Annie seemed to know exactly where she was going, though, and led them with complete confidence until they reached a small, round metal door, like something that might be on a submarine.

"Hang on. Listen," she said as she paused outside. She pointed down; the door was slightly ajar, and a narrow beam of orange light came from inside, along with an indistinct girl's voice.

"...But you probably don't want to hear about all that," the voice was saying. Shiloh couldn't help but think it sounded very familiar. "And frankly, I don't really want to get into it—again! I'd much rather listen to you. Seriously, I'm still here, not going anywhere. I'm listening!"

Very slowly, Annie reached out and pulled the door further open until they could see inside.

The small, round room was lit with a warm orange light and filled with radios, microphones, and a few old, bulky TVs, constant static snow on each screen. In the middle of it all was a chair. It looked softly padded, with thick arms, and its back was to the door, making many more details hard to see. Still, there were two clearly unusual things about it. First, it seemed to be hovering around three feet off the floor. Secondly, a pair of legs in pink leggings dangled over the back, feet constantly jiggling. The feet's toes were painted bright pink too and they were also in continuous, wiggling motion.

"Once again, this is Radio Angel, on board the Radiance ship FireRunner out of Parole, coming to you live from... somewhere on the way, way far-out outskirts of the Tartarus Zone. Sorry I can't be more specific, but I don't have a window in here."

Slowly, the chair rotated until they could see who was in it and Shiloh caught xir first glimpse of the face behind Parole's ever-present guiding voice.

Even hanging upside-down, the girl in the chair remained in constant motion, bright bubblegum-pink hair in pigtails swaying back and forth. As she spoke, dozens of echoes followed, sometimes repeating her last phrase, and sometimes what sounded like entirely different conversations. Some were in different languages; Shiloh caught snippets of Spanish and what might have been French underneath her out-loud English. But they were all definitely her voice. "Probably wouldn't say if I knew anyway, no secrets over the airwaves, because—why? Everybody, say it with me!" She waved her fingers like conducting an orchestra. "*You can never know who's listening!*"

Shiloh almost laughed—xie'd mouthed the words along automatically. Xie looked up to see if Annie and Indra had done the same. It didn't look like they had; Annie was just leaning against the far wall with the most relaxed smile xie'd seen on her face the entire trip. Indra stared in what looked like unabashed awe as the girl with Parole's most famous speaking voice (Evelyn Calliope had the top singing spot) kept the show rolling.

"That, and, gotta say, we haven't heard from anyone in a long time, and we're getting a little worried about all of you back home. If you're talking, we're not hearing it." A plump ball of pink energy, she was never still, entire body working toward one goal: getting a clear signal. She had a microphone in one hand, other hand pressing one earphone against one ear. She gingerly stretched out a leg—Shiloh caught a glimpse of what looked like burn scarring on her bare ankle—and hit a button with her big toe, then waited expectantly. When nothing happened and the static remained unbroken, she sighed, and slumped a little. When she spoke again, her voice sounded a little less cheery and more tired. "But we're still listening! So keep trying, I'm here! I'm always here."

She stopped talking and waited. After around five seconds of silence, she shut her eyes and let herself go limp. Even her toes stopped moving.

"Hi, Kari," Annie called in a soft voice Shiloh had never heard her use before. It went nicely with her smile.

Slowly, Radio Angel raised her head, then carefully sat right-side-up to face the three people in the doorway to her small realm. "Wow," she said quietly, as a smile slowly spread across her own face. "That was fast."

"Not really." Annie smiled back, blinking hard as she stepped over the raised metal threshold. "Would have been home a lot sooner, but—"

"It's fine. You're home now." She clasped her hands above her head, stretching out an ache along her spine, and they could see the front of her pink T-shirt now. Handwritten in black sharpie, it read: EVERYTHING IS GOING TO BE OKAY.

"Sorry," Annie said, taking another slow step. Her voice sounded thick, like the words were suddenly hard to get out once she found them. "I know you've had... a hard month too."

"Oh, honey." Kari sank back down into her chair with a sigh that might have been from fatigue, or relief, or both. "You're back. That kinda makes it a good year. Now come *here*!" She flung her arms out. "Every second you spend not hugging me is unacceptable!"

Annie laughed and rushed into her arms, only pausing to avoid jostling her legs. The floating chair rotated from the momentum, and Annie lifted up her feet to let it take her along for the ride. Life in Parole tended to age people hard and fast. Even teenagers could seem twice their age after what they'd endured. But sometimes, in moments like these, when Radio Angel pulled Annie close, pressing a kiss to her cheek as they spun, years fell away. The children they hadn't gotten the chance to be shone through.

"There," Radio Angel said when they finally stopped spinning and Annie's feet were back on the floor. "That better?"

"Yeah." Annie nodded but didn't move away or release the hug after she touched down. Instead she rested her head on the other girl's shoulder, looking up into her face as she spoke. "A lot. Sorry, that wasn't too rough, was it?"

"No, no, never stop tackling me!" Kari laughed, pink pigtails swaying as she shook her head. "My legs feel a lot better! They hardly hurt at all anymore. And walking's getting easier too. Can't complain."

"Really?" Annie took a step back now, looking her over with a skeptical gaze. She rapped her knuckles on one of her metallic shoulder braces. "I sure can. And I don't even have any burns."

"Fine, I'll complain." Kari sighed, smile fading. "It sucks. EDS sucks. Wiggly, sore joints suck, bruises and bleeding if I bump into something wrong sucks, and it's super cramped in here, so I bump into stuff a lot more now. It's never *not* gonna suck. And it sucks even more with burns on top of it. But I'm dealing, and you're sweet for asking. I'm ridic lucky for even getting out at all. And look!" She stuck her leg out, pulling up her legging a little to show off more of the fading burn scars. She wiggled her toes at Annie and smiled again, almost as convincingly as before. "I can do that without screaming, couldn't do that before you left. They're good for button-pushing too."

"I saw." Annie nodded, looking caught between fondness and impressed wonder. "You haven't changed at all."

"Everything's changing too much, too fast." Kari dipped her head down to touch her forehead against Annie's. "Somebody's gotta stay the same."

"Yeah they do. Oh," Annie said, like she'd just remembered something important. "I was gonna say, we would've been here sooner, but my shield broke down."

"Oh no, I hope you got a new one! Running around with no shield is super dangerous."

"Uh-huh," Annie said, nodding slowly. "We had to stop at Radiance HQ for a new one."

"You did?" Kari's eyes widened; she might have been alarmed, intrigued, or something else Shiloh couldn't quite identify.

"Lucky for us, Lakshanya's helpful as ever."

Kari took in a quick breath. "She helped you?"

"She gave us a new shield, yeah. I'm glad she worked with me—Celeste probably could have gotten more, but she's still out of commission."

"You did great," Kari said after a split-second pause. She seemed deep in thought. "Maybe I should try getting in touch too."

"Good idea. But first," Annie rolled her head to the side to look at Shiloh, who still hung by the doorway, not sure yet if they were invited or intruders.

Indra hadn't even come in from the hall. "I brought some new friends. Guys?"

"Hi," Shiloh said, still smiling as xie stepped over the threshold. Ever since xie'd heard her voice in person, xie hadn't been able to stop. "I—I know you. From the radio."

"You sure do, hon." Kari's pensive expression faded, replaced by a warm smile. She managed to wrestle one arm free from Annie's continued hug and extend a hand to Shiloh. "Hi. They call me Radio Angel. But *I* call me Kari."

"Nice to see your...face." Shiloh immediately internally kicked xirself. Why had every coherent word suddenly dropped out of xir head? It was a very good thing xie'd worn xir sunglasses inside today, because she couldn't see xir eyes widen in horror. After a moment of blank-minded paralysis, Shiloh realized her hand was still waiting, and quickly took it. There, that part was done. The next part was easy, xie knew this information at least. "Shiloh!"

Annie shook her head, not bothering to hide her own grin. She turned toward the open door, where Indra still remained in the corridor. "Anyway, there's one more out there. Come on in!"

"Hey," Indra called, but didn't step inside. "Sorry, I'll be right in. I just—I'm not entirely great with closed-in spaces, that's all."

"Oh wow, you doing okay on the ship?" Kari called. "I know we've got some tight halls and rooms, especially down here. You totally didn't have to come all the way down here just to see me!"

"Pff—it's fine! I'm okay, mostly, but this one room is just—no offense, it's a great room, it'll just take me a minute here."

"Take all the time you need!" Her tone stayed light and airy but her expression turned puzzled and a little troubled. It looked like she was trying to place his voice like the melody to a half-forgotten song.

"No, I'm good," Indra said, audibly taking a deep breath outside and letting it out fast. "I am good. And I'm coming in." A moment later he strode inside looking perfectly cool, confident, and in-control as if there were no walls around him, closing-in or otherwise.

Kari looked up into his face. Her mouth fell open, but no sound came out.

"Pleased to meet you, Miss Angel," he said, giving her an easy smile. "I'm Indra. Lakshanya's my sister, heard you know her already. And from what I've heard of you, you more than live up to your name."

Her blue-green eyes were huge and round, pink-glossed mouth hanging open. The constant white-noise background chatter of the other radio signals and Kari's voice, carrying on its dozens of conversations at once, had fallen silent. Her distress-call multitasking and whatever telepathic link she had with her radio frequencies had been severed or at least interrupted, all because of seeing his face.

"Um... is everything okay?"

"I'm fine," Kari said quietly. Behind her, the speakers slowly began whispering her messages again. Her voice requesting help crackled back onto the airwaves. She made herself smile, but it was shaky. "You remind me of someone, that's all."

"Well, I am a twin," he said, smile dimming somewhat. "If you've worked with my sister, that's probably where you've seen me before."

"I haven't seen..." she trailed off, still staring.

Indra gave a resigned sigh, not looking nearly as happy anymore. "So it's gotta be my brother right?"

"Well, y—" She cut herself off. Kari stared for another second, then shook her head as if to clear it of cobwebs. "I mean yeah, you really do look like him.

That's—wow. Wow. Does Jay know? Have you talked to him yet?"

"Jay as in Shiloh's uncle, right?" Indra shot xir a puzzled glance. "I haven't seen him at all, unless he was around when I was all sick and out of it. Why?"

"Uh... I think I'll let him tell you." Kari let her eyes travel over the three of them and, now that she'd overcome her momentary shock, her happiness was clear and genuine. "Wow. I don't remember seeing this many people in person before. Or talking with them, since Parole stopped answering."

"You'll hear from Parole again," Annie reassured her. "On the radio or in person. A lot of people will want to thank you to your face. Maybe even see your face."

Kari smiled and shook her head. "That's sweet, but it's okay. I don't think people really think of me as a person, if that makes sense. And I'm fine with just being a friendly voice on the radio."

"You're more than that," Shiloh insisted, relieved to note that xie could speak in complete sentences again. "Everybody knows your voice. My mom and I listened to you every day and I know everyone in Parole does too. You're a real superhero."

"Ugh, I never liked that word." She rolled her eyes—then gasped, as if realizing something of incredible importance. "Hey, did I hear right? You can boost signals?"

"Yeah!" Xie nodded, unable to stop the huge grin that spread across xir face. "That's how my mom and I heard you all the way in Meridian. But that's just for every day. The super-concentrated energy blasts are for more—"

"Special occasions?" Kari was smiling too, and seeming like she was trying not to giggle. Shiloh couldn't tell whether she was laughing with or at xir, then decided xie didn't care. She was smiling.

"Well, I was going to say 'emergencies', but sure, special occasions are good too!"

"We have to try working together," she said, and the urgency in her voice made it clear that this wasn't just a request for fun. "We just have to. I've been trying to get through to Parole for weeks—but I haven't heard a word. That's *never* happened, not getting an answer. I've never had to deal with silence before. But this whole time, I haven't heard a single..." She stopped, eyes widening in what looked like fear for the first time. "That's not true. I did hear something once."

"So did we," Shiloh said, feeling xir own excited happiness slip away along with xir smile. "I tried boosting our radio signal once, so we could talk to you. Don't think it really worked, but we did hear a man—"

"Sharpe." Annie spoke the name in a whisper, but it cut through the small space and left an uneasy silence in its wake.

"We couldn't tell who it was," Kari said at last. The room was oddly quiet, Shiloh realized. All the voices that had been talking over one another when they'd come in had fallen silent. "Just that he had to be talking about you. And that meant...one of you was dead. We didn't know wh—"

"Yeah." Annie folded her arms and looked at the floor. "I know."

"Um, I just remembered something." Indra reached into his pocket, seeming grateful to break the awkward stillness. He pulled out the small envelope Lakshanya had given him and handed it to Kari. "So here, before I forget."

"What is it?" Her pink eyebrows came down as she took the envelope and turned it over in her hands, looking for some identifying writing but finding none.

"I don't actually know," Indra said, clearing his throat. "But my sister said to get it to you. She hopes it helps. And so do I."

Without waiting another moment, Kari tore open the envelope and shook out its contents. A small black cylinder with a red button on one end fell out into her hand.

"Hey, that's one of my mom's mini teleporters," Shiloh said with rising excitement. "Could she have—"

"Wait, stop!" Annie shouted, reaching out toward Kari, but it was too late. She'd pushed the button.

They all held perfectly still. They also held their breath. But the room remained silent except for the constant static hiss. Slowly, Kari lifted her thumb from the button and sheepishly looked up at the others.

"Sorry," she said, giving an apologetic shrug. "I just... got kind of excited."

"I was just going to say," Annie sounded relieved and exhausted at the same time. "Wait until Jay can scan the thing at least. Then push the button."

"Well, at least it didn't explode or anything," Indra sighed. "Which is what I was kind of afraid of this whole time."

"No, it wouldn't..." Kari started, then trailed off. Slowly, she put the device back in its envelope and put it aside, as if she didn't want to even look at it anymore.

"What was supposed to happen?" Indra couldn't help asking.

"I don't know. It didn't happen." Kari turned back to her radio controls and started manipulating dials seemingly at random. She didn't look up at Annie, but she wasn't looking at what she was doing either. She didn't seem to be seeing anything at all. "Listen, I'm going to keep trying to get a signal out."

"I'm sorry, Kari, we'll go in a minute," Annie looked almost as disappointed at the button's failure, but worry had entered her voice for the first time since they'd entered the small room. "But you really don't know what's blocking our signal?"

"No," Kari said, voice short, a vast departure from her usual bubbly chatter. "I don't know if the problem's on their end or mine. Starting to think it's mine. Maybe Tartarus interference, maybe something else."

"So then," Shiloh said hesitantly, refusing to let xirself hope. "You haven't heard from my mom and dad either? Captain Aliyah said if anyone would know, it'd be you."

Kari was quiet for a moment, then shook her head without looking up. "I'm sorry. I'll tell you if that changes."

"And I'll tell you if we hear anything more from Celeste," Annie said, steering Shiloh out into the hall, and nodding for Indra to follow. "Come on, guys. Lots more to see."

"Um, I'll help you with that signal boosting later," Shiloh called, casting one last glance over xir shoulder. "If you want!"

"Cool-great-thank you." Kari answered so quickly Shiloh wasn't sure if she'd heard at all. Slowly, she tipped over to hang upside-down again and pointed her toes toward the ceiling.

"Is she gonna be okay?" Indra sounded slightly concerned as they headed toward their next destination. "I mean, I know she's Radio Angel and all, but nobody can handle everyth—"

Somebody coming around the next corner walked directly into Indra, effectively interrupting that sentence, and nearly knocking them both to the floor. Annie and Shiloh narrowly avoided being dragged in and toppled like dominoes, and in the confusion it took a moment to even see who they'd so unexpectedly met. But they did hear him right away.

"Sorry, sorry!" Jay said with only a little embarrassment as they all attempted to untangle and regain their balance. "Totally my fault, I got turned around again, this place is a freaking maze. And I never expect to run into anybody down here, or at least nobody sneaks up on you, Radio Angel hovers, and you can hear Rowan coming a mile aw—"

He stopped mid-word.

"It's okay, don't worry about it," Indra assured him with an equally embarrassed chuckle. "I'd get lost every day even if I lived here. Maybe we should start... carrying around some balls of string..." His smile faded, replaced by concern. "Hey, you okay?"

Everyone else had found their feet quickly. Jay, however, didn't seem nearly as steady. He wavered like he'd lost his equilibrium, like he stood on the pitching deck of a ship in a high gale at sea, still holding onto Indra's shoulders.

"Uncle Jay?" Shiloh stepped closer, trying to get a better look into his face. Worryingly, he seemed almost sick or disoriented, at the very least. "Are you all right?"

Jay didn't answer or look up, not even registering that he'd heard at all. He was staring directly at Indra, for the first time since any of them had come on board. His eyes were wide and fixed on Indra's face in what looked like shock, or maybe horror. Now, he slowly pushed Indra away to arm's length, then stepped back. He continued to back away slowly, then, without a word, turned and walked quickly back way he'd come. When he reached the end of the corridor, he sped up, rounding the corner at almost a flat-out run.

Indra stared after him, looking quite understandably dumbfounded. "What the hell was—"

"Nothing. I don't know. Don't worry about it," Annie said quickly, moving past him and turning right, to head in the opposite direction from where Jay had disappeared. "Come on, lots more to see."

Shaking his head, Indra followed, seeming glad to leave the strange encounter behind them. Shiloh kept quiet, absorbing everything xie'd just seen, knowing right now that letting any of this go was out of the question. Xie couldn't quite think of an un-awkward, inconspicuous way to ask xir uncle about any of this but this conversation definitely had to happen, and as soon as possible. Shiloh remembered having that look on xir own face not long ago. Out in the Tartarus wastelands, staring into something that wore xir father's face, but didn't have his eyes.

It looked like Jay had seen a ghost.

CHAPTER 9

Rocks and Hard Places

"COME ON, NEXT STOP!" ANNIE GRINNED, PRACTICALLY BOUNCING ON THE BALLS OF HER FEET AS she led the way down one of the FireRunner's corridors. It sloped down and was an even tighter squeeze than most of the ones they'd seen yet, windowless and not quite as well-lit. "I've been waiting to show you this for days."

"Is it another new friend?" Indra asked with something between excitement and apprehension, walking down the center of the small, windowless hall and keeping his eyes forward.

"Uh, maybe," she evaded, almost laughing as she reached a heavy metal door with a round wheel in the center, which squeaked as she began to turn it. "It's always been a friend of mine."

She opened the door and they stepped through.

"Holy crap," Indra murmured, eyes widening and mouth falling open.

"I know, right?" Annie smirked. "I was gonna tell you but, really, you had to see for yourself."

It looked like they'd stepped into another world. The innermost depths of the FireRunner held a huge, metal-walled cavern, ceiling arcing so far overhead it was almost lost in the low light. It had to be an emptied water tank, Shiloh realized—and converted into some kind of in-ship forest. Full-grown trees rose up from the center of the room on a hill covered in grass and thick bushes of roses. The growth was old and extensive. Clearly, the garden here had been taken care of for years if not decades. And, above it all, rose a towering tree, its branches stretching up into a darkness so velvety and complete it looked like the night sky, the soft lights like stars.

There was grass underfoot, and the air was cool and damp, and carried the delicate fragrance of the hundreds of pink roses climbing the metal walls. The only sound was softly running water; somewhere there had to be an actual stream. A soft glow came from above and Shiloh looked up to see strings of tiny bulbs like Christmas lights and paper lanterns, clustered like stars or iridescent moss. It felt like going deep underground or maybe another planet—one that was quiet, peaceful, and very, very safe.

"I didn't think this was real," Shiloh whispered, staring up at the huge tree in the center. It seemed as tall as the crow's nest on the deck above but, more than that, it was familiar. Shiloh knew this tree. Xie'd sat in its branches in a dream. "How did this... happen?"

"It took a long time. Rose—one of our friends in Parole, she's incredible—started it, like just to see if she could do it. Guess she could. That was like, what, five years ago?"

"All this in five years?" Shiloh marveled, turning xir head to stare at a small but thick bunch of huge Venus Flytraps that rose around five feet into the air on snakelike stems. Xie could swear they moved to follow xir, almost like they were 'staring' right back.

"Yep. Rose is the best. Just about every plant Parole has left came from her. But this is the nicest garden, way bigger than anything Parole has. Look!" Annie smiled, pointing up at a hammock hanging from a sturdy branch. She looked more confident and comfortable than either of them had ever seen her, as if she'd stepped onto solid ground the moment her boots had hit the metal deck. "I love hanging out up there—that is the best spot on the entire ship for naps. It's also mine. Rowan says it's theirs. It's not. It's mine."

"Hey, what kind of tree is this?" Shiloh asked, trying not to laugh as a sudden pleasant suspicion dawned. "A rowan?"

"No." All the energy went out of Annie's suddenly flat voice, all the excitement and light faded from her eyes. Her smile faded too. "It's an ash."

Instantly, Shiloh wished that instead of manipulating energetic fields or signals, xie had the ability to go back a few seconds in time and un-ask that question. "I'm sorry, Annie."

"It's just one of those things." She shrugged and stared down at the thick green grass between her shoes. But no matter how rare and lovely grass like this had to be to someone who had spent over half their life in Parole, Shiloh wasn't sure she actually saw it.

"So, Ash was Rowan's brother, right?" Indra asked abruptly after a moment, forcedly casual tone only clashing further with the suddenly uncomfortable silence.

"Yeah. And my godfather." Her words sounded almost memorized. Like she was forming the syllables, but unable to focus on their meaning. Dropping them for others to figure out. "My parents don't trust anybody, really, that's probably how they're still alive. But they trust Ash. Trusted. They trusted him."

"What was he like? You don't have to tell me," Indra quickly amended, seeming to realize too late exactly what he was doing and how fragile of ground they might both be treading upon.

"No, it's okay. He was..." Annie didn't look up or continue right away but the way her face slowly twisted into a grimace spoke volumes of unspoken tension, grief, and the monumental effort required to hold the storm of emotion inside. Or maybe the opposite. Maybe expressing it was the hard part. Maybe nothing about this was easy at all. "Funny. Brave. Nice–God, I don't know!"

"I'm sorry." Indra held up his hands, but didn't step back, no matter how much he looked like he wanted to. "I shouldn't have–"

"It's not you!" She shook her head so fast her uneven hair flew. "It's him! It's my mom and dad still stuck in that place, it's everyone missing–what am I even supposed to say? You get so used to a thing, or a person–if they're good to you and they're a part of your life, then they're what your life is made of! How do you even describe something that's always there, so much you don't even think about it–they're like a part of your body! You don't think about it until it hurts! Or air! You don't think about it until you can't breathe!"

Indra didn't say a word. Neither did Shiloh.

"When Ash was around, things felt normal." Annie's voice was flat again. It didn't sound any happier than her painful desperation. "I'd look up and he was there. Now he's not."

"But you're still here." Indra spoke quietly, looking, not at her, but up at the very familiar tree where they'd met so many times in dreams.

"Yeah. I sure am." Annie's voice was bitter. Shiloh's heart ached at the sound but didn't know what to say, what would help or hurt. So xie kept xir mouth shut. Indra didn't, but his tone was so low both of his friends almost had to lean closer to hear.

"You got home safe," he said slowly, proceeding with caution. "I gotta believe he'd be happy about that. And want you to stop beating yourself up about this."

"You don't know that." She folded her arms around her upper body. "Nobody can know anything he would have thought about anything, not anymore. And you didn't know him."

He nodded once, as if conceding her the point. "No, I didn't. And I've never had a godfather either. But a good, funny, brave guy who you look up to and makes you feel safe and normal… that sounds like a good big brother. And I had one of those." He shrugged, let out a soft sigh. "Takes one to know one."

Annie didn't answer. By unspoken agreement, Indra and Shiloh looked in any other direction but Annie when she dragged her sleeve across her eyes, gave a loud sniff, then wiped her eyes again. The three of them stood together looking up at the tree's spreading branches and soft lights for a long time. Nobody wanted to be the first one to leave.

☆

Shiloh headed across the top deck, followed by the fast, heavy click-clanks of Toto-Dandy's huge paws. The late afternoon was warm and windy and, although xie carried an oxygen mask like everyone did while above-deck, they hadn't reached any Tartarus outskirts concentrated enough to make wearing one a necessity. Couldn't be too careful, but the air was safe for now.

"Hello there," a voice called down and Shiloh looked up, shielding xir eyes. Even behind xir sunglasses and the subtle darkness that cloaked the ship, Shiloh's sensitive eyes felt a pang at the direct sunlight. As if in response, the shade intensified until the area around them seemed washed in low purple twilight and the pain faded. With the bright light dissolved, Shiloh could clearly see Captain Aliyah on a nearby higher level, up a metal stairway and looking out at the horizon.

"Come on up!" She waved. "I want to show you something."

Remembering Annie's same words from not long ago, Shiloh complied, wondering what lay in store out here. Dandy paused at the stairs but didn't follow. Instead, he looked up at Shiloh and the captain with a tilted head and cocked ear, gaze bright and oddly intense. Then he turned and headed off with purpose, pursuing his own mysterious errand. Not for the first time, Shiloh had to wonder exactly how intelligent these synthetic-but-alive animals were and what that one in particular saw with those cold blue eyes.

"Finding your way around all right?" the captain asked when Shiloh came up level. Beside her on the wide, flat railing rested a large metal coffee pot and steaming cup with another one beside it.

"I'm getting there," Shiloh said, thinking about the labyrinthine network of corridors below. "Annie's been really helpful. Everyone has."

"Glad to hear it, not surprised. They're a good bunch." She gave a satisfied nod. "Coffee?"

Shiloh glanced at the one half-full cup—black, no cream or sugar around.

And the sun was going down but xie wasn't about to rudely refuse anything the captain offered, not after she'd also offered her ship and home. "Please—and thank you."

She poured one cup and took a few short sips of her own. The metal cup was warm and comforting in Shiloh's hands but the liquid inside was like an electric shock to the tongue. To say it was the strongest coffee Shiloh had ever tasted would have been an understatement by about a million degrees—coincidentally, that also seemed to be its temperature.

"A bit strong?" Aliyah asked, eyes glinting with amusement.

"Just a little," Shiloh rasped with difficulty.

"Well, thank you for joining me anyway. Not many people left on board who'll take me up on this offer. Can't imagine why." Behind her, Aliyah's wings spread out wide, each golden feather stretching to catch the sun that filtered through the protective field. Her pinions spread like rays of a halo, gleaming until it looked as though she were wreathed in golden flame.

"Thank you, Captain," Shiloh said in a slightly stronger voice. Though surprisingly strong and hot, the coffee had an aftertaste that wasn't at all unpleasant and xie soon realized xie was gearing up for the next sip. "I mean, for this and everything."

"Quite welcome—and it's just Aliyah. Ma'am in a pinch. 'Captain' is reserved for official channels, strangers, and those who've really annoyed me. And that's not you, not yet anyway." She stretched one wing up and over her head, casting a welcome shadow in the hot sun over them both. "You're a guest here and among friends. So if there's anything you need, give a shout."

"Well, there is one thing," xie responded after a brief hesitation. "Arnold-Chiari Malformation. That's what these are for," xie tapped xir dark lenses.

Nobody else wore their sunglasses on board; apparently Shiloh was the only one with a physical need. "And I take meds for the pain, which help a lot. But I'm starting to run low and getting refills out here might be a problem." It was a fear that had been on xir mind for days. But in all the bizarre and life-altering events of the past several days, mundane needs like this, even urgent ones, tended to get overlooked.

"Not as hard as you'd think." Aliyah gave an easy shrug with one shoulder and corresponding wing. "A great deal of our time and energy is specifically dedicated to getting people the help they need. Or was, until we were volunteered for this specialty task."

"Seriously?" Shiloh had to ask in some disbelief, but it was happy disbelief.

Now she grinned; clearly this was a source of some pride. "What do you think we're transporting right now? It's not just water. Antibiotics, vaccines, hormones. Tell Rowan what you need, they'll help you find it. Failing that, we can probably recreate something fairly close."

"Wow, okay." Shiloh had been ready for something devastating or at least to start problem-solving. The lack of a crisis was momentarily off-putting. "I kind of expected that to be more of a problem."

"I understand why you would. The world's an unfriendly place even if your body and mind aren't trying to trip you up every day. But nobody's getting left behind just because they need a bit of assistance. Most of us do in some way or another." She gave Shiloh a quick nod as if to say that was the end of it. "And I'm anticipating a smooth trip otherwise. Not much to worry about until we get into Tartarus proper. Hopefully, we won't even do much of that."

"No on ozone, yes on toxic storms, right?"

"That's correct." Aliyah looked out toward the open horizon and the setting sun. "But we'll burn that bridge when we come to it and we've still got a few days to procure working shields before we press on."

"How about Eye in the Sky?" Shiloh remembered the intimidating man outside Radiance HQ and suppressed a shiver despite the warm afternoon. "Is there a chance they might come after us?"

"Really on top of things, aren't you?" She looked over with a slight eyebrow raise. "Granted, it could get a bit exciting if anyone catches wise that we're not strictly on the Radiance up-and-up. But we've been at this a good while. I wouldn't worry."

"I'll try not to," Shiloh said and tried to smile as well. "It's just getting a little harder."

"Isn't that the truth. But it's not all bad—we're finally seeing some success at containing Tartarus. Five beacons down, five to go. It's a stopgap measure at best, I know, but having that thing boxed in will buy us some time at least." She was quiet for a moment. When she continued, her tone had dropped just enough casualness that Shiloh suspected this was the real reason xie'd been invited into this conversation. "Shiloh, perhaps you can help me with something. You and your mother have something of a unique perspective on Tartarus and its ghostly inhabitants, correct?"

"You could say that. We've never actually been inside but she probably knows more than anyone about what it's made of." Shiloh thought about the burn-like poison wound spreading across Indra's arm and wrapped xir hands more firmly around the warm cup to stave off the sudden chill. "But not everything."

"Ah, but none of us have ever gotten quite so up close and personal." Aliyah didn't sound envious exactly, but definitely intrigued. "At least, not on speaking terms."

"You want me to tell you about the ghosts." Shiloh quickly took another sip of coffee to cover xir surprise. It was just as strong as before but Shiloh must have been acquiring a taste for it because it went down much more easily, for which xie was also grateful.

"If you wouldn't mind. I'd ask Annie, but I want to give her more time to recover from what had to be... a challenging trip."

"Challenging is right." Shiloh frowned, trying to sort out a concept with too many unknowns and not enough answers. "Uh, my mom's always thought they were trying to communicate. But not with the repeated words they actually said."

"And is she right? The most we know about them is that inhaling the air around them can be extremely toxic." Her face darkened slightly. "As your friend Indra would no doubt agree."

"It only attacked after it got scared," Shiloh said hurriedly. Why xie suddenly felt defensive about this, xie wasn't sure, but it did seem important. "Just like before, the first one. In Meridian. Eye in the Sky shot at it, and *then* it attacked. And then later, I know your big robot wolf—Dandy?—he thought he was helping, but he scared it. It wasn't going to attack us, at least I don't think so. It was talking to us. Then everything went wrong."

"It was speaking to you? You mean mimicking?"

"No, like actual new words. It said 'exchange.'" Shiloh paused. "It... it looked like my father at the time. So it was definitely talking right to me. Then it pointed out the lights that led us here. I think it wants us to help it."

"Help it do what?" Aliyah was watching Shiloh now with a shrewd gaze but xie didn't get the feeling she was studying xir directly. Instead, it seemed like she was adding all this to an already-half-completed puzzle, trying to make sense of a much bigger problem.

"'Turn out the lights,'" Shiloh said slowly, unsure of xir own meaning. Xie was having trouble even with this small piece; xie couldn't even guess at the larger one.

"Well, it sounds to me like it turned the lights on."

"I know. They're hard to figure out. But it pointed us in the right direction. It led us right here. Why would it help us?"

"You'd have to ask a ghost itself, I suppose, but they've never actually spoken to us."

"Well, that one did!" Shiloh said eagerly, somehow glad to have something nobody else did, even a single word. "It said something else, too. 'Icarus.'"

"Well, now, that *is* interesting." Aliyah's black eyes widened.

"The ghosts said it twice!" Shiloh felt an excited thrill as xie saw the recognition on her face. "The first one we saw, back in Meridian, then later when they showed us the lights!"

"I do have to wonder how they knew about that," she said thoughtfully. "Can't imagine anyone would have told them. That word symbolizes one of Parole's greatest victories."

"What does it mean?" xie asked, fairly vibrating with excitement. "It sounds really important."

"Oh my, yes. It's..." She thought for a moment, then gave a slight shake of her head. "Ask your uncle. It was his big day, mostly. Wouldn't be fair to steal his thunder. It is a good word, though." She glanced up at her wing, the sun beyond it. "Of course there is another meaning I prefer not to think about."

"I'll ask him! But isn't that a good sign?" Shiloh wasn't ready to let xir point go yet. "Talking about your best day ever doesn't sound evil to me."

"Perhaps not." She seemed about to say something else but thought better of it. When she didn't continue, Shiloh pressed on instead.

"Can I ask you something now, Cap—Aliyah?"

"Of course. Though I can't guarantee you'll get a good answer. There's so much we don't know."

"Which do you think is more dangerous? Tartarus, or the ghosts that live in it?"

She paused in the middle of the sip she'd been about to take and slowly lowered her cup. "Putting me between a bit of a rock and a hard place, aren't you?"

"Sorry—I just can't stop thinking about them. Or wondering if they're actually evil."

"I believe evil exists," Aliyah said softly. "But I will agree that it too often doesn't look evil and it doesn't hide under the bed. If you and your mother are right and the ghosts are trying to make some kind of deal, promising us help…well, men like Turret use lies and communication breakdowns to their advantage every day."

"The SkEye officers who shot at it didn't want us to communicate. And Lakshanya told us Major Turret approved of us lighting up the beacons."

"She's correct." She folded her arms. "That…man is very eager to see this project done. It's the first thing he's said in years that isn't monstrous. He's been quite helpful, actually."

"So he signed off on this plan," Shiloh said in a conversational tone. "And now the ghosts are trying to talk to us."

"I know what you're thinking." Her wings gave a brief twitch even if her face remained impassive. "But look at the facts. Tartarus is still extremely dangerous. No matter what the ghosts say, simple exposure to its toxins is often fatal. If we don't stop that poison spread, thousands more die. Needless to say, that's not an option. And with every beacon we upgrade, the toxins recede. Our path would seem clear."

Shiloh weighed xir chances, then took another. "Even if it's exactly what Turret wants?"

"Just keep your eyes and ears open." For the first time, her expression hardened into a grim glower. "If the ghosts speak again, listen and report. But be very careful. The enemy of my enemy... is not necessarily my friend."

"Then what is he?"

"A liar, at the very least. At most..." She took another sip, longer this time and more pensive. "I said this is the first thing he's said or done in a long time that wasn't monstrous? That's because we're dealing with a monster." She set her cup down with a decisive *clink*. "But we work with what we know. And we know we need a new shield. Tomorrow Jay and I will see if we can't dig one up before we have to get a move on."

"Sounds good," Shiloh said, remembering Annie's desperation for one—and wishing xie had Aliyah's apparent ability to simply close these troubling subjects and move on. "I'd really rather have one than not."

"So would I. But we can't always get what we want." She glanced up at the sky where the sun was nearing the horizon. Overhead, the glittering stream of light continued into the distance, and Aliyah nodded upwards, giving Shiloh a brief smile. "They're up there, aren't they? Your mother's flashing arrows. I can't see them, of course, but that's what I've always pictured."

"Uh, it looks more like... kind of the Northern Lights?" Shiloh struggled to put the beautiful image into words, suddenly hit by the realization that not everyone could see what xie did. "And glitter. Like a sparkly comet trail and the Northern Lights, leading way off that way."

"It sounds lovely," Aliyah said, sounding a bit wistful. "I do wish I could see it firsthand. Might have to beg Jay for a peek through those goggles of his sometime. But that's something, isn't it? We're still going the same direction Maureen's leading. So we're bound to meet up."

Shiloh was quiet for a moment. Finally, xie said something xie hadn't told anyone yet, not even in a dream. "I really thought she'd be here, waiting for me. My mom and my dad."

"I'm sorry. Had to be a blow when they weren't. But they're out there, you can see that clear as day even if I can't." Aliyah sounded certain about most things she said, and this was no exception. "And the moment it's safe, you'll be back together."

"Thanks." Shiloh had to smile. Somehow, hearing this from her was even more reassuring than looking up and seeing the continuing lights. They definitely led somewhere but nothing helped as much as hearing xie wasn't alone. "I'm trying to hold onto that but sometimes it's nice to be reminded."

"Well, I'm good at that. Now, you'd best get inside before the temperature drops along with the sun." Her eyes narrowed slightly and Shiloh could tell she was running back over the ominous puzzle of Tartarus, Turret, and the ghosts. "Thank you for the talk, Shiloh. It was most... well, question-raising, not-much-answering."

"Okay. Sorry I couldn't be of more help." Shiloh couldn't help feeling a little deflated as xie turned to go. A minute ago, xie'd been so confident and excited that xie held the key to figuring out this whole mystery. Now xie wasn't so sure. Or even sure they were doing the right thing at all anymore.

"Oh, it's quite all right," Aliyah said, quickly and easily. She didn't seem to share any of Shiloh's doubts but she wasn't looking at xir anymore either. She'd turned back out to face the horizon. "We've run on much less before. Sometimes I think this crew does its finest work in the dark."

"Are you coming in?" Shiloh was halfway down the stairs before xie realized she wasn't following either.

"In a little while. Lots to think on. Coffee to finish. Go get warm."

CHAPTER 10

The Smoking Gun

PEOPLE SAID YOU FELT TARTARUS APPROACH BEFORE YOU SAW IT. THE OZONE LAYER THINNED THE closer you got to its corrosive atmosphere, nights got darker and colder and days got brighter and hotter. Even inside the resupply outpost's protective bubble, the change was noticeable.

But not in CyborJ's makeshift command center. The single, round window was shuttered, edges taped over to keep out the sun's glare, the only light a pale blue glow from a solid wall of computer screens. It was dim enough for Shiloh to take off xir sunglasses and take a good look at one of the strangest rooms xie'd been in on this strange trip. The cramped space was invaded by dismantled motherboards and huge piles of wires and tubing looped like lazy

snakes. On all sides, active consoles and displays. And it was very cold. Icy air blasted through a vent in the ceiling and when Shiloh exhaled xie half-expected to see xir breath.

"Climate control's important, ok," Jay said a little distractedly as xie gave an audible shiver, not looking up from his current screen or stopping his consistent typing rhythm. "Gotta keep it frosty, even the best rigs run hot sometimes. And this Radiance junk is *not* the best, let me tell you. Mine is—was. Back in Parole. But keeping cool's a lot easier out here, I will say. No random fire bursts. Yes AC." He stopped then and turned to look up at Shiloh, seeming to fully register both xir presence and that not all humans enjoyed the same temperature extremes. He stepped on a pedal on the floor and the ceiling vent hinged shut. "But I guess I can take a break if my nibling made the trip down here."

"Thanks." Shiloh gave a sigh of relief and unclenched xir shoulders as the freezing air blasting down on xir head and shoulders finally stopped. The cold lingered in the room but at least xir ears weren't threatening to go numb anymore. Finally free from brain freeze, xie was able to process Jay's entire last sentence and smiled. "Hey. 'Nibling.' It's kind of amazing to hear that out loud."

"Kinda amazing to say it." Jay kicked off from the floor and rotated in his chair, sticking his feet up on a console opposite the one he'd been working on. "Lemme know if you figure out something better, huh? Hey, I'm saying 'xie' right, right?"

"More just like 'zee,' no 'ex' sound at the beginning."

"Xie? Xir, xirself..."

"Yeah, that's it, you got it." As cold as the room had been a moment ago, xie couldn't help but feel warm. CyborJ was one of Parole's most vital, beloved, and borderline-legendary figures, responsible for rebuilding and maintaining the city's communication infrastructure, free information, and foiling SkEye's deadly operations through misdirection and technological brilliance. The fact that hardly anyone had ever seen his face or even knew if he was a single person, an entire infamous Syndicate, or a human being at all (nobody had ruled out the possibility of a sentient AI yet) only added to the mystique. But the man behind the machine, Jay, was incredibly easy to talk to. After seeing xir uncle in person for just this brief time, Shiloh could hardly believe xie'd been so nervous.

"You know what's not amazing, though?" Jay's expressive face screwed up into a scowl, and he swiveled back over to face his original screen, glaring at it like it was solely responsible for every bit of the world's substantial suffering. "This freaking disk!"

"Um...problems?" Shiloh asked, not sure whether to smile, offer help, or back away slowly. Even in frustration, Jay's entire existence was animated and energetic perpetual motion. It was almost entertaining or would be if he wasn't clearly upset over something incredibly important. Especially if the kick he aimed at the wall console was any indication.

"Always! Just when I think I'm getting somewhere, no!" Jay glared, hands going fully back to the keyboard as he tried a few different tactics. "Another level, another layer, specifically written to drop-kick anything that even looks like Radiance out the door."

"But we're not Radiance, at least you're not." Xie shook xir head in confusion; the numbers in this equation made sense but the answer certainly didn't.

"*This ship is!*" There was a metallic clank as he kicked the bulkhead this time. Shiloh glanced down. There were a few more dents in it at foot level xie hadn't noticed before. "And all I have to work with are the ship's computers! And the disk sees Radiance Technology trying to crack it open, so it thinks it fell into enemy hands, it locks down even tighter!"

"Are you saying you can't open this disk?" Without quite knowing why, Shiloh dropped xir voice and moved in closer as xir heart began to pound. This entire time, Jay opening Maureen's encoded disk with its lifesaving information had been such a given, Shiloh hadn't even considered the alternative. Now xie did and the thought made xir insides shrivel.

"No—maybe—I don't know! Do not tell anyone I said that! I have a reputation here. Damn!" Jay arched his back, dragging his hands down his face. "I don't know what to do here. I don't know. Freaking Radiance machines, can't live with 'em, can't take a sledgehammer after 'em!"

"Should I go?" Shiloh glanced toward the door, wondering if now would be a good time to retreat while xir uncle blew off some steam alone.

"No, I'm sorry." Jay sighed, rubbing his closed eyes and waving in a 'have a seat' gesture, except that he had the only chair in the room. Shiloh leaned against the curving metal wall instead and waited. Eventually, after mumbling under his breath for several seconds, Jay looked up. He didn't look aggravated anymore, just exhausted. "Your mom did the right thing. The smart thing. She designed it so nobody nasty would get a look at what's on this thing—and so that I'm, get this, *I'm* the only one who *should* be able to open it." He gave a faint smile but it had none of his usual confidence or wry humor. "And if I was back in Parole, with my own setup, my systems, my *cat*—I'd have this thing open before it knew what was happening! But I'm not..."

"Probably a really dorky question, you totally don't have to answer," Shiloh started tentatively. Xie couldn't believe there was much Jay hadn't thought of but xie couldn't ignore the impulse to ask, find out more, help if possible, and, failing that, somehow at least make him feel a little better. "But do you think you could once we get to Parole? Or is..."

"No, I don't know if my stuff's still there." Shiloh immediately regretted asking the question that prompted the flat, abrupt answer. "I don't know if anything's there anymore. The bottom dropped out, we grabbed what essentials we could, and ran. Not like we weren't prepared, not like I didn't have a million backup plans, because come on, of course I did." His shoulders dropped another inch or two. "But you ever had every single backup plan fail at once? It's... a hell of a thing."

"I'm so sorry," Shiloh said, fumbling for words and knowing as soon as those were out that they meant essentially nothing. Not after someone had been through something like that, xie'd found that out multiple times on this ride. There was some pain that words couldn't express and words couldn't really heal it either. But it would still be nice to find ones that helped even a little.

"It's all right," Jay said, looking up at Shiloh with a much different smile than the pained, sardonic one he'd had a minute ago. Fatigued, but real. Starting to look like himself again. Amazingly, Shiloh had the feeling that maybe xir nothing-words hadn't been nothing after all. "I'm still gonna beat this. I can do anything I set my mind to." He slowly started nodding as if confirming it beyond a doubt. "Especially if it involves a keyboard and some stubborn code. But I don't have much to work with, so it's just gonna take me a while. Damn, I wish Seven was here."

"Seven?"

Jay nodded to a picture Shiloh hadn't noticed before beside one of his several screens. In it, a fluffy cat sprawled on its back across a keyboard, exposing a furry belly and looking up at the camera. It looked like a Himalayan. It also didn't look entirely real. Patches of fur had worn off the pointed ears and fuzzy sides, revealing complex metal inner workings. The cat's eyes looked like Toto-Dandy's as well, intricate gyroscopic spheres that shone a bright green.

"Best little techno-helper in the world," Jay said, sounding fond but looking far from happy. "She'd have this thing open so fast. Pretty sure she thinks encrypted files are mice or some kind of treat, she goes after 'em even when I don't want her to. Maybe a box."

"Is that... a real cat?" Shiloh couldn't stop staring at the half-robotic-looking animal.

"Of course she's real!" Jay sounded mildly indignant, then seemed to realize what Shiloh was asking. "I mean, no, she's not organic or anything. Danae made her—she made Dandy too, and lots of other cool stuff."

"I was wondering that." Shiloh smiled, happy to have been right. Xie was catching on. "Looks kind of like Stefanos's arm and eyes."

"That's cause they all come from the same place. Danae can turn just about anything metal into a..." He stopped, looking a bit confused. "Well, I don't really know how 'alive' her stuff is, we think it's an AI thing. But most of it's nowhere near as complex as Seven. *She's* alive, that's for sure."

"Is she..." Shiloh stopped, remembering the answer to xir own unspoken question. "She's back in Parole, isn't she?"

"Yeah." Jay's expression immediately darkened. "She was... busy. I dunno where exactly, but too far away to catch up to us before we had to leave."

"I'm sorry." Shiloh didn't know what else to say. Nothing would make it hurt less, xie knew that well enough every time xie thought about xir parents. It wasn't the same but the worry and heartache were.

"It's fine," Jay said, though it clearly wasn't. "She's kind of a therapy animal too. Scans your vitals, goes for help if you get hurt, purrs you right out of panic attacks—literally, she can purr on 12 different frequencies depending on your distress."

"She sounds amazing," Shiloh said and meant it. "I really hope you find her again."

"Or she finds me. She's programmed to prioritize human survival, everything else comes second. So, she understands why I'm not there. I hope." Jay slumped a little in his chair. "But that won't stop her from looking." He shook his head as if to clear it. "Never mind, enough sad-sackery. I don't have Seven, or any of my own stuff, and that's gonna make it harder to open this disk. I'll get it eventually, I'm just gonna complain a lot while I do it."

"Well, maybe you don't have to do it alone." A memory rose to the surface of Shiloh's mind, long buried under all the chaotic events between then and now. "Mom said you'd need a little help from a friend."

Jay tossed xir a half-skeptical, half-pitying look. "Nobody on this ship knows how to pick virtual locks better than me, they'd get in the way. Not a brag, just a fact."

Xie shrugged. "I dunno, that's just what she said. And that you'd know what that meant."

"Well, we lost contact with a lot of people in the collapse. Kind of running low on friends at the moment." His eyes slid away and past Shiloh and xie turned to look too. The one of Seven the cat wasn't the only photo Jay had in his room. The entire opposite wall was full of them.

Most were people Shiloh didn't recognize, but there were two xie certainly did. In a small but dense cluster, several younger versions—ten years or more—of Maureen, Garrett, and Shiloh's own round, happy baby face, smiled out at them. Shiloh actually recognized a couple, and wondered if the black 'Bad Reputation' shirt xir tiny baby self had slept in was the same one Jay'd worn when they'd met just a couple days ago. Xie hadn't seen or thought about any of these in years. Now xie had to wonder if xir parents did. Jay obviously had, every day.

"You kept all of these? I thought you lost everything when Parole collapsed."

Jay shrugged now but he was smiling, seeming caught between embarrassment and tentative happiness that Shiloh had noticed. "Yeah, well... Like I said. Kept the essentials. Um, you can go ahead and look, it's fine. You'll meet every-most of them, eventually, uh. Hopefully."

Feeling warm inside, Shiloh turned back to look over the rest of the wall. There were a few more familiar faces but a lot more xie didn't recognize mixed in. Some strangers were very strange-looking, but maybe not for Parole. A person who looked like they were made of stitched-together parts of other people—different skin tones, hair, and eyes—was lowering their black hood and leaning down to listen to a younger man with bright orange hair, while Aliyah shot them a fond gaze.

A pink-haired girl in a floating, somewhat futuristic-looking chair—Radio Angel; Shiloh was still having to remind xirself that the voice had a person attached—spun under colorful lights, holding hands with a girl in black from head to toe. Even inside she wore a black-visored helmet and, for a moment,

Shiloh thought it was Annie, but realized the skin of her exposed hands and lower jaw was darker and her build taller and more willowy. Strangely, where Radio Angel was lit up in rainbows from the lights, her dance partner's suit reminded Shiloh more of the eyes of the Tartarus ghosts. It didn't reflect a thing and this mysterious girl looked almost like a shadow herself.

Shiloh looked further and started to see a common thread. Xie didn't recognize him, but one man kept showing up in group photos; tall, muscular, dirty-blonde hair and bright blue eyes, usually surrounded by several dogs, seemed to be missing at least part of one middle finger. Usually with an easy smile or the most relaxed one in the room in any given photo. Shiloh was about to ask who he was, since he was obviously important—then xie saw the shark tooth hanging from the chain around his neck. It was the same one Annie wore, the one she held onto like a lifeline when her fear and anguish reared its head. When she remembered Ash. Shiloh kept xir mouth shut and moved on.

Most of the rest were Jay's selfies. But these were usually with at least one other person, and several with Seven. Everyone Shiloh had met on the FireRunner showed up at least once, along with many people xie didn't recognize. It took a moment to figure out why these felt unusual. It wasn't just because of the angles or awkward poses. The first time Shiloh had ever seen Annie giggle, completely happy and unworried, or Rowan smile at all, was on this wall.

Shiloh's eyes settled on one of Jay, but what had to be a teenage Jay; he didn't even quite look Shiloh's age yet. He was caught in the middle of a laugh and had something in his hand—an unfinished project that looked like the custom goggles he often wore now, or a prototype—but that wasn't what made

Shiloh almost do a double-take, then squint to get a better look. It was just as surreal the second time. The young man with Jay had a wry, victorious-looking smile on his face, like his joke had just landed exactly right. Shiloh had seen that look several times by now but, even without it, he would have had a striking resemblance to Indra.

"Is that–"

"Mihir," Jay cut in immediately but his voice was uncharacteristically soft, almost a mumble. "He saved a lot of lives. More than I ever did, that's for sure. But, uh, we keep doing the work and, we still got good people back in Parole doing the–oh! Here's some over here."

Stefanos's face smiled out of an older photo on the other side of the wall, unmistakable–except for the lack of golden eyes. Apparently they'd once been a deep blue. Both his arms were flesh and blood and one was wrapped around a young, fiery-redheaded woman's freckled shoulders. Although he dwarfed her smaller frame, something about the shared determination in their smiles made it easy to see the resemblance, though hers seemed a tad more wolfish.

"Stef's little sister Danae–she basically made about half this ship. And his limbs. Did he tell you that? Anyway, she made a whole bunch of other cyborg people walking around Parole." Jay nodded to the next photo. In it, Danae, two other women, and a little boy all cuddled together on the stairs leading up to a brightly lit entrance, a sign reading EMERALD BAR overhead. On one side of Danae and the toddler was a beautiful dark-skinned woman with flowers and vines twisting through her long, curly hair and around her shoulders and arms. Her legs were reminiscent of Stefanos's limbs, except even these were decorated with greenery and blossoms. The little boy in Danae's arms wore a crown of the same flowers that cascaded all around her and she was tucking another one behind his ear. Her flowers seemed to have gotten everywhere, including all over the pink-haired, punk-rock-looking (and more-than-vaguely familiar) woman on her other side who pressed a kiss to her cheek. Nobody really seemed to mind. The only other thing keeping the family portrait from being ordinary was the air filter masks they all wore.

"Hope they're all okay," he said, smile fading a little. He sounded apprehensive, like someone who'd heard too much bad news in too short a time. "Last thing we heard from Parole was something about them getting separated. That's...just never good."

But it was the picture next to the family photo Shiloh couldn't stop staring at. A spotlight cut through the dark and lit Evelyn up on a night that looked a lot less jazz cabaret and more rock concert than the last time xie'd seen the Emerald Bar. But it was unmistakable. Her rose-violet hair rising in a curling cloud, one arm stretching to the ceiling and one fist around the mic stand, mouth wide open in a climactic note. On it was written: *To The One And Only CyborJ With Love*, above a large, looping signature.

Shiloh tried to speak but no words came out. Jay never seemed to have that problem.

"I don't know what Maureen's talking about, though, a little help from a friend? None of them would be able to help with that disk. Only one who might is Celeste." Jay gnawed on his lower lip and slowly swiveled his chair in deep thought. "And she's been missing for a month. I mean yeah, she knows a few tricks, I guess." He shrugged, conceding the point in what was clearly an understatement. "Couldn't have pulled Operation Icarus off without her, that's for sure."

Shiloh's mouth dropped open and xie turned so fast xir head spun, mental alarm bells going off so loudly xie couldn't hear anything but that one word, the driving question since this all began. "What is 'Icarus'?"

"Hm?" Jay frowned, taking a moment to regain his lost train of thought. "A program that, uh, Celeste and I wrote ten years ago. Parole's one secret... not a weapon, what's the opposite of a weapon? Not a shield so much—also kind of the opposite of a shield..."

"Uncle Jay..." Shiloh cut in very quietly but desperately. Xie felt like xir entire body was vibrating all the way down to the soles of xir feet and, considering what happened when xie was around electronics, or especially excited, that might be the case. "I think that word is really important, and you're the first person I've met who might tell me what it means. What is Icarus?"

Jay sat perfectly silent and still. Shiloh knew then beyond any doubt that he'd been deliberately stalling before, distracting, because he said the next words with no flash or pretense. "It dropped the barrier around Parole for one minute."

"It's how we escaped," Shiloh whispered, suddenly feeling as if all the gravity in the small room had disappeared along with the sun. "My mom and I. Ten years ago, that's how we... I remember looking up at the barrier and thinking it was so bright, everyone was so scared and I was too, but I kept thinking it was pretty. I almost wanted to touch it. And then it just—it wasn't there. So we ran."

"Yeah." Jay nodded, but he wasn't looking at Shiloh anymore. He stared at a spot on the floor or maybe at something from many years ago. "Gave you all the time we could."

"Thank you." Shiloh still felt off-balance, like the room had just been spinning at a high speed and xir equilibrium hadn't adjusted. "If nobody has told you that yet. I don't know if I've ever said—"

"Eh, CyborJ gets loving multitudes every day." He shrugged one shoulder, flashed his teeth in something that wasn't quite a smile. "But, uh. Me, not so much. Thanks. It was nothing." The not-smile faded. "I mean that. One minute..."

"You got us out. And I don't even know how many other people, a lot, it has to be a lot. You dropped the barrier. You did what nobody thought could ever be done."

"Twice." The look on his face was another new one. Grim determination. Hard. "We knew that thing wouldn't stay dead but we thought we'd have more than one minute. We didn't. Came back in such a hurry we thought hey...practice makes perfect. And in the collapse last month, we tried again. Icarus. It's the last thing she did before she disappeared." Now he looked up, seeming caught between tentative hope and vague suspicion once back in the present. "Why?"

"I know that word's important. The ghosts keep saying it," Shiloh said, carefully watching as Jay sat back in his chair farther away; any open curiosity in his face closing off as well. "First when one showed up in Meridian, as a dragon. Then later when it—the same one, I think?—pointed out Mom's lights in the sky."

"Ignore 'em," Jay said through the corner of his mouth, sounding like he was clenching his teeth. "They never have anything good to say."

"Yeah, except Gabriel said it too."

Now Jay looked over and Shiloh could see the moment when the puzzle piece clicked into place in his head. "Dreams. You said something about that way back before any of this—" he broke off, eyes dropping to the floor. "And I didn't lock onto it."

"You had a lot going on," Shiloh said easily. It didn't even seem particularly generous considering the circumstances. And it wasn't as if they'd had a lot of time to talk.

"Yeah. Yeah, we did." He nodded, the faraway look creeping into his eyes that Shiloh was coming to recognize. It meant Jay had slipped a thousand miles away and a month ago, feeling the ground crumble into flames far below. Then he seemed to snap out of it, eyes narrowing. "Still. I could've listened instead of burying it just because I didn't want to talk about..."

"What?" That last part Shiloh hadn't expected.

"Dreaming about more dead people just wasn't something I was prepared to deal with right then," Jay said in what was clearly supposed to be a return his usual light, quick tone but just came out sounding strained and tired. "And I thought Gabriel was dead. I stand very much corrected. I thought a lot of things I now stand very much corrected about."

"*More* dead—"

"So what'd he say about Icarus?"

"Uh, sorry." Shiloh paused to catch xir breath and bearings, even though Jay was the one who'd just been talking so fast xir head spun. "Yeah. He said it the same way the ghosts did—Tartarus ghosts, I mean. By itself, really important, and like I should already know. That was the last time we saw him. The day Parole collapsed."

"Okay." Jay was almost always focusing directly on something. A screen, a new and interesting development in a puzzle or twist of their lives, peering into somebody's face with several layers of meaning and usually humor in his own. Right now he just stared into space, seeing nothing. But he didn't seem to like this particular kind of nothing and Shiloh didn't like the way it made his face and entire energy level drop. "I wasn't listening before... I am now. Tell me about these dreams."

"It wasn't the first time we had them," Shiloh started, unable to keep from smiling. "I remember them from a long time ago. Like, years ago, right after we left Parole."

"You had them all this time?" He shot Shiloh an incredulous kind of please-say-no look, as if this pushed the very boundary of possibility, even in their strange lives. Fortunately, nothing was quite that strange yet.

"No, they stopped for a long time. But then they started again, same as I remembered."

"Well, I don't remember this," Jay mumbled with a little shake of his head. "But back then... we all had a lot going on, like you said. Nothing ever changes. When'd they start?"

"A few weeks before Parole collapsed. Then a really intense one the day of. Then nothing... until Annie and Indra showed up in Meridian. Once we were all together, we started dreaming again, ending up in the tree, the one down in the water tank."

"Annie. Damn." Jay was shaking his head. "She never said a word. Not to me, anyway. She had to have told somebody though, that's just not the kind of thing you keep to yourself—well, maybe she does. She's not really a sharer. If she told anyone, it was probably..." He didn't quite finish that thought, but Shiloh followed his eyes this time. He wasn't staring at nothing after all, but an old picture of a much younger Annie. She was riding on the shoulders of the tall, blonde man xie'd seen in several pictures, but nowhere on the ship. He wasn't wearing the shark tooth yet, and had all his fingers, but it had to be Ash.

But significant and painful as that realization was, the people in the picture weren't all that caught Shiloh's attention. Xie leaned closer, squinting at the somewhat faded, dusty (perhaps smoke-damaged?) surface. "Those curtains. They're still there."

"Huh?" Jay looked like he was halfway back in a reverie again, staring at the photo. One he might not really want to leave.

"The Emerald Bar. The last dream we all had, it was there. Those look like the same curtains, that's all," Shiloh said, but xie was moving on already. That dream had stayed burned into xir brain ever since for a much more important reason.

Jay swiveled partway around to face xir, looking almost sheepish. "Okay, I don't know much about this—I really don't know much about powers at all, everything I know comes from just hanging out with a bunch of people who do have them, so you're probably better off asking—"

"He was there too," Shiloh cut in, softly, definitely. Xie'd finally found who he was looking for. He was an unexpectedly hard person to spot even in photos.

"Who was where?"

"Him." Shiloh pointed. In it, a thin, green-scaled man with yellow eyes and a loose frill of skin around his neck lounged in a beanbag chair with Rowan, curled tight against them under several blankets. He contentedly rested his head on their shoulder, sleepy eyes looking like they might slip shut the moment after the photo was taken. Rowan held a book in front of both of them, and though it was always somewhat difficult to tell where they were looking, their smile didn't seem to come from something they'd read. "He said his name was Regan."

"*Regan?*" Jay lurched upright, both hands clamping down on the arms of his chair to push himself forward. For a moment, Shiloh thought he might jump right out; of the chair or maybe his skin. He seemed almost like he'd been jolted with an electric shock. Jay was usually an energetic presence but this sudden tension was a complete shift and not necessarily a good one. "You *saw* him?"

"Yeah. He said he was safe with friends, but he couldn't come back yet," Shiloh said carefully, watching to see how the words landed. "Gabriel's with him, and someone else. I can't remember who. I know it was kind of a weird name, though."

"Zilch?"

"Yeah, I'm sorry, I can't remember."

"No, I mean did he say Zilch was with him? That's a name."

It was a weird name, but not the right one. "I don't think so."

"Danae? Evelyn?"

"Not those either." Shiloh shook xir head, hoping Jay wasn't going to keep asking.

He stared in rapt hyper-focus usually reserved for screens with lines of puzzling code. He waited for a moment for Shiloh to continue, furrowed eyebrows shooting up when xie didn't. "And?"

"And that's it. I wish I could tell you more," Shiloh said and sincerely meant it, not least because all of this was maddening to xir own unsatisfied curiosity. "He said he was sorry."

"Great." It didn't sound great when Jay said it and Shiloh doubted the apology was accepted. "He happen to say *why* he was sorry? Or am I supposed to guess that too?"

"About Rose," Shiloh said slowly, trying to recall foggy dream details. "Something about...he couldn't take back what he did to her. Or maybe–didn't do? And he couldn't come back. Not until he did something. I don't know, I'm sorry."

"It tracks." Jay's voice dropped almost to a whisper. "It all tracks. The footage was real. No wonder I couldn't find evidence of... *Shit.*" He was quiet for a moment, perfectly still except for a few shaking breaths. "Anything else? Anything at all?"

"He did seem upset about one thing." Xie recalled one detail that previously had been shaken out of xir head by the ghostly encounter and nearly-deadly fight immediately following the dream. "So much that I think it woke us all up."

"What?" Jay sounded a strange combination of half-annoyed, half-afraid of what the answer might be.

"Annie was still wearing her shark tooth in the dream. When he saw it, he seemed... I don't know, scared or something. He asked why she had it, and she wouldn't tell him, and then he started to ask something else." Shiloh stopped, trying to collect several scattered, increasingly fuzzy pieces. Xie wasn't sure if xir head was aching from the effort or the unpleasant memory. "But we woke up, and the ghost was there. Maybe it was the ghost that did it?"

Jay didn't answer right away, looking troubled and maybe a little sick. When he did, he gave a slight jump as if startled back into the present or waking from an ominous dream. "Yeah. Yeah, maybe. Listen, this is important... did Regan say where he was? Anything? Anything at all else that you can remember?"

"He..." Shiloh hesitated. Xie hadn't talked with Indra or Annie about this part, and never really expected to with anyone. Somehow this didn't seem like xir message to pass on, but it also seemed important. "Regan said he loves you. You and Rowan."

“Okay.” Jay’s single-word answer was bland, seemed intentionally neutral. That alone told Shiloh xie wasn’t seeing, and didn’t know, even the very tip of this iceberg. He let out a long, slow breath but didn’t move or speak for a few full seconds. For the first time, he looked at a complete loss for what to do next, either in the future or in the next moment. “Well, if you see him again... just tell me if you see him again. We got a lot to talk about.”

Shiloh had never seen the heavy, bitter look in his downcast eyes before, not on Jay or anyone else. Xie never wanted to see it again, especially once the hard realization hit of exactly what to call it. Haunted. “You don’t trust this Regan guy at all, do you?”

Jay swiveled his chair around to face Shiloh, then back away again, shaking off eye contact and his strange reverie. “Hey, remember those stories I told you not to ask about when you first came on board?”

“Yeah. So—”

“Don’t ask about them. Safer.” He started typing again, an off-rhythm accompaniment to his too-flat voice. “Stories are just stories. In real life, good people die. One just did. And he’s lucky, we actually knew his name. I’m not trying to bring you down, Nibling, I’m just making sure you know exactly what you’re walking into. There’s normal life and then there’s life down here, where we all might as well be wearing red shir... God, never mind, I’m depressing myself.” Jay sighed, head hanging low. The two of them fell silent. Suddenly the small room felt even smaller, as if the walls were pressing in under the weight of the chaos outside. For several long seconds, neither one spoke.

“Kirk or Picard?” Shiloh finally asked in the light, conversational tone Jay had used so often before but couldn't seem to muster now.

"What?" He looked up, but it was slow, hesitant, as if the simple question had to be some kind of trick or trap or hidden snare.

"You were going to say in this story we should all be wearing red shirts," Shiloh continued, surprised by how difficult it was to stay upbeat while even half-thinking about these terrifying realities. How did Jay do it all the time? How much energy did it take? "Well, I know what happens there. So if we're all wearing red shirts, who'd you pick to get us out of this mess in one piece?"

Jay just stared with his mouth open but no sound came out. Shiloh had the feeling this was not a reaction anyone commonly received. Somehow that felt like a good sign. "I know everyone's gonna basically automatically pick Picard, because... of course they will and, yeah, there's probably some diplomatic solution to all—" Jay actually laughed, though he still looked stunned. Shiloh had to smile at the interruption xie'd absolutely hoped for. "But Kirk beat the one-and-only Kobayashi Maru, a situation designed to be impossible, no positive outcome, total death and destruction the actual only ways out."

"He cheated," Jay murmured, stare unbroken. He didn't move, blink, or seem to breathe.

"Yeah, Kirk cheated, because surviving is more important than following the rules. If the rules say you die, you change the rules and live, right? So is he your pick?"

"You first," Jay said, voice still very faint, and sounding a mixture of wary and impressed. "So I know you're not just telling me what I want to hear. Kirk or Picard?"

"Neither." Shiloh's smile was tired but genuine. "The Sisko, of Bajor."

"He's not one of the choices."

"I didn't like the rules."

Slowly, Jay's face lit up into one of his smiles that resembled Maureen's triumphant grin that beamed out at them from the wall. "Wow. We might actually survive this after all."

"So, Kirk?" Shiloh asked in the casual tone they both knew wasn't casual anymore.

"No." Jay's smile turned sharp, almost wolfish. "You need somebody to rise to the challenge, do the things that can't be done, save the Kobayashi Maru—and Parole, which has to be even tougher? You need me!"

"You can't pick yourself! You're not even in Starfl—"

"Rewriting the rules, remember? Sure, James T. had the right idea, but CyborJ is better than he'll ever be!" He actually laughed and Shiloh felt weak with relief, as if somehow xie'd passed some impossible challenge as well. "Hey, how did *Enterprise* end? That's about the time Parole got cut off from—no!" Jay shook his head, but with renewed energy. "Don't spoil me. Some things are worth risking a torrent for. Especially now I actually got someone to discuss with. *Trek* and everything else. I've been dying to catch up with you, honestly. See what I missed." He faltered, eyes dropping. "I'm—listen, I'm sor—"

"Don't apologize," Shiloh said firmly. "My mom always said you were the reason Parole still existed at all. And you got us out, we got to Meridian, we were safe there. And we did fine. It was never home," xie had to admit, but didn't much feel like going back there, even in xir mind. "Not without you or my dad, or... Parole was home, that's all. But my mom never let me think for a minute that we wouldn't get back there, or see you again, or that anything we did was for nothing."

"Thanks. You, uh—you did great." Jay nodded a few times, before his face dropped into an expression as close to defeat as he'd been to triumph moments before. "Nibling—Shiloh, can you just kind of, insert an inspiring parental thing here? I'm trying to think of what your mom would say if she was here and if our lives were normal, 'cause I've never been good at saying the right or responsible thing, that's Maureen. Getting you guys out of Parole was pretty much the one right and responsible thing I've ever done. And then I wasn't around for the rest of—anything." His fingernails rapidly drummed against a nearby metal tower; he cracked a knuckle on his other hand. "So, I'm trying, but I'm not great at this and I want you to have a normal life and that's basically impossible by now, and—"

"Uncle Jay. You're doing fine." Shiloh spoke quietly; suddenly xir chest felt heavy. "I miss my mom too. But seriously, don't worry about it. You don't have to be her. Or my dad. We'll find them and then... it'll just be different. Better. We'll all catch up together."

Not for the first time since they'd met face-to-face or even in this conversation, Jay was looking at xir with a mixture of surprise and respect. "That sounds perfect. I mean, not sure how well I'll fit in with the whole normal-family picture but it's a nice thought."

Before Shiloh spoke next, xie took a moment to check the math. Numbers didn't lie, but some answers were hard truths to process. "The first 'Icarus' run was ten years ago, right? When you dropped the barrier and let us escape?"

"Yeah, so?"

"You would have been what, seventeen?"

His eyes flicked away. "Yeah, so?"

"You stayed behind. You let my mom and me escape so we could have a normal life and you stayed in Parole to help." For one of the first times Shiloh had known xir uncle, he didn't say anything at all. "Sounds pretty—what'd you say? Right and responsible?"

"Well, then I guess I have de-responsibled nicely." Jay's smile came back, almost too quickly, and just as quickly he turned away, re-orienting himself in front of the disk's stubborn encryption screen. "Anyway, I should probably get back to it. Haven't tried that Radiance message you gave me yet, figured your mom's info was the priority. Might have better luck there. Pretty sure Lakshanya actually *wants* me to open it."

"Okay, I'll let you work." Shiloh stepped over a pile of cables toward the door, figuring that was what passed for a subtle signal to wrap things up. "It was really great talking to you though."

"Yeah, it was." Jay stopped typing and looked up. "Uh, door's open. If you want, tomorrow or whenever—I mean, it's not gonna be much fun, just me banging my head against a wall until this thing's open, but..."

"Sure." Shiloh smiled, feeling that xie'd just gotten an invitation not many people ever did, even on this ship. "See you tomorrow."

Jay cracked his neck again and settled back in front of the keyboard, looking much more serene and less drained than he had before Shiloh's visit. He inserted the thumb drive with Radiance Technologies logo, and as predicted, it opened with none of the difficulty he'd had up to this point.

A moment later, a recorded voice issued from the computer speakers.

Jay replayed the message. Twice. Three times. He grabbed a pair of headphones from a tangle of cords and strips underneath the console and jammed them onto his ears, then replayed it several more times. Each time, his eyes widened in equal parts shock, panic, and recognition.

Then he scrambled out of the cramped room like it was on fire.

☆

Annie was right where Jay expected to find her but he wasn't about to disturb her. Not even after the shock he'd gotten from that recording. The hammock swung gently from a thick lower branch in the huge tree in its dry water tank and from here he could see the top of her head and tightly curled hands. She slept with them balled into fists and covering her face, but she looked peaceful, maybe even smiling a little.

"I haven't even told her how brave she was yet," Rowan said quietly, eyes on her sleeping face and slow breathing. They leaned against the tree below the hammock, sitting on the large, curving roots. They hadn't moved when Jay had stumbled up and he got the feeling they'd been there for some time. "We asked too much of her to begin with. She must have been so scared. And then it turned into more than... any one person should ever..." They trailed off, watching her sleep and sway.

"She did so good. But she wasn't alone." Jay knew it was a risk. He said it anyway. "Not on the way there, or back. And she's home now, she's safe and sound." The unspoken hung between them. Jay had never been good at enduring that, or any kind of silence, so he continued. "I figured you'd still be in the infirmary."

"Indra's doing much better." Rowan hadn't looked away from Annie, sounding so far away they might as well be the one lost in a dream. They didn't look over when Jay shifted uncomfortably and scratched his face, as if he'd suddenly remembered something unsettling. "Stable, recovering, the antitoxin's doing its job. I'll check on him again soon, but he's going to be fine."

"No, I mean I thought you'd be with, you know." He gave an awkward shrug, hands spread, then closing as if he could pick the words he wanted out of the air. "The jars? The new one. Figured you'd just want to hang onto that for a while."

Rowan didn't answer right away. Finally they did turn to face Jay, though it seemed to take some concentration and effort. He hadn't expected to find them down here at all and he didn't expect them to look this tired when he did. "I had to get out of there for a while, that's all. And I wanted to spend some time with her. Even if we haven't gotten a chance to talk much yet."

"I hope you get some quality time." He made himself turn, made himself take a step away, but stopped at the rustle of grass and soft sound of hooves behind him.

"Wait. You don't have to leave." Rowan kept their voice down and Annie didn't move in the hammock overhead, but suddenly they seemed more present, more engaged, focused. Any chance Jay had to make a clean exit was quickly disappearing. The really inconvenient thing was, he wasn't sure if he wanted to. "We haven't gotten much time together either. I'm sorry, I've been..."

"Hey, we've all been busy." Jay knew what would happen if he turned around. Rowan would immediately see the struggle surface in his face. Emotional turmoil and futile resistance. And he'd see Rowan's painful exhaustion again and everything beneath it. And then his arms would be around them, and it would be such a relief he'd forget why he'd come down here in the first place, and both of them would be a hopeless mess instead of getting anything done, and this was important, this was *serious, dammit*. "And it's a big ship."

"Not that big. And we haven't been that busy. Even back in Parole, with everything falling apart every day, we made the time. And it's much quieter out here." Especially on an empty ship, in the middle of a deserted wasteland. They seemed to have nothing but time and not much to fill it. Somehow the vast water tank was starting to feel as claustrophobic as Jay's small room.

"I just wanted to ask Annie something." He just wanted to go to sleep and wake up to find all of this had been a bad dream or distant memory. He wanted to see Rowan smile. "But she needs the rest more than I need answers."

"She'll probably sleep for another few hours at least. Can I help?"

"No, it's nothing. Don't worry about it." Jay knew what would happen if he turned around. Knew it. But the thought of going back to his room full of screens and not enough resolution was more than he could stand. And now so was being alone. Usually that was all he wanted. Everything was different now, even him.

"It must be important to get you away from your work. Especially now." When Jay didn't answer, they tried again, lowering their voice and stepping closer to still be heard. "I know how much you need answers, Jay. At least... I think I'm starting to understand. As much as anyone can."

"You mean Regan." Jay turned around. Warning lights went off in his head. Soon there'd be no getting out of this conversation. He ignored them and looked up anyway. "And Zilch."

"Yes." Rowan nodded after a small pause, their face a calm, enigmatic neutral. Jay recognized that look. It was the same one he was focusing most of his attention on maintaining. "I'm hoping when Annie wakes up, and has had some time to recover, obviously, she can tell us more. Anything might be helpful to figure out where they are, even if she didn't realize at the time." They took a breath, spent a half-second to ensure their composure hadn't slipped. It mostly hadn't, except for the last sentence speeding up with excitement or maybe desperation. "Is that what you were going to ask?"

Jay hesitated, holding very still. He held his breath too. The only way out of this now was to lie. Simple, fast, this would be over and he'd be back in his room before he knew it. Annie would still be asleep. And Rowan would still be here. Under this tree, waiting and keeping the fear out of their face, just like him. "No, not exactly. It was more about Ash."

Rowan didn't respond right away. Their face remained relatively blank—but now it relaxed somewhat, tension fading and, for a moment, Jay was happily surprised. He'd expected something much worse. Anything would have been worse, really. But his relief didn't last long, because he soon realized where else he'd seen that face. Jay had only been in the library's infirmary once or twice when someone had come in with a terrible injury. Usually a burn. Rowan defaulted then to a calm, compassionate, professional mask that revealed nothing. It let both of them, Rowan and whoever looked on, function through a crisis. Reaction, emotion, even a breakdown—that all came later. And it almost always did.

"Oh." Rowan's voice sounded as serene as the rest of them. Jay felt sick. "What about him?"

"I wanted to ask her where he died," he said as casually as he could, hating the words and hating that his voice sounded anything like Rowan's unnatural calm. "Get an idea of everyone's position while they were out."

"Oh," Rowan said again, then paused and, for a moment, Jay thought that somehow, mercifully, that might be it. He'd just started to half-turn away when their voice stopped him again. "Why does it matter?"

"I just want a clear picture," Jay said, trying not to clench his teeth. "When and where."

"Because we know how."

The words hit like a punch to the center of his chest. Jay shut his eyes for a second. "Yeah. Yes we do."

"It was outside Meridian." Rowan's voice wasn't calm anymore. It was flat, almost a mechanical monotone. People sometimes had a hard time telling where Rowan's all-black eyes were focusing. Jay never really did and now was no different. They stared past him, maybe through him. At something he could only guess at but didn't really want to. "That's what she said. They were almost there."

"Meridian..." Jay murmured. "That doesn't make sense..."

"What doesn't?" Rowan asked, much more sharply than he would have expected from their near-trance.

"Nothing. Don't worry about it." Jay realized his mistake much too late and quickly made a second one. The moment he took a step away, a flurry of hooves followed him and suddenly Rowan was in front of him instead of behind. Kicking himself inside for forgetting how fast Rowan could move—even, apparently, after looking near-catatonic with grief—Jay stopped and looked them in the eye. "You're worrying about it, aren't you?"

"What doesn't make sense about Meridian?" Rowan's expression hadn't changed much from its tight control from before but now their voice was just as tight. "We knew that's where it happened already. Did you figure something else out?"

"I'm not trying to get a position on Ash and Annie," Jay said slowly, determined not to make a third mistake. For the first time, he found himself wishing Rowan wasn't quite this quick, in several ways. It would make this a lot easier. They'd never had to match wits on anything before, and almost any reason would be better than this. "I'm trying to track Sharpe's movements. So I needed to know when and where, that's all."

That stopped Rowan for a second. Now Jay saw a change. They lowered their head very slightly, as if they wanted to charge something with their huge horns. Their jaw worked, as if they were clenching their teeth. Jay didn't move. "We knew he was in Meridian too. Since they were. He'd have to be."

"Yeah," Jay said quietly, wondering how in the hell he was going to get out of this. "So I just needed to confirm his starting point. So from there I could—"

"You were going to ask Annie," Rowan actually cut in, very quietly. "If Sharpe was really near Meridian?"

He didn't answer. His eyes went from the tree, the gently swinging hammock, Annie's fingers curled around the cloth edge, back down to Rowan's unbroken stare.

"Jay," they asked, and now instead of intense, even instead of their crisis-mask of calm, they just sounded exhausted, entirely and bone-deep. "What is going on?"

"About ten minutes ago, I opened that message from Radiance HQ Shiloh gave me. I know, I thought I'd focus on Maureen's disk first—that was a mistake. I shouldn't have waited. It was a recording. Just a couple seconds long." He took a deep breath, like the last one right before diving headfirst into deep, dark water. "It was from Regan."

Rowan's eyes opened wide; for the first time, Jay had the feeling they were completely present and painfully aware. When they spoke, it wasn't in their tightly controlled voice anymore, and Jay actually had to lean a little closer to hear their faint whisper. "How? What?"

"I don't know," Jay said in as level and calming tone as he could manage himself, hoping it would ground both of them. "There was nothing else on the drive, no background noise, nothing I could trace—"

"What did it *say?*"

Jay faltered, then made himself speak the words that had chilled him to the bone. "'Blood in the water.'"

Rowan nearly took a step backwards, seeming to fall off-balance for a moment, as if someone had slapped them in the face. When they recovered, their hands were balled into fists, and their breathing quickened. "He said that? You're absolutely sure?"

"Yeah. Just four little words." Jay smiled, but it didn't feel good at all. "Not much mistaking what they mean."

"And you're sure it was him?"

"Not much mistaking that either."

"I want to hear it for myself—no I don't," they said quickly. "Because it's not real, it's just another trick. What do we always say about this place? Tartarus lies—"

"Not this time," Jay maintained, hating every word. "It's him. That was an official Radiance drive, Lakshanya Chandrashekar's own encryption, nothing gets past her. And I ran voice recognition, about eight times. I analyzed every millisecond. It's Regan's voice, without question, nobody could make a fake so perfect I wouldn't catch it. And it's not like I wouldn't know his voice anywhere, there's that too," he finished in a mutter.

"Then he needs help. If that's really Regan, saying—*that*—then it confirms beyond a doubt that he's out here somewhere and we need to find him, right now, before—"

"Yeah, that's been on my list for a while." Jay still didn't raise his voice, but it was getting harder not to. "I'm working on it. Believe me, I'm really, really working on it. I'll talk to Radiance, find out when and where but you know how tight-lipped they are about their contacts. That's why I started with Sharpe's position first instead of just asking them about Regan. If he's a 'contact,' we're not getting anything else."

"We have to at least try! Regan was there, we know that!"

"And I will. But that's not our only priority anymore, it can't be."

"What's a higher priority than finding Regan again?" Rowan stared at him as if he'd suddenly started speaking another language, one neither of them had heard a word of in their lives. "And Zilch? And their heart? Everything else is secondary, even..." They stopped, as if they weren't sure of their own words anymore. "Even Sharpe."

"Listen, I know Regan's important to you—he is to me too!" Jay remembered not to shout just in time. He froze for a full second before continuing, in as loud a whisper as he dared. "Was, is, I don't even know, that last runtime was—"

"Regan is important to me the way breathing is." Rowan's voice was soft, but it surprised Jay into silence anyway. "And I know you feel the same. Even after all this."

Jay held very still, afraid of giving some wrong answer, or answering at all. Finally, his shoulders sagged and he nodded, letting his head drop so far down his chin almost touched his chest.

Rowan stepped forward and caught his hands in both of theirs. Jay hadn't even realized he was shaking, or that he'd been holding his breath, until he could breathe again. "This has been hell on all of us, but you saw him last, the night this all started. And now that message, saying..." They stopped, shaking their head as if to clear it of the words they didn't want to remember. "But what are *you* saying?"

Jay kept his eyes on their hands and held them tight in his own as he carefully chose his next words. "This isn't Parole. We don't know how things work out here. We don't know anything. Be careful who you trust."

"Of course I am." Rowan looked up at him with the first real reaction to break through their careful control, aside from shock, pain, or grief. Confusion. "I trust you. And I trust..."

Jay said nothing. He was holding his breath again.

"No." Rowan let go of his hands. "No, that's not—"

"That message might not be a call for help. It might be a warning."

"Yes, exactly, he's warning us about Sharpe, he's still trying to keep us safe!"

"No, Rowan. That message is a red flag, but Regan's not the one waving it." Jay forced his voice to stay hard but level, and keep saying the words. The sooner he said them, the sooner they'd be out of him like poison. "When we find him...Regan might not be Regan anymore."

"What?" Rowan heard him. He knew they did. And couldn't blame them for a second for wanting to deflect, but he couldn't stop either.

"Maybe he didn't betray us on his own free will." Now it was Jay's turn to try to access some of that control Rowan had in spades, or had when they'd started this awful conversation. Keep his eyes and voice level and steady and don't crack, break, or run. "How long did SkEye have him under their thumb?"

"That's not fair, Jay. That was years ago."

"Fine, you're right, let's not go back years. How about just a couple months?" Jay stopped to catch his breath, surprised that he even had to. Suddenly it felt like he'd sprinted beyond his comfort zone. All of this was far beyond it, anyway. "Listen, I know nobody wants to talk about this, but it was only a couple weeks before Regan disappears and everything breaks out—"

"No," Rowan interrupted, seeming to instantly know where he was going with this and not liking it at all. "That has nothing to do with—"

"Sharpe grabs him! Two days in a detention center. He's recaptured, re-addicted, re-clean—"

"Yes, exactly, he survived Sharpe, he survived another round of withdrawal, he escaped, he made it home even though it almost killed him. Regan did all that."

"Sharpe had him," Jay said, stating the fact as if it were the only real one left. "For two whole days. Right before all this started. We're really supposed to just let that go, like it's all a coincidence?"

"Stop," Rowan said simply, very quietly.

But Jay couldn't, not once that particular dam had burst. "And what did Sharpe do to him? We don't even know! Regan didn't know! What the hell could somebody do to a person, so they don't even remember?"

"I remember. You don't have to remind me." Their voice had defaulted to their triage detachment again. Jay forced himself to ignore this red flag and focus on the original.

"So we can't rule out the possibility he's been compro—"

"No."

"No? Just—no?"

"*No.* I do not accept that."

"Okay!" Jay tipped his head back to look up at the dark ceiling and bright, soft lights in the treetop for a moment, fighting the urge to break into helpless, borderline-hysterical laughter. "All I know are the facts. And now we have a new one to consider."

"Well, here's one more fact: Regan did not betray us." Rowan folded their arms now, and Jay could swear they were digging their hooves into the ground.

"I'm not saying he did!"

"Then, once again, what are you saying?

"There are so many possibilities here, and not a whole lot of good ones, okay? We just have to look at this from every angle and be ready for whatever—"

"There are possibilities I'll accept, and ones I won't—like Regan being a traitor!" Rowan started shaking their head and Jay almost took a step away from their horns. But like before, he didn't go anywhere. "And I won't abandon him. Not when he needs us most. How can you even think that, Jay? After—"

"You think I like even considering this? You think this is fun for me?"

"Then why are you doing this?"

"Because what Regan pulled on that last runtime caught me totally unprepared, bam, never saw it coming! I had a plan for anything—except that!" Jay leaned closer and whispered, so harshly it hurt. "And so this time we can maybe be ready, if it all goes to hell again! I hope it doesn't! But we need to be prepared!"

"I'll never be prepared for that." Rowan shut their eyes and kept them squeezed shut as they spoke, as if the possibility stood directly before them beside Jay, the tree, and Annie as she slept. "We might lose Regan forever out here and I can't. I just can't."

"Rowan… I just don't want you to get hurt. Again. Like I did." Jay took in a slow breath, disturbed at how much it shook. The exhale was just as bad. "We might have already lost him."

"No!" Rowan half-shouted, voice nearly breaking. Annie shifted in her sleep but didn't wake up. "Regan is alive—and so is Zilch, we can see that, we have solid, concrete evidence, so—"

"That's not what I mean. You know it's not."

"And I won't accept it, because it's impossible. *Regan didn't betray us.* He hasn't been brainwashed, nobody is controlling him. When we find him—*he'll be him!*" Jay sometimes wondered if tears from all-black eyes that had been turned from Tartarus vapors would be clear or black themselves. He'd never seen them; he'd never seen Rowan anywhere near crying and that was probably the way they liked it. But that might be about to change. "And he'll be alive! Blood in the water or not. We'll get him back. We have to."

"Okay. Fine." Jay held up his hands, then let them drop. He'd never been so glad to let a conversation drop either. But the unanswered questions and a decade of memories seemed to hang around them like heavy curtains. Just like the Tartarus wastes, everywhere they looked tonight, they saw ghosts. "So where does that leave us?"

"I don't know, Jay." Rowan's voice was flat again, as lifeless as it had been at the beginning of this entire ordeal. "Where does it leave us?"

This time, when he turned to go, Rowan didn't try to stop him.

CHAPTER 11

Find The Queen

THE NEXT DAY CAME AND THE FIRERUNNER HAD YET TO SHIP OUT. RESOLVING THAT IF ANY working shield existed anywhere in this outpost, they would find it, Aliyah and Jay set out in the now-familiar disguises of ponchos and sunglasses. Everyone else was free to stay on the ship, join in the search, or keep an eye out for anything else useful while they were still in a friendly port. It would likely be a while before they saw another.

Seeming moderately panicked at the realization that they'd soon be confined to the ship, Indra was quick to follow. Shiloh didn't come close to sharing his cabin fever but was relieved to see him excited about anything after the ordeal at Radiance HQ. Xie had no idea what he was looking for but

readily agreed to help him find it before they left.

There wasn't much to see down on the street leading to the docks. Like Meridian, this barrier-domed outpost was little more than a single main street, though the prefab buildings and parked trucks made it look even less established and more like it was made to be dismantled at a moment's notice. A few people passed by, mostly Radiance volunteers.

A short distance away, Annie and Rowan—in a large, ill-fitting trench coat, ears and horns covered by a hat even bigger and floppier than Shiloh's, and hooves in even worse-fitting boots—conversed in low tones. They'd chosen a shady spot under one of the few trees in this protected bubble; Shiloh wondered if it reminded them of the huge one in the FireRunner's tank.

But xie didn't have time to wonder for long. The sound of a deck of cards being loudly shuffled came from behind xir and, for a moment, Shiloh wondered if xie'd fallen asleep. The last time xie'd heard that sound was in a dream. But xie felt awake and alert as xie turned to see Indra with the cards xie'd heard, shuffling them in midair with more skill and ease than Shiloh had ever seen in person.

"You're really good at that," xie had to say, watching as cards streamed from one of his hands to the other, none of them falling to the ground.

"What?" Indra actually looked puzzled as he continued shuffling—he wasn't even looking at what he was doing, Shiloh realized. It seemed a lot more like a nervous habit, like when Annie twirled her hair around her finger, finding comfort and relief in the repeated sensation. "Oh! Thanks. It's just something I do to calm down. Been wound a little tight lately."

"I could never do that." Shiloh couldn't help staring now, at the way the cards seemed to float between his hands, the way his motions seemed so automatic and effortless, the small glittering trails the cards left in the air—

"Everybody needs a way to blow off steam. This is mine. Usually for an audience, but even—woah!" Indra clapped his hands together, cards between them. Still, tiny bright lights danced around his hands, like sparks that didn't burn. "Was that you?"

"Ah, sorry!" Shiloh blushed, clamping down on the unconscious energy flares like blowing out a candle xie hadn't noticed was burning until it caught something on fire. "I didn't mean to do that. I was just watching, and..."

"Don't worry about it! That was awesome. Actually..." Indra smiled slowly, a little mischievously, as if he were putting something together for the first time, something he liked. "Can you do it again?"

Five minutes later, Indra stood in the center of a growing crowd, demonstrating exactly why the sound of cards and coins usually accompanied his words in dreams.

"Pick a card! Any card!" Indra's voice carried well even over the sounds of engines and the excited crowd. Any last bits of wandering attention were caught in his sweeping, flourishing movements. "Any card in the world—no, actually, just any card in my hand! Pick any card and I will match it, find it, bring it home. Everybody's looking for something and today's looking great for cards..."

It worked like a charm. While Shiloh remained unobtrusively off to the side with xir head down, Indra stood in the spotlight—a quite literal one that Shiloh focused on maintaining. Subtle enough not to set off anyone's suspicion but flashy enough to catch attention. When Indra's hands arced through the air, faint flashes followed their movements. When cards flipped over, they flared in small showers of sparks.

"Is this your card? No, of course it's not, they're mine!" He said with a laugh that actually sounded genuine. "But it's the one you picked, isn't it? Yeah, that's what I thought!"

Not all powers came from Chrysedrine. Indra's ability to manipulate everyday objects, making them appear and disappear seemingly at will were uncanny, but not supernatural. But he did command another kind of magnetism, Shiloh's influence aside. It came from a brilliant smile, an engaging charisma, and an infectious laugh.

"Yes, this is the lost and found desk. Did you lose this Queen of Hearts? 'Cause I found it—Yes! Yes, God, I get tired of being right!"

And he did glitter. It hadn't taken long to figure out that Indra's natural showmanship and Shiloh's energetic spark was a winning combination. With every spark, the gathered people let out appreciative *ooh's* and *aah's.*

"What did I tell you?" Indra glanced over his shoulder and shot Shiloh a grin as equally dazzling sparks cascaded around him. "Sometimes all you can rely on are your wits and your hands. Lucky mine have the Midas touch."

"Your wits or your hands?" Shiloh couldn't stop smiling either. Not when he looked like that. After Radiance HQ and then the infection scare, Shiloh had been actually afraid xie might not ever see Indra's smile again. There were still dark circles under his eyes but today they were lit up with Shiloh's flares and his own kinetic energy.

"Both. And a little help from my friends." He winked, revealing the Jack of Spades with a flourish. He turned his smile up another few watts and went back to his hustle. "No, no tips necessary, good people! Your delight is a far better reward!"

Shiloh watched, hypnotized, as his long, nimble fingers manipulated the cards and pulled threads of chance, so enthralled xie almost forgot to keep up the fireworks. Indra had obviously been practicing this for years. This at least partly explained how he'd been able to float from place to place for as long as he had. Alone.

"And that's all folks!" Indra raised his voice a minute later, flipping the cards back into his hand with a final flourish. "We had some good times, good memories, a few laughs. Thank you, we've been great!" As the small crowd dissipated, he busied himself in collecting the cards, not looking up.

"Nice job," Shiloh said quietly as the crowd dispersed, and Stefanos's large frame appeared from the back of the audience. Shiloh wondered if he'd been there the whole time. He hadn't had the best viewpoint from where he'd been standing, but then, with his eyes, maybe he hadn't needed it. "That was a great idea."

"Not really, it was reckless and idiotic and could have gotten us all caught and killed, especially 'cause we don't even need the money," Indra groused, his performer's smile disappearing as fast as his cards up his sleeve. "But if I didn't find some kind of creative outlet, I was gonna find a tall object and walk off."

Shiloh felt a cold shock of alarm. "Indra, if you're—"

"No, no, I didn't mean that, I'm sorry," Indra said, holding up his now entirely non-glowing hands. Now that he met xir eyes, he was clearly more than just tired. He looked brittle, wound tight as a string that might snap. "Just been a hard couple days. Family stuff. And then...you know." He dropped one hand but kept holding up the one that until recently had cracked and peeled with the Tartarus ghost's poison.

"Yeah," Shiloh said, every bit of happiness and excitement from a moment ago faded as fast as their spotlight. "It's still bad?"

"It's not great." His eyes flicked down to his arm, then away again just as fast. There were no lasting marks, and he'd just demonstrated full use of his hand easily enough, but he still looked haunted. "Helps to think about anything else. So thanks for helping me out there."

"It's okay," Shiloh said gently. It wasn't hard to believe xir friend was still in pain. With Indra's showmanship energy dissipating, the bags under his eyes and the heaviness in his movements were clear. Exhaustion radiated off him in waves. "For a while, you looked happy. I mean really happy. It's a good look on you."

"I was. For a minute. I'm okay if I stay with people," he said quietly. "I think one reason I got so bad over the years is I was alone so much. Too much quiet, alone with everything that hurt. I..." He looked down at his hands.

"It gives you too much time to think, doesn't it?" Stefanos asked as he came over to join the other two. His low voice carried only a hint of a mechanical whirr underneath. And with the same dark glasses and gloves he'd worn when they'd met, he easily passed for an ordinary, enhancement-less person, cybernetic or otherwise.

Indra cast the big man a wary look. "I suppose you're gonna chew us out for drawing attention like that, huh? Don't bother, I know it was a mistake."

"But did it help?"

"Yeah."

"Then it wasn't a mistake."

That didn't seem to be the answer Indra expected, but he still looked a little leery. "It's something I'm good at. One of the only things. And if I keep busy, things almost seem normal."

"No such thing as normal anymore. Normal died when Parole was born.

Good riddance." Stefanos chuckled at his own small joke. "But you feel how you feel. Forget the rest."

"What if I don't really know how I feel?" Indra's frown looked pained as he looked away. "My brother kind of died when Parole was born too and I still don't know what to make of that. Never have. Ever."

"Then you don't," Stefanos said simply, but it didn't sound dismissive or blunt like it might coming from someone else. "Nothing wrong with that either."

"Yeah, but it's kind of annoying." Indra gave a sigh that certainly sounded it. "Being numb doesn't hurt, exactly, but eventually it's like okay, ready to feel something, just to get it over with."

Shiloh wasn't sure what to say to any of this, and xie hated it. Xie'd hated it back at Radiance HQ and xie hated it now, even not knowing how to say that Indra didn't really seem numb. He did seem incredibly driven to see what his brother had seen, as he'd put it. His pain, anger, and grief almost felt tangible, even when they weren't connected in their dreams. But if Indra said numb, that was really the only word that mattered.

"I was nine when it happened," Indra continued, still sounding frustrated. "So I don't really remember a whole lot about Mihir. You know, from before..." He stopped, eyes dropping to the ground. His shoulders slumped and his hands, so quick a moment ago, hung down at his sides.

"And we don't have to talk about him now either," Stefanos reassured him. "Not if it'll do more harm than good."

"No, it's fine, it's just..." Indra said faintly, then cleared his throat and tried again. He didn't sound irritated anymore. Now he really did sound numb, resigned, and very tired. "I never—I don't know. I hope it didn't hurt, that's all."

Stefanos's gears whirred audibly as his brow furrowed. "How much do you know about what your brother did that day? When Jay and Celeste saved Parole from the Waste blast?"

"Just that it was the last thing he ever did," Indra mumbled. "And right before, he and my dad had a fight. Something big was happening in Parole. My dad didn't want him to go, but Mihir went anyway. I remember..." His eyes went to Shiloh, and xie could almost hear wind in the branches of a towering tree, the crackle of flames far below. "Mom and Dad fighting. Somebody coming to tell us... I don't know. I think I didn't want to know."

"It didn't hurt." Stefanos fixed both eyes on Indra. "Happened all at once. Fast. Clean. Turret tried to destroy Parole once and for all. And at the same time, Jay initiated Icarus, the program that would drop the barrier and set us all free. Celeste gave him all the time he could. One minute. And if Mihir hadn't been there, it wouldn't have been fast or clean for any of us. Your brother was—is—a hero."

"My dad always blamed Parole." Indra sounded faraway, head dropping and shoulders rising as he spoke, seeming to cave deeper into himself and memory. "He said it would get Mihir into trouble. And Mihir said what Turret was doing was wrong. He and my... both of them. They were both wrong."

"Turret *was* wrong," Stefanos said firmly. "In every single way someone can be. But I'll give you an unpopular opinion. Your mother wasn't the enemy. Turret was."

"What?" Indra stared, eyes widening as he raised his head. "You don't think it was her fault?"

"I think she was trying to navigate an impossible situation with minimal bloodshed. Talk to someone else—even on this ship—and you'll get a different story. But you think I don't know what a powder keg that city was?" He shook his head. "The only wrong thing your mother did was leave. I know why she did, I understand it. But we were still left alone at Turret's mercy. And he doesn't have any."

Indra looked at the ground, said nothing.

"Without your mother, we didn't have a chance. She was the only thing keeping Parole remotely stable." He held up his huge gloved hand and then opened wide, miming an explosion. "That's when Turret's iron fist closed. The second he took over, everything went up in smoke. You know the rest of the story. Parole is what it is today, because of him."

"But my mom..."

"Was instrumental in making sure that God-awful place didn't spread any further." Stefanos looked over at Shiloh, and smiled. "Both of your mothers. They were already working together to save millions, they just didn't know it yet."

"But did she know what Turret tried to do?" The note of desperation hadn't left Indra's voice. "I mean, yeah, she left Parole because losing Mihir almost destroyed her, I get that—because hey, same. But before that. I wish I knew what she was thinking."

Stefanos hesitated, wheels turning in his head. In his case, this may have been literal. "You make up your own mind. But some things we know for sure: Parole needed Mihir. We needed Icarus. And that means we needed Jay and Celeste. Those boys were heroes, your brother just didn't get to keep being one. The rest is history."

"Nice to know there's one hero in the family," Indra said with a dry smirk that faded fast. Shiloh stayed quiet and watched as worry returned to his face. Xie couldn't shake the thought that something was odd about what Stefanos had said, but it was hard to focus on abstract weirdness when Indra looked so troubled. "But I can't stop thinking about my mom. Did she sign off on Turret's plan? Did she just decide hey, it's better if this place just disappears?"

"I don't believe that." Stefanos shook his head. "And I won't. The Rishika I know wouldn't have written us all off like that. Why she left us in his hands... you'd have to ask her."

"I will," Indra said, voice filled with determination for the first time. "First chance I get."

☆

A short distance away, Annie and Rowan stood together under the shade of a small tree, half-watching the show but not really seeing it. She'd taken off her helmet and Rowan didn't wear the sunglasses they'd brought; Indra's magic show attracted enough attention that they could converse with some low-level strangeness relatively unnoticed.

"Thanks for getting me out here," Rowan said, shifting a little awkwardly in the boots they wore over their hooves. "It's good to get out and see the world a little, if we're here. Even if takes some doing."

"Yeah." Annie nodded. "Gotta get some fresh air sometime, enjoy it while it doesn't smell like smoke or Tartarus poison."

They were quiet for a minute. Annie looked over at Rowan a few times, started to say something, and then stopped. Nothing was coming out exactly right and she wasn't going to actually say anything until it did. Rowan didn't question or pressure, just waited. Annie could have always turned around and pointed at her jacket; that usually worked, but some things she just wanted to say herself.

"You don't have to worry," she said abruptly after a while. "I'm really fine."

"But I'm still going to." Rowan's smile was tired but genuine when they turned. "It's too late now. In too deep. Couldn't stop if I tried."

"I'm really doing okay, though. Haven't even freaked out or collapsed super bad or anything." She shrugged. "Couple nights on the road sucked but I picked myself back up again. I'm fine if I keep moving."Annie reached under her shirt and pulled out the chain and its dangling shark tooth that hung hidden but close to her heart. "And I really did mean for you to take this."

She held it out to Rowan as she had before. And as before, they shook their head and turned away as if the mere act of looking at it hurt.

"It's yours, not mine," they said, voice barely carrying over the noise of the nearby crowd. "It's what he'd want."

"No it's not." Annie's face was flushed as she let the tooth drop but she tucked it back under her shirt, hiding it from view again. "It was the same with Indra's family. They said all the same things about Mihir, except they'd been saying them for ten years. Always arguing about what he would have wanted, and trying to—what'd Indra say? Stand where he stood." She jammed her hands in her pockets and stared at the ground. "Well, I was right there with Ash. I did stand where he stood and it didn't change anything."

"Annie," Rowan started gently but she cut them off with a frustrated noise that sounded like it had been building up inside her for some time.

"I'm not talking about blaming myself, I'm just saying it doesn't matter if you're there or you weren't. I was with him and I still don't know what he'd say or do, because he's not here anymore. I just know that he wouldn't want... *this.*" She pulled out her hands, raised them in a helpless gesture to where the tooth hung, then to the both of them, then let her arms drop.

Rowan shut their eyes for a moment and took one full breath before speaking. "He'd want you to get back to us safe and sound. That's done. He'd want me to get you home, back to your parents. I'll do my best. And he'd want us to finish what he started, get Zilch's pancreas and heart and all their organs back together, make sure they're safe."

"Yeah," Annie said a little shakily, face falling again. "Yeah, I'm sorry. We looked everywhere, the heart just wasn't on that ship."

"And that was not your fault." Rowan looked up and directly into her eyes as they spoke. "None of it was. It's no one's fault but Sharpe's."

"We still can't go back without Zilch's heart." She swallowed hard. "Or Regan."

Rowan was silent for several seconds and their eyes drifted away again. When they snapped back to Annie's face, they still didn't look entirely present, like they were looking at her but seeing something, or someone, miles and months away. "You didn't see any sign of him out there, did you? Anything at all?"

"There was this dream..." Hesitatingly at first, Annie told them what she'd seen and heard in the Emerald Bar, or the place that looked like it in her head. When she was done, Rowan didn't respond right away. They'd closed their eyes again and seemed deep in thought, or maybe trying not to reveal their feelings, whatever they may be. "But it might not have been him. Maybe it was just a dream. Not like I haven't dreamed about home before."

"But your friends were there?" Rowan sounded caught between tentative excitement and worry, as if they couldn't decide whether any of this was a good or bad sign. That Annie wasn't sure herself didn't really help. "They saw this too?"

"Yeah. Usually when we all dream the same thing... I dunno, we pay attention."

"Was he..." Rowan stopped, seeming to struggle at finding the right words. They'd been doing that a lot lately and it was a strange and somewhat unsettling thing to watch. Annie was used to wrestling with words, trying to fit them into an order that made sense, but Rowan always seemed to know what to say, how, when. Their words came out right. They could even be beautiful instead of just functional, a strength instead of a frustration. And now they weren't. Another change. She didn't like it. She waited, feeling slightly sick, until Rowan found the words at last. They were simple but important. "How was he?"

"He seemed... okay," Annie attempted, immediately realizing this was annoyingly inaccurate. Now it was her turn to search for the right words and come up emptyhanded. "Uh, tired. Worn, um, not ragged, but like, something that's—that's—"

"It's all right. Take your time."

She did. She made herself take a deep breath and take one word at a time like slow steps. "I think he's been running really hard. Pushing himself. Harder than back home. But he was happy to see me and that's what made me think it was him, at first, him for sure. It felt so real. And then he got scared—as soon as he saw this." She pulled out the shark tooth again, this time letting it swing from her hand back and forth. "He got so upset, I thought he was going to go invisible, like he does. But instead I think it woke us all up."

"So then...assuming it really was Regan," Rowan said slowly, studying the tooth as if they were trying to puzzle something out as they spoke. Or perhaps they'd already found the answer, hadn't liked it, and kept searching for any other possibility. "Did you talk about what that meant?"

"No. We didn't have time." She lowered the chain but didn't let it go, hand curling tightly around the tooth's sharp edge. "And I don't think I–I mean, I couldn't–"

"Don't worry. I don't think I could have either." Rowan reached out and covered her hand with theirs, the shark tooth within them both. "It's better that he hears... in person, anyway."

"If there is a better." Annie sniffed. "I'm so sorry."

"You have nothing to apologize for," Rowan said firmly, giving her wrist a gentle squeeze so as not to cut her hand on the tooth. "And we have everything to thank you for. You did more than anyone should ever be asked to do."

She shrugged and said nothing, but let go of the tooth to squeeze Rowan's hand back. Somehow, standing under this unfamiliar tree in a place she'd never been, surrounded by strangers, she felt like she'd come home in a small way after a very long time.

"I should get back to the ship," Rowan said after a while of easy quiet. They still held her hand and didn't let go or step away yet. "This so-called disguise won't fool anyone who looks too closely, and... well, it's time for another round of organ checks. Are you coming?"

Annie considered that for a moment, thinking about a much taller tree with lights in its high branches and a hammock in its lower ones. Then she heard laughter across the street–Indra's, she realized a moment later–and caught a glimpse of something sparkling when she turned to look. She'd see the big tree in her dreams tonight anyway. "Think I'll stay here for a while."

☆

"Hey, we heading in too?" Shiloh asked as Annie came up to join xir and Indra and Rowan disappeared down the street that led back to the FireRunner. She'd missed the end of the magic show but caught the way Indra scowled at the suggestion.

"We got a while before it gets dark," she said, giving Indra a searching look. "You gonna do some more tricks?"

"Probably not." He shook his head. "But I'm still pretty wired, so best thing to do is keep going at something else until I'm too exhausted to think. Then I'll crash, nice and easy."

Xie disliked both the dark circles under Indra's eyes and the return of his haunted look. "Listen, whatever'll help you feel better, we'll do it. Right, Annie?" Xie looked up, raised eyebrows visible behind xir sunglasses.

"Drugs, no," she said in a tone that left no room for argument. "Murder, no. Suicide, no. Sex, no. And we can stay like an hour—"

"An hour?" Indra shook off his returning glower long enough to whine. "Seriously?"

"Because Rowan and Stef are going back to the ship," she said, as if she hadn't heard his interruption or accompanying groan. "And we should get back too before it gets dark."

"Fine. Okay." They stood together on the sidewalk for a few more seconds—and then Indra saw it. "That's it," he whispered.

"What?" Annie didn't sound like she entirely trusted his revelation.

"I see a sign." Electric blue neon flashed from a nearby bar window, lights just coming on in preparation for the sun set. It might not quite have been a divine vision but it was just as welcome in his time of need. He moved forward as if in a trance. "Karaoke."

Annie shook her head before meeting Shiloh's pleading gaze, following it to where Indra's face was lit up by both the neon glow and a real smile. Slowly, she wiped her hand across her helmet to make the visor go dark and turned up the audio insulation. "One song."

☆

It was actually several songs before they called it a night.

"Eight in a row," Annie marveled as they hurried toward the towering ship. Thanks to the unexpectedly long, cathartic karaoke break, it was long past sundown. "I get coping. I respect it...but was that much Queen really necessary?"

"Can't even believe that's a question," Indra snorted, but he was smiling, seeming truly relaxed and happy for the first time since they'd left the Radiance tower. Maybe the entire trip; his face was open and serene and comfortably sleepy without a hint of anxiety—or performance adrenaline. "Besides, Freddie Mercury was Indian, bisexual, ridiculously talented, brilliant, gorgeous, possibly an actual angel descended from the heavens to rock an undeserving Earth..." He stopped counting off on his fingers and sighed contentedly, gesturing to all of himself. "And here I am. Some things are just meant to be."

"You sound like you've got it all figured out," Annie said with what sounded almost like envy. "Who you are and junk."

"Well yeah, kind of." He looked over, her unusual tone clearly breaking through his post-performance bliss. "Took me a while, but it's worth it. You haven't really?"

"I dunno. All I know is," she shrugged, shook her head and scowled in frustration. "I don't know what I don't know. I don't get people, I told you that. But I *really* don't get the whole romance... sexy... thing. I don't get why it's a thing we have to do. And I don't really want to do it."

"Oh! Ace?" Indra held up one of his playing cards, the Ace of Hearts.

"What?" Annie eyed it with equal parts suspicion and confusion. "Is this one of your card tricks? I thought we were done with that."

"Uh, no." Indra stopped walking, looking every bit as confused as she did. "No, I was just going to... um, never mind."

"You can do it, just tell me what you mean." She was looking at him now, still with confusion but not the same suspicion as she'd regarded the card. "What am I supposed to do here?"

"Nothing you don't want." He shrugged easily. "I was going to use the cards as a... visual pun, I guess, for asexuality. Or a metaphor or—a joke, basically. Just a joke."

"Oh." She seemed to relax. "Okay, I get that. Thanks for explaining. That's funny."

"Thanks! And don't worry, everyone deals with the hand they're dealt. You can't really lose."

"I don't even know the rules, though."

"Well, do you have an idea of what...suit?" He paused. "If you want me to keep talking in, uh, cards?"

She considered this for a second. "Yeah. It's dorky but it makes talking easier."

"Okay, that's fine, whatever works for you. Do you like something a little more...Aro-mantic?" he held up a second, the Ace of Spades, with an arrow motif.

"Do you have any with a big question mark on them?" she asked. "Sometimes I don't even know what game I'm playing."

"So, the joker then. That's pretty wild."

She smiled, but aimed it at the ground. "How long have you been sitting on these?"

"Since I figured out it made asexual and aro friends actually laugh instead of hurt." Indra watched Annie twirl her hair thoughtfully, shuffling through the cards and studying every one. She stopped on the Ace of Spades and held it. "Bad puns are better than bad names."

They were glad to get back to the ship. After not seeing much of xir uncle all day, Shiloh was also happy to catch sight of him walking across the deck a short distance away. But apparently Jay wasn't nearly as happy to see any of them, because he kept right on walking, clearly pretending he hadn't seen, but not doing a very good job.

"He definitely saw us, right?" Indra said, sounding as baffled as he had a day ago, when their paths had crossed in a much more literal way, very suddenly and all at once. "And he's definitely avoiding us. Again."

"I'm sure he's just, uh–Uncle Jay!" Shiloh called. "Hey, are you... he's gone."

"I'm gone too," Indra muttered, turning and heading off the opposite direction. "Dunno what his problem is, but I'm pretty sure it's me. And I'm done. Good night."

Annie and Shiloh watched in some confusion as both Jay and Indra quickly disappeared, but there was no time to dwell on why.

"Ah, there you are!" Aliyah's voice came from the opposite direction and all three turned to see her striding toward them, her expression determined, decided and thoroughly Captain-Mode. Stefanos followed, face set in a hard mask meant to reveal nothing but its contrast to his usual warmth spoke volumes in itself. "Glad to see you back, I was about to come find you myself. Nobody leaves the ship for the remainder of the night, or tomorrow morning, understand? Actually, nobody leaves, period, not until we settle in again."

"Why, what's going on?" Annie picked up on the tension immediately, mirroring it in the way her shoulders stiffened and hands curled into fists, as if she were anticipating an invisible-but-immediate threat.

"Nothing's wrong yet," the captain explained in a slightly calmer voice, wings that had been partially flared behind her coming to settle around her shoulders. "But I'm afraid we can't wait any longer to get moving. We've sat on our hands here too long as it is and we don't have the luxury of time. We ship out at first light tomorrow and make full speed for the next beacon."

"We can't," Annie said bluntly. "We don't have a shield."

"Yes, I'm aware." Instead of sounding angry at what could very easily be called insubordination, Aliyah just sounded somewhere between ironic amusement and fatigued resignation. "But it's a much bigger shield I'm worried about. Every minute we spend twiddling our thumbs and not lighting up those beacons, Tartarus has time to advance. Even worse," she said with a brief glance up toward Stefanos, who sent an inscrutable golden stare down toward her in return. "Parole goes it alone without our help. The faster we get moving, the faster all this is resolved and we get home."

"Traveling without a shield's a recipe for disaster, that's for sure." Stefanos folded his arms across his broad chest, eyes narrowing, but not in a glare aimed at any of them. "But so's sitting around here any longer than we need to. Time to get this show on the road."

"Don't worry," Aliyah said before Annie could object again. "This isn't a crisis yet, or anywhere near. We'll still be able to steer well away from Tartarus with any luck."

"But what if it changes around?" Annie asked anyway, voice as tight as her fists. "Like it did on me and—like it did before? Those storms move so much faster than they look. One snuck up on us and if we hadn't had a shield..."

"You don't need to tell me, dear. I did say with any luck. Sometimes that's all it comes down to." The nod Aliyah gave wasn't unsympathetic, but it was a clear sign the discussion was over. She turned on her heel to head toward the stairwell leading up toward the bridge but stopped for one last word. "But we focus on the positive, the productive, and what we can actually control, instead of worrying about what we can't. And we keep moving forward. No way out but through."

She disappeared up the stairs and Stefanos turned to follow. Just then, Shiloh realized exactly what had been bothering xir since they last spoke.

"Wait, can you hold on for one second?" xie called, hurrying after Stefanos as he took his first long step after his captain. He stopped but didn't turn or speak, and Shiloh figured that was xir cue to speak fast. "Before, when you told me about Celeste, you said 'he' brought down the barrier. I thought Celeste was a girl? Did I have that wrong?"

"Oh, that." He hesitated, but so briefly Shiloh couldn't be sure if xie'd imagined it. "'Celeste' is an alias. More like a title. Ten years ago, the first Celeste was Mihir."

CHAPTER 12

Third Options

"CELESTE WAS MIHIR," SHILOH PANTED. XIE'D RUN STRAIGHT TO JAY'S ROOM IMMEDIATELY AFTER hearing and now leaned against the doorframe, trying to catch xir breath.

"Who's what?" Jay asked, rotating his chair around to face Shiloh and sounding too studiedly casual and innocent to have actually misheard.

"Mihir," Shiloh said again, more clearly and less breathlessly. "He was Celeste. 'It's more like a title.' He was the first. That's why—"

"Who told you?" Jay asked, dropping all pretense.

"Stefanos—what?"

Jay was rolling his eyes before the name was even out. Still, he didn't seem very upset, or even surprised. "Of course."

"Was it supposed to be a secret?" Shiloh asked, worried xie was treading somewhere xie didn't belong.

"Yeah—I mean, no!" Jay groaned. "No, it's not a secret, everybody knows—everybody on this ship, and that's fine, of course you were gonna find out, I was just hoping we wouldn't have to talk about this so soon." He sighed. "Or maybe ever."

"I still don't really know what we're talking about," Shiloh admitted. "Or not talking about, I guess."

"It means Turret is a murderer." Jay's eyes were cold and Shiloh didn't have time to ask why before he continued. "But he didn't just kill Mihir. And he didn't just cut Parole off from the world behind that barrier. He wrecked the outside world with the Tartarus Blast and set us up to take the fall."

There was only one thing Shiloh could think of to say. "Tell me everything."

"You gotta understand," Jay started, sounding apprehensive. "That night, the night we broke out Icarus and dropped the barrier? It was chaos. Thousands of people rushing to escape. Mihir—Celeste the first—managed to get the thing down for one minute. Just sixty seconds, but some of us made it. Not enough."

"Mom and I did." Shiloh recalled crowds, large bodies jostling xir small one until xir mom picked xir up and ran. Everyone running. Smoke. Suddenly, clear sky. "I thought I remembered you being there but I'm not sure how much I remember is real."

"That part's real. Your mom couldn't find you, so we looked together. So I wasn't around when Mihir..." Jay fell silent, staring at something Shiloh couldn't see. "Don't get me wrong, I wouldn't have missed getting you out for anything. But sometimes you wish you could do a night over. Anyway." He seemed to shake the memory off and looked back up at Shiloh. "You and your mom got out. I stayed in Parole. So did Mihir. And Turret killed him."

Shiloh stayed quiet, trying to piece everything together, before realizing this was impossible without a few more pieces. "How—why? For dropping the barrier?"

"No." Jay's eyes went very hard. "Mihir was a stepping stone. Turret killed him and used him to grab power from Rishika, who up until then was keeping him in pretty good check. Turret tries to wipe Parole off the map and, when that doesn't work, he goes to his Plan B. Tartarus." Jay leaned forward. "There is a smoking gun out there. And I'm gonna find it."

Shiloh tried again to make sense of the cause and effect. It didn't work any better the second time. "I'm sorry, I'm trying to get it, but—"

Jay flopped backwards again with a frustrated noise. "What happened to Parole after the Tartarus blast?"

"It disappeared," Shiloh said after a second of puzzled thought. "To most people, anyway. Nobody can get near it because of SkEye and the story is that Parole was one of the first places Tartarus destroyed—"

"Exactly," Jay cut in. "It wasn't destroyed, but it was definitely supposed to be. First, Turret tries to nuke us. Someone—Mihir—tries to disarm it. It should have worked. But something went sideways, because the thing went off somewhere else."

"The Tartarus Blast," Shiloh said slowly. "So instead of one city, the whole country got burned?"

"Right, which *distracts* everyone from Parole. Everyone forgets we exist." Jay's shoulders sagged. "And then he kills Mihir. Says he's so sorry he couldn't save their son, but this *proves* that this horrible city full of monsters has to be controlled. Rishika abandons Parole in grief and Turret takes her place. He blames Parole's disappearance on Tartarus and blames Mihir's death on us... on me."

"The CyborJ Syndicate." Shiloh felt a now-familiar tinge of dread. "That's what Indra's parents said. We didn't believe it, of course—at least I didn't. I don't see how anyone could, everyone knows you've done nothing but good for Parole."

"Enough people believed it," Jay said, sounding resigned and bitter at the same time. "Which isn't that big a group, contrary to popular belief."

"But I mean, does he know who you were?"

"No, kept it away from SkEye so far. Since I'm still, you know. Alive. There's no way Mihir's family knew. Pretty sure his parents just saw me—like, *me* me—as a harmless teenage nerd. Which is still just fine."

"What about everyone else?" Shiloh was still missing an important puzzle piece, xie could tell. "Everyone in Parole seems to think you're a hero—or CyborJ is, anyway."

"Right. But it's the same here; I'm alive because there is no me, there is only CyborJ. There are like six people who know the truth and most of them are on this ship."

Shiloh still wasn't satisfied. "But wouldn't someone notice if CyborJ was accused of murder?"

"Oh, they noticed. But nobody believed it because, first of all, this is Turret talking. And second of all..." Jay almost smiled. "Celeste wasn't even dead."

"Wh..." Shiloh stared at him. So far xie'd been keeping up pretty well but not because Jay made it easy. "But then, if he's not dead, why...?"

"Mihir was dead. But not Celeste. Some things are harder to destroy than others."

"It's more like a title," Shiloh whispered as realization struck. "He was the first Celeste. But there's a new one now."

"Right. And nobody is gonna believe CyborJ killed anyone if the alleged-victim is still walking around." He almost-smiled again. "Plus it totally threw off anyone who was actually onto Mihir. Can't be Celeste if he's dead. I think Turret's still mad about that."

"But who is it now?"

"Celeste runs on secrets." Jay almost-smiled again. "And that's one of the biggest."

"So why don't you tell everyone the truth?"

"What would happen if I did that, right now?" Jay returned, then answered his own question. "It would be bad. The baddest bad. Even if everyone in Parole believes Turret's to blame—which they probably would—I still need proof. And the only proof I have is my word against his. CyborJ's word," he corrected. "Because the only way I'm still alive is by keeping every eye on the CyborJ show, so they're not looking at mild-mannered me. Or at Celeste 2.0."

"Even if you both said it? If she backed you up—"

"It would mean connecting a bunch of dots that should never line up. If I say 'Turret killed Celeste,' it puts 2.0 *and* me back in the hot seat, because the only reason I was cleared is because the new Celeste stepped up to shatter the suspicion. How can I have killed anyone when Celeste is right here? Turret's claim auto-debunked. Going 'no, not *that* Celeste' undos everything."

"And nobody knew who the first Celeste really was, did they?" Shiloh asked, connecting a couple of those dots. "People would start to wonder."

"Exactly. If I say 'Turret killed Mihir,' everyone asks 'so, what does he have to do with anything?'" Jay shook his head. "And I'm not letting that secret out. He wouldn't want it. I know that for sure."

"You think people would be mad? Why, I thought they'd be grateful."

"It's not Parole I'm worried about. It's the outside."

"But nobody knows Parole exists."

"Exactly. Because this is Turret's private kingdom where he gets to do or destroy whatever he wants, only because it's a total secret. If that secret got out, if Turret lost control for two seconds, what ammo would he use to get it back?"

"Tartarus." A few more dots lined up. Shiloh didn't like the picture they were making. "He'd blame it on Parole."

"Because like he said, Parole's a horrible city full of monsters and now he has a new excuse to hold onto absolute power. He's got dirt on us, Nibling. Sure, it's all lies, but my word only means something in Parole. Outside?" Jay shook his head. "I can't make a move until I get some dirt on him."

"I think I get it," Shiloh said, hoping this was true. "At least I get why you're doing all this. You don't want to clear your name if it means Turret can blame everyone else and make life in Parole worse."

"That's why I *should* be doing it." Jay rubbed his face, pressing the heels of his hands over his eyes, and gave a sigh that swept through his entire body. "But all I can think is, Turret wouldn't just blame Parole. If he forces my hand, and Celeste-Two and I have to step up—Turret would do one of two things. Either blame me *and* Mihir for the Tartarus Blast, which the rest of the world will be ready to believe, once they find out who lives in Parole... or he'd blame me for Mihir's death. And that's not something I'm prepared to deal with. Not again."

"And—oh no," Shiloh realized mid-word, but asked anyway, hoping to be wrong. "Celeste—the new one—she's missing, isn't she? Nobody knows where she is?"

"She's alive," Jay said without hesitation. "She's just out of contact for a while. But yeah. Can't say a word of this without her to back me up. If I do..." He covered his face with his hands. "Turret shifts the blame back to me. And Mihir this time. I can deal with suspicion and loathing. I can't deal with that being slung at him. Even for the greater good or whatever. Guess I'm just not a good enough person."

"You're trying to clear his name too. You look pretty good from where I'm standing."

Jay looked up, peered at Shiloh through his fingers. Cracked a smile. "You're a good kid."

"He was important to you, wasn't he?"

"Sure." Jay shrugged. "He was important to all of us; a lot more people would have died without his help."

"Have you told Indra any of this?" Shiloh asked, trying to sound casual and actually having success.

Jay blinked. "No, it's, uh, never come up."

"Probably because you never talk to him."

"I don't know what you mean." Jay spun his chair around and stared at the nearest active screen.

"Stefanos talks to him." Shiloh continued talking to the back of Jay's head, remembering all the times xie'd seen it as Jay scrambled to escape being in the same room with Indra. "So does Radio Angel. Rowan and Aliyah too. The only person I've seen who hasn't talked to Indra is you. So am I right?"

Jay slowly turned back around, gaping at Shiloh like a fish out of water. "I—

you—that was a long time ago, and you are way too—for your own good!"

"Too what?" Shiloh grinned. "Perceptive?"

"*Nosy.*" Jay was shaking his head, but he didn't look upset. More like impressed and a little awed. "We are *so related.*"

"Really, Indra would probably love hearing about his big brother." Shiloh's smile faded into something more serious. "I bet you have some good memories too."

"Yeah—a bunch?" Jay dragged his hands down his face. "But it just sounds weird? 'Hey, kid, I've dedicated the last ten years to finding proof that your brother didn't screw over the entire country and maybe the world, your bro's a hero, not a traitor *or* a careless rube—it's a whole big conspiracy theory, kind of an obsession, and yeah I was in love with him, and you don't need to know any of this'—no. Keeping my mouth shut. It's less painful for both of us. And less weird."

"He still needs to hear it," Shiloh insisted. "And deserves to, honestly. He said the whole reason he's going to Parole is to see what his brother saw. 'Stand where he stood.' Indra needs to hear the story."

"The story isn't finished, I haven't found my proof," Jay protested.

"He knows Mihir died, but not why," Shiloh said simply. "Not the truth. You gotta tell Indra it wasn't random, or a mistake. He died a hero."

"I don't want to get his hopes up," Jay muttered. "That's one of my rules too. Don't ever get your hopes up ahead of time. And you know I'm all about changing the rules but some can't be broken or even bent. Sometimes there is no third option."

Shiloh couldn't think of what to say to that, so instead, they just sat together in rare, unbroken silence.

☆

The FireRunner pulled out of the docks and began following the continuous glittering stream in the sky. With the huge sails open, it truly seemed like they were sailing across the ocean of poisoned sand, beneath the blazing white-hot sun. The air was still but the solar energy the sails were actually meant to absorb moved the ship along without a breath of wind. As the miles went by, the scorched earth graduated slowly to a powdery, gray ash. Occasionally, they passed abandoned structures that might have once been small houses or outposts, buildings crumbling and metal frames stripped.

Where these stood, there were usually at least a couple graves, bleached white like bones in the sun. Whatever cataclysmic poison had destroyed these structures was long gone, but even without the threat of toxic storms or ghostly assaults, the environment was harsh and unforgiving. At night, when the sun dipped below the horizon, the place almost seemed tolerable. There were around five minutes of sweet relief from the endless glare at sunset—until the temperature dropped, bringing a chill that cut to the bone.

Shiloh grew more and more excited as they followed the glittering guideline in the sky, until it was almost impossible to think of anything but what lay at the end. It was definitely pointing the way to the next beacon, which had to be a sign it was pointing to xir parents too. Xie'd find them waiting at the end of the stream and then they'd all continue together. It was simple.

The next day as the sun was nearly setting, the end of the stream came into view. Just as expected, a beacon waited. But there were no other ships or signs of life and Shiloh started to feel a tinge of worry. Xie wanted to get out and search every inch of the beacon and surrounding area—but there was no time.

The beacon was the priority and they were losing daylight fast.

Reluctantly satisfied with the promise that they'd make a thorough sweep once the location was secured, xie waited and watched from the safety of the top deck as the FireRunner's crew approached, evaluated, and launched into action. Annie had given xir a general idea of what to expect, but said nothing could really compare to seeing it done. She was right.

The air was clear, but everyone still wore portable oxygen masks and tanks. Storms could come on without warning and this operation left them all vulnerable. Success required efficiency, coordination, and very precise timing. Once they started moving, they moved very fast.

First, something flared bright red on the end of Stefanos's arm—a laser-like beam that he used to cut through the thick metal door with surprising speed. Once he was done, all it took was one kick. Once the way was open, Jay quickly slipped inside and went to work. Stefanos remained outside and projected something else from another arm extension; the dampening field resembled a sphere of darkness enveloping the tower's base. Immediately, the beacon's light flickered and went out, as if someone had actually unscrewed the gigantic lightbulb. It flickered briefly back to life, only to die again as Jay disabled the backup generators and interior security systems.

Right on cue, several faint, ghostly figures started to appear on the ground and move toward the tower. The ghosts ignored the FireRunner, instead seeming drawn to the beacon like moths, but not to its light. Their attention was captured by the dampening field and whatever was going on inside it. Small flashes lit up the field's inky darkness as Stefanos and Jay fired off some kind of very bright ammo rounds. Long, twisting, serpentine shapes appeared in the tiny lightning flashes, but they didn't strike.

With the curious ghosts handled, Aliyah shot a hundred feet in the air up to the tower's top, pausing only for the few seconds it took to secure a climbing line. Then she jumped off just as quickly, falling like a stone only to level out and circle about twenty feet in the air, waiting.

Below, secured to the other end of the line with a harness and safety belt, Rowan waited. The moment Aliyah was clear and the line in place, they started to climb. But their movements weren't the slow, careful steps of an ordinary mountain climber–here, Rowan's hooves were in their element. They moved in fast, graceful bounds, speeding around the tower at an angle and ascending much faster than should have been possible. Aliyah followed, and together they spiraled up.

It only took around a minute for them to reach to the top. Then they both disappeared inside the lighthouse-like top chamber to complete their task as Jay and Stefanos held position at its base. About ten very tense seconds went by as the beacon remained dark. Then it flared back to life, but not the same life as before. Instead of a white beam, an electric violet string issued from the beacon, traveling out into the distance. It would connect to the last, previously lit beacon and both their rays would intensify, keeping Tartarus and its ghostly inhabitants at bay.

But as the beacon lit up the sky, another change took place–though most of the crew would never see it. The FireRunner had followed the glittering stream where it led, here, clear to all who could see. It didn't disappear now, but it did change direction. It now curved off into the far reaches of the Tartarus Zone. And the next beacon.

When Shiloh saw this, xir heart sank. Xie had never been farther from home, but xie'd been sent right back to square one.

☆

The temperature dropped sharply as night fell outside, but Radio Angel's room was as cozy and warm as the last time Shiloh had been here. It was a good place to be, xie thought. Anywhere else would have felt as desolate as the cold Tartarus night.

"I'm so sorry," Kari said, turning away from her dozens of radios and microphones to give Shiloh her almost-undivided attention. Her ever-present echoes continued after she stopped speaking, but they were lowered to background whispers. "This had to be a punch right in the heart."

"Pretty good way to put it," Shiloh said with a faint sigh, still reeling from the blow. "I don't get it. We followed the lights, they pointed right here. So my mom and dad should be here too—but they're not. Now it's pointing somewhere else and I'm starting to wonder if they'll even be where it leads next. I don't know, maybe I'm doing this wrong."

There were no windows in this small room but xie knew the glittering stream was still out there, bright against the night sky and leading off into the distance. And xie felt another rush of anger and heartsick despair. Once the sparkling stream had been beautiful. Now it was just a reminder that the journey wasn't over—and shiny promises weren't always to be trusted.

"We'll find your parents," she promised. "Nobody's giving up. Honestly, if they're not out here that's kind of a good thing. Tartarus isn't a place you want to be any longer than you have to. Maybe they made it all the way to Parole already."

"My mom would definitely want to help," Shiloh said thoughtfully. "But my dad risked everything to escape Parole. I don't know why he'd go back now."

"It would be a lot easier if we could just call and ask if anyone's seen them," Kari said with a little sigh that echoed Shiloh's from a minute before.

"You've been trying to get in touch with Parole for a long time, right?"

"Yeah, basically ever since we left." Instead of the excitement and joy she'd radiated when Annie had first introduced them, she just looked sad and tired. Even only knowing her briefly, Shiloh had the feeling that was a recent change. "But I haven't heard anything from anyone. That's never happened before. I don't know what's wrong, but I'm starting to worry."

"I know the feeling," Shiloh said with a sad nod. "I think the not knowing is the worst part."

"Exactly. But sometimes no news really is good news." She took a bracing little breath and smiled. It looked like it was a concerted effort. "And Parole's still full of good people. Even with everything falling apart, they look out for each other. If your parents are there, they're safer than we are. And someone there will know."

"While we were out and caught a little bit of your broadcast, I heard you say a name." Shiloh hesitated, somehow feeling xie was treading on secret ground. "Celeste?"

"Yeah." Kari's smile turned a little sad. "If anyone could help, it'd be her."

"Who is she?"

"Information specialist," Kari said after a split-second pause. "I guess that's what you'd call it. Espionage, finding out what SkEye's doing next, keeping track of everybody and all the most important secrets in Parole."

"Annie said she usually handled her Radiance contacts, so I kind of pictured someone like you." Shiloh was still having a hard time picturing exactly what Celeste did but maybe that was the point.

"Ha, oh gosh, no." Kari gave a little giggle but it died away fast. "She's way more hardcore than me. All I do is sit here and talk but Celeste is on the ground, right in the middle of bad guy central—and she's brilliant. Strikes fast, then gone in a flash. Almost an urban legend." Her voice sounded dreamy. "Secrets are her specialty. She can hack into anything, sneak anywhere, spy on anybody, find out anything—that sounds creepy, I know, but she's on our side. Nothing like SkEye."

"I believe you," Shiloh assured her. "I heard she's the one who dropped the big barrier for one minute so some people could escape."

"Yeah she did." Kari sounded proud as if she'd done it herself. "We would've lost a lot more people in the collapse without her and Icarus."

"That's the program, right?" The sequence of events was a little tricky, but Shiloh was getting a better grip on it all the time. "The one that dropped the barrier ten years ago too?"

"Yeah. But that wasn't Celeste," Kari said, shaking her head. "I mean it was, but ten years ago she was just a kid, we all were. There were—let me back up." She shut her eyes and rubbed them. Shiloh couldn't help wondering how much she'd slept since the collapse, or before. "Celeste—my... our Celeste... wasn't the first one. The name's more of an alias. A title."

"I know. Uncle Jay told me. The first one was Mihir, right? He did it the first time."

"Yeah. And Celeste—our Celeste—and Jay did it again when..." She trailed off for a moment. "During the collapse. She's how I got out."

"Sounds kind of like a superhero." Shiloh smiled, only half-joking.

"No powers. But she saved about as many people as the big ones. Me, Celeste, and CyborJ. Kind of a dream team." She cracked a smile. "We worked together for a long time. Running the networks, the public and secret ones, keeping people safe. I ruled the airwaves, Jay had the internet, and Celeste had...secrets."

"I bet Parole has some big ones." Now that xie actually thought about it, xie was getting curious too. Water was supposed to be currency there, but in a place like that, information might be worth even more.

"Oh, yeah." Kari nodded, actually smiling back. "Celeste would disappear, do her invisible magical girl super-spy dance for a while, and come back with locations for half our missing persons list, and a ton of treasures we didn't even know we needed. Then she'd look up at me with this 'what, like it's hard?' smile, and just...make genius look easy all over again the next day."

"I really hope you find her." Shiloh meant it. There seemed to be a lot of missing people now, in every sense.

"Oh, I know where she is. She's alive." Kari sounded convinced but her smile faded. "She just can't come back yet, I guess. Or answer. I'm sure she has a good reason." That last sentence didn't sound nearly as convinced, or hopeful. "Anyway, you wanna do this?"

"Oh—yeah!" Shiloh gave an embarrassed chuckle as xie remembered exactly what they were doing and why xie was here. "Sorry. You go ahead, start talking or broadcasting and I'll boost the signal."

"Thanks, Shiloh," Kari said, sounding tired but genuinely grateful. "Maybe someone will actually hear me this time."

Shiloh reached out and put a hand on the nearest radio display, this time anticipating the crackling energy that swept through every machine in the room and made the lights flicker overhead. "Okay," xie said as soon as the surge stabilized. They weren't listening for a signal this time, Shiloh reminded xirself.

Focus everything on sending, transmitting, broadcasting. Out, not in. Loud and clear. "I think we're good."

Kari turned to stare at a single microphone on the console in front of her. She took a deep breath, then began to speak. Her words didn't overlap in her usual mode of voices layered over one another; she spoke in one single voice. Just her own.

"Hello, Parole. So, it is...wow. I'm sorry, I have no idea. Is it Tuesday?" She shot Shiloh a questioning glance, and xie nodded as soon as xie realized the question was directed at xir. "Okay, it's Tuesday. Now I'm trying to remember how long I've been away from Parole, and I don't know that either. A month? Time does funny things now. I hope you all know if it's Tuesday or not. I just hope you're okay.

"We're pretty far out, in the middle of a whole lot of nothing. It's quiet. If I can be totally cliché, it's too quiet. I'm used to the noise of the city. I've never been outside of Parole until now. Ever. When I was a little kid, there would be trains and sirens and traffic all around. Then Chrysedrine happened, and the barrier happened, and people with powers and men with gas masks and guns...happened. Everything's loud back home. I don't know what to do with the quiet out here, I can't sleep."

She wasn't looking at Shiloh anymore and xie held perfectly still. Suddenly it seemed like xie was hearing something xie shouldn't. Xie felt like an eavesdropper even though xie'd been invited, guilty without knowing why. Radio Angel's focus seemed like a fragile spell that might break if xie made the smallest sound.

"And the sky is so big and full of stars. Or blue. Just endless bright blue," she said, voice falling to just above a whisper. "You look up at it, and...it's so open. It makes me feel so small. Like I'm a tiny mouse and any minute a huge eagle is going to swoop out of the sky and snatch me up in its talons and fly me away to eat me."

She laughed, and seemed almost as surprised as Shiloh. "Sorry—that was weird. I just thought you all might like to know what I'm seeing. I wish I could show you. Even the weirdness. Remind you that there's a world outside of Parole. It's real and it's here and it's waiting for you. Someday you'll be here to see it. I'm gonna help you see it, I promise, even if all I can do is talk."

Kari fell silent then. The seconds stretched into nearly a minute and Shiloh thought she was done, until she leaned forward until her lips were almost touching the microphone, speaking in a voice so quiet xie almost couldn't hear.

"Celeste...I miss you so much. I'm still here. Talk to me. Please." She was quiet again, sitting and waiting for a reply that didn't come. Finally, she sighed and leaned back in her chair, looking exhausted. "Um, that's all. I hope somebody heard this."

Shiloh kept the connection open for just a few more seconds before finally letting it go.

"I can try again tomorrow," xie offered once the radios fell silent and dark. "Maybe we'll have better luck then. I hope you find her."

"Thanks." Kari fiddled with a sparkly doodad in her puffy pink hair and didn't look up. "Me too. When Parole collapsed—when I lost her..."

"Yeah," xie nodded, feeling vaguely sick. Xie didn't quite know if it was empathy, or just being reminded of things xie'd rather not dwell on. "I know that feeling too."

"I bet you do. A lot of people from Parole do. Even if they haven't been there in a while." She swallowed and kept staring at the floor. "But I'm okay.

Mostly. Getting over it. It's all you can do when people fall through the cracks."

Shiloh laughed, but it wasn't a happy one. "I hate that saying."

"Yeah, especially 'cause in Parole, the cracks are literal, and they have fire underneath. But there are a lot of different kinds of cracks to fall through."

"Listen, when we heard you, just before that guy Sharpe took over?" Shiloh made xirself say the name despite the bad taste it left behind. "You said 'good night, Celeste.' If we could hear you, maybe she could too."

"That thought is all that keeps me going sometimes," she said with a shaky breath. "It's why I keep talking even when nobody answers." She sniffed, let her head fall forward. "And maybe that's selfish. I should be doing it for all the thousands of people who need help."

"Thousands?" Shiloh said a little faintly. Somehow xie hadn't quite put together the sheer number, but nothing else made sense. "That's how many people you talk to every day?"

"Not anymore. Not if I can't get through."

"Sorry, I'm just..." Xie shook xir head, mind boggling. "Thousands. I'm still trying to wrap my head around that."

Kari shrugged one shoulder. "Everybody needs a lifeline."

"Yeah, but nobody needs that kind of pressure."

She shrugged again, smaller this time. "It's what I do."

"You do pretty well from what I've heard. They don't call you Radio Angel for nothing."

"I didn't pick that name. People just started calling me that. It stuck." Kari let out a long, deep sigh that came from her very core. Her round shoulders sagged, head dropped, pink pigtails drooping. "She was wrong. I'm not a hero, or an angel. I'm a girl who can talk. I'm just trying to say things people need to hear. But no one can hear me now, so why does it even matter?" She curled her pink toes, pulled her scarred legs up on the chair to cross them gingerly underneath her.

"You said 'she' was wrong," Shiloh realized slowly. "You didn't pick the name Radio Angel. Celeste did. Didn't she?"

Kari's eyes filled with tears. "I just thought if I could make my voice loud enough, if I had a megaphone so big that I could talk to the whole world, then maybe she'd hear me! Maybe if I just kept talking, someday she'd talk back! And that's selfish, and wrong, because there are so many other people who need help, and they're going to die if we don't help them—and all I can think about is her!"

"That's not..." Shiloh's head spun. For the first time xie felt the full weight of responsibility and tension that filled this small room. The pressure. "Come on, nobody's going to die because you don't..."

"Yes, they will," Kari filled in, remarkably calmly. Her blue-green eyes looked very old and very young at the same time. Shiloh wondered if anyone listening to her voice on the radio ever guessed. "My channels are so important to Parole's survival. And Parole's in the middle of its worst crisis ever. And I'm not there."

"You can't be there," Shiloh said firmly, pleased to find xie believed the words entirely. But it was always easier saying them to someone else. "Not right now. There's nothing you can do about it—anyone, really. But we'll be back soon and then you can keep doing your job and helping people. And you'll get an answer."

"You sound pretty sure." She didn't sound sure herself but when she looked up at Shiloh it was with faint hope instead of tears.

"I just have to believe you will," xie said simply. "Like how I have to believe I'll see my parents again. Or at least hear their voices on a radio. They..." Shiloh stopped, feeling xir own eyes begin to sting. "I thought they'd be here at the end of the stream. They're not. And every time I think we're close, the light stream says we have to keep looking. But they're somewhere. And I gotta believe we'll be together again, because if I don't..."

"Then you can't keep going." Kari picked up where xie left off. "And the only way you'll find them again is if you keep going."

"Exactly. So let's just keep believing we'll find everyone we love, because if we stop, we definitely won't. I can come back tomorrow and we can do this again–somebody has to hear us eventually. Maybe Celeste, maybe my parents. Maybe Parole."

"Thank you, Shiloh." Kari sounded tired, but nowhere near as sad as she'd been. "I wish you could power everything up like that, and make it better, brighter, stronger. The whole ship. Parole. The people in it..."

"That would be pretty great." Xie didn't even want to think too hard about that; it only led to disappointment and feeling useless. But now that the idea existed, Shiloh could tell it would stay in xir head like a too-catchy song. "I don't think my power really works like that, but you never know, I guess."

"Still glad you're here," Kari said, looking a little less hopeless with every word

"Yeah. Me too." Shiloh had to smile back, because for the first time xie realized this was entirely true.

CHAPTER 13

Dark Clouds on the Horizon

STEFANOS TOOK A DEEP BREATH, METALLIC HUM ACCOMPANYING THE INHALE, AND HELD IT. HE held a small blowtorch in his flesh-and-blood hand, the flame at its tip a bright violet instead of blue. Similar to the frequency that repelled ghosts, flames with certain chemical additives worked well at dissolving Tartarus toxins. Most people just didn't use the fire on their own bodies. Small sparks flew as he applied it to the black, rust-like corrosion built up in his mechanized hand and arm's deceptively delicate working parts.

"Need a hand?" Jay asked from where he lounged across the room, waving.

"Awful pun," he replied, shooting Jay a glance with unusually bright golden eyes. He'd turned on the high-beams to focus on his task, and Jay laughed,

throwing up one arm to block out the flash of light. "Just awful."

"Ahh! All right, point taken." Once Stefanos's eyes shifted away, Jay opened his own. He watched Stefanos work for a second, looking thoughtful and unaccustomedly serious. "Seriously, how's it looking?"

"It'd be a lot better if you'd quit worrying," Stefanos said through the side of his mouth, focusing on the slow progression of the violet flame. The poisonous buildup fizzled and dissipated without damaging his prosthetic arm, or the rest of him. The smoke it gave off wasn't toxic but it sure could smell better. "Both of you."

He didn't turn around, but gave a nod to where Rowan stood behind him, carefully inspecting a row of clear, reinforced jars. Each one held an organ suspended in slightly greenish liquid, and their number now included the recently-returned pancreas. Rowan was absorbed in their work and didn't react. They stared at the lungs specifically, seeming entranced by the continuous inflate-and-deflate rhythm, as if it were the most important thing in the world. Maybe the only thing.

Jay watched them for a moment with a look of clear concern and started to say something but seemed to think better of it. Instead, he shook his head and turned back to Stefanos. "What's our next step?"

"Well, there's two possibilities," Stefanos said, flexing his newly-repaired hand. "Option one, we light the beacons and lock up Tartarus, according to plan."

"Or option-the-second," Jay continued, tone light and almost convincingly casual. "We head straight back to Parole and do damage control there."

"Couple problems there." Stefanos shut off the blowtorch's flame. "We're only halfway around the beacon ring. And if we don't finish what we started

Tartarus keeps expanding. And everything goes up in smoke."

Jay watched as Stefanos gave his clean hand another experimental flex. "How long before you need a total overhaul?"

"Arm and leg? A week. Two if I push it," Stefanos said as he inspected his repaired joints with a satisfied nod.

"You always push it. How about internal?" Jay almost sounded afraid of the answer. "Lungs. Eyes. Heart."

"Built to last." Stefanos's metal fingertip tapped against one gold eye with a soft clink. "Danae does good work. So we have two weeks. After that, exterior workings will lock up pretty good and I don't know if I'll be able to unlock them with what we have on hand."

"Great." Jay smiled but it was nervous and faded fast. "That's just great."

"Hey." Stefanos's voice softened as he looked up at Jay again, this time without the eye-beams. "This isn't self-sacrificing heroics. Just practicality."

"Not very practical if your limbs get wrecked when they don't have to. Or, you know. You."

"Exactly," he said levelly. "I'm not going to die so someone else can live. Not even a thousand, not if I can avoid it. I'm a lot more useful alive than dead."

"I don't care about your usefulness." Jay folded his arms and tucked his chin down, but didn't look away. "I care about you."

"And I intend to survive."

"Glad to hear it. 'Cause Rowan's a doctor, not an engineer. And neither am I." Jay snorted. "Not for robot arms and legs. I do keyboards, not wrenches."

"And nobody does them better." Stefanos smiled.

Jay didn't seem to hear, however, muttering his next words primarily to himself. "I can *kind of* keep cybernetic implants and prosthetics functioning–if they're already working. If there's something actually wrong with them, and there is..."

"We need Danae."

"Of course we do." Jay sighed and tipped his head back to lean it against the wall. "Except... I'm not saying she..."

"Except she disappeared along with half of Parole." Stefanos started rolling one pants leg up, revealing his synthetic leg and the corrosion clinging to its intricate workings. It wasn't as severely gummed up as his arm, but the residue was still significant. "But that's the one thing I'm not worried about. She's survived so much worse. When we get home, my sister will be holding the place together."

"Well, maybe we compromise," Jay tried. "We drop you off in Parole and you find Danae. We ship back out and finish the job. Shouldn't delay us more than a couple days."

"We've been over this." Stefanos shook his head. "We can't split up, you need my metal bits to maintain the ship and fight off the ghosts—and the human monsters wandering around out here. We need Aliyah's wings, your tech, Rowan's hooves, my everything else. No spare parts here."

"Fine. Fine, whatever." Jay held up his hands. "You're right, we can't go dropping anyone else off, especially now that..." He shut his mouth, eyes flicking up to Rowan, then away just as quickly. "But okay, all that aside, our job is to get Maureen's disk to Parole as soon as possible. That's what Annie risked her life for. And Shiloh. And Maureen, for that matter."

He didn't mention the other life risked and lost. He didn't have to.

"And we've all got unfinished business back home," Stefanos conceded. "Maybe you most of all."

Jay opened his mouth to reply, then stopped. He shifted to a more comfortable position, ending up resting his chin on his fist and half-glaring back. "That's not why I brought it up."

"Wasn't a judgment," Stefanos said with a half-shrug. "You've got your priorities, that's all. And we'll focus on your mission—and my repairs—as soon as we finish this one. First, ring around the beacons. Then, home."

"We can't go home yet," Rowan said quietly, looking up for the first time.

"Why is that?" Stefanos looked up, seeming encouraged at first to hear Rowan joining the conversation, but his smile faded when he saw the rigid tension in their shoulders and the grim look on their soft face.

"Because—!" Rowan's answer was unexpectedly loud, apparently surprising even themself, because they shut their mouth quickly and dropped their head. Their hands had closed into fists, which they slowly opened, forcing themself to relax with a slow breath. But when they spoke again, their voice had lost none of its intensity. "I know we need to go home soon, the collapse was devastating, thousands must be dead and thousands more need help. And Jay needs to get back to his search and you need actual repairs. This is just a stopgap, even I know that. For us, and Parole."

"But...?" Stefanos pressed gently.

"But we can't go home unless we all go home together."

Jay and Stefanos waited for an explanation, but it didn't come. Rowan wasn't looking at either of them anymore; they'd gone back to staring at the row of jars. Their breathing matched the rhythm of Zilch's lungs, which was at least slow and regular.

Eventually Stefanos filled the silence, voice low and gentle. "Tartarus took your brother. You think it's going to take more people you love. That about the size of it?"

"It wasn't Tartarus." Rowan spoke through clenched teeth. "It was Sharpe."

"Ash died protecting Annie," Jay said, voice dry. He cleared his throat before going on. "So she could live. I mean, that's something, right?"

"Yes." Rowan shut their eyes briefly. This seemed to help them regain some calm. "It's everything."

"So try to focus on that." Stefanos picked up where Jay left off. "She's alive and safe. And Ash would want you to be—"

"I'm grateful she's still here," Rowan said, but their voice was flat. "More than words. But Sharpe's still here too. That...is unacceptable."

"He's not here," Jay said a little more firmly. "And he's not coming back, that's not how he operates. He wouldn't attack a whole ship. Annie's safe. We all are."

"No," Rowan's voice dropped almost to a whisper. "We're not."

"What are you talking about?" Jay sounded equal parts wary of an answer he knew he wouldn't like and resigned to the fact that he already knew it.

"Blood in the water."

Jay suppressed a groan, but had to look away anyway. "I should never have said anything."

"Sharpe has to die." Rowan's voice wasn't panicked, or angry. They didn't even seem upset, but this wasn't their tightly controlled crisis-face either. It seemed much more like a moment of perfect clarity. "He killed Ash. There, I said it."

"Yeah you did." Jay was staring at them now, concerned for a different reason. "Didn't expect to hear you say that. Not Ash—the other part."

"Sharpe," Rowan said again, as if once they'd said the name, they found it hard to stop. Each time reinforced their certainty. "Sharpe needing to die."

"Yeah. Never heard you talk like that before."

"I've never lost a brother before." In yet another first, Rowan's voice was more bitter than Jay or Stefanos knew it could be. "Or a partner. Both of them at once."

"They're not lost," Stefanos maintained. "We'll find Regan, and Zilch, and all their missing pieces. Don't write them off now."

"I'm not. Sharpe is." Rowan's voice rose slightly, but lost none of its unaccustomed edge. "Ash is dead. Annie was almost dead. If Sharpe has Zilch's heart, they're dead, even if they're still breathing." They paused, eyes landing on the lungs still in motion in their jar. Then Rowan forced themself to look away and move on. "And he's going after Regan next. That's the only thing his message could mean."

"Even if he is," Jay started slowly. "And I'm not saying he is..."

"Well, I am," Rowan said, folding their arms; instead of a challenge it looked more like they were trying to hold themself together. "Of course Sharpe's after Regan. That's all he's ever done—why would he stop now?"

"We can't go after Sharpe," Jay said flatly. "That's the opposite of what we should do. The only way we're going to make it out of this alive—"

"Is with Sharpe dead. And we can't go home until he is."

"All right, just take a deep breath." Jay held up his hands. "Let's take a time out for now, we can talk about this when you're—"

"I won't be able to breathe, not until we're all back together safe. And that will never happen while *Sharpe* is breathing." With that, they turned and walked out the door, sounds of their hooves receding on the metal floor.

After they were alone, Jay and Stefanos looked at each other again, exhausted in several ways. Stefanos sunk down to sit on the ground, leaning his back against the wall.

Then Jay sighed and flopped down beside him much faster, laying his arms across his knees and letting his forehead drop onto them. "I hate this. We never used to fight like this. Now it's all we do."

"We're all stretched to our limits. Eventually we're bound to snap." Stefanos gave a tired nod. "Wouldn't really call it a fight, though."

"Fight, drama, breakdown, blue screen, system malfunction. What the hell happened to us?"

"Parole. The collapse. Tartarus. Ash. Regan. Zilch. Sharpe." He counted off on his metal hand, extending a corkscrew and switchblade when he ran out of fingers.

"Okay, so there've been a few... developments. But you know, back before all this started? I dunno, I thought we were heading some direction. A good one. We get hitched," he bumped Stefanos with one elbow without looking up. "And for a while everything just seemed—good? Like, actually good, not just Parole good."

"I know what you mean."

"And there was me and Regan, obviously," Jay continued. "Him and Rowan and Zilch, also obviously. And you and me, and—it's like everyone was just clicking. Rowan and us, even. Especially leading up to everything."

"But then 'everything' happened," Stefanos said gently, firmly, simply.

Jay was quiet for a second. "We were going to be something. All of us, in different ways. I don't even know what, but something good. I was just starting to think we had a chance."

"So was I. Even a month ago, I would have agreed. I know Rowan would've."

"I hate it when Parole lets you think you have a chance."

"We might again. But now's not the time."

"It'll never be the right time." Jay looked up, eyes haunted and fatigued. "Not while it feels like we're running out of it. Never mind. You okay to move?"

"No, gimme a minute. Or thirty." Stefanos shut his eyes for a moment and took in another deep, whirring breath. They rested together for a few moments. The only thing rarer than loud outbursts was uninterrupted quiet.

Jay wasn't good at keeping quiet for long. Soon he couldn't stand it. "We're a mess."

"Grief doesn't make sense," Stefanos said quietly. "You see how close to the edge we all are. Everywhere you look is a worst-case scenario. A sign of another hit coming. But if anyone can find a way out, it's you, CyborJ."

"Sure. Yeah. You meant what you said?" Jay asked, voice uncharacteristically tentative.

"What?" Stefanos laid his warm hand on Jay's back and felt him take a deep breath beneath it.

"You'll really be okay? I mean, all that crap in your limbs, it has to be torture."

"An inconvenience. Living in Parole under Turret's boot, that was torture. Danae locked up in a cage—more torture." He started counting off on his mechanical hand again. "Working for SkEye to stay close to her, keeping my head down and mouth shut while Turret lays waste to my home city and uses my baby sister to make bombs. Transitioning in the middle of all that. I did it, but not because they made it easy. Never knowing if I'd survive long enough to know what it was like, living as the man I was meant to be—or at least die as myself. That's torture. This is life."

"Just because it's life doesn't mean it's a good life."

"It's exactly the life I want. I can get by without futuristic cyborg parts. Did fine with plain old prosthetics before Danae figured out how to work her magic. If these break down, that's all they'd be. Still work, just no fancy upgrades. And I've been in...'transition maintenance mode' for years, believe me, the hard part is over." He looked over with a smile. "You're just spoiled after living with a man with a Swiss Army knife hand."

"I do like to be prepared." Jay smiled back, but not for long. "But you really do intend to survive? No redemption, no heroics, no needs-of-the-many-outweigh-the-needs-of-the-few...nothing like that?"

"Do I intend to survive? No." He felt Jay tense beside him. "Not just survive. I intend to live. I've had more second chances and more miracles than most men could ever dream of. I'm exactly the man I was meant to be and I'm exactly where I want to be. I'm working to protect that, not throw it away." He smiled. "Contrary to popular perception...I'm the happiest man I know. That means I'll fight the hardest."

Jay let out a sigh and lifted his head enough to give Stefanos a kiss and sank back against his broad chest, listening. Stefanos didn't have a heartbeat anymore; instead there was the steady, constant whir of life-sustaining valves.

"Good. I kind of like having you around."

☆

Aliyah stared at the bottom of her empty coffee cup but made no move to refill it. "Lamb, which do you think is more dangerous? Tartarus, or the ghosts inside it?"

"Um... I think both of them are good things to avoid." Rowan squinted in the last of the sun as it dipped beyond the horizon. Night came on fast and cold here but they still had a warm thermos and strong coffee. They'd go inside when they could see their breath. "And they usually go together, so if you avoid one, you're mostly safe from both."

"Mm, that wasn't really an answer. But it was very sensible. Then let me add something else to the equation. Which is more dangerous? Tartarus, the ghosts, or Major David Turret?"

"Sharpe," Rowan said without a moment's thought, then took another sip of their own coffee, hands wrapped firmly around the cup to absorb its warmth.

"That was quick!" Aliyah laughed. "No deliberation at all, no weighing the–"

"Don't have to. It's Sharpe."

"Well, all right, one last puzzle. Is 'dangerous' and 'evil' always the same thing?"

Now Rowan hesitated, before setting down their cup and looking up at her. "You're having second thoughts about all of this, aren't you?"

"More like third. Us, working with Turret, in any capacity, ever? Honestly, has the world gone even more mad?" She rustled her feathers in an agitated sort of way, then took a slow breath to settle them back down. "Believe me, when Shiloh started asking me why we were going along with all this, I was hard-pressed to answer. Wasn't going to let on, of course, but xie's really got a point–why is that–that *man* so eager to see this whole thing blocked off?"

"Well, I want to see it blocked off because it's a virulent toxic wasteland and it's spreading–"

"Oh, of course that's why *you* want that, because you're a good and decent person, but Turret is neither! So what's he after? What's he hiding? He's *always* hiding something, and he *never* wants what's best for us or anyone else, so if we seem to be heading in the same direction, we'd better check for extremely certain that we're not headed straight off a cliff!"

"Agreed. One-hundred percent." Now Rowan looked up at her with a smile, though it wasn't a fully confident one. They reached out to smooth down a ruffled feather. "Not all of us have wings."

Aliyah sighed and leaned forward against the metal railing, wings settling down to lie flatter across her back under Rowan's hand. "I've got arms, they're good for catching," she murmured. "Not many cliffs out here anyway. Still, Shiloh's right about one thing. Can't shake the feeling that there's more to these shady specters than meets the eye."

"And you're starting to think we're going about this the wrong way?"

"I don't know." She rested her chin on her arms and stared out at the horizon, eyes tracing the jagged shape of a distant mountain range that grew hazy and indistinct in the gathering dark. "I don't know what I think."

"Well, I think you've never steered us wrong before," Rowan said, smiling as her feathers calmed further from their voice as well as their hand. "And no matter which way you take us, everyone on this ship is right behind you."

"That's exactly what I'm afraid of..." Aliyah's eyes narrowed and she pushed herself upright, rocking back on her heels. "Ah. Would you look at that," she said as if she were making a mildly amusing observation. She pointed to where a thick layer of what looked like very low clouds gathered on the horizon, heavy and dark. "Tartarus decided to change 'round on us again."

"Can we go around?" Rowan's voice was tight, sounding like it came from deep in their chest, as if the temperature had dropped below freezing even faster than usual and they were struggling to keep warm. "I know I don't need to remind you, but… no shields."

"And no time." She didn't look over, but her once-light, conversational tone dropped until it was nearly as low as Rowan's. "Next beacon's a straight shot dead ahead. Altering course would add another day at least."

"So we're heading straight through." Rowan stared at the oncoming wall of vapor so thick it blocked out the stars. "Had to say dead ahead, didn't you?"

"Thought I'd say it so nobody else had to." She sighed, a visible puff in the chilly air, but neither of them moved from their spot.

Cup and metal thermos clinking together as their hands shook, Rowan poured them both the last of the coffee.

CHAPTER 14

Ghosts in the Machine

THREE A.M. SILENCE STRETCHED OVER THE DARK EXPANSE AND THE SHIP RAN QUIETLY THROUGH the night. Except for a small room packed with too many computers and not enough answers. Inside, screens glowed bright and everything vibrated as Jay stomped on a floor pedal. Both the volume and bass pounding out of the nearby speakers increased and so did the tempo of his keystrokes. Soon they were more driving than any rock rhythm, almost frantic. Perfect.

CyborJ was brilliant 24/7, but some hours contained more brilliance than others. True works of genius were reserved for three A.M. Even in Parole, with its weakened sunlight thanks to the barrier and smog. Even with the windows blacked out and no natural light anywhere near. And even out here in the wide

open space and blazing Tartarus sun, his circadian biorhythms knew the truth. He didn't get going until now. And then he couldn't quit. The habit was too ingrained.

Runtime started at three a.m. Or that's how it was supposed to go.

"Can't work under these conditions," he murmured, breaking his typing groove with one hand to rub a sore eye. "Awful. Totally unacceptable."

Eye-burn from too-bright screens wasn't the problem. That came with the job description. (Along with public adoration—for his alter-ego, at least—and the satisfaction of occasionally triumphing over evil.) But he needed familiar screens. His screens.

"Smooth, shiny, sleek Radiance crap. Oh, look at me, somebody mass-produced me and a billion like me with my spiffy chrome trim and I'm definitely not gonna spy on you while you sleep or anything!" He leaned back in the chair—not his chair, this thing was hell on his back no matter what position he contorted into. "Probably built right in to be impossible to open on these things, freaking disc probably senses I'm trying to get it open with a... key that it hates." He was too tired for clever comparisons.

"She'd do that, though. Totally would. I know you know what I'm talking about here." He swung the chair around, turning to look down at the floor, as if expecting to see a small animal sitting by his foot. There wasn't. Confused, he was almost about to look further, when he stopped. All the energy and even the frustration slipped from his face.

"Oh. Ha. Yeah..." Jay rubbed at the headache building in his temples and let his head fall forward until his chin was almost touching his chest. "Figures, I finally get out here but everything I need's stuck back in that hole in the ground. Actual flaming hole. I should just call it quits right now, but... No. No, no, no, is CyborJ a quitter? No, he's—"

A sudden blue light flashed against his closed eyelids. Jay opened his eyes with a start, holding his hands up as if touching anything might make it explode. He couldn't see anything different about the screen or room in front of him but something had definitely happened.

"IC-A-RUS," said a voice from behind him. It wasn't human. But without even looking, Jay knew the voice at once.

Jay froze, afraid he'd been hearing things, afraid to turn around and find nothing again, afraid of raised hopes followed by disappointment. He had to be sure. "Seven?"

Something half-furry, half-shiny jumped into his lap and Jay almost collapsed with joy and overwhelming relief. "AF-FIR-MA-TIVE."

Jay had never programmed his cat to exclusively meow or deleted her leftover robotically-spoken responses. Or even let Danae make her 'final adjustments' before taking Seven home. Her partly-unfinished long Himalayan coat with its occasional bare-metal spots were original and unchanged. He'd never felt the need to 'upgrade'; Seven was perfect the way she was. She did everything she was supposed to: provided extra signal masking when he was on a dangerous job, swamped SkEye sensors with garbage data to cover his movements, ran constant searches for content relevant to his activities, and acted as her own wi-fi hub. In all their joint operations, Jay had only come up against a couple security protocols beyond his ability to bypass. He'd never met one that could keep Seven out.

At an unprecedented loss for words, Jay hugged his fluffy assistant, therapy animal, and best friend close to his chest, burying his face in her soft fur. She purred up a storm on anti-anxiety frequency #4, so loudly she sounded like a tiny motor. If it were possible, Jay would have purred back. It took several minutes for him to do anything but pet her fur, confirm it was really her and really here and he wasn't dreaming—and make very emotional noises that didn't begin to be coherent. Despite the fact that she was being held in a most undignified manner and the top of her head was now damp, Seven continued to purr and rub her head against Jay's wet face.

"How did you get here?" he asked when he finally remembered how words worked. "How are you even—you can't just beam in out of nowhere! Someone must have zapped you here with one of those mini-transporter things. *Celeste?*" Jay turned his chair around now but aside from him and Seven, the room was empty. Still, he felt prickles on the back of his neck. "Celeste, this was you, wasn't it? Hello?"

He looked down as Seven hopped off his lap and onto the keyboard. It was almost an ordinary cat move but, like her human, Seven's attention was immediately absorbed by the screen and the locked disk. She sniffed at the encryption display, then at Jay's lines and lines of failed attempts to unlock it, as if examining it for errors.

"If you think you can do better," Jay said, scratching down her back to the base of her tail. Now that she was back, he couldn't stop petting her soft fur and smooth metal patches. Robot cats enjoyed this just as much as their organic counterparts and she arched up against his hand, fluffy tail curling up over her back. "Which I know you can—be my guest. Decrypt that thing! Engage!"

Hearing her command-execute word, Seven bumped the monitor with the metal patch on the top of her head, rubbing her face against the corner.

The lock screen instantly disappeared. The screen went entirely black, suddenly plunging the room into darkness. Jay just had time to let out a startled noise at the empty screen before something filled it again. A word appeared, flashing in huge, bright white font that lit up the dark room like a lightning strike every second.

I C A R U S

I C A R U S

I C A R U S

Just as fast, the word was gone and the screen changed again. Several windows appeared. Security bypassed, disk accessed, secrets revealed.

"Holy..." Jay whispered. "Thank you, Celeste. And thank you, Seven."

She didn't reply except to bump her head against his hand, which, although still engrossed in the new, finally open disk contents, he automatically started petting. "Okay, let's do this."

Jay took his hand back, cracked his knuckles and dove in. Detailed diagrams. Elaborate plans. Blueprints. Lines of figures and labels and explanations and steps. His eyes—suddenly wide awake—traveled over every inch of the information he'd poured hours of sweat and tears into unlocking. But it wasn't immediately obvious what all this actually was. Most of it looked like complicated formulas Maureen, or someone else who wasn't Jay, would easily understand. He'd need a week to get through it. From what he could tell from this first peek, it all looked geared toward building something. One huge device, made of all the different, confusing pieces put together.

When he was done he leaned back in his chair and put his arms behind his head. "I don't know what any of this means," he said to Seven, one of the only beings in the universe who would ever hear him admit this. It felt good not to be talking to himself anymore. "But someone will."

"NEW-MES-SAGE," Seven replied.

"Huh?" Jay looked back up at the screen where a popup box alerted him that he had an unopened message with two files inside, one audio, one text. It was the first time he'd seen anything like it on the ship's computers; nobody knew to send anything to him here and, even if they had, the communication breakdown from Parole would have kept it from being delivered. "Is this from you? I mean, did you bring this with you?"

"Mreh," Seven said, voice actually resembling a cat's meow this time, as it usually did when she didn't have a set verbal response. She stared up at him, bright green eyes round and unblinking.

"Okay. Let's do this again." Holding his breath, Jay opened the text file. "Come on, Celeste, tell me something good."

It wasn't from her. Or anyone he expected to hear from, not in a million years. But he did know who sent it, from the very first line.

"J—

The water's clear now. But I'm still in too deep to come up for air.
Sorry I had to disappear. I'm too good at that.
I promise I'll resurface. But not until I find what we were looking for.
I'm almost there. YOU WERE RIGHT. I wish you were here to see it.
I'll find your answers, then I'll find you.
Someone once told me there was enough air. They were right.
Keep breathing, J. See you soon.

Love, R."

Jay stared at the message for a long time, face betraying nothing, even to Seven. He didn't even respond when she nudged his hand. When he finally spoke, it wasn't to her. "It's not very anonymous if you use your actual initial, and sign it 'love.' You dork lizard."

"Mah," Seven seemed to agree.

"Exactly." Jay pulled Seven into his lap as she resumed purring, shutting his eyes just as they began to sting again. It was getting hard to read the message anyway. "He's a wreck without me."

☆

Ten years ago, even in dreams, Parole's skyline at night had a postcard-from-a-distance beauty, but nobody would call it unusual. Lights shone from buildings, head-and-taillights, strung across bridges like strings on a Christmas tree. But the city wasn't calm. The roads and sidewalks were packed, skies filled with the thrums of helicopters, darkness cut by flashing blue and red. Sirens. People running. Then it wasn't dark anymore.

The barrier appeared in an instant, like a bolt of lightning. But instead of going out like lightning's transient flash, it stayed. The glowing, iridescent dome encapsulated the entire city without ceremony or warning. One moment, people in Parole could look up and see the sky, the next moment they couldn't. Screams and crashes from the city below rose to a crescendo.

"I hate this dream," Indra murmured, but he made himself look anyway.

"Just wait it out," Annie said, heavy boots scuffing at the ground like she wanted to run. "It'll be over soon."

Time passed in a heartbeat, a jerky, disjointed time-lapse. A few seconds for them, a week for Parole. The barrier held—until it didn't. It disappeared in a blinding flare, like a giant strobe light overloading and burning out. The sky was clear, the moon and stars bright once more.

"Icarus," Shiloh whispered. "I remember everything flashed really bright, then so dark I couldn't see where we were going. My mom picked me right up and started running."

"A lot of us didn't get out," Annie said grimly.

A high-pitched keening rose through the air and, in an instant, the barrier returned, more radiant and impervious than ever.

"Well, shit," Indra sighed. "Every time I hope it'll be different. Really wish I knew why we kept having this dream, maybe then we'd stop having it."

"I don't know. But there we go again," Shiloh said, nodding to a sight they all knew, one that never got any easier to watch, or on some level, believe. "Mom kept saying don't look back, we keep running and don't look back...but how do you not look back at something like that?"

"You can't," Annie said just above a mumble. "People always look back, no matter what you're running from. You have to."

Ten years hadn't changed Dr. Maureen Cole a great deal, aside from the white Radiance uniform she wore now, along with a look of mingled fear and determination. She still carried Shiloh, a small, chubby-cheeked nine-year-old, who buried xir face in her shoulder as panicked crowds rushed past. Just as predicted, they and many others turned to face the barrier they'd just barely escaped, the city left behind. Shiloh slipped down out of her arms and stood on xir own but kept hold of her hand. Xie squinted at the much-too-bright energy dome without dark glasses—then xir eyes opened wide in shock.

Breaking away from xir mother's hand, Shiloh sprinted back the way they'd come. Directly toward Parole, the barrier, and two other small shapes beyond it.

"Here we go," xie said now, in the present, resigned to watching the scene unfold. "I always kinda wish this would be different too."

Shiloh's hands had been much smaller ten years ago too. Now their little palms slammed directly against the barrier without hesitation, pressing against the crackling energetic surface as easily as if it were a harmless plane of glass.

"We should have been dead from that thing." Indra almost smiled as his and Annie's younger selves cautiously reached up to touch the barrier between them and Shiloh's hands. "Or about a million other things. We really shouldn't even be alive by now, you guys know that, right?"

"No, we shouldn't." Annie stared at the wonder on her own decade-younger face. She had eyebrows then, and a head full of long hair that reached down to the small of her back. "This night. Every night since then in Parole. And then the collapse. Why did I... why did we survive when so many other people didn't?"

"I don't know," Shiloh-in-the-present said, as Maureen-in-the-past scrambled up to the strange scene a split-second later— but stopped herself from grabbing her child's small shoulders, as if afraid touching Shiloh while xie was in contact with the barrier might somehow cause xir pain. "And I don't know why this dream keeps coming back. But I think this is how they started."

"What, instead of killing us, this thing connected us?" Annie almost sounded angry at the thought, tearing her eyes away from the bright light of the barrier and the slowly building red glow behind it. Parole was catching fire and this time she wouldn't watch.

"I always figured my power was something like... siphoning," Shiloh said slowly, words difficult to find even in dreams where meaning came fast and easily. "Absorbing, releasing it in other forms, that's what I did here. I knew the barrier wouldn't hurt me. And I just wanted to get back to you so bad. But I didn't know it would link our heads together too."

"That's because you didn't," said another voice from behind them. They turned to see a boy with sad, dark eyes, floating a few inches off the ground. "I did."

"I knew it." Indra grinned up at Gabriel but his smile soon faded. He was even more transparent than the night of the collapse. Stars shone right through his face, as if he wasn't entirely solid, semi-opaque as the barrier but nowhere near as deadly. "What's—"

"Shiloh was right," Gabriel said before he could ask the obvious question, looking over at xir quickly. He seemed almost embarrassed by his transparent appearance or at least had more to say first. "Xie saved everyone's lives ten years ago. But xie couldn't have joined them. I made a—a chain linking us all together. And back here."

"Yeah," Indra conceded with a sigh, looking back at Parole and its intensifying red-orange light. The fire was growing stronger below. "I would definitely say we're chained here."

"Gabriel, what's happening?" Shiloh immediately felt foolish for how tentative xie suddenly felt, somehow not wanting to alarm him about the fact that he was increasingly transparent. Surely he was aware of it. "It looks like you're fading away."

"It's getting harder to come here." Gabriel's brow was slightly furrowed, as if it was indeed an effort just to stay present as he was. "And I can't stay long."

"Is that why we haven't seen you in a while?" Annie spoke fast, urgency making her voice sharp. "Where have you been?"

"It's—hard to explain." Gabriel seemed to struggle with a complex or troubling subject, shrugging and shaking his head. "Just listen. I'll be here as much as I can but I might have to disappear again. But I'll come back and... even if I'm—different? I'm still me. I might look different but it's still me, remember that."

"Okay, we'll remember," Shiloh agreed, though xie had to wonder exactly how much a boy who hadn't aged in ten years, and apparently no longer had a physical body, could possibly change. "No matter what changes, we'll believe you and we'll know it's still you."

Gabriel seemed to struggle to find the right words again, or maybe whether or not to tell them something. He ended up saying nothing, simply looking frustrated and a little scared.

"We'll still be your friends," Shiloh assured him. That part at least xie had an easy time believing. "That hasn't changed."

"But you did," Gabriel said at last, looking down sadly into a small, red-glowing crack in the ground. With every next word he spoke, he became a little bit fainter, fading away before their eyes like stars after sunrise. "You all grew up and I didn't. I fell. Then I fell asleep. When I woke up, I was a ghost. But not a Tartarus ghost. Just a dead one."

"You're not just a ghost!" Shiloh almost surprised xirself with the strength of xir words. Almost. "And we could never forget you. Dreams or no dreams."

"You've been helping us all this time, you brought us together in the first place—you warned me about the collapse!" Annie almost shouted, every bit as sure as Shiloh with even more conviction. "If I hadn't run when you told me, I'd be dead!"

"You kept us alive, so we'll find a way to keep you alive," Indra promised. "It's okay, Gabriel, no matter what you look like when you come back, it'll be you, and..."

He was gone before Indra finished speaking, but his smile was the last thing to go.

☆

Indra woke from the dream and lurched upright, but stayed half-asleep long enough to wonder if he was still dreaming. He didn't recognize the room or the far-off engine noise. He didn't know why the floor and walls were metal or where he'd been before this. He'd woken up in enough unfamiliar rooms on his search for Parole that this wasn't entirely unusual. But it would never stop being disorienting. At least he was alone this time; nobody for him to embarrass himself in front of, 'centaur' or otherwise. And his arm was healed. He was safe. He'd gotten to the ship... called the FireRunner.

Once everything came back, Indra flopped down and tried to go back to sleep. But it was no use; lucid dreams with Annie and Shiloh (who might still be hanging out without him) left him drained and wired at the same time. Sleep wasn't happening. So he climbed out of bed and left his room without even putting on shoes.

The FireRunner was dark and quiet this late at night; it had to be around three A.M. and Indra seemed to be the only one awake. He wandered through the empty corridors, not sure if he wanted to run into someone or just needed some alone time. He did manage to make a circuit of the level without getting lost, an improvement from the past few days.

When he passed the stairwell leading deeper down into the ship and up onto the bridge, he decided to take it. He'd only gotten a glimpse of the bridge on Annie's brief tour and it might be fun to get a closer look at all the buttons and levers. Without touching, of course.

But when he reached the bridge, he stopped, staying half-hidden in the darkened stairwell entrance. The bridge wasn't empty.

Someone stood motionless on the far side, facing the large window. Jay, Indra realized. He didn't have to see his face to know. He'd seen the back of Jay's head often enough as he ran away. But he wasn't running now; he seemed deep in thought as he stared out at the starry night sky. Indra held very still, trying to decide whether to back away or take a step forward, say something, see if Shiloh's uncle would frantically avoid him even now.

"Can't sleep?" Stefanos's voice, deep but soft, came from the opposite stairwell on the other side of the bridge before Indra could say a word, or move. Indra froze. He didn't want to eavesdrop on a conversation but if he stepped away, he was sure someone would see him—and think he had been anyway. So he tried not to move or breathe too loudly.

"The lockbox is open," Jay said without turning around. "And it wasn't me."

"Really?" It came out a little louder and a lot more excited than his previous soft question. He didn't bother trying to stay quiet as he strode across the bridge. "What was on it? And what do you mean, it wasn't you?"

Jay turned; his face was drawn with exhaustion, and the circles under his eyes were deep and dark, but he was smiling. Now, Stefanos and Indra could both see that he held a cat in his arms.

"Seven!" Stefanos exclaimed, sounding as happy as he was surprised.

"Where'd she come from?"

"Celeste. Beamed her right over with one of her little teleport thingies." Jay scratched behind Seven's ears, which seemed to relax both of them. "And she did exactly what I kept saying—opened that thing in two seconds. Like it was nothing. I spent days on that thing and got zip. If you were human," his voice shifted up a little as he directed the next words to his cat. "I'd be so cheesed off at you, showing me up like that. But you're not, you're the best cat in the universe! You're—" he stopped, looking back up at Stefanos with something almost nobody ever saw on his face: embarrassment. He cleared his throat and spoke in his normal voice. "Sorry. It's been a while."

"Don't stop on my account," Stefanos chuckled. "Sure has been a while, way too long since I've seen you smile like that. You deserve it."

"I dunno." Jay shrugged, turning his attention and scratching fingers toward Seven's chin. "But I gotta say, it feels good."

Stefanos watched them for a moment, golden eyes fond. He seemed reluctant to break up their reunion and his voice was gentle when he spoke. "So, let's have it. This big important data we're all risking our lives for."

"I've never seen anything like it," Jay said, sounding awed. "The plans on that thing."

"Plans?" Stefanos raised his eyebrows, golden eyes flickering as he focused in closer on Jay's face.

"Yeah." Jay hesitated, looking troubled.

"Whatever it is doesn't leave this room," Stefanos reassured him.

"It's big. Powerful." Jay paused, eyes wide. "My sister wasn't wasting all this time, I'll give her that."

"A weapon?"

"No. Not her style. Too many of those in Parole anyway."

"Then what is it?"

"I..." Jay looked distinctly nervous for the first time since Seven had reappeared from thin air. "I'm not sure. Exactly. Maureen's designs—she was always on another level, okay? Like a whole different nerd-tier, a different language from me, like, except for the occasional shiny gadget, I work with stuff that already exists, I navigate established rules and how to get around them, but she's all about inventing stuff that doesn't exist yet, probably shouldn't even work but does, and..."

"You can't tell what it is at all?" Stefanos prodded gently after a couple seconds.

"Like I said, it's big," Jay said with certainty. "Like a huge tower. Almost looks like a beacon, but not. It's definitely gonna do something. And whatever that is, Parole must need it or everybody wouldn't be making such a big deal about this thing."

"All right," Stefanos said, voice a steady anchor for Jay to hold onto while everything else shifted and spun. "Then only one thing matters. Is it worth it?"

"It better be. No," Jay amended, eyes narrowing into a look of unwavering determination. "Maureen spent years on this. Shiloh came a thousand miles to get it here. Annie risked her life—and Ash gave his life for this. I'll *make* it worth it."

"There it is." Stefanos smiled at the fire in Jay's eyes. "That's the look that belongs on your face. I missed that. Probably as much as you missed Seven."

"Yeah..." Worry replaced Jay's conviction, as if he'd just remembered something he wished he hadn't. "This is great. This is fine, major victory here. Big win for the good guys."

"But?" Stefanos said, fixing him with gaze now that was studying, curious, instead of hopeless.

"It wasn't just Maureen's plans on the disk." Jay didn't sound excited anymore. Or determined. Or even hungry, eager to chase a new lead. He just sounded tired. "There was something for me too."

Stefanos's eyes were tinged green as they studied him, slipping into momentary, unconscious scanning mode. "The smoking gun?"

"No." He stared down at his cat for a few seconds. Her synthetic eyes didn't look back; Seven had closed them and gone into sleep mode in Jay's arms. "I was so sure when Celeste contacted me again, she'd have the most obvious, flashing neon sign—here, good buddy, let me just do you one big solid, take a load off—but..."

"But she didn't."

"No," Jay said again, looking up at Stefanos. He seemed calm, but in a way that suggested this was so overwhelming he had no idea how to react. "Regan did."

"Regan?" Stefanos's golden eyes widened and their delicate rotating parts started to move and whir, a clear sign he was surprised and thinking fast. "He's here too?"

Jay didn't say 'no' this time, just shook his head and let it drop slightly. "He sent a message. In what he probably thought was a secret code. He said..." Jay took a slow breath, in and out. "'The water's clear now.'"

"No blood?"

"No blood." But Jay didn't look very hopeful. "But he can't come back yet, because he's looking for something. And I think it's... what I thought Celeste was going to send me."

"Proof." Stefanos folded his arms, still in deep-thought rapid-eye mode. "Solid dirt on Turret? For Tartarus, Mihir, everything?"

Jay gnawed his lower lip. "He said he'd find my 'answers.' Well, there's only one answer I really want. He knows what I want, it's what we were trying to find for eight years."

"So that's where he's going. Back to Parole, after escaping?" Stefanos shook his head with a faint smile. "Regan always did do things a little differently."

"I'm not getting my hopes up," Jay said, sounding more sure of this than anything he'd said yet. "I can't. Why would he be able to find anything now, when we never could before? And that's if he gets there—he's been out in Tartarus this whole time? He might never make it back to Parole. The message might not even be from him. Could be a fake."

"You don't actually believe that."

Jay shut his eyes briefly. "No, I don't. He said 'there is enough air.'"

"It's really him..." Stefanos's voice was so quiet it barely carried across the bridge. "Regan's alive. He met up with Celeste and now he's going home. And he never stopped thinking about you, Jay, we can see that now. Everything he's doing is somehow for us."

"Sure seems that way."

"This is another major victory right here," Stefanos said, then seemed to realize Jay didn't share his optimism. "But it's not what you were hoping for. Was it?"

"Those great big plans will save Parole. Everybody wins. CyborJ's brilliant, and delivered us all from certain death once again, and everybody's happy. Or maybe I don't have to save everyone, because Regan says—basically, under the cryptic bullshit—that he's got it covered. Or something. And I'm supposed to just trust this." He stared down at the floor, eyes out of focus. Finally, he shut them. "I'm tired."

Stefanos placed two warm fingers under Jay's chin, tipping his face back up to look at him. When he opened his eyes, they looked at each other for a moment. Jay shrugged, shook his head a little, and said nothing. Stefanos held his gaze and held his cheek in the palm of his hand.

"I messed up," Jay whispered at last. "I did what I always tell everybody not to do. I got my hopes up. I should've known better. I *do* know better. And I did it anyway."

Stefanos paused. Then, as if he were making the most important decision of any of their lives, he leaned down and kissed Jay fully and fiercely on the mouth. The smaller man gave only the shortest of surprised noises before relaxing automatically into his arms. Like all their motions around each other, the kiss was natural from long years of practice. As they held each other, they seemed to believe just for a moment that nothing terrible haunted their dreams or made their waking lives a nightmare. When they finally moved apart, it wasn't fast, or far.

"I don't know how, or when," Stefanos rumbled, still gently holding the side of Jay's face. "But justice has a way of finding what it's looking for sooner or later. Just like you. Turret can run on for a long time, but his time *will* run out. Don't give up, Jay. We're not giving up on you—what's so funny?"

"You. A lot of things." Jay was smiling and it was still in a different way than Stefanos expected to see. "Uh, none of this ended up how I expected. But I also have Shiloh back. I can give xir some important answers. Which is more than I've given in years. And I have you."

"Yes you do," Stefanos promised. "You always have me."

"And you!" Jay said in a higher-pitched voice than usual. Stefanos looked confused until he realized Jay wasn't talking to him anymore. Seven had woken up after being jostled by the kiss and now looked up at her human with vaguely indignant green eyes. "And we still have Rowan, even if everything's a little messed up right now. Or a lot messed up."

"We do, and that's not all. Annie's safe and sound. Somehow, Mihir's little brother made it here of all places—and Indra's a great kid all on his own. Radio Angel's still speaking out, and someday someone will hear. Aliyah's still steering us through the storm. We've lost a lot, but not everything."

"Yeah." A smile spread across Jay's face, slow but real. "I might even have Regan."

"And he's right. You will find your answers and you won't be alone when you do. No matter what they turn out to be."

They were quiet for a while, just standing together in the very-early-morning stillness.

"I'm sure about one thing," Jay finally said.

"What's that?"

He took Stefanos's hand and ran his thumb over the wedding band he wore. "Still glad you said yes."

"And I'm glad you asked."

☆

After Stefanos left a couple minutes later, Indra emerged from the outside corridor and quietly stepped onto the bridge. Jay caught the movement out of the corner of his eye and looked up, mouth already open—then he shut it again and looked away as soon as he saw who it was.

"Uh hi," Indra said, stopping in the middle of the room and giving an awkward wave. "Please don't leave. I've been wanting to talk to you this whole time."

"I'm not going anywhere," Jay sighed, setting Seven down and pinching the bridge of his nose. She sat directly on his foot. "Here I am, you caught me. Now how much did you hear?"

"Enough to know you knew my brother." Indra gave a small, humorless laugh entirely unlike his real one. "But I didn't even need to hear anything to know that."

Jay looked up, studying him for a moment, then threw up his hands in defeat. "Fine, I'll ask: how do you know I knew your brother? We haven't even been in the same room for more than five seconds this entire trip—totally immature on my part, yes, I'll admit, and I'm sorry. I'm sorry for a lot of things, believe it or not."

"Well, there's that," Indra shrugged. "You run away every time I walk into a room. And you won't talk to me, you won't even look at me. You do the thing where you look at my face real fast, then look away, like anywhere but—there, that! You're doing it right now."

Jay stopped mid-motion, seeming to realize for the first time exactly what he was doing as Indra described it. "Okay. I might have done that. Couple times. I said I was sorry."

"You don't have to apologize." Indra shook his head, hair brushing across his shoulders. "I get it a lot. People do that when I remind them of him. I know we look a lot alike and it freaks people out. You're not doing anything my whole family hasn't done for like, years. Just a little more obviously. Never had anybody actually run away from me before."

"I don't know what I thought I was doing." Jay stared at a point on the floor. "Just that I didn't know how to have that conversation with you. Or any conversation. I guess I was hoping somehow you wouldn't notice? Until I could think of what to say?"

"Seriously?" Indra almost laughed.

"I don't know!" Jay groaned. "Listen, this isn't how I wanted to—"

"It's fine." Indra was serious again in a moment but his voice didn't shake or falter. "Forget it. We're talking now. And I want to talk more—like about what you were saying a minute ago. About proof and what really happened the night he died."

Slowly, Jay turned to face him. "I don't even know if it's true. So don't get your hopes up, okay? It's just a theory."

"Sounded like a pretty good theory to me." A very slow smile spread across Indra's face and Jay's eyes flicked away again. "Anyway, it's better than the alternative. I'd much rather believe my big brother died a hero trying to prevent a catastrophe, than for no reason at all. That's a way better story."

Jay was quiet for a moment. "Even if we find out it's not true?"

"I still have to see what he saw." Indra's eyes stung, but he didn't move an inch. "It's just gonna bug me otherwise. Don't you hate not knowing how a story ends?"

"Closure is a hell of a painkiller." Jay's shoulders dropped. "I mean, I assume."

"And I'd *really* like to know who killed him. And what we do about that."

"Now, that we can agree on."

Indra spent a few seconds deep in thought. When he spoke next, it was in a much lighter tone than before. "So, there was so much going on before, I never really told you, but I've always been a big fan of your work."

"Oh, really?" Jay looked up, raising his eyebrows and brightening somewhat as well. "Your brother tell you tales of cyber-chills and techno-thrills, or do the legends speak for themselves? They're all true, by the way. I try to live up to my own hype, but let me tell you, I do not make it easy."

Indra stared at him for a second. "I just lost a bet."

"What?"

"I thought he was making it up. I thought nobody could actually talk like that in person. But there it is." He nodded, looking pensive. "I owe Mihir ten bucks."

"So he did tell you about me," Jay sounded hesitant, as if unsure whether that was good or bad.

Indra nodded. "He said he had a friend named Cyborg. He was super smart, super cool, and knew everything about computers. Cyborg was so good he could talk to anybody in the world, open any door, find out any secret. He saved a whole lot of people in Parole. Basically a superhero. Even if he didn't have powers, when almost everybody else did. Didn't need 'em. Did it all by himself."

Indra paused to glance up at Jay, who was staring into space. "Except he had one problem. Cyborg couldn't shut up to save his life, and he had this...really funny way of talking. Mihir told me about it once—I was only, what, nine? I was nine and I didn't believe him. I thought he was making you up! I bet him ten bucks you weren't real, nobody talked like that—*sorry*, no offense—and he said okay, fine! I'll take your ten dollars, and I'll introduce you to Cyborg, and you'll hit it right off. He'll make you laugh, he'll tell you awesome stories about hacker adventures, and you'll love him, because he makes me happy too."

"That's...thanks for that. I, um. Wish we'd gotten..." Jay cleared his throat and took a moment. "Except, it's 'Cybor-Jay.' Not Cyborg. Say the hard 'G' part like 'Juh'. Jay."

"Sure," Indra nodded easily. "Like 'JIF'."

Now it was Jay's turn to stare at Indra, whose careful poker-face slowly spread into a wide grin. "You little troll, you set me up. You knew I'd take the bait, and I..." Slowly, Jay shook his head. "The resemblance really is uncanny."

"Sorry!" Indra's shoulders were shaking and this time he wasn't sobbing. "I had to. I just—I had to, ever since—I got so confused. See, Mihir never called you by your screen name, just Jay. And I only ever saw 'CyborJ' written out later, so I didn't know...I just never connected it in my head. So..." He gestured vaguely, then just shook his head, laughing some more. "Never mind. It doesn't matter. I just thought it was funny."

"And from the confusion...brilliance." Jay let out a long, contented sigh. But then, uncertainty crept back into his eyes along with ten years' worth of grief. "But was any of it true? Or was it just a setup for a punchline?"

"It's all true." Indra wasn't laughing anymore, but he wasn't in pain either. "Some things you don't joke about. But some things you do. Maybe the most important things."

"Easier said than done," Jay said quietly. "And coming from me, that should say something."

"I just don't think he'd want you to feel nothing but pain when you thought about him, you know? That's the opposite of what he'd want." A faint, genuine smile crossed his face. "When I was a kid, and Parole first—happened? I think my brother knew it was about to get bad. But he wanted me to have some good things to hang onto too. He gave me my first deck of cards. He always tried to make sure I felt safe. And laugh when we could. So...I dunno, that's just something I try to tell myself, anyway. Feeling good and happy is a way of keeping his memory alive too. He'd be cool with that. It's okay to laugh."

Jay smiled.

CHAPTER 15

The Eye of the Storm

ROWAN LAY IN A HAMMOCK THAT SWAYED GENTLY BACK AND FORTH. ABOVE WAS A HUGE, THICK tree limb covered in moss and, past that, the softly glowing lights. This tiny oasis of peace could have been a dreamy scene from the outside world they'd left behind long ago. But the hum of the ship's engines mingled with the faint howling of Tartarus' rising winds picking up outside.

"Should reach the next beacon soon." Above, leaning against the huge, moss-cushioned trunk, Aliyah spread out one wing and separated its long, gleaming pinions one by one, carefully running her fingers down each smooth feather and ensuring none had bent or, worse, broken. Even a single bit of

moment, an off-kilter turn could be deadly.

"What?" Rowan said after several seconds.

"I said," Aliyah leaned forward a bit to peer down at them. "Next beacon coming up quick. Feeling up to it today or shall we cool our heels here for a bit, make sure we're all at our sharpest?"

Even if Rowan was looking up toward her, they clearly weren't in the present. They stared past Aliyah, past the tree and flower-lights, past the dark ceiling. After another moment of silence, Rowan gave their head a little shake, large horns bumping against the hammock sides. "What?"

"Nothing," Aliyah sighed and went back to straightening out her wing. "Question answered."

"I'm sorry." Rowan sat up a little, and now they looked her in the eye. "I was somewhere else. But I'll be fine when we get to the next beacon, really. Today's fine."

"You sure?" She fixed them with an appraising stare. "I'd much rather wait and go out fresh and focused than rush out before we're ready."

"I'll be focused. It's good for me to focus on something and stay in the moment. Adrenaline's good for that."

"I'll give you that one. And I suppose nothing gets the adrenaline pumping like running straight up a very high tower. Still..."

"I'm fine. Really. I'll be clear and alert and we'll get it done. Everything else stays behind on the ship." They gave a rueful smile and sank back down. "It'll be there when I get back."

"It's all right to not be fine," Aliyah said in a level tone after a few seconds of quiet. "We've got a job to do, yes, but that doesn't mean you have to keep it all in."

Rowan didn't reply.

"It's all right to say nothing at all," she continued. "Sometimes words fail. But if you ever find the words, I'm listening."

Still no response. Aliyah wasn't sure whether she'd gone too far or not enough. She didn't know what to make of that either. Rowan had never been hard for her to read, and vice-versa.

"I know our circle seems frighteningly small at the moment," she said, trying one more cautious advance. "But it's not gone. You do have people still right here with you. Me, for instance. Annie." She watched Rowan's face as she spoke, but they remained unusually enigmatic. "Jay, Stefanos."

"I know," they said at last, and their voice was quiet but controlled instead of the tight near-sob she expected. "I haven't forgotten you. Or them. But times change. We've all changed too. Especially Jay and Stefanos—and me. My circle was always small, but they're in it. Regan, Zilch, you... and them. That should say something."

"It certainly does. You've been in firmly established domestic bliss with two of that circle for eight years... and then there's us." Aliyah shot them a grin. "I'm sure the remaining two would be honored to know they're in such good company."

"They know." Rowan's voice was much more short, flat, and low than she expected. "Or knew, at least. It doesn't matter anymore. Not after all this."

"One could argue that times like these are precisely when strengthening the bonds of love and togetherness and all is most important. One does, in fact."

Rowan shook their head, horns rustling against the hammock fabric. "Maybe if things were different. But so much has changed, it's like we're different people. I don't recognize any of us."

"Some things never change. They still love you. They still want you to be happy."

"I know. And I miss that—sometimes I actually miss *them*. Because now it's like we're all in the same room, but miles apart. And I can't even think about..." Rowan did seem to be thinking hard, however, brow furrowing as it did whenever they searched for an elusive perfect word. "I can't believe Jay really thinks Regan's a traitor."

"I don't think he does either. I believe he's just planning for every possible worst-case scenario, as he is most prone to doing even in the best of times."

"I know—if he really thought that, I'd..." They stopped, and even she had trouble reading their expression. For a moment they seemed frozen in place, then shook it off, and continued. "I don't know what I'd do. But that's not the point. I just never thought I'd hear him say that."

"A lot of things happened we didn't plan. We knew the collapse was coming but that was about it. Everything else, we're making up as we go along."

Rowan was quiet for a few seconds, finally speaking in slow, measured words. "When Parole collapsed, it felt like everything else collapsed with it. Including whatever we had. Or started. Or might have been. We're just not who we were."

"All right." Aliyah held up her hands, wings spreading slightly as well. "You all know yourselves best, so I'll back off. Maybe it's a captain thing, wanting to sort out her crew, smooth and streamline. I just hate seeing you struggle like this, especially when you used to actually prop each other up, like a three-legged stool."

"Well, that's the other thing." Rowan gave a soft, humorless, exhausted laugh. "I did have exactly that. Regan and Zilch. They are always on my mind—

the absence of them. They're missing stool legs. Until they're safe and I'm not falling over every second, I'll never be able to think about anything else."

"And that I do understand." Aliyah gave an apologetic smile, though she felt about exhausted as Rowan looked. "Triage. Take care of immediate injuries, conserve your energy and dedicate it to the most pressing need, focus on what you can save, decide what to let go. Been a while since EMT training, but it comes back."

Rowan sucked in a breath, looking up at the illusion of the starry night sky through eyes that blurred and stung. "I'm so glad you're here."

"Some nights I'm not very glad to be here," she said wearily. "I'd much prefer a private beach or five-star hotel, a lovely spa, anywhere without the constant looming threat of death. This particular vacation spot gets three stars at best. There's a terrifying military force outside and a toxic wasteland devouring the world! Unacceptable. Yes, I have several complaints, now that I think about it."

"Our sincere apologies, Ma'am." Rowan sniffed, but they were smiling.

"The company, however, gets me much closer to 'glad'." Satisfied with the state of her wings, Aliyah sighed and leaned back against the tree, arms behind her head. "Though I still have some grievances for the front desk."

"Listening and ready."

"Well, let's see. Workplace environment is creatively and personally fulfilling, I suppose—but safety standards are abysmal." Her voice dropped. "Has failed to meet professional and personal expectations. I signed on for a continued happy life with a noisy, chaotic, but loving family, parents, sister, cousins, aunties, several little tiny sprouts running about. Life interrupted by unforeseen circumstances in form of hellish dystopia. Most dissatisfied. Are you getting all this?"

"Taking detailed mental notes, Ma'am. Anything we can do to improve your stay?"

She grinned and her voice brightened again. "Well, let's see. They say 'a good woman is hard to find'—and I don't think that's true, not in the slightest, have you seen women lately? Marvelous. But I haven't seen any, not out here in this blasted place. I suppose she is hard to find, at that."

Rowan actually laughed. "A good woman? No, she really isn't. You're so much braver than I am—or you're better at hiding it."

"That's rich. I'm scared to death every minute."

"But you do it anyway." When Rowan smiled at her, it was much more tired than happy.

"Oh, do not turn the captain's big chair into a pedestal! Much too lonely up there. Listen, the moment I step on the bridge I'm supposed to be detached and make snap decisions with my head, based on logic and strategy, but it doesn't work that way. The heart rules as well. If I recognize that, it makes it a little easier to actually make good decisions instead of awful ones."

"I'm glad you told me. You don't have to be bulletproof all the time, Aliyah."

"Have to be if the bridge is yours, or the bridge falls down," she sighed. "Doesn't help anyone if I burst into tears at the drop of a hat, much as I'd like to some days."

"You can if you need to. Everybody does sometimes."

She looked over at them, mouth open, then seemed to think better of what she'd been about to say. Her next words were in a softer tone than her last. "It's always easier to say that to someone else, isn't it?"

"I guess so." Rowan wasn't looking at her. Or listening anymore, their vacant expression and murmured reply would suggest.

"We just have to complete this one mission," Aliyah reaffirmed, more to herself than Rowan. "This one dreadful, ghastly, most distressing mission. Nothing lasts forever, not even storms—and it's a good thing. I've had it with this vacation too, just as much as you have. Time to get back home where we belong."

"Home..." Rowan paused for a few seconds. Then there came a loud thump as they rolled out of the hammock and dropped down into the grass below.

"Yes, home." Aliyah shot them a nonplussed look. "I thought you'd be jumping to get back there, start putting our lives back in order."

"Home's not there anymore. The library burned to the ground, like the rest of Parole. But even if it were still there it wouldn't be home without Regan, or Zilch, or..." They'd begun to pace around in a small circle, but now they stopped and looked back at Aliyah. "No, I'm not just devastated that it's gone. I am, of course, but it just doesn't make sense!"

"You and Jay, same coin, I swear, not even different sides..." Aliyah murmured under her breath, then raised her voice. "This has to do with Regan's disappearing act, I'm guessing?"

"He barely left the library except for Runtime! And now he left Parole? He's out here somewhere, alone, in a world that hates—no, in a world that doesn't even know who or what he is!"

"Yes. It's terrible. Doesn't bear thinking about," Aliyah said in a tone that clearly suggested she tried not to. She shut her eyes and wondered when the last good night's sleep she—or any of them—had enjoyed.

"It's not just terrible, it's impossible!" Rowan's aggravated noise indicated just as clearly that they could do nothing but think. "I wouldn't believe it if I hadn't seen him leave on that recording! Because he wouldn't do it! Not if he was acting of his own free will!"

"Even an agoraphobe will leave the house if that house catches fire," Aliyah said slowly and studiedly patient. "And Parole's been on fire for some time."

"No. Not Regan. Not without a note or a sign or just—something explaining at least part of what he was doing! He wouldn't just disappear, with nothing, not if it was his choice! Or if he had any other choice! Ever!"

Aliyah stared at the dark ceiling for a moment, then shook her head and sighed. "All right, I'll bite. You sound quite sure of that, much more than I would be in your sh... hooves. Why?"

"Because that's not how his mind works. He gets scared if you do something without telling him and then without telling him why. He doesn't like being kept in the dark. So I don't do that, nobody who cares about him does that, we always tell him what's going on, so he knows we're safe and he's safe. And he does the same for us, not because we need it, but because that's what we do for him. If someone left him like that, he'd..." Rowan stopped. When they didn't continue, Aliyah looked over to see them staring into space, with no apparent intent to go on.

"You know him pretty well," she said, annoyance gone. Now she tried to smile and had some success. "Understatement, I suppose."

"Of course I do." Rowan still wasn't looking at her. Even if they had, she doubted they'd see her. "Better than myself, some days. Especially these days. That's the other reason none of this makes sense. He'd never leave... It would be like me doing this to you, Aliyah—well," now they looked at her, some of the pain dropping off their face, replaced with something near embarrassment.

"Not exactly like—Queerplatonic and romantic relationships, they're just—I'm not saying one's more or less important, that's not it at all, they're just different, they're on a different frequency, almost, and Regan was my first-"

"Oh my—Rowan, stop!" Aliyah almost laughed, then turned it into a very unconvincing cough. "We've been over this. Several times. In any case, you don't need to explain any intricacies while you're mopping your heart up off the floor."

"Okay, I just don't want you to think..." They sighed, words failing. "You're important to me."

"I believe we've been over that before too."

"Regan's just..."

Her smile turned a little wry. "You love us both, but you want to kiss his fool face and marry him under the stars while you shake him for putting you through this mess."

"Not even shake him. Just ask him why. I don't like being in the dark any more than Regan does. Not when it's him that's in danger." They sank back down onto their spot on the tree root. "Kiss him though, yes. Hold him, wrap both of us up, warm and tight, so his eyes are the last thing I see as we fall asleep. Marry..."

When they didn't continue, Aliyah looked over with a quick smile. "Well, now you've got my attention. You've actually been thinking about it?"

But Rowan only met her eyes briefly and without any answering excitement. "No. Not even when we were all... no, we weren't."

"Why not? Parole doesn't give a fig. Not about most things but it *really* doesn't about who marries whom, or in what combination. Ask anybody to name a highlight of the past ten years, nine out of ten'll agree—Evelyn, Rose, and Danae tying the knot and the concert-party thereafter. There's a few good women right there." She gave her wings a little flutter as if she were shaking off the temporary glow of rare, good Parole memories. "It's really none of my business and I don't know the first thing. But I know you. And I know how you are with Regan and Zilch. Some things do make sense."

Rowan seemed to relax as she spoke, warmed by thoughts of home and the people who survived its fires every day. Now they did try to return her smile, but it faded quickly. "You know, I've been trying to remember the last thing I said to Regan? Or what he said to me? I can't. Zilch either."

"That had to be over a month ago." It was hard to state such a sad fact in a reasonable, reassuring tone, but Aliyah managed it.

"Regan was six weeks tomorrow." Rowan abandoned their botched attempt at optimistic agreement and resumed staring into space. That seemed to come a lot more naturally. "I can't remember if I told him to be careful going out that night. Or kissed him goodbye."

"Well, I wasn't there, but knowing the two of you, I can make an educated guess."

"So can I," Rowan conceded. "And I hope we're right. It's just... I can remember the smallest, most random details–how he shakes out his frill and scratches under it a certain way and, like clockwork the next day, he'll start shedding scales. But I can't remember if I told him I loved him."

"He knows," Aliyah said firmly. "Even if you didn't tell him that night. You didn't have to."

"And I can't even remember," they continued, as if they hadn't heard. Their voice grew increasingly bitter with every word. "Exactly where I last saw Zilch. Because by then it was chaos. We were all in such a panic, in and out... looking for Regan. I have no idea what I said to them. Or what they said. Or when they were gone. And then—the collapse. We were gone. Even if they came home… I was gone."

"Listen." Aliyah flared her wings in a fast *whoosh* and dropped down to a lower branch to look them more closely in the eye. "What Regan knows, Zilch knows, and they know you'd go through Hell and back for them—oh! Look! Look at what we're doing right now, us sailing across Tartarus as we speak. And if our luck holds and all goes as planned, you'll get to tell them again."

"The plan was to forget them," Rowan said, more pensive than downcast. "We agreed on that eight years ago. Even in a city that doesn't exist, we don't exist. And if one or more of us disappears… whoever's left moves on. The others were never here."

"Rowan."

They looked over into her doubtful, concerned face and shrugged. "It was the safest way. You have to understand what their—our lives were like. They were constantly being hunted by SkEye—"

"You think I don't know that?" She almost laughed. "You don't need to explain this to me. It's not that I don't understand, it's that I think it's utter nonsense. You don't just cut off part of your life like that and move on like nothing happened."

"You do if you want to survive," Rowan said slowly, patiently, as if it were something they'd repeated and rationalized hundreds of times, if not more. "And we were all more valuable to Parole alive than dead. And if we wanted to stay alive, we needed to stay secret. So no significant connections, no evidence that could be used against anyone, no… nothing. We loved… we love each other. But we still had to plan for the worst."

"And what's that they say about best-laid plans?" Aliyah sighed, shaking her head and turning back to her now re-mussed feathers. She'd have to start again, but it was worth it. There was nothing like a good wing-flap for emphasizing a point. "You can plan all you want, but it doesn't work like that, does it?"

"No. It doesn't. I can't just forget them." The change in their voice was so clear it made Aliyah turn and look right back. Rowan sounded hard, determined, as if they'd just come to the most important conclusion of their life. "So I won't."

"Well, good." She nodded, a little bemused but pleased. "Fighting for the ones we love can only help us win the day and save Parole."

"No," Rowan said again, sounding just as resolved but further away. "Not Parole. I can't go back. Not without Regan. And not without Zilch's heart."

"You can't save everyone. I can't save everyone. Saving myself is hard enough." Aliyah spoke every word deliberately, as if trying to imprint them on her own heart as well. "We try. We do the best we can, we keep as many alive as possible, and we love them with all our hearts. And when we lose them, we carry on—"

"Maybe we can't save everyone. But we can save some of them. And I have to at least try-"

"Rowan, this is a war." Her voice was hard, left no room for argument. "A secret one, a quiet one, but it is! And in a war, you have to look at the entire map. Focus our attention where we can do the most good."

"I know!" Rowan almost shouted. "I know we have to focus on the greater good, Parole, thousands of people, the mission, the beacons, Tartarus, all of it. But I can't—I don't want to see the bigger picture if Regan and Zilch aren't part of it!" Rowan stopped to catch their breath; suddenly it seemed like they'd just made a breakneck sprint that left them exhausted.

"I know it's hard." Aliyah kept her voice level and didn't let herself echo Rowan's increasing desperation, but this was getting harder too. Especially after everything she'd just said about remembering, honoring the past. She believed it wholeheartedly—but it was the future that worried her now. "But we simply must stay objective. We knew this day would come, when we'd be scattered to the winds, forced to choose between finding one another or moving forward. There's only one way we survive this, and it's by focusing on the mission and getting it done. If we don't, it won't matter if we're together or not. There'll be no together. There'll be nothing left at all."

"I have nothing left if they're gone," Rowan said, every bit as unyielding. But there was a plea in their voice instead of steel. "I'll forget them when they're really gone, but right now I don't know that for sure, they could still come back."

"Yes they could," Aliyah said quietly. "A lot of things could happen. But we need to—"

"They're not gone yet," Rowan insisted. "And I can't give up on them until they are. Not while I'm still here." Now their eyes narrowed, as if they'd just realized something even worse. "Or while he is."

"Sharpe."

Rowan didn't answer. Instead they slowly nodded, fear and pain in their face slowly transforming into a cold fury Aliyah couldn't remember ever seeing before. She never wanted to see it again, either. It didn't look right on their face.

"Which is it?" she asked at last.

"What?" Rowan was lost in a reverie again, a much darker one than before.

"Which is more important? Finding Regan and Zilch's heart, or taking Sharpe down?"

"I... both. We have to find them, and we have to kill him. Neither one are even options."

"Suppose you could only pick one. What's the priority—rescue or revenge?"

Rowan's eyes widened, then narrowed again. "Would it change anything? Would you say yes to either one, even if I was being, what—one hundred percent objective? Fine," they continued before she could answer. "Objectively, Sharpe is a... danger that has to be addressed. And Zilch and Regan are allies we have to recover. That's all true."

Aliyah said nothing.

"So if we take emotion out of the equation, why doesn't it add up?" Desperation came back into Rowan's voice immediately. "We've never lied to each other, don't start now. Please. If you won't let me go, then is there any chance we could stay out here just a little longer before going back? Just a few days, not even a week, to look for Regan? And Zilch's heart? We know they're out here, we have proof. Can we just... try?"

She shut her eyes and didn't speak for several seconds. She almost kept them closed, but some answers, with some people, you had to hand down looking them straight in the eye. "No."

"Why?" Rowan didn't shout. She almost wished they would. "Why won't you let me go at least?"

"Do you really want to know the answer to that question?"

"Tell me."

"Because you are too valuable an asset to lose," she said, voice sounding about as exhausted as she felt, but still unwavering. "You're one of our only medics left. You will save hundreds, thousands of people with those skills alone. You and your prototype antitoxin. And we need you to contain Tartarus. That's thousands more lives right there. I cannot allow you to risk your life, because it risks all of them. They outweigh anything else, including my feelings."

"And Regan and Zilch?" Rowan asked in a whisper.

"We don't know where they are. We don't even know if Regan is alive, not for sure. We do know that thousands will suffer and die if we break off to save two."

"So that's it?" Rowan stared at her. They gave a short laugh, but it wasn't a happy one at all. "It just comes down to math?"

"There is no other way of looking at this. Chances, risks, loss and gain, we have to think like this if we're going to survive. Or I do, rather." She gave just as sardonic a smile in return. "I think like this so you don't have to. Or that was the plan."

"We're really doing this? Writing them off because they're too big of risks, with not enough reward? And what about Sharpe?"

"Also just one man. A venomous, treacherous man, but only one."

"He does enough damage for a hundred. And he will never stop."

"Maybe not. But we're not the ones to stop him."

"He killed Ash," Rowan said, in the coldest tone she'd ever heard from them. Maybe from anyone. It sounded wrong in Rowan's voice. "And he almost killed Annie. Now he's after Regan. The odds are good that he has Zilch's heart. This is my family, Aliyah. I need them safe—and I need Sharpe gone."

"And so do I," she said with every bit of conviction she could muster. "I need it for you, and for me, and for them, like I haven't needed much else in my life. But that is the problem. We need. Not 'they.' Not Parole. The difference is too vast. The risks are too great. And the odds were never on our side. I'm sorry."

Rowan didn't retort or challenge her again. They didn't say anything at all. Silence stretched between the two of them like it never had before.

Suddenly, the lighting changed dramatically, making both of them jump in surprise. They looked up and out a high window in time to see another flash of lightning streak across the sky.

"A storm?" Rowan gaped outside, where the previously-bright afternoon suddenly looked dark as night. "Right now?"

Lightning flashed again almost before they'd finished speaking. They both jumped, scrambling to get around each other and up the hill to the door. Just before they hurried through, Aliyah caught Rowan's arm.

"We're not done here! This storm is a temporary reprieve, that is *all.*"

"Fine," Rowan agreed. "Bookmarking the breakdown for later."

Aliyah took a deep breath and readied herself. "Right, let's go batten down some hatches."

☆

The FireRunner came to a halt in the lee of the next beacon tower. Its looming shape gave them some shelter from the high winds and the reassurance of having their backs against a solid wall. When the sky cleared, they'd light it up. But for now they had bigger concerns.

When a storm rolled in, ghosts came with it.

It was nowhere near sunset, but when the FireRunner crew, including Toto-Dandy, came above deck, it was almost dark. The storm front blotted out the sun and trail of light, forming a solid wall of dust. The oncoming mass traveled over Tartarus's dry desert like a tidal wave. Dark, ghostly shapes flitted in and out, leaping and diving like porpoises in sea swells. And dipping toward the ground, reaching down like a sea monster's tentacles, were dozens of thick, swirling cyclones of toxic air.

"You've heard me say 'no orders except in a pinch,'" Captain Aliyah shouted to be heard over the growing noise, talking fast. The wind howled; they could all feel it in the bones of their chests and the soles of their feet. "Well, it is indeed pinch time! But don't fear, follow Captain's orders and we're all going to be fine! Have you got that?"

When the affirmative came back over the wind, she gave a sharp nod and moved briskly on. "Right, then! Changes today are as follows: One! We've got two new recruits learning the ropes!" She cast a wide grin at Shiloh and Indra, who huddled together, slightly excited and very nervous. Shiloh nodded anxiously and Indra gave a nervous grin and salute. "Shiloh, you're with Jay. Eyes on the oxygen tanks and lines, very important job, making sure we all don't die!"

"Yes ma'am!" Xir voice didn't shake, but the rest of xir certainly did.

"Good. Indra, I want you with Stefanos, making sure every air vent and water gate is completely airtight and uncontaminated!"

"Got it." The big man with the golden eyes waved for Indra to follow as he headed toward the railing. Then he held up his other hand, the synthetic one, and gave it a nod. "I'm also in charge of dampening cover from the flashbangs and any ghosts that get too close."

"Flashbangs? Ghosts?" Indra repeated as he followed, looking a bit seasick. Dandy followed after him and Stefanos at a bouncy trot, seeming excited about all the activity. Shiloh wished xie could trade some of xir rising tension for that unworried, doggy happiness.

"No time, explain on the job!" Aliyah called. "Because change number two! Without a shield, our automated mechanisms have started to corrode. That means we have to button everything up by hand! Now! Less standing around, more getting to business! Move out!"

The solid-looking storm drew closer by the second. Now Shiloh could see individual ghosts flying through the air. Some were shapeless blurs, some looked like skeletal horses or birds of prey—or dragons.

"Don't worry." Annie grinned as she ran past, looking actually excited to face the terrifying maelstrom. She held something like a missile launcher but with an enormous bulb at the end of its barrel. "This is gonna be fun."

Shiloh followed Jay around the main mast in the middle of the FireRunner's deck. It anchored most of the solar sails, along with their complex network of metal cords. The sails were slowly closing themselves, as if the ship were curling up defensively. Jay hurried to the ring-shaped plastic tank that encircled the mast's base.

"First stop, everybody grab some oxygen," he said, passing out masks similar to the ones people wore in Parole. Instead of only filtering out smoke or toxic gas, these were connected to small personal oxygen tanks that strapped securely around the waist and shoulders. They also had an attached earpiece and microphone. "And switch your headsets to public. Stay on it as much as you can unless you really need a private line. Maintaining voice contact is good, nobody knowing if you need help is bad."

"Don't we need suits or something?" Shiloh asked, worried at the minimal protection.

"If we were closer to the center, yeah," Jay explained, securing his mask and headset. "But the air isn't toxic enough out here to bother your skin. Just don't breathe it in. Lungs and insides are another story." Next, Jay began passing out what looked like climbing harnesses, like the one Rowan wore to run up the side of the last beacon. "Second step, everybody into a harness. Police your lifelines, keep them neat, no tangles."

"Masks and lines secured?" Aliyah asked from behind her own. Unlike everyone else, she wasn't wearing a safety harness. Shiloh immediately realized why when her huge wings unfurled behind her.

"Yes, Captain—sorry," Shiloh nodded, glad for the mask that hid xir blush. "I'm just—it's..." Xie looked back up at the wall of storm.

"Deep breaths," she reassured. "There's plenty of good, clean oxygen. You're doing fine. Just relax, safety first, and we'll get through this all right."

"Aliyah," Rowan said quietly and she turned to see them standing behind her, the only one not hurrying to fulfill her orders, because she hadn't given any. "How about me?"

She hesitated, then reached out to put both hands on Rowan's shoulders. "Stay by the comm line. We need someone in contact with Radio Angel, in case anything else goes wrong."

They just looked at her for a moment, then slowly nodded, eyes dropping to the ground. "Aye-aye."

"I meant what I said before, Lamb." Aliyah spread her wings to their full span, turning to leap into the tossing sky. At the last second she looked back, face softening. "Hang on. Nothing lasts forever."

Rowan gave a tired smile as she lifted off. "Not even storms."

Aliyah's powerful wings battled the winds as she leapt from sail to sail, ensuring that each was furling closed correctly. From high up on the mast, she had an extensive vantage point of the entire ship and kept an eye on everyone's operations.

Down the length of the ship, Annie pounded up the stairs to the highest deck. Vaulting up over the last few steps, she dropped down to kneel beside the metal railing, resting her large flash-gun barrel on it for stability. She put her eye to the aiming scope and followed the storm as it bore down on the ship, and the things leaping inside.

They seemed curious about the ship, but mostly kept their distance. Until one ventured away from the group, swooping down toward her—and she fired a blast of light. It didn't hit the ghost directly; instead the sky lit up as if lightning had struck. The ghosts shrieked and scattered away from the light, fleeing in all directions. Throwing her head back, Annie yelled that yeah, they better run, and loaded up another volley.

☆

"Just keep close to me," Stefanos called to Indra, giving his lifeline a tug to ensure it was tightly secured. He looked over the edge and stretched out his metal hand to point at a row of open vents, just below the lip of the deck. Someone would have to hang over the edge to reach them. "See those grates down there? They're vents for air and water, they connect to the tanks."

"Yeah," Indra said, fear making his voice tight. "We gotta close those, right?"

"I do. You don't have to worry about them," Stefanos reassured him, voice and stance steady. He positioned himself so he was standing upwind of Indra, huge body taking the brunt of the gale-force winds. "I'm going to rappel down there and close every one of them tight. We wouldn't have to worry about this if our shields were operational. But we do what we gotta."

"Sounds safe enough!" Indra shouted over the noise, face tensed into a grimace. "What do you need me to do?"

"Just spot me," Stefanos answered with a smile, golden eyes glinting as he watched Indra visibly relax. "Keep an eye out, make sure I'm still there, and give a shout to one of the others if I'm not!"

"Okay." Indra nodded, watching as the huge man heaved himself over the railing and started to descend. "Um, I'll be here. Anything else I can do to help?"

BANG. The world flashed bright as Annie fired off another halogen round at a ghost that had gotten too bold. Indra stared, unable to look away from the dark shapes and twisting cyclones that seemed to reach out toward them, threatening to wrap around the ship and swallow it up.

Stefanos stopped climbing over the railing and came back, big hands on Indra's thin shoulders. "You all right?"

"Fine!" Indra yelped, voice unnaturally high. "Yes, I'm fine. Fine!"

Stefanos didn't seem convinced. "If you need to get out of here, just—"

"*No!*" Indra shook his head, took a step back. "No. I want to help. Please, let me stay. I'm good for something." He gasped, shut his mouth so fast he bit his tongue. "I mean, I'm good, I'm fine."

Somehow Stefanos's cold alloy eyes were warm. "You can do this. Don't look up at the storm. Annie's got us, the ghosts can't hurt you. And don't look down. Jay and Shiloh have the other end of your lifeline. You won't fall. So just keep your eyes on me. Can you do that?"

"Yeah. Got it." Indra pointed two fingers at his eyes, then up at Stefanos's metal ones. "Just. Keeping the eyes on you."

"Good. This won't take long." Stefanos gave him a last nod, then climbed over the edge. Indra watched him go and held on tight to the railing to keep his hands from shaking.

☆

Across the deck, Shiloh was finding it hard to stand still and wait. Despite the vital importance of watching the lifelines and emergency oxygen supplies, there wasn't much to do except stay ready and watch. Everyone had their jobs and Shiloh's didn't start until someone ran into trouble. It was somehow boring and nervewracking at the same time.

("Turn out the light...")

"What?" Shiloh jumped, looking around wildly for the source of the words sending shivers down xir spine.

(Icarus,) the voice said. *(Turn out the lights.)*

Shiloh couldn't move. Couldn't think. Xie only remembered the rest of the world—and the storm—existed when Jay almost bumped into xir, actually knocked off-kilter by a particularly strong gust of wind.

"Sorry," he said as he regained his balance. "This is one of the windiest I've ever seen. You doing okay?"

"Did you—?" Xie stared at Jay, unable to put xir anxiety into words.

"What?" he asked, eyebrows raised in confusion. "I didn't say anything."

"I know!" xie said, switching to his private channel. Xie couldn't say why but xie just didn't want to broadcast this. "I mean, did you hear that?"

"Didn't hear anything either. I mean, I hear a lot of things, the storm, Annie shooting off—"

"No, I mean the voice!" Finally, Shiloh's real fear clicked into place. "It sounded like Mom!"

"It..." Now it was Jay's turn to stare in slowly dawning horror. "What'd she say?"

"Icarus, turn out the lights, same thing the ghosts keep saying! So it's gotta be a ghost, right? It can't be her—can it?"

Jay was nervously scanning the churning skies above and didn't answer. Then he switched his radio to public frequency, broadcasting his voice not only to Shiloh but everyone. "Aliyah?"

"Yes, you've got me." Aliyah was currently 50 feet above the deck but everyone heard her loud and clear.

"Might want to keep an eye out for any ghosts who get too adventurous."

"As we speak!" Aliyah carefully made her way along a thick crossbeam, wings pressed down against her back to keep from catching the wind.

"No, I mean look extra hard. We just heard something weird, might be ghosts getting salty."

"Right, message received. Stay sharp."

"As we speak." Jay shut off the connection and turned back to Shiloh. "See? Everything under control."

☆

Aliyah reached the central mast and paused in the crow's nest, taking advantage of both its shelter from the tearing wind and its unbroken panoramic view. From here she could see the whole ship from end to end, a good place to check on her crew's lockdown progress and scan for any ghostly forms that didn't belong.

The solar sails were wrapped up and secure. Down near the aft, Stefanos and Indra were around halfway through sealing the top-deck air vents. Annie waved from the far end, sitting in the bow and catching her breath during what looked like a lull in the surrounding ghost frenzy. Not one had come anywhere near breaking through.

Nothing to explain what Shiloh had heard.

"Everything's looking ship-shape from up here," Aliyah called. "Knock on most tentatively-optimistic wood. Rowan? How's the weather down there?"

"Windy," Rowan called back. "But we should be in the eye pretty soon. If we–"

They stopped mid-sentence, staring at the grey, shadowy figure standing straight, tall, and very still on the top deck's metal railing.

The man in the storm should have been tossed instantly overboard. Instead, he stayed perfectly balanced on the narrow rail without the help of wings, ropes, or anything else. At the very least, the wind should have torn at his long overcoat and long hair, but they both stayed still. All of him did. It was as if he were standing in his own calm room, away from the gale, away from the chaos and the ghosts, away from the entire world.

His back was turned and there was no color in his form, only monochrome grey and stark black and white. But there was no mistaking him.

"*Ash?*" Rowan's whisper was choked with tears.

Slowly, the ghost turned. Rowan knew, long before his face came into view.

They didn't need to see this man's face to know him, here, or in a burning city or in dreams, or any other world. He'd always been there before, standing beside them in their darkest hours, and here he was again—or at least something wearing his face. A human face, with dark, deeply alien eyes.

"*God...*" Rowan breathed and then their breath started to come faster until they visibly swayed on the deck.

The ghost with Ash Price's face slowly tilted his head until it hung at a quizzical angle, staring as Rowan slowly stepped closer. Like all ghost eyes, this one's were black, but these empty hollows were nothing like Rowan's eyes. He stretched out his hand—the one with only four fingers—and Rowan did the same. The distance closed between them and within seconds, Rowan's hand slipped into his. At the contact, Rowan's face twisted, their own eyes closing and mouth opening in a silent grimace. But instead of pulling away, Rowan stepped carefully up onto the railing.

"Why are you doing this?" Rowan whispered, several kinds of pain filling their voice. "What do you want?"

(*What...you want,*) Ash's voice returned. It might have been an answer, or an echo.

"You're not him." Rowan shook their head, panting and shaking. They finally let go of the burning hand and clutched their own, injured one to their chest. "Are you alive? What are you? Tell me!"

The black eyes held Rowan's gaze, staring. Then the specter of Ash Price opened his mouth to speak from beyond the grave.

A bloodcurdling howl split the air. They both looked up in time to see Toto-Dandy hurtling toward them, metal fangs bared. Rowan scrambled backwards on the narrow metal bar, hooves quickly re-balancing them on the railing. The giant wolf leaped for the ghost—and seemed to have miscalculated, because he hit the railing at an awkward angle. Unable to reconnect in time, Dandy narrowly avoided slamming into Rowan, but the miss was near enough he brushed against them. He sprang away from the railing and turned, snarling and ready for another lunge, but stopped with an almost human look of shock.

Rowan teetered wildly on the railing, reaching out desperately for something to grab, and finding nothing but empty air. They'd been knocked too far off their precarious balance to recover, and now they began to tip over the edge—

Until the Ash-ghost reached out and caught them, but not by the hand. His spectral hand was wrapped around Rowan's neck. Their face contorted in a silent scream and the ghost tilted his head and frowned, looking confused at Rowan's distress.

The keening shriek of a bird of prey came from above. Aliyah's face contorted in horror as she dove, arms outstretched. She plummeted like a thunderbolt, diving through the storm so fast they could almost hear the whip-crack of her wings slicing the air. "*Let them go!*"

The hand opened. Rowan slipped over the edge without a sound. Without hesitation, Aliyah followed.

The ghost who looked like Ash Price stood on the railing with stunned bewilderment on his borrowed face, staring at the empty space where Rowan had stood a moment ago. Then the edges of his form started to distort, like a thin layer of oily smoke.

(S...orry.) Then he was gone.

"*No!*" Jay's voice rang out, desperate and choked despite his easy supply of oxygen. He almost fell to his knees in his frenzied scramble across the deck and reached the railing a half-second later, catching himself against it and desperately looking over the side...

Only to immediately stumble away, nearly falling over backwards. Aliyah's huge, golden wings flared as she shot upwards, like a dolphin breaching the ocean's surface, and she wasn't alone. Rowan hung in her arms, limp and very still.

"What happened?" Annie pounded up beside Shiloh, staring at the scene in horror.

"Just keep them off her!" Jay shouted, reaching out for Aliyah as she hovered. Her teeth were gritted and hands balled into fists in Rowan's clothes, every fiber of her being focused on keeping them aloft. Her small frame and mostly-hollow bones weren't at all designed to lift much of anything, much less a person bigger than she was. But, fortunately, her powerful wings were. They flapped with all the strength Aliyah could muster, slamming back and forth to keep herself and Rowan steady in the howling winds.

Shiloh just had time to wonder what Jay meant by 'them,' before it became horribly clear. The Ash-ghost was far from alone. Small, smoke-edged figures surged up from below, flights zigzagging and erratic; it looked like they'd been whipped up into a frenzy by the storm. Flashes of light erupted as Annie fired off flashbang rounds, scattering ghosts before they got too close.

"Hey, all of you!" Jay pointed at Shiloh and Annie, who stood together, frozen in horror, as Indra joined them. "Help me get further out there!" They rushed to comply, holding him steady as he leaned out far over the guard rail, stretching out both arms. "Come on, Aliyah! Drop Rowan on me, then get down here!"

She inched closer, buffeted by the gale-force winds and shadowy shapes as ghosts swarmed around them both like sharks that had caught the scent of blood. With Annie's covering fire, she slowly drew level with Jay's outstretched arms. Finally they were close enough to lock eyes, silently communicate the vectors, the precision timing it would take to safely transfer Rowan, then get Aliyah safely landed—

A stray ghost flew into Aliyah's face. When it ripped away, it took her oxygen mask with it.

Her mouth fell open in shock—and she couldn't help sucking in a tiny gasp, pure instinct and reflex. The breath was small, but in this storm, one small breath was all it took. Aliyah's wings faltered and they started to dip.

"Just a little closer!" Jay's voice shook almost as badly Aliyah's wings. Annie was still firing photo-rounds rapidly, but it was too late. She was out of targets anyway. True to their name, they seemed to have faded into thin air. "Keep trying—*please!*"

But it was too much. Aliyah couldn't keep both herself and a full-grown adult airborne. Feathers trailing, she dropped below the surface of the deck and out of sight, taking Rowan with her.

Everyone stared in silent, paralyzed terror. Now none of them could breathe.

Then, an arm reached up over the edge of the FireRunner's windswept deck and grabbed onto the railing. An arm made of metal. In his other strong arm, Stefanos held Aliyah and Rowan, safe and sound.

"*Yes!*" Indra yelled, reaching out to grab his wrist. "I got you! I got you all!" Laughing, or maybe crying, he dug in his heels to pull them up and the image might have been funny if it wasn't so dangerous—slight, skinny Indra desperately trying to heave the enormous Stefanos carrying two other people up over the edge. "But we could use a little help!"

Annie was there in an instant. Shiloh and Jay charged forward, grabbing ahold too, and together they all pulled Stefanos, Rowan, and Aliyah safely onto the deck. Stefanos rolled onto the flat of his back, exhausted from exertion and adrenaline. The first person he saw when he looked up was Indra and his golden eyes crinkled into a smile.

"Thank you, spotter."

"Any time," Indra panted, bent over, exhausted with his hands on his knees, but he was smiling.

But the storm wasn't over. On all sides, shapes roiled and surged in swarms so thick it looked like the ship was surrounded by a solid wall. The FireRunner's battered crew, terrified passengers, and growling dog huddled around Aliyah and Rowan, preparing for the next wave.

"Jay, count of three, fast as you can." Stefanos's high-beam eyes flashed, pointing the way across the deck. It wasn't far, but right now, feet looked like miles. "And hold the door."

"Right. Okay." Jay nodded tensely, eyes so wide the whites almost showed all around, face was slick with sweat.

Stefanos kept one metallic eye on Jay and one on the ghosts that flew around them like circling vultures. "Annie, cover him, and I'll cover you. You two..." He looked at Shiloh and Indra. "Keep your heads down, soon as there's a break, follow Jay. Don't look back."

"Where'll you be?" Shiloh couldn't help the question that slipped out.

"Carrying them." Stefanos crouched by Aliyah and Rowan, ready to pick them up and run. "One, two—"

Another howl. Before any of them could stop him, Dandy bolted from their small huddled group and charged down the length of the ship.

"*No!*" Annie yelled, jumping up and taking a couple steps before she was pulled back down by several hands. As she watched in horror, Toto-Dandy ran to where the Ash-ghost had stood and reared up, huge front paws coming down on the railing with a metallic clatter. His blue eyes beamed out into the storm, like miniature beacons in the heavy gloom, and he howled again, sharp teeth flashing.

The wolf's cry seemed to shock the storm itself. Every single ghost stopped their wild circling and floated where they stopped, as if hanging suspended in the air on strings. Even if only a few of them had clearly defined heads and eyes, it seemed like they were staring at the FireRunner crew, and waiting.

"What's happening?" Shiloh whispered, staring. "What do they want?"

"I don't know." Annie shook her head. "And what's Dandy doing? I've never seen him do this before. Stef?"

Stefanos didn't answer and didn't let go of her shoulder either. On his other side, Jay and Indra silently watched the wolf toss his head, flare his blue eyes, and wave his tail like a banner—as did hundreds of ghosts, all around. Then Toto-Dandy leaped overboard.

Every frozen ghost snapped back into motion, flying after him as the shocked humans stared in confusion and horror. Shiloh shielded xir face, covering xir eyes as the ghosts whipped past. The noise was deafening; hurricane winds melded with Dandy's fading howls. But gradually, the roar faded. After around ten seconds, it was calm enough for Shiloh to open xir eyes—to find that while the storm still raged, Toto-Dandy and the ghosts were gone.

"What the hell just happened?" Indra held onto the railing, shaking.

"Figure it out later. Take care of them now." Stefanos nodded at Aliyah and Rowan, immediately shifting the focus from the remaining storm and toward their injured friends.

"Wait one second," Annie said quickly as she replaced Aliyah's oxygen mask, covering her nose and mouth. She checked Rowan's mask as well, but froze for a second, startled. There was a dark, hand-shaped lesion forming around their throat.

"Are they breathing?" Jay repeated through clenched teeth.

"They're breathing. So we get them inhalers," Annie murmured fast, eyes narrowing at the handprint mark around Rowan's neck. "I don't know what that is. I've never seen that before."

"Me neither!" His voice was tight with increasing panic. "Maybe because it shouldn't exist!"

Annie looked up, seeming much calmer than Jay, but no less grim. "It does. Help me get them to the infirmary."

Without a word, Stefanos bent down to pick up both unconscious forms and, after a moment, Jay jerked out of his shocked reverie to help as well.

Shiloh looked up and squinted in the suddenly bright sunlight. Xie'd never been so glad to feel the answering stab of pain in the back of xir head. The sun was beginning to break through the angry thunderheads, filtering through the dissipating Tartarus vapors. The howling wind died down; soon the air would be still and silent as ever. Tartarus' storms came on without warning and moved on just as quickly.

They had to move on quickly too. The skies may be clearing, but the danger was far from over.

CHAPTER 16

The Calm After

THE SKIES WERE CLEAR AND WINDS CALMING. OUTSIDE, AT LEAST. INSIDE, THE STORM continued. but the crisis was far from over. Running largely on adrenaline dregs and muscle memory, the shaken crew pushed through their fatigue to get the FireRunner to a safer location—minus a few very important hands. Meanwhile, Annie readied the sickbay for the unconscious Aliyah and Rowan, closing the infirmary door tightly behind them and denying any offers of help. Shiloh probably would have waited there nervously anyway, but at least now xie had the excuse of being assigned to wait and worry. When xie asked how xie could help get the ship moving, Jay's second answer (less unbearable and more productive than 'sit tight and don't touch anything') was to wait here and see if

Annie emerged with updates or if she needed anything.

It sounded like a good plan at the time. Or would have been if it were anyone else doing the waiting.

An hour later it was almost more than Shiloh could stand not to knock on that door, if only to ensure everyone behind it was still alive. Xie thought xie'd left this kind of helpless, frustrating indecision behind along with Meridian's barrier. But here xie was again, waiting for an answer. It hadn't gotten any easier since. Hands behind xir back to resist the temptation, xie instead stared as hard as xie could, willing it to open—and terrified at the same time what would happen if and when it did.

"Leave it until she asks. You'd just get in her way."

When Shiloh looked up, xie caught the glint of Stefanos's eyes as he turned away with a slight shake of his head. The last remaining oasis of calm in a sea of anxiety-fueled chaos, Stefanos stood staring out a window halfway down the corridor at the clearing skies. Like Shiloh, he clasped his hands behind his back like a soldier in an at-ease position. Unlike Shiloh, he didn't look like he was trying not to jump out of his skin. So xie headed over to stand beside him, hoping to somehow soak up some of his resilience like taking shelter beneath a sturdy tree.

"Is she really okay working alone? Is there anything we can do to help?"

"Ordinarily, Rowan's the medic. But Rowan's down." Stefanos's voice was as level and unshaken as the rest of him but it was flatter, more lifeless than Shiloh had ever heard it. "Annie's spent years learning everything she can from them. She knows what she's doing. The rest of us, not quite as much." He shut his eyes, extinguishing their golden shine.

"But they'll both be okay...right?" Shiloh turned xir attempt at reassurance into a question at the last second, like veering away from a road xie had no business going down. Not when xie couldn't quite believe the comforting words xirself. Now that they were standing closer together, xie could much more easily see the exhaustion in his face and realized the hands clasped so tightly behind him were shaking. Both of them. "You have to have seen this a lot, people—"

"Physical contact with a ghost is unprecedented." His eyes opened with a soft whir but he didn't look down at Shiloh, staring out the window as he spoke. "Or it was, until Annie told us what happened on your way here. We don't know why they're becoming solid. They shouldn't be..." He was silent for a moment, seeming caught on the edge of too many complications to voice. When he spoke again he sounded more focused, grim but determined. "We know inhaled vapors wreak havoc on the body. Tartarus gases sear the inside of the lungs, the esophagus, everything. People can lose the ability to speak. Or breathe on their own. We can get them clean, keep them on purified oxygen. Humidifiers. Annie's a competent field medic, but even with a real hospital there's just not much you can do."

"What about that new antitoxin?" Shiloh grasped at one last hope. Fortunately it seemed like a good one. "Indra said Rowan was working on an injection, isn't that supposed to be stronger?"

"It is. Yes. It's also an untested prototype."

"But it's at least worth trying, right?" xie pressed, slightly surprised at xir own tenacity.

"Under normal circumstances, I'd be right with you." Now Stefanos did slowly turn his head to look down and focus on Shiloh's face, and xie was struck by how even miraculous mechanical eyes could look so haunted. "But it's what I said before. Normal died when Parole was born. And Tartarus is another animal entirely. Yes, I've seen Captain Aliyah recover from things that should kill a man twice her size but that's when she's at her best. Nobody has been at their best out here for a long time." He folded his arms across his chest and his eyes narrowed in a hard, cold glare. Xie almost took a step back but soon realized this quiet flare of frustration wasn't aimed in xir direction. Or any. That might be part of the problem. "And Rowan… I don't know."

"You don't know if they'll make it?" Shiloh didn't feel at all energized or determined or tenacious anymore. Now xie just wanted this conversation, and this entire nightmare, to end.

"I don't know anything, because what happened shouldn't be possible."

"Because ghosts aren't solid objects." Shiloh didn't veer it into a question this time. Instead xie remembered the nauseating *crack* of Annie's bat as it connected with very thick bone. Lakshanya's warning that unless something contained Tartarus now, nobody could predict how it or the ghosts would advance next. Now it wasn't the look in Stefanos's eyes making xir shiver. "They're not supposed to be real."

"That's right. We don't know what happens with bites, or scratches, or… *that.* Because they don't happen. This wasn't *supposed* to happen." Stefanos shook his head, turning to face the window again but with none of even the illusion of his previous calm. The motion was jerkier than his usual deliberate smoothness and another slight movement caught Shiloh's eye—a sudden twitch in his mechanical hand that he immediately curled into a fist and re-clasped behind his back. "In a whole lot of ways."

"So we're just giving up?" Xie couldn't help one last try. The words just came out.

"Nobody's saying that," Stefanos said, but his voice was heavy with fatigue instead of its usual warmth. "But I'm saying... just be careful where you place your faith. Untested prototypes, long shots, gambles like that?" He seemed to catch himself or maybe catch the slow-dawning despair on Shiloh's face, because a tired one spread across his own. "Well. Maybe it just means we're happier when the long shot pays off, that's all."

With that, he turned and walked down the length of the corridor and up the stairs leading to the bridge. Shiloh started to follow him then, as xie'd been doing so much in the past hour, stopped short. Instead, xie turned to rush up to the infirmary door and knocked—much more quietly and slowly than xie wanted to.

"Annie?" xie called, not at all sure if this was the right choice but sure xie couldn't stand another moment of not making one. "Could you use some help? I don't know much, but...I'm here if you need me."

The door opened after a few seconds to reveal her pale, exhausted face. Her eyes were dry, but her thousand-yard stare was one Shiloh hadn't seen since their first day together and never wanted to see again. Xie'd seen it much too soon, just now on Stefanos's face.

"That sounds great," Annie said in a dry whisper, hand shaking as she opened the door the rest of the way. "Thanks."

Before they could move, wailing alarm klaxons broke the quiet and flashing lights bathed everything in an urgent red.

"Everybody who can hear me, proximity alarms are going off!" Radio Angel's voice came through the P.A., layered so it sounded like several of her were yelling the words, while more of her echoed the warnings. "Looks like a SkEye vessel, right behind us and gaining super fast—pretty sure we're about to have company. You know what to do!"

☆

"Who is it? Who's after us?" Indra panted, hurrying to catch up with Shiloh and Annie as she led the way down one of the FireRunner's innermost corridors.

"Turret." Annie almost spat the name. "Who else? I knew we couldn't trust him, even if it looked like we were on the same side! I knew it!"

"He's coming after us with a whole ship? Like with people, soldiers?"

"Of course he is!" Annie shot him a glare that probably wasn't really aimed at him, before turning a corner and continuing down a tight stairwell. "This is a raid! He's bringing everyone he's got. Now, I locked the infirmary, it's got its own shields. Nobody's getting in there. Aliyah and Rowan should be safe. Radio Angel too, she's barricading herself. Safest places on the ship. Follow me and I'll get us safe too."

Troubled by something else, Shiloh had only been half-listening, and almost missed the next step. "Do we know who that is? Who's with him?"

Annie didn't answer right away, just kept pounding down the stairs. When she did, her voice was hard to hear over the noise. "If Kari's right, and she usually is... Your friend Brianna's on that ship." She didn't see Shiloh's look of equal parts dread and nausea because she was turning to face Indra. "And so is your mom."

"Why?" Indra managed after a few shocked seconds.

"I don't know, you'd have to ask her." Annie stopped in front of a long, featureless stretch of metal bulkhead that looked the same as every other section on the ship and started studying it as if it were also the most interesting section.

"I—well—that doesn't mean she's on his side!" Indra stammered. "What if she's really just here to talk? You're right, Annie, I should just ask her myself."

"You don't want to do that," Annie said shortly. "She's not the only one here. There's at least a dozen SkEye creeps boarding us right now and if they see you—just don't let them see you."

"But my mom—"

"Made her choice, if she's here with him. Same for your friend," Annie continued before Shiloh could cut in. "It sucks, but that's how it is."

"No, I can't believe that." Shiloh finally found the words to object. "Brianna's not SkEye, she wouldn't follow him by choice—she's not here because she wants to be! She's in a lot more danger here than any of us!"

"And we have to take care of ourselves first," Annie maintained, not looking up. She ran her hands across the metal wall as if searching for something she couldn't see. "Or else we're no good to anyone."

"So shouldn't we get behind a barricade or hide or something?" Shiloh didn't like the idea of hiding instead of helping, but liked standing around out here in the open even less.

Annie felt around for one very specific seam in front of a particular section of metal bulkhead. She slipped a hand into a hidden slot, and pulled. The wall swung at an angle on hidden hinges, revealing an opening wide enough to squeeze through. "Yeah."

Indra hesitated as Annie and Shiloh started to climb into the hidden crawl space. "It is very dark in there. And very small."

"Uh-huh, most good hiding places are." Annie looked back at him and waved impatiently for him to follow.

"But—what about the captain? And Rowan?" Indra looked increasingly nervous, and it could have been for several possible reasons. The most pressing one, however, looked like the crawlspace. "They haven't woken up yet, they'll be—"

"Fine," Annie cut him off. "They'll be fine, the infirmary's under lockdown. Nobody's getting in there. But *you* have to get in *here!*"

Indra didn't move. "My mom's on board," he said in a much smaller voice.

"Yeah," she said, looking increasingly frustrated. "She's right here with Turret. And you are definitely going to get caught if you don't hide, now!"

He shook his head and took a step backwards. Still shaking his head, he turned and hurried back down the hall.

"Indra, come back!" Shiloh started after him, but Annie grabbed xir shoulder.

"We have to get out of sight. Now."

"But he's—"

Annie jabbed a finger at the ceiling—or the stairwell they'd just come down. Clanging footsteps were growing louder from above, as if someone were descending the stairs in heavy boots.

Reluctantly, Shiloh ducked down out of sight and Annie closed the crawl space door behind them. It was dark and small inside and very quiet except for their shallow breathing. They couldn't hear the footsteps outside anymore or the ever-present engine hum. The entire ship was waiting.

☆

Rishika stood on the bridge of the FireRunner like she belonged there, even with her heart pounding and adrenaline burning through her veins. Back straight and eyes steady, she surveyed the pair opposite her and opened with a conversational tone. "Where is the Captain? I was hoping she'd be the one to greet me."

"She's indisposed at the moment." Stefanos stood front and center and just as still. His large arms were folded across his chest and he stared back, pokerfaced, revealing nothing. "Where's your Major?"

"Turret requested permission to search the vessel for contraband alongside his men."

Stefanos snorted. "Well, good luck to him."

"Yes, I doubt he'll find much or you lot wouldn't have had nearly as lengthy or notorious a career."

"Good excuse to get rid of him, though."

"Something like that." She had to smirk. "And wasn't there one more of you? The one with the goat's horns."

"Actually they're more like a bighorn sheep," Jay said, leaning back against a navigation console and staring out one of the large bridge windows at the vast Tartarus expanse. "But no. You get us. How can we help you today?"

"Charming as ever, Jay, I have missed that, believe it or not."

"But not enough to actually answer my calls. Or come back to check on us, not once in ten years."

"You know very well why. If you loved my son the way you said all those years ago, even for a moment, you know why I had no choice."

"Yeah, I sure do. I distinctly remember trying to tell you all about it–the truth, not whatever story Turret spun you. Thanks for listening. Oh, wait!" He made a noise halfway between laughter and disgust, but still didn't look at her. "That part I don't remember."

"This isn't why I'm here and we've been over it anyway." Annoyance started to enter her tone for the first time. "But I'm listening now. What do I need to do to convince you?"

"You could lay the blame where it belongs. Mihir died to save Parole but it didn't kill him. Not the city, not the CyborJ syndicate, whoever they are." He amended the last sentence quickly and continued just as quickly. "The smoking gun—and the guy holding it—they've been right in front of you the whole time. And he won't stop until nothing stands between him and absolute power. That means you, sooner or later."

"David Turret is many things, most of them unsavory. But he is not a murderer."

"And the syndicate is? They've done nothing but good in Parole for ten years, why would they kill one of their biggest allies? You have to admit it doesn't add up. Besides, you know nothing about them, that's kind of their deal."

"Exactly. Your friends haven't shown where their loyalty lies. He has. I don't pretend to know Parole's shadow players and secret agendas or who would stand to gain from Mihir's death, but I know Turret isn't among them." She spoke briskly, clearly disengaging and ready to move on.

"Taking control over a whole city isn't gaining from it?"

"He's rigid, ruthless, and appears to have mishandled his position, possibly quite badly. I'll believe almost anything about him—but not this." She hadn't risen to his bait and the finality in her tone indicated the matter was closed.

"Then I guess we have nothing else to say to each other after all." Now Jay looked over at her, his expression bitter, disappointed, but not surprised. "You good with ten more years of radio silence?"

Rishika gave her head a rueful shake before turning to look up at the much taller other man. "Hello to you as well, ex-Lieutenant Argyrus."

Stefanos inclined his head. "Ma'am."

"You look like you're doing well for yourself."

"I am." His eyes flashed into life for the first time. "Despite everything."

"Glad to hear it. You were a good officer and agent. And a friend."

"Don't." He shook his head. "We *thought* you were our friend. Until we all nearly died, a hundred times over. Turret gutted Parole to within an inch of its life and he's still doing it. And through it all you were nowhere to be found. Until today." He smiled grimly. "People don't commandeer each other's ships just to kiss and make up."

Rishika looked from him to Jay and back, probing. Stefanos looked away again, shaking his head. Jay watched her out of the corner of his eye and now his expression darkened, eyes narrowing, gradually revealing the beginnings of old pain and fury behind the superficial lightness and control.

"You saw what I was trying to do once," Rishika said, matching Stefanos's serious tone but not the darkness under it. "To heal everyone who was hurting. That's what Chrysedrine was for. You know I have only the absolute greatest good in mind—for all of us."

"You had good intentions. You and Garrett Cole both. And his medicine did save lives." His golden eyes narrowed, extinguishing their gleam. "But you can't just drop a bomb like that and walk away. You can't shake the earth like that, then just let it go."

"There were extenuating circumstances." Rishika's voice hardened for the first time.

"You're damn right there were. And we all had to live with the consequences." Stefanos's voice had grown to a steady rumble like tectonic plates moving underground. "We were lost without you. And without you, Turret moved in. What did you expect? The moment you started allowing innocents—children—to get caught in the crossfire, you crossed the line."

Rishika took a breath. "It's for children that I'm here. My child."

"Indra came to us for help and that's what he got." Stefanos folded his arms and shot Jay a sideways glance, receiving a slight nod in return. "You know why we're here and what we do. Same thing we've done for years. Save lives. Protect anyone who needs it—or asks for it. Make a better life. That's all we've ever wanted."

"And I want to know my son will be safe."

"He's on our ship because it means something to him. He wants to find sanctuary in Parole."

"Sanctuary in Parole." She smiled sadly. "That's a phrase you don't hear every day."

"What do you want, Rishika?" Stefanos sighed, sounding as if he felt about as old as the earth they sailed across. "We're not handing Indra back if he doesn't want to go. We'll never force anyone off this ship, you know that."

"No. And I'd never ask you to."

"Then what is it you want?"

She stepped closer, holding Stefanos's golden gaze. "I want to see the state of the world for myself. Somebody told me recently that things are much, much worse than I knew. I've been hiding myself away in my tower for far too long—and it's time I ventured out and took a look."

"Good," Jay said suddenly and they both turned. "I spent so long wondering if you'd ever come to your senses, come back and save us. You know, I really thought you would. But I was wrong, every day! And it never got less painful, or confusing. The Rishika Chandrasekhar I knew would never let the people she cared about—no, not just us, that whole city, thousands of people, she'd never let them suffer like that, not if she could help it!"

"And now I'm moving to address that," she said firmly. "I'm not sure what else I can say."

"I kept asking myself, what happened?" Jay wasn't done, voice climbing in pitch as he grew increasingly agitated. "Were you dead? Did Turret actually kill you too in his grab for power? That was my working theory for months! One of the better ones!"

"You never did lack for theories," she said with an almost fond shake of her head, but he just kept going.

"This kind of devastation, you had to be dead, you'd never stand by and let it happen otherwise. But no, once I finally broke through the Radiance firewalls and found out you were alive and well—and still in charge, *that* was the kicker, *that* one hurt—"

"Jay," Stefanos said softly, turning his focus from Rishika for the first time.

"So then what, if you were alive—did you just not know?" Jay went on as if he hadn't heard. "Did you really *not know* what he'd done to us, that we were quarantined, trapped over a fire that never went out, and the ground crumbling under our feet, with his soldiers there to make sure we just stayed in line *until we all fell in and died?*" He shook his head and took in a fast breath, face shining with sweat.

"I didn't know," Rishika said in a measured voice while he recovered. "I still don't. I'm going to see for myself."

"What do you mean you still don't know? Our word isn't good enough?"

"I need to see for myself."

"Didn't you ever wonder how we were doing? A whole city that you—you zapped with this power, these tons of variables, these things we shouldn't have had, you made Parole what it is! Then you disappeared. Say what you want about Garrett, at least he actually *stayed!* You let us deal with the fallout, wondering if you were there or could hear us when we cried out for help—"

"Sounds downright Catholic when you put it that way," Stefanos muttered. He was staring at the ceiling now, as if resigned to Jay's catharsis. He looked down to see both of them staring at him with nearly-matching expressions of incredulity, then sighed and rubbed a hand across his eyes, waving the other one in a 'go on' gesture. "Never mind."

"How could you not know how important you were?" Jay went right back to staring at Rishika and shook his head, slowly at first, then faster. "What losing you meant? Your protection? What that *murderer* did the second you were gone? Why did you do it, Rishika? Why did you leave us?"

"You know why!" Her voice cut through Jay's and the dead air. Almost imperceptibly, her hands had begun to shake. She clasped them behind her to steady herself. "I've already lost one son to Parole. I won't lose another."

"It wasn't Parole that killed Mihir and you know it. It wasn't us." When Jay broke the silence it was in a very low, hard voice that didn't sound like it belonged to him. "Turret killed him. Turret sentenced an entire city to burn and Mihir died so it was just one person instead."

Rishika didn't answer. Or move. But she did steadily meet his eyes.

"Parole still burned. But not to ashes." Jay's voice was quiet, slow, but filled with hope. "His death was not in vain. We haven't let it be, not for one day. We haven't wasted his sacrifice, or forgotten, and we never will."

"I still don't know if his choice was the right one," she said. Her eyes were wet. "Or if I'll ever understand it—or heal from it. But I know that you honor it. Which is...good to see."

"Does that really come as a surprise?" Jay asked, looking at her hard. "We loved your son. Even before he died, he was important and he knew that. And we loved you." He shook his head, expression softening, not quite a smile but something about halfway there. "Even when you made it hard."

Rishika swallowed and blinked but when she spoke her voice still didn't shake. "My word is good. I *am* talking about saving lives. And I *will* save your family, if you help me save mine."

"You mean hand Indra over to you." Stefanos's voice dropped several degrees as he focused on her last words.

"No, I'd never ask you to do that," she said calmly, parting her hands. "I just want to speak to him. If he wants to stay, he stays."

"And what if he doesn't want to—"

"It's okay," said a new voice from the doorway and they all looked up. Indra was pale and shaking, eyes wide but unwavering as he looked at his mother. "I'm here. I'm listening."

Rishika opened her mouth, eyes as wide as her son's. For once, she had no words. Instead, she shut her mouth again and opened her arms. A moment later he rushed into them.

"I'm sorry," he said quickly, voice muffled from where he buried his face in her shoulder. "For everything I said back there, at the Chicago center, I shouldn't have—"

"No," she curled her fingers through her son's hair, palm warm on the back of his head. "You were right. You and your friend Annie, you were right. You opened my eyes. I've been asleep for a long, long time, Indra. And now it's time

I woke up and saw how the world has changed." Her eyes narrowed. "And who changed it."

"Thank you. I'm—I'm so glad…" his voice broke, and she held him tighter.

"Hush. It will be all right. I will make it all right." Her eyes set into a determined stare over his shoulder. "It's certainly the least I can do, after everything."

"You could always come with us," Indra suggested. His mother stepped back to look him in the face, smiling with what looked like the most tentative optimism.

"Or you could come with me," she countered, still sounding cautiously hopeful. She stepped back to look him in the face. "We could both face the damage, and decide the next step."

Indra's eyes dropped. "Sorry, Mom. I just—"

"You need to do this for yourself. Yes, you told me. And you've found…friends here?" Her gaze flicked up to Jay and Stefanos, who stood quietly off to the side, giving them privacy but remaining ready.

"Yeah." Indra's smile was faraway but his nod was certain. "We have to see this through together."

"I understand. Just as I hope," she continued, more slowly and carefully. "That you can understand…why I did what I did, ten years ago."

"Easy." Indra's smile faded and his eyes slipped to the floor. "Mihir was gone. We all got…messed up."

"I was devastated." She shut her eyes. "And angry. I turned my back on Parole, yes. I couldn't look at that place for another moment. So I left someone I trusted in charge, let him deal with it. And that was a mistake."

"And you're trying to fix it now?"

"Yes. I'll do my best, and just pray my best will be enough. From the sound of it, the damage is extreme."

"I know." Indra nodded, still looking frightened but steady on his feet. "I've heard the stories. I know I'm heading right into a war zone, and it's..." He swallowed. "People don't run *toward* Parole. Ever. But I am. I have to."

"Because you need to see it for yourself. Just like me."

"No," he shook his head. "We're both going–but not for the same reason. You want to see how bad it is. I want to see how good it is. Mihir gave his life for it. Something made him want to do that. Parole didn't kill him...he died so it could live."

"Nothing I can say will stop you, will it?" Rishika asked, very softly. Everyone on the bridge held their breath.

Indra thought long and hard, as if looking for a reason to stay. "No. It won't."

"Then go. See for yourself. And I will do the same." She closed the distance between them again and pulled him close. Squeezed her eyes shut tight, but couldn't keep the tears from falling into his hair. "I love you, Indra."

"Love you too." His fingers curled tight around the fabric of her coat. "See you in Parole."

Rishika held him at arm's length and looked into his eyes for a few seconds, then turned and strode toward the door, only stopping when Indra spoke again.

"What are you gonna do now?"

"We can all agree that there is one person making life much more difficult than it has to be," she said without turning, the hint of a smile pulling at the corner of her mouth. "I'm going to take care of him. It's been a long time coming."

CHAPTER 17

Teeth

"UM, HELLO." BRIANNA CLEARED HER THROAT, STARING AT THE MICROPHONE IN FRONT OF HER AS the P.A. system crackled to life. When she glanced up, her father's stare was as unyielding as ever. She turned back to the microphone and tried to focus on nothing but the words.

"I'm...this is Major Turret's—I mean, this is Bri," she corrected and the knot in her stomach loosened. "Because this is me talking, not him. Not Eye in the Sky. And this is really just to one of you. Shiloh. You're my best friend, I love you and want you to be safe. And this doesn't have to be hard, it doesn't. So the best thing for you to do is..." She stopped. Remained silent and still, until she could feel her father's stare on the back of her head. Then she slammed her

hands down on the console.

"*Run!* Shiloh, this is bullshit!" Brianna yelled, her soft drawl slipping back into her voice as it did when she was upset. "He's making me say this! My father's here, he wants me to draw you out so he can catch you, and—"

Turret snatched the microphone from her hand and she whirled around, grabbing at it fruitlessly.

"*No!* No, give it back—Shiloh, RUN! Keep running! Don't look back!" Brianna screamed into the still-broadcasting microphone. "Get to Parole, don't stop—"

"That's enough!" Rishika's voice cut through the noise, and they both turned to see her standing in the now-open doorway. "David, I'd ask what in the world you were doing, but I'm not sure there's an explanation I'd accept. Step away from the intercom."

"Ma'am," Turret started, but he did put the microphone down. "This is—"

"Now step away from her."

Turret held absolutely still and kept his eyes fixed on Rishika. Neither one blinked, but she did raise her eyebrows expectantly after one second too many passed.

"Ma'am, if you would listen to the facts—"

Turret did take a step then, toward Rishika. The moment he moved, so did Brianna. She sprinted past him, darting out of his reach and kept going. She scrambled across the small room, slipped past Rishika and out the door before either of them could move. Turret made no effort to catch her but his already-pale face faded and his jaw worked with a clear flare of silent fury. Rishika turned to watch Brianna go, then focused back on Turret, eyes narrowed and arms folded.

"Facts, you said? I'm listening."

"Ma'am, I don't know what you've heard," Turret recovered fast and began in his customary level tone. "But the Parole situation is well in hand."

"Is it? I'm beginning to wonder."

"You trusted me. You were grieving, you needed a friend." His voice dropped a fraction but remained cold where anyone else might have softened. "Someone to handle the mess so you didn't have to, while you processed and healed—"

"And I've processed," she shot back, tone just as civil but with an increasingly sharp edge. "I've turned myself inside out, ripped myself to shreds, rebuilt myself from the ground up, and done it all over again. And now I'm ready to re-evaluate my position. *Both* of our positions."

"There's no need for you to trouble yourself with Parole," Turret maintained. "As I said, it's well in hand."

"But I am troubled and we haven't even gotten there yet."

"You'd be a lot more if you knew what that place was really like."

"All the more reason for me to have a look! I'm quite curious about how you've been holding down the fort."

"As I said, Parole is under control and any remaining threats are being neutralized as we speak."

"Really. Control, threats, neutralized. I suppose that does line up with what I've heard so far." She almost laughed. "But why is it that I didn't hear anything from you? Yes, I cut myself off from the rest of the world. They couldn't reach me. But *you* certainly could. So tell me, why such a *disparity*? They couldn't all be lying. Could they?"

"Ten years ago, I tried to save your son." Turret didn't rise to the challenge aside from a slight narrowing of his eyes. "We lost a lot of good people that night and a lot more every night since. And that's just Parole, before Tartarus devastated everywhere else. Now if I were you, I'd want to put that far behind me and make sure it never happened again. I'd leave someone experienced in charge."

"You do not need to remind me about any of this." Rishika's voice dropped as well, every word slow and deliberate. "I am well aware of how it began. And I am aware of the cost. My...*experience*...in this area is beyond compare."

"With all due respect, you've been out of the game a long time, Ma'am."

"Thank you for your input, Major." She put the slightest emphasis on the title. "It's noted, believe me. But it's also long past time I rejoined play. Before we all suffer quite a penalty."

"Ma'am—Rishika—"

"David...*shut up*." She crossed the room and took the microphone in hand.

☆

Shiloh sprinted down the corridor, panic growing with every step. It seemed like xie'd been lost since the moment xie'd burst out of the hidden crawlspace. Every single hallway and corner looked the same down here and, with each turn, xie got more confused, more lost, and more desperate. Xir footsteps clanged on the metal floor, echoes repeating until the noise was a jangling mess just as disorienting as the labyrinthine maze itself.

"Bri?" Xie risked a shout, voice only adding to the confusion. "Bri, I'm here!"

The P.A. system was still going, Turret and Rishika's voices yelling over one another in unintelligible, garbled messes of words xie doubted made much sense even in person, much less in metal ship interiors. Finally, completely turned around and frustrated, Shiloh came to a stop outside a large door—and at the same time realized exactly how bad a choice xie'd made. There were soldiers on this ship. A ship xie still got lost in about every ten minutes. And xie'd just yelled xir presence to everyone within earshot, echo-chaos or not.

But here was one tiny piece of luck: xie did recognize this door. It led to the central tree tank. Couldn't get lost in there and it would make a good place to hide until all this was-

"What the hell are you doing?" Shiloh almost jumped out of xir skin as someone slammed into xir from behind, and almost took off running again before xie realized it was Annie's voice, and her hands grabbing onto xir shoulders.

"Brianna—she's here, I have to—"

"So you just run around yelling with SkEye everywhere?" Annie at least kept her voice down to a furious whisper. "Are you actually trying to get caught and killed? We have to get back where-"

"No!" Shiloh shook off her hand. "You heard her on the P.A.! She tried to help me and now she's somewhere on the ship, so I have to help her!"

"No, you have to get back where it's safe and let someone who knows what they're doing—"

"She'd do it for me!" Shiloh almost abandoned whispering again, feeling a mild electric surge run up xir spine. "I can't just leave her here!"

Annie's eyes widened and her mouth fell open, but no sound came out for a second. When it did, she wasn't whispering anymore either, voice low but resolved. "Okay. Let's go get her."

They opened the door to the tree tank together and stepped quietly through.

Brianna was the first thing Shiloh saw. She was under the tree. It was as if they'd planned to meet here, as if she'd somehow known where to wait. Shiloh smiled immediately and Brianna was running toward xir almost as fast. They threw their arms around one another, nearly falling over and taking Annie down with them.

"Shiloh!" she cried, laughing, but crying at the same time if the tears Shiloh felt on xir cheeks were any clue. "You heard me!"

"Yeah, I did!" Xie squeezed her, and thought maybe not all the tears were Brianna's after all. "I can't believe you're here!"

"I'm so sorry for saying those awful things, even for a second, I didn't want to-"

"I know, don't worry, I know you didn't! That's how I knew it was a trap after the first second, because you'd never say that, this is super basic kidnapping logic 101 stuff."

"But you came out anyway!" She laughed, shaking her head. "I think you fail that class."

"We're *all* gonna fail." Annie's warning tone brought them both back to the present. "If we don't hide and shut up right now. There's SkEye troops sweeping the ship still, remember?"

"Right, come on, Bri!" Shiloh couldn't stop smiling. "We'll wait this out, then we'll introduce you to everyone on board, the whole crew's really great. We have this one mission, I guess, but we're heading to Parole when it's done—for real, Bri, Parole! I still can't believe it!"

"Shiloh, wait." She stopped as xie tried to take her by the hand and lead her toward some thick rose bushes, looking overwhelmed and troubled.

"What?" Shiloh looked back, trying to hold onto the swell of joy xie felt slipping away as xie saw the look of doubt in Brianna's eyes. "This is what we wanted. And now it's happening. We couldn't do it before but now we can, this is real!"

"I still can't," she said, hand slipping out of Shiloh's as she took a small step back. "I'm sorry."

"I don't understand," Shiloh said, throwing Annie a slightly desperate look, maybe a plea for help. She gave her head a little shake as if to say she didn't get it either, but then, there was a lot she didn't get about these things. "Why'd you run away just now if you weren't coming with us?"

"I just wanted to see you..."

Shiloh stared for a second, incredulous. "You're staying with your father? After all this?"

Her eyes fell to the ground. "I'm not with him. But I don't know where to go either. If I stay with you he'll just follow, he'll never leave me alone, he'll never leave you alone! I can't stay here."

"Parole is still there, Bri," xie tried to infuse every word with conviction, get her to believe it even a fraction as strongly as xie did. "We've all seen it. It's alive. Gabriel is alive."

"I can't believe it," Brianna whispered, though she looked like she was beginning to. "What about my family, everyone my father said was dead? Are they alive too?"

"Liam's there," Annie said, giving Brianna a contemplative but not suspicious look. "Not the most popular guy in town, but he's—"

"My brother is alive?" Brianna turned to look fully at her for the first time, eyes wide and hopeful. "You don't understand, I thought he was dead all these years, everyone told me he was dead, him and my mom and whole family and friends and everyone, and then my father says the city is there but destroyed and has to stay destroyed and it's evil, but I don't think that's right, that can't be right, and Shiloh's the only one who says different, but I can't just..."

"You can't get your hopes up on something so good," Annie said slowly. "Because letting yourself hope and then getting hurt is so much worse than never hoping at all."

Brianna didn't say a word. But shakily, she nodded.

Annie smiled, crooked and slow. "I don't know about everyone, but Liam's there." Her smile grew as Brianna let out a sob, but she was smiling too. "A lot of us are. Parole's a mess, especially now, but people are still hanging on. And we don't turn anyone away... even when we probably should. So are you coming or not?"

Brianna didn't answer right away. Her expression was one of intense concentration but didn't reveal a decision either way. Finally, she opened her mouth to answer—and gasped at something over Shiloh's shoulder.

Cold dread gathering, xie turned around. Standing where Brianna had been beneath the huge, starlight-filled tree was a perfectly average-looking man. He wore a SkEye uniform and the same scrutinizing, somehow predatory stare he'd had when he'd passed Shiloh, Annie, and Indra coming out of Radiance Headquarters several days ago.

But he didn't move and neither did they. Shiloh couldn't if xie tried. It was a wonder xie could even breathe under his penetrating gaze.

"This is Rishika Chandrasekhar, CEO of Radiance Technologies. All SkEye personnel, withdraw immediately." Her voice issued surprisingly loudly over the

P.A. and all three of them jumped—but not the man in the uniform. He continued to hold perfectly still, focus unbroken. "Yes, that is an order and, yes, you do answer to me. Since I was the original authority over the 'Parole Situation,' as it's apparently known to everyone *but* me, I'll be rescinding the Major's temporary position and retaking my own. Isn't that right, Major?"

"Orders confirmed," Turret replied, voice neutral and controlled as ever. "Follow them as if they came from me."

"Thank you. We will disembark in an orderly fashion and return to your—our vessel at once. You are then to hold position here on the ground while I continue to Parole, where I will evaluate the ground status and oversee an appropriate response. Repeat, all SkEye personnel stand relieved, both here and Parole. FireRunner crew... carry on."

The speaker shut off and the first hint of anything besides cold calculation or a smug smirk crossed over the SkEye officer's face. His eyes narrowed and his hands curled into his fists, as if he wanted to lash out at the sound of her voice despite having no target. But, just as suddenly as it had come, the flash of anger disappeared and the silently intimidating man turned to go.

As he did, something caught his eye. He stopped mid-step, pale blue eyes zeroing in on the chain around Annie's neck that had come out of her shirt as she and Shiloh ran. On the large shark tooth on the end. Like the flare of temper, his hesitation only lasted for a moment and he was soon striding away from them toward the other end of the tank.

But before he left, he smiled. This time, he showed teeth.

They seemed too large to easily fit inside a human mouth.

And they were very sharp.

"No..." Annie's whisper was barely audible, but it still cut through Shiloh's shock, and xie turned to see her staring with the most haunted, horrified look xie'd ever seen on her face, even in a journey full of horrors. She didn't move except for her shaking legs, which looked like they couldn't decide whether to propel her forward in a desperate sprint after the man or buckle under her, leaving her in a heap on the ground.

"That's him?" Shiloh asked, immediately frustrated because of course it was, it could be no one else. And he was walking away, further all the time. In another minute, he'd be off the ship and gone. "We have to tell someone, we-"

Another sudden noise—rapid footsteps—made xir turn back around. The man with the shark teeth was gone and Brianna was running again, this time in the opposite direction from where he'd disappeared.

"Bri!" Shiloh cried, helpless panic surging back with a vengeance. "Stop! Don't—"

"You were right, Shiloh!" she called back, sounding happy of all things, excited, alive. "Parole is still there! Liam's alive! My family, Gabriel, everyone! I have to find them—I have to see what my father tried to hide!"

"So you're going with him?" Shiloh took one frantic step after her, then saw Annie, and took two back.

"No!" Brianna laughed. "With her!"

More confused than xie'd ever been and sick to xir stomach, Shiloh looked up at Annie, who looked even worse than before. Tears streamed down her paled face and she was hanging onto her—Ash's—chain again.

"We can probably still catch them," Shiloh said, though xie was believing that less by the second. "Both of—all of them. Bri, Turret, and Sharpe. We tell everyone right now and if we hurry we can catch that whole ship, with the guy who killed Ash on-"

"Let him go," Annie said in that same faint whisper, shaking her head. "We don't stand a chance without Aliyah and Rowan. We never really did without Ash. We're hurting so bad, going up against him now... no." She sniffed, and let her hand drop. "There's enough blood in the water already."

☆

As promised, they left the ship unharmed. On the ground, Brianna watched the FireRunner's lights disappear into the inky night with a smile on her face and tears in her eyes. Then, all at once, every light disappeared, as if dropped behind a cloak of shadow. There was no chance of catching them now if they didn't want to be caught.

"So, the queen returns," Turret rumbled from where he stood beside her, staring out after the receding lights and engine hum. He glanced down. "And you demonstrated your capabilities and intent very clearly."

Brianna sucked in a breath and tensed, standing at attention before she even looked up to see the angle of her father's squared jaw above her. "I'm not one of your soldiers."

"No, you're not. Mine know how to follow orders and show the loyalty their position demands."

"Like how they're all loyal to Radiance now?" Brianna wasn't sure where she found the guts to say the words, but she did, and braced for the fallout. "If I was one of your soldiers, I'd be obeying Rishika Chandrasekhar. Would that be better?"

"They won't listen to the first thing she says." The corner of his mouth gave the faintest twitch.

"You said they should follow her orders like they came from you."

"Exactly. I would never hand down the disasters she's about to. If I did, it would mean I wasn't fit to command. Or I'd been otherwise compromised."

"So then what...?" Brianna almost didn't want the answer. She shivered, and it wasn't because of the suddenly-bitter cold after sundown.

"They'll rebel." He let out a rush of air through his nostrils, the closest to a chuckle she'd heard from him in years. "She wants to wear the crown? Fine. She can have it. And everything that goes with it."

Eyes widening and blood draining from her face, Brianna ran over everything she'd seen and heard. The logic was simple, terrifying. Finally, there was only one thing left that mattered. "I still couldn't let you do it. Shiloh's family."

"Our family died with Parole," he said, voice dropping faster than a Tartarus nightfall. Given how softly he spoke, she never expected him to move so fast. "That's not difficult to remember."

"I remember a lot of things," Brianna said through clenched teeth. "I remember Mom, and Liam, and Aunt Cass—"

He released her, not with a flash of hot anger, but the cold detachment of disdain and disappointment. Then he turned and walked away without a word, to where a silent figure waited. Before they both disappeared, she caught the flash of a sharp-toothed smile in the dark.

Brianna held very still until they were gone, then quickly switched on her shortwave radio. "Madam Chandrasekhar?"

"Yes?" came Rishika's clear, clipped tones. *"Who's speaking? Is this Turret's line?"*

"This is his—this is Brianna Turret. Ma'am, if you're headed to Parole..."

"Speak quickly, please, we're about to get out of range."

"I want to come with you. My father is wrong, he's been wrong for a long time, and you're going to Parole, and I just—I want to be there. I want to help. I… I have family there."

A long pause. Brianna held her breath.

"I'll see what I can do."

CHAPTER 18

Turn Out The Lights

ALIYAH WOKE UP AROUND A DAY LATER. SHE WAS WEAK, AND COULD BARELY WHISPER, BUT FROM the moment she opened her eyes, she fought to stay conscious and present, refusing to rest until she'd been fully briefed on the events she'd missed. She was battered and bruised, but her ship had been invaded without her knowledge and she was still the captain—and she was now very firmly awake.

Rowan wasn't. Not then, and not the next day.

The angry, dark handprint-scar around their neck was stark as ever and the skin around it had the same burned-paper texture and black veins that had appeared on Indra's infected arm. But unlike his arm, Rowan's neck didn't seem to respond to the treatment.

"It's because it actually grabbed them, and we don't know how to deal with that," Annie explained bluntly. She sprayed the antitoxin aerosol directly onto their skin every few hours and ensured their oxygen contained a mix of clean air and vaporized medicine. The burnt-looking skin did recede and heal over, but scarring remained. Even once their dark veins faded, the skin above and around them kept the marks of handprints. Both of them had only four fingers.

An early stroke of good luck came with Annie remembering the injection-form antitoxin prototype. Stronger than the aerosol or vapor, but untested. Thinking this emergency was exactly the right time to test it, Annie gave Rowan a small amount and continued her careful watch. Their hand showed some small improvement, but they remained unconscious, with no sign they would wake up in a day, a month, or at all. Crushed and frustrated, Annie stayed in the infirmary for a full day before she was finally persuaded to sleep with the promise that someone would always be watching Rowan, and would call her at the first sign of change, for better or worse.

That change hadn't come by the time Aliyah was awake. She still had to spend most of her time in bed, so Annie, Jay, and Stefanos came to the infirmary and took turns filling her in on the storm aftermath, Turret's boarding, and Rishika's role in averting certain violence. She remained silent, though clearly troubled by the events she'd missed. Her eyes narrowed when Annie confirmed that not only the Major, but his Lieutenant, had set foot on her ship.

Shiloh came to the informal 'meeting,' but not for the same reason. Xie had an idea.

"It's something I've been thinking about for a while," Shiloh started, only a bit hesitantly. "It's actually something Radio Angel said, about boosting stuff? I can't believe I forgot to tell anyone, it's been such—" xie broke off, seeing Aliyah's focused stare, but exhausted everything-else, and finished quickly. "I think I can not only light up the next beacon, but all of them at once."

Aliyah said nothing in reply. But her eyes did widen and she raised her eyebrows, prompting Shiloh to continue.

"So far you guys have been doing them one at a time, right?" Shiloh continued to talk fast, not wanting to burn through the captain's energy on non-essentials. "Well, it's just like when I boosted Kari's signal—I think I can do the same thing to the beacons! If somebody turns it off, I can turn it back on and power it up to the new frequency."

Xie paused, watching Aliyah's face. She was frowning, but looking deep in thought instead of outright disapproving.

"It's because the new beacon frequency is really close to the one my mom used for the stream, the one we've been following," Shiloh explained. "Almost ultraviolet—I'm sure I can copy that." Xie wasn't actually entirely sure. But even a slim hope was better than none.

"We need all the boost we can get," Annie added, still looking exhausted. She might have left the infirmary but clearly hadn't slept. "Rowan's down. And..." She cast a wary glance at Aliyah, who readjusted her feathers in an indignant sort of way. It seemed like an acknowledgement. She probably shouldn't have even been sitting up, but insisted on hearing everything while as upright as possible. She studied Shiloh for a moment, then shot Jay a questioning look.

"I mean, it sounds like a good idea," he said with a slight shrug. "I dunno if it'll actually work, but when's that ever stopped us before? If it works, we could be done in a day instead of a week."

Aliyah looked over to where Rowan still lay and watched their chest rise and fall. The movement was slow and easy to miss—as Annie had already discovered a few frightening times—but still there.

"Yeah," Jay said, sounding like he wished he were saying anything else. "The sooner we get back to Parole, the better." Aliyah looked back at him and the worried, pained expression she'd turned toward Rowan now sharpened into something firm and resolved. There was still a question in her face and he continued with even more reluctance. "And if it doesn't work—we could undo everything we've done so far."

"Maybe one of us should go ahead," Stefanos suggested, not sounding any more hopeful than Jay. "Take Rowan back to Parole. Everyone else can finish the job."

"We knew that was bull when Rowan said it," Jay snorted. "And it doesn't work any better coming from you. Like Annie said, we need all the help we can get, with half of us out of the action."

"Then what would you suggest?" Stefanos didn't sound challenging, just tired.

"Listening to Shiloh," Jay said immediately. "I mean, what are our options? Go home now and Tartarus keeps spreading. That's bad. Finish lighting 'em up, and we lock Tartarus up, but the longer we spend out here..." He glanced over at Rowan, then back toward Aliyah, who still watched him carefully but was beginning to slump with fatigue. "That's also bad. And when both options are bad..."

"It's time to take a third." Shiloh was actually smiling. "Change the rules."

"That's right, Nibling." Jay grinned back, anxiety in his face overruled by pride. "We might have a chance yet."

"Fire everything at once and save the day?" Shiloh felt a shiver of excitement. Already the air around xir crackled with an electric charge. "Let's light it up."

Aliyah took a deep breath and spoke her first slow, whispered words since the storm. "Worth a shot."

☆

The FireRunner stopped around ten minutes before sunset. Before them loomed one of the dormant towers, stretching up into the vast sky. The gradual movement of the beacon's long shadow marked the hours like a giant sundial. After the sun dipped below the horizon it would feel like all the light and warmth in the world had been extinguished. Shiloh didn't have much of a problem with that. But it was still this crew's job to make sure not every light went out.

Aliyah stood on deck straight and tall, firmly holding the guard rail. "What do you need?" she asked, voice somewhat improved but nowhere near recovered.

The question was overwhelming, as was the growing pain in xir head. The bright sun was painful, but anxiety made chiari symptoms grow worse as well, until it could no longer be ignored. But everything had a first step and Shiloh knew that one at least. "I need to be closer."

"Done." Aliyah gave a sharp nod.

"We're doing this now?" xie asked, suddenly apprehensive.

"Almost sundown," she said, clearly trying to cram a great deal of thought into brief, difficult words. She nodded toward the beacon, then headed away in the direction of the bridge. "I'll tell Stefanos and Jay to begin."

As the ship rumbled toward the tower, staying in its long afternoon shadow, Shiloh stood alone, stretched out xir short arms, and prayed this would work. Xie could hear Jay's voice loud and clear; *we are so related.* "And I am so scared."

"Shiloh!" Indra's voice cut through xir reverie and xie turned to see him hurrying up the nearest stairs from a deck below. "Figured you might want some company for this. Annie's coming in a minute too."

"I..." Shiloh just looked at him. Suddenly xie couldn't think of a single word that would possibly be enough. But xie could smile.

"You doing okay?" Indra checked in, sounding about as anxious Shiloh felt.

"I need to..." Shiloh wavered, chewing xir bottom lip. The deck vibrated underfoot as the ship moved toward the tower. They'd reach it in just a few minutes.

"What do you need?" Indra asked quietly.

"Not just closer..." Shiloh hesitated, trembling. Xie knew the answer, but didn't want to say it. But xie made xirself turn toward the central mast. On it was the P.A. speaker and intercom for the top deck and a metal ladder leading up—to the crow's nest. "I need to get higher."

"You sure? Like, absolutely sure?" Indra asked, looking up, and up. "That thing's half as tall as the beacon."

"I know. I've never been this sure about anything," Shiloh said, teeth clenched to keep them from chattering. "Listen. Ever since we woke up together in the tree, it's been the weirdest, best time of my life. I know you understand."

"Yeah. Even when I'm awake."

"Then you have to know I'm serious about this. Help me. Please."

Indra hesitated, eyes wide, and mouth open with no sound coming out.

"Or don't. Because I'm going up anyway." Here it was again. The uneasy, standing-on-the-edge-of-a-cliff feeling that everything was about to change. Like the calm before the storm, or the collapse of Parole, or the dragon in Meridian. This moment was the surface of a lake and there was something huge moving way down deep.

Xie watched as Indra's apprehension slowly faded into the smile xie knew would come. "And I'm right behind you. Ready?"

"Yeah." Shiloh put a hand on the first ladder rung, then stopped. "I mean no..." xie stammered and that stopped Indra too.

"I'm right here. What else do you need?" Indra asked quietly, stepping closer, both hands on Shiloh's shoulders. The ship came to a halt and everything was very still.

Until a metal door banged open a level below. Annie stomped out, craning her neck straight up and shielding her eyes from the harsh setting sun. "Crap, it's bright out here."

Shiloh smiled and the tension in xir shoulders melted away under Indra's hands. "Her."

"What are you doing?" Annie yelled up at them.

"Shiloh's gonna light it up!" Indra called back, waving and pointing up at the crow's nest. "All the way up!"

"From up there?" She was either glaring or squinting in the bright sunlight. Shiloh still couldn't tell which as she started up the stairs toward them alarmingly fast.

Shiloh shot Indra a nervous glance, wondering if this was actually the good idea xie'd thought. "Uh, we thought—"

"Without me?" Annie grinned, not a trace of doubt on her face. "Highest place on the ship. Really dangerous thing. But why?"

"It's the only way to get up level with the beacon!" Shiloh insisted, but slightly less confidently.

"You're sure?"

"Listen, I know how it sounds, I know you guys think I'm—"

"I don't care how it sounds," Annie said with the certainty Shiloh wished xie still felt. "I'm asking if you're sure you can do this."

Shiloh looked up at the tower stretching up into the sky, almost too high to see its top—then down at Annie and Indra, their faces filled with worry, excitement and faith. "I can do this."

Annie gave a firm nod. "We won't let you fall."

All at once, the light overhead was gone. Like a massive candle being blown out, the beacon stood dark and dormant, and the world was much darker.

"That's Stefanos and Jay." Annie nodded toward the extinguished light. "Whatever we're doing, we better do it."

"Okay." Shiloh gripped the first rung and immediately almost let go—even with the ship idle and the tower dim, the ladder was vibrating from the concentrated energy. But xie started up, hoping xie wasn't about to topple to the hard deck below and die, taking xir friends down too.

It felt like hours and vertical miles before they all found the relative safety of the crow's nest. Eyes squeezed shut, Shiloh took a few seconds to orient xirself in this new height, holding on tight to the metal railing. Then xie looked up at the beacon. Xie absolutely did not look down.

"You don't have wings," someone said, a rough voice coming from a speaker in the crow's nest Shiloh hadn't noticed. Xie carefully looked down to see Aliyah standing below, beside the mast's lower intercom. She looked very small.

"Shiloh needed to get higher," Annie said back into the crow's nest speaker.

"It'll work better from up here," Shiloh added.

Alilyah paused, probably evaluating the very solid danger versus yet-insubstantial rewards. Then she spread her hands and wings in a gesture that looked like a shrug. "First thing goes wrong, you're down here. No arguing."

"Understood," Shiloh said, not sure if xie was relieved or terrified.

"Work careful, but work fast. Not much time."

"Is something wrong?" Annie leaned a bit over the guard rail, peering down at the captain, who even from up here seemed tense.

"Not yet." Aliyah shut off the intercom and it fell silent.

The wind was picking up. It howled around the high mast, rushing around them like a fast-moving current. Even with the light dormant, the beacon's energy sent a piercing vibration through the air.

"I can feel it," Shiloh shouted to be heard over the sound. "But I need..." Suddenly xie didn't know.

"Words aren't doing it anymore, are they?" Annie asked when Shiloh hesitated. She smiled. "So don't use them. They'll be here when you get back. So will we."

"You got this," Indra said, arm going around xir shoulders. "You got this, and we got you."

Shiloh smiled and closed xir eyes. One more moment of quiet. One more deep breath. "Okay, I'm ready."

Shiloh raised xir arms and the keening grew so loud Indra had to cover his ears. Annie plugged one with her free hand and pressed the other ear against

Shiloh's shoulder to shut out the noise. Shiloh stretched xir fingers to the sky as if drawing power down from the sun for once instead of just pain.

Just like in Meridian, xir heart started to race. Xie'd felt it a hundred times now, the sense that they'd all been here before. The three of them stood together, higher than any of them had been in their lives. The tree from the dream was far below them. Everything was below them. Everything but one another.

"It's just like at the barrier," Indra said in xir ear. "But now we're on the same side!"

Shiloh smiled as another familiar feeling rushed back. A beautiful, warm, electric surge flowing through xir veins; the opposite of fear, the opposite of suffocation, stillness, or death. It began in xir palms but it didn't end there.

Light rushed from xir hands, streaking up toward the beacon in long, flowing strings, energy sending shivers rushing down their spines, a wave of goosebumps so intense it hurt. Shiloh's hair didn't just feel like it was standing on end, but floating. All of them were floating. Like everything in the world was weightless, lifted by the most powerful magnetic force imaginable, charged and eternally linked.

Above, the dormant beacon flared to life, answering Shiloh's signal with all force. Instead of a plain, stark white, its light was now neon purple, so bright it seemed like a second sun had come down to earth, washing it an unearthly violet. Shiloh laughed, head spinning in a rush, feeling free, high, small, and terrified all at once. Xir hands curled into fists around the glowing cords and held on.

"You got this," Indra kept whispering to Shiloh, arms wrapped tight around xir instead of the railing. His teeth chattered and his voice shook with every syllable. "You got this, and we got you."

Annie planted her feet, one hand on his shoulder and one on Shiloh's, her straining eyes fixed on the new light. "It's working," she said quietly. "But when does it–"

The world disappeared in a flash of brilliant light. It took several painful seconds for their eyes to re-adjust. When it did, everything had changed.

As before, the raw energy split from a single bright flare into a violet stream stretching out across the distance. But there were many now instead of just one, arcing up into the sky, crisscrossing and weaving together to form a huge network like a giant glowing spiderweb. Between the strands was the same iridescent, bubble-like forcefield as the one over Meridian. Maureen's designs, power just turned up many, many notches. Shiloh smiled, soaking in the warmth of the energy strings flowing from xir hands all the way up to the beacon, and didn't let go or look away.

Below them, Aliyah was staring too. She didn't move but she did spread her wings, feathers seeming to reach for the light.

"There it is." Shiloh stared in awe at the incredible sight. "I did that. Do you know how that feels?"

"I kind of think I do," Annie whispered back, shaking. "You okay?"

Shiloh slowly nodded, face shining with sweat. Xir chest was filled with a tossing storm xie couldn't begin to sort into words. Xie didn't open xir fists, keeping the stream flowing.

"*Continue lighting the beacon,*" a voice suddenly commanded. It was not Aliyah's and it didn't come from the speaker. Maintaining the streams, Shiloh turned to see the sun had set, and now bright searchlights sliced through the gathering dark. The harsh white beams, and the voice, came from another ship, and the distance between them was shrinking fast.

"This is of the highest importance." Major David Turret's amplified voice cut through the wind and humming energy. *"Thousands of lives depend on your success."*

"What?" Shiloh whispered, turning to look back at the oncoming ship. Xie was so lightheaded and absorbed in the light streams, Turret's words were almost nonsense syllables.

"Oh no." Annie's grip tightened until she dug her fingernails into her friends' shoulders. None of them seemed to notice. "Oh, God. Why is *he* here?"

One of the searchlights landed on the crow's nest, lighting them up as harshly as the beacon's light, and blinding everyone inside.

"Everything is going according to plan." Turret's voice sounded calm, but it still sent shivers down Shiloh's spine. *"Once the barrier is in place, Tartarus will be contained and neutralized."*

"That ship," Annie continued, sounding near-panicked. "That's Turret's voice, but Sharpe's ship! Sharpe is here, these are the lights, no, no—"

"What does that mean?" Indra yelled, covering his face to block out the light with his free arm.

"Get down!" Annie cried, falling to her knees and trying to drag Indra and Shiloh down with her. "Sharpe is a sniper! We're in the spotlight! He's aiming a gun at us right now!"

"Raise the barrier!" Turret's voice was getting more intense; the ship had to be nearing fast. *"Turn on the lights!"*

Shiloh didn't move. Even with Annie and Indra both trying to pull xir down behind the minimal safety of the crow's nest wall, xie stood firm, keeping the stream of light flowing up to the beacon and new barrier.

"Get down!" Annie, or maybe Indra yelled, xie couldn't tell anymore. "He killed Ash, he'll kill you too!"

"*Raise the barrier,*" Turret repeated at the same time, words all jumbling together until they meant nothing.

"No," Shiloh whispered, staring at the new barrier dome; the light reflected in xir mirrored lenses. "That's not right."

"Shiloh, get down!" Definitely Indra. "Forget the barrier! Forget the lights, forget the ghosts, forget Icarus, all of it! Just get down!"

"Icarus..." Shiloh's heart began to pound, fists trembling, not from pure adrenaline, but realization. "They want me to—"

"Turn on the lights!"

"No!" Shiloh fell backwards, wrenching xir hands away. The long stream followed behind, but it didn't break. Xie almost let out a panicked yelp—now instead of controlling the energy, it held xir in place. The energy stream had become a tether and Shiloh was chained to the barrier, unable to break the connection. Both fists were locked, paralyzed, and xie couldn't stop the stream no matter how xie tried.

"What do I do?!" Shiloh yelled, voice straining and heart pounding. The overwhelming power was terrifying now and xie couldn't turn it off. The barrier's curve blazed so brightly it seemed about to eclipse the entire world. Xie could almost feel the crosshairs on the back of xir head line up with the spotlight. "It's too much!"

The answer came, but not from anyone xie could see. It didn't even come from Turret.

(Turn out *the lights.)* Shiloh heard the new voice without hearing it. It felt

like someone was whispering in xir ear and from far away at the same time. Or maybe from a tree in a dream. Xie remembered dragons.

"How?" Shiloh called again. Xie tasted salt and realized tears were streaming from xir eyes. "How do I do it?"

(Icarus.) Suddenly all Shiloh could hear was wind in branches and crackling flames. Back where it all began. Clutching a branch instead of a stream of searing hot energy, trying just as desperately to hang on. Letting go meant falling into darkness and fire below. Hanging on a second longer meant bursting into flame.

(Trust me. Trust you.) Shiloh recognized the voice now. It was Gabriel's.

Everything had led to this. Looking up to see a dragon in Meridian. Following the shining ultraviolet stream in the sky. Meeting people whose faces xie knew, but not from the waking world. Dreaming of a tree with lights like stars.

Shiloh closed xir eyes. *Please, let it all not be for nothing. Let it be enough.*

(Let go.)

"Okay."

Xir fists opened and the lights went out. All of them. The night, once overpowered by blinding light and energy, plunged into darkness. The beacon was dark. Everything was still; both the FireRunner and Turret's ship's engines had fallen silent, and the wind had died. Sharpe's searchlights were extinguished. And the barrier was gone.

One silent second passed. Two. Then Shiloh's knees buckled. Gentle arms caught xir on both sides and helped lower xir to the crow's nest floor. They huddled together against the wall and waited.

"Shiloh," came Indra's frightened voice in the dark. "What did you just do?"

"The right thing?" Xie tried to reassure him, but it just came out sounding scared. "I hope."

The night was dark and still and, for several more seconds, nothing seemed to happen at all. Then, something appeared beside the dark beacon, just visible against the near-night sky. Something big, with a serpentine neck and huge black wings.

"Oh no," someone whispered. Shiloh couldn't tell who; maybe xie'd said it.

Hovering level with the crow's nest, staring directly at them, was the dragon. Its dark eyes were the same as in Meridian, the same as when they'd looked out of Garrett Cole's face. The rhythmic, regular wingbeats seemed too slow to keep the gigantic shape aloft. The frantic pounding of Shiloh's heart was much, much faster.

Annie's clenched fists were drained as white as her face and she looked like she might vomit or scream or both. Beside her, Indra gasped for breath, trying to speak, move, or do anything, and failing at all attempts.

But Shiloh couldn't see them anymore. Xie couldn't even see the dragon.

All xie saw was the figure riding on the dragon's back.

It wasn't Gabriel.

But it was someone Shiloh knew.

"Mom!" Shiloh yelled, half-delirious with exhaustion, confusion, relief, and joy. Astride the dragon, holding into its thick neck with gloved hands and staring them down, was Maureen.

Aliyah was saying something from below but xie didn't hear the words. Annie and Indra were speaking too, but Shiloh heard nothing, saw nothing except xir mother's face. Xie couldn't believe it, this was too good to be true—

(Icarus.)

Shiloh's heart sank as xie realized. It really had been too good to be true. Maureen's form was stark black and white, a monochrome facsimile of a person. Her faded jeans, work gloves, boots, T-shirt were all here, but they weren't real. She wasn't real. When Shiloh looked into her eyes—black, inhuman, un-shining—xie didn't know what looked back, but it wasn't xir mother.

"Why?" xie whispered, staring at the ghost with the too-familiar, too-alien face. "Why are you doing this? Why would you show her to me? This isn't real!"

No reply. The dragon-ghost simply kept hovering in place, huge wings moving much too slowly to actually keep it aloft. And both of them continued to stare at Shiloh, mute and unwavering.

"Didn't I do everything right?" xie said, fighting back more tears. "Why isn't this real? Why aren't you here?"

BANG!

A gunshot ripped through the stillness before either ghost could answer, loud and sharp. Annie screamed and fell to the crow's nest floor again and, this time, Shiloh and Indra both followed. No searchlights illuminated their position anymore, but the shot still sounded like a very near miss.

"Stay down! Keep still!" On the deck below, Aliyah shouted into the P.A. speaker despite her sore voice, wings flaring. "Kari, are Stefanos and Jay back yet?

"*We made it,*" Stefanos's voice answered instead. "*And I have the bridge.*"

"Then get us out of here!"

The FireRunner's engines roared in reply and the ship slowly began to move away from the dormant beacon. The ghost with Maureen's face, and her dragon, stayed hovering in place, impassively watching the inky dark shape of Turret's ship grow larger.

"I did everything you wanted," Shiloh whispered, not caring if the ghost heard, or anyone heard. But both of them, the dragon and the image of xir mother turned their heads to stare again. "I turned out the lights."

The ghosts stared at the small humans. Waiting. For what? Suddenly Shiloh remembered another ghost. The one that looked like xir father, Garrett Cole.

"Exchange?"

Neither ghost answered, but Shiloh was sure xie'd caught a flash of Maureen's smile. The dragon flared its massive wings and they both shot up into the sky with astonishing speed. The dragon-ghost rose hundreds of feet in the air—then fell in a streaking blur directly onto Turret's ship, like an enormous undead eagle attacking its prey.

"I can't..." Shiloh whispered, staring at Turret's ship, where dark shapes gathered like a swarm of angry locusts. More gunshots sounded, but they weren't aimed at the FireRunner anymore. "I can't believe it worked!"

"I can't believe we're still up here!" Indra gave both Annie and Shiloh's shoulders a shake, which finally snapped them back to reality and the urgent need to get down to solid ground, or at least a more-solid deck.

Aliyah waited at the bottom of the ladder, steadying them as they reached the deck one by one. Together they all hurried toward the door as the strange gunfight broke out in earnest behind them. Several more gunshots split the air, followed by a louder boom like a cannon. The ghosts shrieked, like tired souls who'd finally found something to fight for.

Aliyah held the door and they all staggered through. The FireRunner rolled on, leaving the noise, the chaos, and the still-dark beacon far behind.

As the door closed, Shiloh realized why the sky was so completely dark. For the first time since they'd seen it, the glittering stream was gone.

CHAPTER 19

Miracles and Repairs

JAY RARELY WENT ANYWHERE WITHOUT HIS FINGERLESS GLOVES AND THEIR SELF-DESIGNED holographic interface for all his virtual needs. Now he took one off to smooth Rowan's hair back from their face and feel their forehead. "No fever. I dunno what I expected, hasn't had one for days."

"Then why do you keep checking?" Stefanos sighed from where he sat on the next bed and leaned back against the wall, eyes firmly shut. "Let them rest. You should rest. Plenty of beds in the room, take your pick."

"It's either do this, or do nothing, and I'm not going to do nothing!" Jay shot him a look that was equal parts exasperation and frazzled exhaustion, then turned back to Rowan, as if expecting some change in the time he hadn't been

watching. There wasn't one. "I wouldn't blame you, you know."

"For what?" Stefanos hadn't opened his eyes.

"I wasn't talking to you." Jay's tone softened and he leaned forward, resting his elbows on Rowan's bed. "I mean, I get it it if you're just kind of hanging out, taking a break. After all that, I wouldn't really want to wake up either."

"So get some sleep," Stefanos tried again. "Think you've had about two hours of decent rest since we left Parole. Rowan too. They're probably making up for lost time. They'll be okay if you take your eyes off them for a few hours, Jay, I'll watch to tell you if there's any change."

"Your eyes aren't even open," Jay said without turning around.

"Don't have to be. Danae stuck in some X-ray vision at my last tune-up."

"Just go to sleep." Jay gave a little laugh, but it was more work than it was worth and it died away fast. He slowly let his head drop forward and rested his forehead in his hands. "Snap out of it, Rowan. You're always saying we gotta find Regan—well, what's he gonna say when we find him, and you're... like this? You can't miss that. You gotta see him. And he has to see you. And I have to..."

He stopped and nobody picked up where he left off. Rowan didn't answer. Stefanos was as quiet as they were.

"Everybody's falling asleep on me," Jay sighed, sitting back and looking over to where Seven sat, green eyes bright in the low infirmary light. "One more point for you, I guess."

"STABLE," she replied, following Jay's gaze to Rowan, who was apparently the most interesting subject in the room to her health-scan mode, which had been continuously running ever since the storm. "VITALS NON-OPTIMAL BUT WITHIN ACCEPTABLE PARAMETERS. INTERIOR DAMAGE TO TRACHEA, ESOPHAGEAL LIN-"

"Thank you." Jay rubbed his tired eyes, then continued the massage up his temples. "We know it's bad. The antitoxin prototype shot didn't even work on the worst of it—I really thought that was gonna be the answer!" He directed the last part to Stefanos, whose only reply was a silent shrug and head shake. "But no, I guess being touched by a ghost is even worse news than anyone thought. Big freaking handprint scar around their neck, kind of a clue." The robotic cat turned away, looking about to hop down onto the floor, when he reached out to pet her ears. "Sorry, Seven, I'm not mad at you. This just sucks."

He half-expected Seven to give her regular reply in the 'AFFIRMATIVE' as she rubbed her head against his hand. She didn't, but her mechanical feline face, though impassive as always, seemed to agree anyway. It was good to have her back.

"THE TIME IS THREE A.M."

"Runtime." Jay nodded, head dropping down to rest on the mattress.

"THE TIME IS THREE A.M. AND FIVE SECONDS."

"Jay," Stefanos called sleepily. "How about you find out what your cat wants? She's going to wake Rowan."

"And that's a bad thing?" Jay grumbled. "Seven, shut u- I'm sorry. I mean what is it? What do you want? Don't tell me what time it is again, I know what time it is, it's Runtime, but we can't, we're not in Parole. So then wh... oh." Jay slowly straightened his back. Hunching over a bed was a lot like hunching over a keyboard and both had their perils. "That other message. The audio one. Forgot. Go ahead and play that."

Seven didn't move or do anything, just sat very still and kept staring at Jay, as if expecting something more.

He gently bumped his forehead with one fist. "God, I'm rusty with my own cat. Engage."

She complied at once.

"Good night, dream sweet..." The voice that played from Seven's small speakers was quiet, tentative, and clearly did not belong to a trained or practiced singer. It was dry and slightly hoarse, as if this were the first time he'd sung or even spoken in some time. Or maybe his throat was sore, more given to a raspy cough than a song. Maybe he just needed water. And maybe Jay needed to stop analyzing for five seconds and focus on the song. Regan still sang it with feeling. That was the important part. "In the morning, I'll be here..."

"I wish," Jay murmured. "Gotta say. I really do."

A ragged gasp made him turn and let out a quiet one of his own. Rowan's eyes were open.

"Don't move," Jay said as they struggled to sit up. "And don't try to talk yet—yeah, I bet your throat hurts, let it rest." Rowan was clearly trying to speak and having no success, but they didn't need words to make that much clear. Jay shook his head and tried not to stare at the dark handprint scar around their neck. "Actually I bet everything hurts. But your whole neck-region got the worst, uh, we think. You're gonna be okay—but you had a hell of a—not quite a week, but close. We all did! Probably a good thing you missed—"

"There was a storm," Stefanos filled in, a little more slowly and a lot more calmly. "And a ghost. They're both gone. Everyone made it, they're fine. Aliyah's fine." Rowan seemed to follow, because they fell back, panting, relief clear on their face. But though they were too weak to move again, they kept looking around as if desperately expecting to see someone else in the room aside from the two of them.

"It was a recording," Jay said a little reluctantly, holding out his hand for

Seven to head-bump. "He's not actually here. I thought maybe if you heard Regan's voice... and I guess it worked. But I wasn't trying to mess with your head, I'm sorry."

Rowan held still for a moment and they did look crushed. But then they reached out a hand toward Jay, which he moved to take, relieved–until Rowan stopped, seeing the same black-vein pattern and burned, paper-like texture that had spread up Indra's arm when he'd come on board. Except Rowan's scarring started at their hand in the shape of a grasping handprint. Like the one around their neck, this one had four fingers.

"Yeah," Jay said, sounding about as exhausted as Rowan. "The ghost looked like him, but that's all. It, uh... didn't get the personality down very well."

Rowan's undamaged hand curled into a fist around the clean sheets. Their shoulders began to shake, black eyes filling with tears. Contrary to what Jay had imagined, they were clear as anyone else's. Somehow that was even worse.

"You were braver than I would have been, you know." Jay tried to keep his tone as light as possible but it didn't work any better than his last attempted joke. "You tried to talk to it. Find out what it was. And yeah, we know they do actually talk now. Sort of. So, really, it might have worked."

Rowan's face didn't change from its mask of grief. The dark circles under their eyes were deep, but they clung both to wakefulness and Stefanos's wrist. He raised a large synthetic hand, wiping the tears from Rowan's cheek with one huge finger, gentle and warm as flesh and blood.

"Except that Tartarus lies," Jay continued. "It gets its fingers inside your head and shows you what you want to see. Or what you're scared to see. But it's not true. That wasn't Ash. This isn't a punishment, Rowan."

They looked up, eyes widening in a look of bemused surprise, and Jay almost smiled.

"Yeah, I know what you're thinking. You weren't there when he needed you, you failed him, and anything bad that happens from now on, you deserve—and he basically showed up to confirm that. Am I close?" Rowan shut their eyes again. Jay was still tired of being right. "That's what I thought. I know, because that's been my everyday for the past ten years."

Rowan reached out with their uninjured hand and Jay met them halfway. Stefanos stayed quiet, watching the two of them with golden eyes whose hard metal had never looked so soft and warm.

"And now..." Jay stopped; somehow this was even harder. "You think you're doing the same thing to Regan and Zilch. Right?"

Their only answer was more slow tears.

"Listen. We can't always be there. No matter how much they need us. Or how much we want to," Jay said, voice quiet but so intense, so sure. "It doesn't mean we're failing them. It just means... Sometimes I don't think it means anything. It just happens. A lot of stuff that happens doesn't mean anything. And that sucks. But it doesn't make it your fault."

Rowan stared down at their joined hands and held very still.

"Hey. You're still here." As Jay spoke, Rowan slowly looked up to meet his eyes. "And so are we. We're not going anywhere and neither are you."

"We?" Stefanos finally asked.

"What?" Jay looked over, raising one eyebrow.

"You said 'we' can't always be there," Stefanos observed. "You weren't just talking about Ash, were you?"

Jay didn't reply immediately. When he did, he didn't meet either of their eyes. But he sounded just as sure as before. "No. I..." he stopped. Then shook his head and almost laughed. "Screw it. I want to find Regan and Zilch just as much as you do, Rowan. I always did."

Rowan was staring at him as if unable to believe what they were hearing. So was Stefanos but his face slowly filled with cautious hope. "Are you saying you changed your mind? You believe Regan's still with us?"

"I don't believe a lot of things. Or trust them. But... I'm starting to trust this." He smiled at Rowan, who looked at him with so much hope and joy it was as if they were finally seeing one another after being apart for years. "And I can't wait to find out if we're right."

"You sound pretty sure. Why the change?"

"A lot of things." Jay gave Rowan's hand a gentle squeeze; they were already holding on as tightly as they could. "Regan's message. The one that wasn't about blood in the water." He nodded to where Seven had curled up and gone into sleep mode on the other side of Rowan's bed. "He's still got my back, or he's trying. So it's just fair I hold up my end. We gotta find him. We find that heart, we find our lizard—and *then* we go home. All together. Whatever the hell that means."

"Still have to go slow and keep our eyes open," Stefanos said quietly, seeming reluctant to spoil this fragile happiness but unable to ignore reality. "We might have a happy ending after all. But we have to find them first and it's a rough road. There are no miracles."

Jay shot him a grin. "But there are repairs."

"Yes there are. And we're good at those." A slow smile began to spread across Stefanos's weathered face, golden eyes glinting like evening stars in the soft darkness. Rowan reached for him and he was there in a heartbeat. They sat up again, this time just enough to lean against his broad chest. Stefanos wrapped one arm around them very gently and, with the other one, pulled Jay close.

Rowan let out a long sigh, closing their eyes and resting their head against Stefanos's reassuring warmth. They hadn't let go of Jay's hand and, for the first time, since they'd been awake or since leaving Parole, their face—all of their faces—were free of worry and pain.

CHAPTER 20

Enough

SHILOH DIDN'T KNOW WHAT TO DO WITH XIRSELF. EVER SINCE OVERPOWERING THE BEACON AND shattering the shield xie had been unable to think of anything else. After destroying it? Temporarily disabling? Xie didn't know. Now xie just existed in a state of numb apprehension. It was over. Xie'd made the choice and had no idea if it was the right one. Now something had to happen, something had to give—but nothing did.

The night stretched on just like every one before it. Maybe a reunion with xir parents had been too much to hope for, Shiloh thought, but answers surely weren't. And yet, neither appeared. No resolution, no confirmation xie was on the right path. Even the glittering stream was gone, although Shiloh had long

since stopped trusting it. Xie wandered around the ship without seeing anything, feeling like a sleepwalker. But there was no comforting tree in this dream and xie couldn't wake up.

It wasn't fair.

Shiloh said as much to xir empty room, voice sounding small and flat in the late-night quiet. "None of this is fair. I did everything right... or maybe wrong. I don't know. I don't know anything anymore." A wave of electricity surged through xir from head to toe, hotter and more intense than usual, almost stinging. Shiloh didn't bother to keep it controlled, and soon small arcs zipped around xir hands, and xie felt static rush through xir hair, puffing it out and up. "Why aren't you here?"

The room's radio speaker crackled on.

Shiloh looked up, not entirely surprised xie'd turned it on accidentally. Xie was about to apologize out loud for barging into Radio Angel's channel without warning, when a voice interrupted.

"Hello?" The signal was faint, and sounded like it came from thousands of miles away. Or maybe another planet, another time, another life.

Shiloh held very still, mouth hanging open. Xie knew this voice. Knew it almost as well as xir own. "Dad?"

"Well, hello there Shiloh." Garrett Cole's voice could shake mountains and boil oceans, but now his words were as warm and easy, casual as if Shiloh had just seen him in the next room, instead of years ago. *"I was hoping I'd hear from you. Figured it wouldn't be long. When your mom showed up, I knew it was just a matter of time. You had a job to do first, that's all."*

"Mom?" Shiloh's head spun as xie latched onto the one part xie could handle. Xie could barely grasp the words themselves; all that mattered was that it was Garrett's voice speaking them. "Mom's there?"

"*Sure am.*" Maureen's voice made Shiloh sink down onto the bed, suddenly feeling weak in the knees. "*I am so glad to hear your voice–and so mad we have to talk like this, instead of in the same room!*"

"It's okay," Shiloh said faintly, a smile starting to spread across xir face. This was real. Xie wasn't delirious. Aside from being deliriously happy. "You're here. Sort of–where are you? What did you do? Tell me everything!"

"*We got the job done, just like you,*" Maureen said after a small hesitation. "*But it wasn't easy. I teleported farther than anyone has business teleporting. I found your dad. And we hunkered down and tried to figure out how to get a message to you without exposing our location. Judging by the light show, I'd say you got it.*"

"What message–the ghosts?" It seemed absurd even as xie put it together. "They kept telling me 'turn out the lights, Icarus'–that was you?"

"*Sure was.*" The pride in her voice came through loud and clear. "*I knew they were smart–knew it! But I had no idea about... well, a lot else.*"

"Tell me everything!" Shiloh wasn't above begging, especially when xie heard her hesitate. "Please. I want to know everything that's happened, all of it!"

"*Well, that's a long story. I've had a lot of adventures,*" Garrett said in what sounded like an understatement. "*Scares and triumphs. And so have you, or so I've heard.*"

"You could say that." Shiloh's head spun. "We were supposed to light up all the beacons and make a giant barrier but we didn't, we dropped it instead. Now it's totally exposed!" Xir heart pounded as the enormity of the situation sunk in. "But I really thought it was the right thing, I swear I didn't mean to ruin everything, but–"

"Hey, don't panic now," Maureen's reassuring voice—anything she said now would be, simply because she was speaking—cut through Shiloh's rising anxiety and brought xir back to Earth. *"We won. I know it doesn't seem like it, but everything actually did go according to plan."*

"Whose plan?"

"Whose do you think?" Garrett asked, and Shiloh could hear the smile in his voice. Xie tried to answer, but couldn't say a thing.

"When the ghosts appeared to you, they kept saying one word, didn't they? Like it was the most important thing in the world?"

"Yeah. Icarus."

"Who do you think told them to say that? It was like a recorded message. It's hard to explain."

"Well—try!" Shiloh wanted to laugh and cry at the same time. Somehow wanted to tear off the wall-mounted radio and shake it until xir father appeared so xie could hug him close.

"I will. I promise. But it's not the kind of thing you say on the air. And it's..." Garrett paused, sounding very tired. *"A long story. Just know that I was trying to get a message out the best way I could after we lost communication in the collapse. I had to improvise. Fortunately, that's what I do best."* His laugh, carried across airwaves and thousands of miles, was as deep and rich as if he were in the room with them. *"I faked my death to escape Parole. The world thought I was a dead man...so I thought I'd use ghosts."*

"Okay." Shiloh said wearily, trying hard to keep up. There was so much to follow there, but xir energy was limited, and xie wouldn't be able to rest until xie got one answer at least. "But...I really *didn't* make things worse?"

"No, you did the right thing," Maureen said immediately. *"You did exactly what*

you were supposed to do."

"Bringing the shield down?"

"It's not a shield if you don't choose it, then it's just a cage. That's what Turret never understood. Parole didn't need one. And we don't need one here."

"But—oh God, what happens if it's not sealed off?" Shiloh persisted. "Even if the ghosts are on our side, isn't the poison going to keep spreading?"

"Not if we can help it," Garrett reassured xir. *"The spread still needs to be stopped, but that wasn't the way to do it. Listen, your part here is done. You kept Turret from setting us all back decades. That's all you need to worry about."*

"You're still keeping secrets, Dad."

"Of course I am."

"You know a lot more than you're saying about the Tartarus ghosts, and Turret, and everything." Even being more relieved and exhausted than xie'd ever been, xie couldn't help investigating the puzzle. It was a reflex, like kicking when xir knee was tapped or shielding xir eyes from the sun. "How are you gonna keep it from spreading without the barrier? How did you talk to the ghosts, were you actually controlling them? Where are you?"

"I can't tell you." Garrett said softly, but his voice lost none of its resonance. *"I want to keep you and your mom safe. That means the less you know, the better. The less anyone knows."*

"That's bull." Shiloh's heart started to pound in time with the throbbing pain in the back of xir head. "Don't give me that. Not after all we've gone through. We haven't heard your voice in over a month—and we haven't seen you in ten years. We've waited long enough!"

I know. I'm asking you to be patient for just a little bit more."

"I'm done being patient." Xie said the word like it had four letters, through clenched teeth. "If I did everything right, why aren't you here? Why can't you tell me what's going on at least?"

"Shiloh, I'm glaring at your dad right now," Maureen said. *"I know, he likes to present a united front, but you're right. You deserve better."*

"You both do," Garrett agreed without hesitation. *"You deserve answers. And stability and safety and all the happiness in the world. And I hate not being there to give them to you."*

"Okay, great. We all hate this. So let's do it and get it done." Xie could envision Maureen's quick, businesslike nod, the one she always gave just before diving into another vital project, sure and determined. *"Next step's same as always. Getting that data to Parole. Getting ourselves to Parole. Countering Turret's next move."*

"What do you think he wants?" Shiloh's frustration gave way to anxiety at the mere mention of the name. "We're sure he's not just trying to contain the poison, like us, right?"

Maureen snorted. *"I'm gonna pretend you didn't just say that. No, he wants walls up. Keeping anyone from getting deeper in there."*

"He's hiding something in there." Shiloh felt dizzy. "Uncle Jay was right."

"Looks that way. And you can actually tell him that one, he's earned it." Maureen chuckled, but it didn't last long. *"Turret is definitely hiding something, about Mihir, and Tartarus, and Parole and everything–and if Turret wants it gone that bad, I want to know what it is."*

"Okay." Shiloh did feel a little comforted. "I hope we do soon. I hope everyone finds each other again soon. People and robot dogs."

"What?" For some reason, Garrett's voice sharpened, sounded more urgent.

"Yeah. Annie's dog, I guess she called him Dandy. He kind of started a big fight with the dragon when he showed up but he was trying to protect us. He thought he was helping. He ran away, though, hope he's okay—"

"*Damn!*" His voice boomed even through the small radio speaker.

"Dad? What's wrong?" Shiloh asked hesitantly, almost afraid of the answer.

"*Hans!*" Static crackled and popped like urgent punctuation.

"What—who's Hans? Regan said—"

"*I thought he was under control—but I should have known he wouldn't stick to our plan. No, he was always playing his own game...*" Garrett paused, apparently to get his head together, and Shiloh did the same. Xie hadn't understood a word of that, but if it had xir father this concerned it couldn't be good. "*You said this wolf protected you?*"

"Yeah, when I was talking to a ghost. First it looked like you, then it turned into a dragon. Then Dandy showed up and I think he was trying to protect us. But the dragon panicked, and breathed some poison at us. My friend Indra got really sick. And then just a couple days ago, the FireRunner sailed into a storm. A—a lot of stuff happened. But Dandy kind of lured the ghosts away. He jumped right overboard, and they all chased him away and left us alone."

"*Interruptions,*" Garrett pondered, sounding tense. "*Misdirections. I'd say Turret's not the only one with a vested interest in breaking down communications.*"

"*Listen, I don't care about Hans or Turret or any of this,*" Maureen said sharply, then softened. "*I care about seeing you again.*"

"Me too." Shiloh frowned, but xir voice was only slightly bitter. Still, xie wasn't ready to let one very important thing go. "I thought you'd be here when we got to the FireRunner. But you weren't."

"*I know,*" Garrett answered. "*I'm sorry. But everything I've ever done, I've done to bring us back together. Please believe me on that. If you don't believe anything else I've ever said, believe that.*"

"So next stop is you?" Shiloh pressed. "No more running around, no more side quests?"

"Shiloh...Maureen. Trust me," Garrett said. *"I wouldn't be doing any of this if there was another way. I want you here with me, right here, right now. I've wanted that since the day we were separated. The minute. All I can tell you is we will be together again. I promise. What you did, stopping that barrier, was a huge step forward."*

"So it was really the right choice?" Shiloh asked in a small voice. "Everything seemed like it was pushing me toward the opposite."

"Maybe. But you listened." At those words, Shiloh felt something xie'd almost forgotten. Relief. The feeling was so profound it almost seemed like a physical force, rushing over xir like an overpowering tidal wave. All at once, xie realized how tense, scared, and exhausted xie'd been since leaving Meridian. Or maybe for ten years. *"That's never wrong."*

"To the ghosts?" Xie curled up and listened to Garrett's steady, reassuring voice, so clear xie could close xir eyes and easily imagine him being in the room. Felt young, felt small, safe and warm.

"To them, to Regan, to the Chandrasekhars, to everyone on that ship. Your friends. Everyone you met on the way. To your mom. To me. You decided who to trust...and who did it turn out to be?"

Shiloh was quiet for a long time. "Myself."

"That's why we sent the messages to you," Maureen said. *"Because you'd hear every side, listen to them, then make your own decision. You know when to hold onto what everyone else tells you, and when to let it all go."*

"That's what Gabriel said when this all started. Trust. Letting go." Shiloh remembered releasing a desperate grip on a branch, while fire rose up through the darkness. Xie remembered words that hadn't made sense until now.

"Sometimes falling isn't the last thing that happens. Sometimes it's the first thing."

"*Yes.*" Garrett's voice was warm again, expansive, like arms open wide. "*And when you did?*"

"Someone caught me. A lot of people did. I'm so glad they were there."

"*And we'll be there with you soon, that is a promise.*" The edge in Maureen's voice wasn't a warning, but a guarantee. Even if Shiloh couldn't trust the shining stream, or anything else in the world, xie could trust her. "*We'll face what comes next together.*"

"Mom... Dad, I missed you so much."

"*Shiloh, there are no words.*" Still, Garrett's reverberated through xir chest, warming xir to the bone. "*I love you. Now hurry up and come home–to Parole.*"

"That's where you are? You made it?"

"*I didn't say that. It's a conversation best had in person, and we will have it, but not where anyone can listen in. You just focus on getting to Parole safe and sound. And if you ever lose your way...*"

"Follow the stream?" Shiloh couldn't help the slight sarcasm that crept into xir tone. Xie hadn't intended it, but it got the point across.

"*No. Follow my voice. You'll never lose that again.*"

Xie was quiet for a second, eyes stinging. "Promise?"

"*Yes. With everything I have.*"

"Okay." Shiloh let out a long, slow breath and closed xir watering eyes. "I'm so tired."

"*Rest, babe,*" Maureen said as Shiloh drifted into a warm, comforting darkness made of trust instead of fear. Soon nothing existed except her voice. "*We're safe. You're safe. You've been running all this time. Now it's okay to stop and stand still.*"

☆

"This isn't the tree," Indra murmured, staring up at Parole's new barrier, crackling energy against the night sky. "It's that one again. God, I hate this one."

"Me too. But we're just gonna keep coming back here, I guess." Annie's eyes reflected the barrier's glow and Parole's flames. "So we just gotta deal."

"We don't have to. We could wake up right now, or at least try. The actual tree is right here on this ship, in reality. I'd much rather hang out there than see this one more night."

"We gotta sleep sometime."

Indra didn't have an answer for that, so he folded his arms and stayed quiet.

"I know what you mean though," she muttered eventually. "We should be past it, we're different people now. We're not those kids. They're gone. We lived, even if that place tried to kill us. None of this should even exist." She stared at their small hands pressed against the glowing shield, at their faces fixed on each other through the barrier like shining glass. Separated but together. Now, joined together forever.

"Maybe it exists more than we think," Indra said quietly. "Maybe we're still those kids. Maybe we're still trying to escape from Parole."

"We did!" Annie snapped. "This isn't real, when we wake up, we'll be outside! We're a thousand miles away, we did escape! You can't leave something much further behind than that!"

"Then why are we still here?"

"I don't want to leave it behind," Shiloh said quietly and the other two jumped and looked up quickly, as if realizing xie was there for the first time. "If this hadn't happened, we wouldn't be where we are. Or who we are. And... I like us."

"You know something?" They felt as much as heard Indra's tentative words. The question felt like the moment before diving into the deep end of the pool, curled toes gripping the concrete edge. "For the longest time, since Mihir. I just kind of stumbled through life in this depressed, numb fog of nothing—and then I had some weird dreams. And I got on a bike. And I started seeing new things and laughing, and *feeling!*" His smile shook; so did the ground beneath their feet. "Do you know how amazing that is? And how *terrifying?*"

Annie said nothing, but gave him a slow nod. He kept going, and as the words fell out of him, a cool breeze blew past. It did not smell like smoke.

"I'm scared all the time." His voice broke. "And I love it. The weird part about feeling that broken is it also kind of makes you feel invincible. It's like nothing can hurt you, like, bring it on, world, I'm already doing worse to myself. Nothing can touch you. But then you did." He smiled and even in dreams his eyes were filled with tears. "So now I'm under pressure because I have something to lose. I have shit to do. And I don't want to die before I do it."

"You're not going to die," Annie said, eyes on him instead of the burning city. "I won't let you. Either of you."

"Told you before, that's not your job." Shiloh shook xir head as stars winked into view brighter overhead, clearer, maybe nearer. "You've done enough."

"So have you." She smiled too, finger going to twirl her hair even in a dream. "You make me feel like I *am* enough. You understand me when I can't make the words work right. Even when I don't have them at all. Even when I'm awake, I don't have to work to get my point across. Words come out a little easier when you're around, but if they don't it's still okay. I don't get scared. It's how it's supposed to be."

"I know the feeling." In dreams, Meridian seemed so much closer. The endless days. The long-distance calls. Constantly looking over shoulders for Turret, for Tartarus, for anything that might ruin so many lives in so many ways. The surge of excitement, realizing that waiting was finally over. Change. "I can't go back to the way I was. I can't go back to standing still. Not after moving so fast."

"And I can't go back to feeling nothing. I want to feel *something.*" As Indra spoke, they heard the whistle-crack as he hurled a rock at a dragon. Felt the flash of recognition the first time Shiloh saw his face. Knowing xie couldn't miss this amazing, brilliant 'Chance.'

"What your brother felt." Annie nodded, echoes beneath her voice. A motorcycle engine mingled with her yell to get on, hurry up. Radio Angel's distorted words, coming from a dragon-ghost's mouth.

"No. What *I* feel." Indra's voice was stronger and so was the wind, cold but fresh like spring water Parole hadn't tasted for a decade. "What I'm feeling right now. You did that. It hurts. But you make me feel like I exist."

"Parole hurts," Shiloh said as the light around them grew. It didn't come from the fire, but from the sky. A crescent moon had joined the stars and no smoke obscured them. Their light did not hurt xir eyes. "But I wouldn't trade it. Not for you."

Something warm touched xir fingers and Shiloh looked down. It was bright enough to see Annie's hand. Xie took it, then Indra's in the other.

"I can't be glad this night exists," Annie said quietly. "But I'm glad we exist."

"I think that's enough for now."

The city fell away into the distance. Its firelight, so terrifying up close, darkened to nothing more than a faint flicker. They stood there together and watched the city fade like a dimly glowing ember into the darkness. The three of them, the moon, and stars remained.

EPILOGUE

Waking Up

"HEY, GUYS. IT'S YOUR RADIO ANGEL. IT'S ABOUT 4:00 A.M. AGAIN, ON A…NO. I CAN'T DO THIS anymore." Kari took her headphones off, unplugged them, and turned up the microphone and speaker volumes as loud as they would go. She wasn't whispering anymore. "I know you can hear me. You could the entire time, couldn't you? I'm not just yelling into the void, the void is listening."

She took a breath and waited. Just like always, silence was her only answer. Hands curling into tight fists on her knees, Kari did what she did best and started to speak.

"Hey Celeste. I'm talking to you. Not Parole, you. You're alive. I can't stop saying those words. You didn't die. They didn't get you. So maybe they won't

get me."

She paused. She was met with silence, just like every other night. And just like every other night, Kari kept talking.

"Jay opened Maureen's disk. With a little help from a friend. Seven. A good kitty. And from you." She picked up the open envelope resting on the console nearby. Jay had been happy to return it, clearly too happy to be reunited with Seven, and occupied with the newly opened disk to wonder why she wanted the envelope back.

"And I got some help from a friend too. From a boy who..." Kari swallowed hard, but fought the tears back for now. "Everybody talks about how much Indra looks like Mihir. Nobody says how much—" she broke off, hands starting to shake. "I pushed the button, Celeste, I know what it's supposed to do. But it didn't happen. Not for me. And when it finally did work, you still didn't come back."

She took another breath and waited again. Again, no answer.

"Okay, listen. I don't even care if Parole can hear me right now. And I don't care if I ever get home. I care about hearing your voice again. And seeing you, and—Celeste, my best friend, my shiniest, most brilliant star in the whole freaking galaxy, superheroine of my—of my heart? I know you think you're protecting us by staying away. Or something. Well..." She bit her lip and tasted salt. Tears. They'd been falling for the past minute and she hadn't noticed. "I'm not safe, when I spend every night wondering if you're alive or dead. I'm not safe at all. It's almost worse, knowing you're there but not...just say something. Please."

She waited. Five full seconds. Six.

"You always had a plan. And then another one, and—just so many plans. So maybe this is part of your plan too. So okay. I'll sit here and wait all night. As long as it takes. But I can't beg anymore, I'm too tired. I'm running out of words. I just...I hope you heard any of this. I hope you're there to hear at all."

Ten more long seconds of silence passed. Slowly, Kari laid her head down on her console and shut her eyes.

Then a speaker crackled. A voice resolved itself from the static like a figure stepping from swirls of thick fog. *"Kari?"*

Kari's heart fluttered, skipped. She knew before asking. "Who is this?"

"You know who it is."

A breath caught in her throat. "Oh my God, you heard me."

"I've heard you every night. Even before Shiloh got there, but that did help, yes. Ever since the collapse."

"Celeste?"

"You have no idea how much I wanted to answer, it killed me not to. I couldn't, I'd be leading the enemy right to you."

"It's fine," Kari sobbed. Suddenly none of this felt real, not even the words she was saying. The only ones that mattered were the words through that speaker. "It's just Parole rules. Gotta make sure you're not followed. You come home alone—"

"Or you don't come home at all, that's right. Well... I'm alone now. But soon, you won't be."

"You're alive! This feels like a dream—no, no, everything else felt like a dream, until right now!" Kari didn't know if she was crying or laughing, but whichever it was, it felt good. "A nightmare! The worst one I've ever had, I kept waiting to wake up and look over and see you. But I couldn't wake up and I couldn't make anything better, it was just—wrong, it was wrong, and I'm sorry, I don't know what I'm saying anymore!"

"Then just listen. I'm so sorry I had to disappear, Angel–But there was so much I had to do. Evil triumphs when good women do nothing." Kari had her ear pressed against the speaker now and eyes shut, trying to sink into the sound. *"And I knew you'd be all right, I knew everything would turn out fine. It was a risky plan, but I knew if anybody could pull it off, it would be you and everyone on the FireRunner."*

"Plan? I was right. You always have a plan..."

"This one wasn't just mine. Garrett Cole brought together about six loose ends. The entire Tartarus ghost business was entirely his idea, credit where credit's due. He's still quite sharp for a dead man. And our friend Regan proved beyond a–"

"What?" Kari sat up straighter now, attention thoroughly seized even through her emotional haze. "Did you say Regan helped you? Is he there?"

There was another pause on the other end, a couple seconds long. *"Regan remains a friend. For everyone's safety, including, and perhaps especially, his, that is all I feel at liberty to say."*

"But he's okay, he's alive? Oh no, you can't tell me about him–what about Parole? Have you heard from them?" Kari gasped. "The beacons! And the barrier around Tartarus, and now Turret knows that we know he was planning something! What's going to happen to Parole?"

"Don't worry about Parole. Evelyn knows what's happened; she'll make sure everyone's prepared for the fallout. And don't you worry either. Just remember what 'Icarus' really means."

"Tell me again," Kari breathed, leaning closer. Her lips almost brushed the microphone.

"A sad little man in a quiet room sees someone threatening his rule," Celeste whispered, and all at once Kari felt very young. Remembered staying up too

late, telling stories by the light of a flashlight under a blanket. Her voice sounded like it had then. "*He sets a fire, our wings burn. We all fall down. But that's not how the story ends. Because I'm here to catch you, Angel. It means I'll always catch you when someone decides you've flown too high.*"

"Celeste, I have so much to tell you, but—never mind me, what did you—?" There were so many words Kari had to say, she couldn't even get one out. "Just, what are you doing right now? Tell me anything!"

"*What am I doing?*" The repeated question didn't sound playful or even thoughtful. Celeste just sounded overwhelmed and tired. But it only took a moment to recover and, when she continued, it was with complete conviction and steely resolve. "*Finally doing things my way, that's what. Press the button again, please.*"

"Okay!" Kari scrambled for the envelope, shook the cylinder out, and eagerly complied. Then she waited. "Celeste, are you there? Nothing happened. Again."

"*Hang on, two seconds,*" Celeste's voice continued, and now it sounded different, louder and clearer through her speakers, like the connection had improved significantly. "*That's much better. Now, you were asking what was going to happen to Parole? Well, I'm not quite sure. But I can say that after tonight, it'll be very fast and all at once, and we'd better be ready.*"

"We don't know what to do, though!" Desperation crept back into Kari's voice for the first time since hearing Celeste's. "There's so much, all at once! Turret, and Sharpe, and Tartarus, and Parole is still collapsed—and everyone's so scattered, so many of us are missing! Or getting hurt! Or..."

"*I know,*" Celeste's previously quick, confident tone dropped. "*I heard about Ash. I'm so sorry, Angel. He was a good man and losing good people is never easy.*

Fortunately," her voice lifted again, as if she were trying hard to lift both of their spirits as well. "*I've found a few as well.*"

"Regan, right?"

"*And Gabriel. They've both been a great help. Without them, I never could have found... well, I think I'll let Jay fill you in there. He did receive the little gift I sent, didn't he?*"

"You mean Seven?"

"*Yes, finally!*" Celeste laughed and Kari did too, even as more hot tears rolled down her face. "*Turret's got a big, nasty surprise coming. And Parole's got a few big good ones. So does Jay. And Shiloh–and Regan, and Evelyn, so many people, they've all suffered enough. And so have you.*"

"What about you though?" she sniffed. "You've been hurting too."

"*I didn't have a choice,*" the voice on the other end was firm but Kari caught the split-second hesitation. "*None of us did. I had to do what–*"

"But you had to do it alone. We just missed you so much."

"*I…I missed you. I miss a lot of people.*"

"So come home. You can come back now. Can't you?"

"*I was so scared of putting you in danger,*" she said in a shaky whisper after a long silence. "*You and Parole and... I just couldn't move. I'm supposed to just reappear like a light-speed heroine with the vital information and save the day, but–*"

"You think being scared stops you from being a hero? Or hurting? You keep moving even when you're scared out of your mind. I think that makes you more of one."

"*God, I've missed you. That was the hardest part, you know. Listening to you every night, hearing you cry and having to cover my mouth and say nothing back. Or worse, hearing you say exactly what I needed to hear, and still stay away.*"

"Hey, Celeste. Guess what."

"What?"

"Everything really is going to be okay." The words came out effortlessly, felt right and real. For the first time in months, she barely thought about them or whether or not they were true. Her chest felt light and warm.

"I believe you." Celeste's voice was clearer than ever and Kari could hear something else underneath it: metallic footsteps. *"Now are you in your room?"*

"Huh? Yeah. I'm pretty much there all the time now."

"All right." Celeste paused, taking a deep breath of her own. *"Here goes."*

Three soft knocks broke the silence.

Kari jumped and spun around in her chair to stare at her heavy iron door. Her heart pounded, blood rushing in her ears. Crossing her room felt like an eternity, like crossing Tartarus itself, like drifting through an endless dream. She'd lost count of the nights she'd prayed to go to sleep and wake up in the morning to find that the last few months had been a nightmare. After all those desperate wishes, her only wish left was that she wasn't dreaming now.

When she reached the door, she did not open it.

"Please don't be a trick," she whispered. "Please don't be a lie. Please don't be a dream. Not after all this. I need it to be you. I need to believe it's going to be okay too."

Stillness stretched. Behind her, the soft hum of white-noise static filled the air. Radio silence on all frequencies. But then, Kari did hear a voice. It did not come from a speaker.

"Angel, open the door."

She did.

And Lakshanya Chandrasekhar—*Celeste*—stepped through.

Many pieces of the world, like its people, were shattered beyond repair, edges brittle and easily broken. But some still fit together, exactly as they should. Radio Angel and Celeste fell into each other's arms, in a dance much slower, much sweeter than their silent embrace on the stage of the Emerald Bar. They fit together like missing pieces finally found. So did their lips.

The FireRunner continued homeward through the vast black void, a tiny point of blazing light against a rotten sea stretching hundreds of treacherous miles. Far in the distance, a city burned. The people inside managed to survive, by doing what they had done every day until this one. They reached into the abyss, and found helping hands reaching back for them.

Somewhere else, a smoking gun still waited to be found. Men in quiet rooms slept very well at night. But so did the dreamers on this ship, safe and sound.

And so did the ones in that far-off city, which wouldn't burn for much longer.

Acknowledgments

Thank you to Moo and Kevie for the never-ending support, love, and bunny-snuggles. And for reminding me to eat, take meds, and generally keeping me alive while this book took over my entire brain. ♡

The Lifeline Signal wouldn't be the same without the lifesaving words and encouraging presence of Claudie Arsenault. And neither would its author. You made everything at least eight times better. (Love you, Kraken Collective! Best octo-friends!)

Thank you so much to Lyssa Chiavari for the graphic design/ formatting magic, and Laya Rose for the amazing cover art. This gorgeous book is gorgeous because of you.

It's time to deeply appreciate Uli for Tsalagi sensitivity reading, content checking, collaborating–and infinitely more. I wish I could spend three millennia thanking you and your generous eye. You helped me find the key to this book, solve its puzzles, and trust in the heart of its pages through the power of friendship. If I can ever return the favor... just give me a ring.

Deepest gratitude to Vivek Shaker and Thrupthy Jacob for their invaluable assistance in writing Indra, Lakshanya, Rishika and Bhanu

Chandrasekhar. Thank you for your time, energy, and words of encouragement.

Thank you to Tabby for the edit-assists, being so excited over this book, and the Oxford-tunities.

Eri, thank you for the endless nerdery, thread-connecting and feels-flails that helped this book evolve into something better than I ever imagined. The more things change…

Thank you to Quinn Phan for the Vietnamese fairy tales, fact-checking, weird coincidences, and memes. Get yourself a badass leather jacket. The bike will take care of itself.

Now you listen to me, Jack. You're gonna rattle the stars. Let this lighthouse in the sea of time light your way.

Tobias, you're welcome for xie/xir/xirself. Thank you for existing.

Thank you to my amazing patrons on Patreon, especially Quinn. You support me while I create things that I hope make the world a little more beautiful and safe, with less fear and pain. That's what you do for mine. (I'm at patreon.com/RoAnnaSylver. If my words helped you, checking that out would help me more than I can say.)

Thank you Intr0. I still hope you're proud. I hope the words came out right.

I could write a book entirely of Thank You's and still need more pages. I'm more blessed than I ever imagined. Thank you for catching me. Thank you for reminding me that falling isn't always the last thing you do. Sometimes it's the first thing.

The moment I let go of it was the moment I got more than I could handle

The moment I jumped off of it was the moment I touched down.

– "Thank You," Alanis Morissette

About The Author

RoAnna Sylver is passionate about stories that give hope, healing and even fun for LGBT, disabled and other marginalized people, and thinks we need a lot more.

Aside from writing oddly optimistic dystopia books, RoAnna is a blogger, artist, singer and voice actor, is an actual genetic mutant (and proud), knows too much about Star Trek, and lives with family and a small snorking dog near Portland, OR.

The next adventure RoAnna would like is a nap in a pile of bunnies.

Printed in Great Britain
by Amazon

35087490R00260